TYRANT

Michael Wilde

FriesenPress

One Printers Way
Altona, MB R0G 0B0
Canada

www.friesenpress.com

Copyright © 2025 by Michael Wilde
First Edition — 2025

All rights reserved.

No part of this publication may be reproduced in any form, or by any means, electronic or mechanical, including photocopying, recording, or any information browsing, storage, or retrieval system, without permission in writing from FriesenPress.

ISBN
978-1-03-832068-1 (Hardcover)
978-1-03-832067-4 (Paperback)
978-1-03-832069-8 (eBook)

1. FICTION, SCIENCE FICTION, SHORT STORIES

Distributed to the trade by The Ingram Book Company

TABLE OF CONTENTS

Harness 1

Tank 95

Yeti 119

Damage Deposit 123

Mulligan 141

Propogation 149

Quick Slice 189

The Twins 191

Brother Wolf 229

Fugue. 255

Dirge 267

Temple. 291

Two Tails 331

HARNESS

It was
A spark from the Generator
Sound
Seed
Buried beneath
Above
Arise the simple cell
Divide and spiral
Churning
Turning
Endless rotations
Resistance
Building mass
Gaining velocity
Momentum
Ratcheting upwards
Crashing down
Coiled tight
Trigger, charge, repeat
Impact fractures
Pulse
Pulverize
Absorb
Destructive decibels
Crack the mantle
Screaming ascent
Bores through
Pours through
Breaking scorched surface
To fall under sun and sky
Inhale
Exhale
Expire
Arrive

TYRANT

BACK TO WORK:

It's a matter of time. Anxiety kicking in. Rising dread. They're gearing up for something. Can feel it. Months removed and he's still recovering from the tower. John Choi isn't ready to leave his family. John Choi needs to work. The next day he gets the call. One-year contract. No leave. In camp the entire duration. Can't say no. They'll find someone to replace him and he'll go back to the bottom of the list. They don't need the money now, right now, but there's always later. Vacation is over. Given a week to prepare. John visits the beach with wife and child the day before departure. They take pictures, build sandcastles, and splash around in the ocean. Hot dogs for dinner. Ice cream dessert. Sun setting. Time to leave. John picks up his son Elroy a.k.a. Little Buddha. Wades knee deep into the water. Father and son facing the horizon. The hope. The dream. The reason why.

Back home. Elroy sleeping. Bags packed the night before. Alarm set. John spends the remaining hours with his wife Lilly. Share a bottle of wine. Music. Conversation. Attainable plans for the future with some laughs in between. Soon they transition to the bedroom. He commits every moment to memory. She's the one. His wife. His life. They found each other. Confirmation.

Inevitable. A beautiful thing while it lasted. Too bad. Sabine's the one but thirty years is a lot of ground to cover. Ren can't blame her. Had their fun for the better part of two years. Surprised it went past the first night. Surprised there was a first night. Everything after was an added bonus. That's why it was so easy. Effortless. She held the cards. He was along for the ride. No bullshit. No deception. Take it or leave it. Simply a matter of time. In five years, he'll be sixty. That's a daunting number considering she's entering her prime. Clean break. No games. Avoid the awkward decline. Sabine. The surprise. Going to miss her like he knew he would.

Another cigarette on the fire escape. Back inside. Kettle whistling. Ren turns off the stove. Tea steeps while he tunes the guitar. A phone call. Not her. Work. Of course. Had to be. Answers. Always does. No choice. Not yet. One-year contract. All in. No leave. A week until departure. Going to be a rough one. She was there after the trauma on the tower. A blessing to come home to. Not this time. On his own. Empty space. Tomorrow morning he'll strap his camping gear to the motorcycle and head for the hills. Park it by the river for a couple days. Do some fishing. Stare at the fire. Get his mind right.

Scanning the listing. Mo wants that truck. Matte black, leather interior, classic rims, raised suspension, all-wheel drive, conversion engine. Put a cap on the back and she can sleep in it. Save some money. Stop paying rent. Add a trailer hitch and she can haul both bikes. Sick of this slowdown. Needs work. Next contract. Getting restless. Racing, running, climbing, swimming, lifting weights. Exhaust. Distract. Occupy. Anything to stay busy. Keep the demons at bay. Usual suspects. Drugs. Alcohol. Timer goes off. Mo collects her clothes from the laundry room. Folding and sorting when her phone starts ringing. It's work. Whatever's available. Good to go.

TRAVEL TIME:

Vibration is location. The chamber opens. Vomit explodes from John's mouth. Never gone this far. Not even close. A base medic administers an injection providing relief from the nausea. Granted a twenty-four-hour recovery period. Escorted to his room by security. Private sleeping quarters. Small. Sparse. Bunk bed, in-wall dresser, folding chair, and a drop-down desk.

Mercifully, the spinning has stopped. Solid ground. After showering in the communal bathroom, John returns to his room and finishes unpacking. He tapes a picture of wife and child to the wall, takes a seat on the edge of the bed, and bows his head in prayer. Gives thanks for safe travel. Asks God to watch over his family. Lays back in bed. Ready for sleep. Rest up for tomorrow's briefing.

From the hull a chamber opens. New frequency. Ren needs a moment. Rarely gets sick but that was a rough one. Warned it would be. Breath in. Breath out. Skunky. Reeks of flop sweat. The kind that comes with travel. Unable to ride it out, he accepts the injection. Too late. Vomit splashes off the floor onto his feet. Fortunately, the purging offers immediate relief.

Finds his cargo case waiting in his room. Retrieves the supplied toiletry kit from the top drawer of the dresser and hits the showers. Hot water. Strong pressure. Good start. Washed up, Ren returns to his room. Sets the alarm. Doesn't bother unpacking. Depleted. Done. Lay low. Lights out.

Going. Gone. The chamber opens. When the seizure stops, the puking starts. A medic administers the antiemetic injection and calmly explains to Mo, still extremely disoriented, where she is and why. As the sedative properties of the injection take effect, Mo begins to acclimatize to her surroundings. Stops struggling. Arrived. At work. Made it. Kept in the medical station for overnight observation, she's escorted to her room in the morning.

SITE ORIENTATION/WALKTHROUGH:

"Here's your phone, which is only to be used during off hours and must be checked in at the start of each shift. The phone has a contact list for all departments. Any photos or videos you wish to send or bring back home must be submitted for approval. Your phone also functions as your pass card. It will open the doors you need to open. Doors it won't open, you don't need to worry about. This base is in the early stages of operation. Still being built. Under construction. Currently, the barracks contain fifty room units, four communal bathrooms, rec room, gym, stationary pool, climbing wall, kitchen, and dining hall. The barracks have connecting corridors to the medical ward, massage and physio studio, transport, department offices, and surrounding workstations. If you're deployed outside these walls, it will be with a security detail. On that subject, the territory has a breathable atmosphere, but it's not much to look at: dirt, dust, barren, bleak. Not a single burnt blade of grass, but you will notice clusters of black spines scattered over the surface like giant sea urchins. These spines are fuglies. That's what we call them. Nasty creatures. Porcupines from hell. Their bite, their quills, their meat, everything about them is toxic. As far as we know, the food chain on this planet begins and ends with them. With no other food source, they resort to cannibalism. Nocturnal creatures, so the feeding frenzy begins at night. A truly awful racket. Imagine emptying a dump truck of feral cats into a junk bin of rabid raccoons for a rough approximation. Open the audio channels in your dwelling unit when the sun goes down and you'll thank God for sound filters."

ALARM:

Alarm goes off. Light goes on. A shower to clear the cobwebs. John hears the sounds of an upset stomach from one of the toilet stalls. Functioning ventilation spares him from smelling it.

Dressed in standard-issue black pants and shirt, John lays back in bed and waits for his orders. On the hour, a voice over the intercom.

"Morning, John. Jim Dunn, site supervisor."
"Morning, Jim."
"How you feeling this morning?"
"Fine, thank you."
"Good. I know that was a rough one. Have some breakfast and meet me in my office in thirty minutes. It's at the end of hall five. To the right."

Caught by the alarm. A rare occurrence. His internal clock usually wakes him with minutes to spare. Travel fucked him up. Still groggy. Ren rolls out of bed and gets dressed. Waiting for the briefing, he unpacks his belongings: guitar, tablet, pictures, trinkets, and keepsakes. On the hour, a voice over the intercom.

"Morning, Ren."

"That you, Jim?"

"Sure is. How you feeling?"

"Well enough I suppose."

"Some serious travel time."

"Indeed."

"Well, if you've managed to muster up an appetite, grab breakfast and meet me in my office. Hall five. To the right."

Why did they drop her keys in the bird bath? The bird bath is filled with blood. Spilling over. No way. No chance. Set up. They set her up. Anger screams through gut-wrenching sadness. Rage. The scale of betrayal. A voice. Whose voice? Calling her name. From where? Outside. Outside of what? Awake. In the dark. Disoriented.

"Margot?"

Over the PA system. Soaked in sweat. Jangled nerves.

"Yes."

"Morning, Margot, I'm Jim Dunn, the site supervisor."

Slow deliberate breath.

"Hi, Jim."

"Rough ride getting here."

"Indeed."

"Glad you made it."

"Me too."

"How you feeling?"

"Better."

"Do you need another day?"

"No."

"Good to hear. Grab yourself some breakfast and meet me in my office for eight. End of hall five. Make a right."

Harness

WORK BRIEFING:

"You're going to have questions. You're going to have doubts. That's inevitable. Rest assured your safety is of paramount importance to us. It takes priority over the entire process. You have my word, my promise, I will not expose you to any undue hardship or harm. That's not saying it will be easy. Called work for a reason. Risk versus reward. Paid accordingly. Nothing forced. As things progress, we will provide the answers and instruction necessary to complete the task at hand while taking every possible precaution along the way. Now let's get into it. You're going to be working in the trachea. That's what we're calling it. The trachea is a giant hole in the ground. Drop something down there and you won't hear it hit the bottom. Eventually this trachea connects to a pair of lungs but there's a lot of work that needs to get done beforehand. Today will be a distant memory by that point. Our first priority is sealing the puncture sites. Patch 'em up. From one wound to the next, all the way down, with some strapping along the way. That's it. Where we're starting. Given you the broad strokes, now let's go through the steps. Step one: Debridement. Clean the puncture. Clear the damaged tissue. Some of these punctures are tiny. Don't bother with any puncture under a three-inch diameter. We can mesh right over them when we start grafting. After you've cleaned the puncture, mark it and measure the perimeter. Point and shoot. The scanner does it for you and with the added bonus of alerting you when a section needs to be strapped. That means securing the compromised section to the one above it. Strapping one level, ring, rib, to the next with thirteen feet between them. Eight straps, sixteen points, connecting each level. Drilling the straps directly into the bone with diamond anchors. To drill each strap times out to roughly a minute. There it is. That's week one, guys. Then we shift over to grafting."

WHEELHOUSE:

Working in the wheelhouse. Massive complex. Given a tour of the facilities and a tutorial on system functions. It starts with the iris, a retractable cap covering the trachea that resembles a giant folding vegetable steamer. Above the iris is the telescopic hoist system, which arms out above the centre of the drop zone. The rigger suits up in the change room and climbs a crossover bridge, which brings them to the end of the hoist arm. That's where they lock/plug/clip the hoist cable to their containment suit/harness system. After finishing a safety check, the hoist lifts the rigger above the bridge, which pulls away from the iris. Once clear, the iris opens, revealing the trachea with a twenty-four-foot diameter and seventy-five-foot circumference. Its outer edge drilled into the ground with metal plating. Granted access, the rigger begins their descent into the trachea. The hoist cable their tether to the surface. This cable (conduit), with a four-inch diameter and 12.56-inch circumference, serves multiple functions. It brings the rigger up and down while supplying power to their harness (which powers their tools and suit). It's also a communications link. Their connection to ground control. The hoist cable is a rigger's lifeline. That line traces back from the hoist through a hole in the wall to its feeder system contained in a massive air hanger that's filled with spools of cable holding fifty-five hundred feet of line standing twelve feet tall with a twelve-foot diameter. The spools lined neatly in rows on interlocking dollies, which allow the line to run backwards or forwards. When a spool is approaching the end of its line, it's coupled to the line of the next spool. Linked together, the spools and dollies function as a mechanized pulley system.

THE NEEDLE:

Doctor Nadri explains how to operate the emergency exit.

> "I was part of the selection committee tasked with screening candidates for the job. A key requirement was the prospect's willingness and ability to work in confined spaces. Your

profile checked both boxes. Mindset matching experience. As you know, each assignment can bring its own unique set of circumstances and challenges. People change along with their work environment. It's a symbiotic relationship of sorts, and we must have certain contingencies in place to ensure crew safety."

Doctor Nadri pulls the one-inch diameter by eight-inch long carbon tube out from his desk.

"Now, you may have noticed the same carbon container is stitched into the leg of your harness suit. Within the container is a hypodermic needle for intramuscular injection. It's filled with a fast-acting sedative to be self-administered in the unlikely event you experience a panic attack while working in the trachea. To be clear, this is not to be taken for anxiety. It's for panic. Panic attacks and anxiety attacks may share some similar symptoms, but they are different conditions. Panic attacks are sudden and intense bursts of fear or terror, while anxiety attacks are characterized by persistent and ongoing worry. Anxiety attacks are typically less intense than panic attacks. Anxiety is something we should address, we should work on, and fortunately this site has the facilities and staff to do so. That being said, our primary concern is panic. Panic attacks start suddenly and peak within minutes. One experiences intense physical symptoms that can feel like a heart attack or life-threatening situation: rapid heartbeat, shortness of breath, sweating, nausea, dizziness, chest pain and tightness, discomfort. The attack can manifest in a sense of detachment from one's surrounding coupled with irrational fear of losing control or dying. An important distinction is panic attacks can happen without any apparent trigger or cause. Typically lasting for a few minutes to an hour. However, several panic attacks can occur in a row, making it seem like an attack lasts much longer. Understand the panic attack itself is no danger but it can create a hazardous situation in a workplace environment.

Which brings this back to you. While working in the trachea, if you feel the pronounced onset of a panic attack, simply unclasp the container, pull out the prefilled syringe, and stick it into the meat of your leg. Right here on your thigh—that's the spot. You hold the syringe like a dart, position the needle at a ninety-degree angle to the injection site. Insert the needle with a brisk, controlled motion. Compress the plunger to inject the drug. Remove the needle. Place back in the container if possible. When the seal is broken, a signal is sent to ground control to bring you back to the surface for a full assessment. Our hope is the needle will not be required during your time here. That its mere presence might provide some assurance, a sense of security, to prevent a panic attack from ever taking place. If one does, rest assured, there is no shame in taking the injection. It's there for your safety. We simply address the cause, make the necessary adjustments, and go from there."

DROP:

Hoist cable attached. John is lifted off the platform. Suspended in the air as the bridge retracts and the iris opens. Looks down at the yawning black pit. Off balance. Fleeting vertigo. Gathers himself. All good. Composed. Using the suit's inboard control, John lowers himself into the trachea. Yellowed dermis stretched over the ribs and spinal column. Waxen. Mummified. Somehow preserved. Can see rock through the punctures. Different layers, formations, the deeper he goes. So many questions but he sticks to the steps. Clean. Mark. Measure. Drop. Cutting away damaged tissue but the dermis itself appears to be in a state of necrosis. Not sure what to make of it. Adopting the neck down approach. Do the work that's been requested and leave it at that. It takes him three hours to pass the mantle. Surface light long gone. John shines his light through a fist-sized puncture. Nothing there. Nothing outside the trachea. No rock. Tiny particles float through his light before the darkness consumes it entirely. A chill runs up his spine. Focus. Here to work. Four punctures within five feet of each other. John triggers

Harness

the scalpel. Cuts off the damaged tissue. Debridement. Let it fall per instructions. Mark and measure the punctures. Drops a hundred feet to the next site. Eight punctures. Clean. Mark. Measure. Drop. Two hundred feet. The scanner pics up nineteen puncture points. Clean. Mark. Measure. Drop. Sixty feet. Thirteen punctures. Clean. Mark. Measure. Drop. Forty feet. Six punctures. Clean. Mark. Measure. Drop. Eighty-three feet. The scanner showing twenty-two punctures. Clean. Mark. Measure. Drop. Seventy-four feet. The display highlighting 156 punctures varying in size and spacing. The smallest, which constitute 126 of the recorded 156, are less than an inch in diameter. Speckling, most of it to John's right. Finished debriding the immediate area, his hunger now a distraction. John takes a break. Sips Nor through the feed tube in his helmet.

Autopilot. The harness system has motion sensors from every angle. Built-in safeties. Shock absorbers allowing it to stop on dime. Takes Ren twenty minutes to reach the last marker. Dropping seventy feet. to the next set of punctures. Twelve of them. He triggers the scalpel and starts cutting. The next drop is sixty-three feet. Nineteen punctures. Five need a trim. Clean. Mark. Measure. Drop. Eighteen feet. Three punctures. Clean. Mark. Measure. Drop. Fifty-four feet. Twenty-six punctures. Working in a corpse. Carcass. Husk. Hollowed out. Where'd its guts go? Ripped out? Dropped out? Ren cuts off a large flap of tissue, watches it fall, tumble, turn, until it disappears into the darkness. Five hours in. Fiending for a cigarette. Not an option down here. Fuck it. Sip some Nor and get back to work.

Mo scrolls through the colour options on her visor's video display: Soothing Lavender, Lavender Grey, Pistachio Green, Powdered Pink, Dark Blue, Sky Blue, just some of the options. There to prevent and help with motion sickness by creating a solid backdrop to block out signals sending conflicting information where your brain doesn't know whether you're stationary or moving. In this case, the line is still, the descent smooth, but the visual of the trachea (ribs, spine, skin) rushing up while you're going down, the passing and registered movement, can create the confused reaction in the brain that makes you feel sick. So far so good. Not prone to motion sickness. A criterion for employment but one never knows. Seeing what her options are. Time to kill. Almost an hour off the top before Mo meets her starting marker and drops eighty feet to the next puncture site. Recoiling at the sight of it. The entire section looking like something took a cheese grater to it. Tattered tissue with thousands of micro fissures dotting the wall lining. The texture beyond disconcerting. Evokes a primordial disgust. Display alert. Section flagged. Needs to strap it. The scanner detecting 1,583 in total. Twenty require debridement. Mo cringes. Disturbed by the sight of it. Makes her skin crawl. Takes a second to recalibrate. Grits her teeth and gets to work. Straps the ribs. Each strap drilled into bone with diamond anchors. Eight points. Eight lines. Ribs strapped, she triggers the scalpel to cut away tattered tissue from the large punctures. To get to the ones out of reach, she extends the grasping claw and scalpel. By the time the section's complete, she's three hours into her first shift and can no longer ignore the pressure in her bladder. Needs to piss. Positions herself in the centre of the tracheas. Puts her feet in the stirrups. Pulls down the flap and lets it fly. Wipes off. Bags the wipe. Drops it per instruction. Hopes she never has to take a shit down here.

SURFACE:

Organ. Instillation. Both. Connected to what? What are they salvaging? John can see the decay, the rot, but what caused the punctures? The damage? Some sections appear slashed and torn while other areas look moth-eaten. Which begs the question: What exists outside the trachea? Fear of the unknown. Nothing he needs to dwell on. Been on thousands of dives, salvage missions or repairs, where he has no idea what he might encounter. Same idea. Why, though? Why do they need to fix this thing? A rotting husk. For what? What purpose? Build a brand-new pipe. A new conduit. This is a massive undertaking. Investment. Seems like a waste of time. What's the return? The extraction? Do they know? Are they still looking? Have to. They have to know what they're after. How far down is it? They don't know or they'd anchor the line. John catches himself. Takes a breath. Once again, not his concern. On a need-to-know basis. Not to worry. Safety reigns supreme. Sure it does . . . That's what they said on the tower. Unforeseen circumstances. Always are. Tragedy under review. The standard recourse. Blame game. Actual remorse or compensation buried under legalities. Oh well. On to the next one. None of this matters. Here to work. Get paid. Get back. John pulls on a hoodie and heads to the chow hall for dinner.

Ren checks out the rec room for the first time. Three large men with shaved heads and beards are playing poker in the far corner. Two white. One black. Assumes they're part of the PSD. Security detachment. Passes two more mercs engaged in a heated digi-pong rally as he crosses the room to the viewing window. The sun a die-cut spotlight casting an amber glow. Hard-packed landscape. Dirt. Sand. Dust. Spotted with spines. Clusters of black quills. Ren zooms in on the fuglies. Was no exaggeration. Nasty-looking creatures. Mangled land crawlers riddled with tumours. Leaking abscesses. Coarse black hair jutting out between their quills. Bags of blood constitute eyes. Mangled mouths filled with beaked rows of gnarled teeth. The desert terrain littered with their tattered carcasses. Ripped apart. Gored and gutted. Entrails splayed and strewn.

"Enjoying the view?" asks one of the poker players.
"Lovely."
"You want to get in on this next hand?"
"Yeah, I'll play."

Ren closes the zoom tab, takes a seat at the table, and counts his chips.

Nervous energy. Mo needs thirty minutes on the heavy bag. Hands wrapped. Gloves on with shin pads. Start slow. Warm up. Build speed. Intensity. Punch and kick combinations followed by a fifteen-minute cooldown in the endless pool. Showered and dressed, she grabs a late dinner. Mess hall almost empty. Recognizes the black woman eating alone at the far table. Straight black braids and a harelip. Mo brings her tray over to join her.

"You mind?"
"Not at all."

TYRANT

Mo sits four seats down and across.

"Transport, right?"
"Yes."
"You brought me in."
"I was there."
"Sorry about that."
"Nothing to be sorry about. Good to see you're alright."
"Thanks. Yeah . . . my name's Mo."
"Kim."
"How do you like it here?"
"I don't."

END WEEK:

John suits up. Clips in. Eight-hundred-foot drop to start the day. Sixteen punctures. Clean. Mark. Measure. Drop. Ninety-eight feet. Twenty-four punctures. Clean. Mark. Measure. Drop Seventy-three feet. Two punctures. Clean. Mark. Measure. Drop. Sixty-four feet. Display alert. Has to strap it. Twenty thousand punctures. More micro fissures. The entire left side is porous. A tissue-thin barrier between him and the abyss. Somehow staring back. Throat tightening. Feels it in his chest. Elevated heart rate. Stop. Snap out it. Focus. Breathe. What's required? Nothing. Not now. They'll have to mesh the whole damn thing. Strap it and move on.

Incremental drops all day. Nothing past forty feet. Small sets. No more than twelve punctures at a time. Steady pace. Next drop. Descending. Ren points the green laser straight down the pipe. See where it stops. Doesn't. Simply dissolves into black. None of this makes sense. The entire order of operations seems completely arbitrary. Strapping compromised sections to secure the structure. So why stop? Why waste time cleaning punctures? Secure it all the way down then start cleanup. Sure, it's sort of annoying working around the strapping but there's still room. The whole thing's a fuckin' mindfuck. Ain't no way to explain it. Above his pay grade.

Seventy-eight punctures start her day. Tedious work. Next drop. Thirty feet. Ninety-two punctures. Clean. Mark. Measure. Drop. Two hundred and thirty-nine feet. Section flagged. More strapping. One hundred and sixty-eight punctures. Fucking dismal setting. This one's messy. Going to take hours to clean. Doesn't matter. Paid by the hour. Do the work. Anchor the ribs. Repair the punctures. Three hours until the next drop. Thirty-three feet. Forty-one punctures. Clean. Mark. Measure. Drop. Sixty-seven feet. Completes forty-three punctures when Mo hears the hum through her headset, announcing the end of her shift. Mo retracts the scalpel and grasping claw and returns to the surface.

RESET (Day of Rest):

John allows an extra hour for the alarm. Starts the day with some basic maintenance. Clips his nails and sweeps them into the waste bin. Shower. Breakfast. Back to his room. Records a quick message for the family. Sends his love and assurance. After submitting the video file to transport, he stops by the rec room to look out the viewing window. Catch the dawn. Not alone. Two mercs playing videogames. Monsters. Giant necks. Traps. Deltoids. Arms. Thick brows. Size of their skulls. HGH and everything else. Tattooed mongoloids absorbed by the digital carnage on screen. John steps to the viewing window. Nothing to see. Still pitch-black outside.

Ren rolls out of bed. Strums on the guitar. Gentle chord progressions. Easy. Nice and easy. Finds a combination that works. Resonates. Pair it with the right lyrics and he might have a song. First one on the first album. Plans to write it during his stay. Records what he has. Makes some notes. Lets it rest. Ren puts the guitar down. Skips breakfast. Brings his coffee to the rec room. There's an attractive young woman in a baggy hoodie and jogging pants lying out on the couch staring up at the ceiling, arms crossed, jaw clenched, mouth tensed. Ren decides to interject.

"It's not that bad, is it?"

She tilts her head and meets Ren's eyes. Not annoyed but a far cry from friendly. He continues their introduction.

"How long you been here?"
"First week."
"That makes two of us."

Mo looks up at this lanky character. Late forties, early fifties maybe. Sharp features. Angled nose. Brown eyes. Kind eyes. Grey beard with some black left in it matching his streaked hair pulled back in a bun. His name's Ren. Veteran rigger. Fifteen years' experience. One of his teeth, the lateral incisor, is chipped and crooked. Endearing. Adds character. Something about this guy, his voice, has a presence that puts her at ease. Keeps the conversation going.

"Where were you stationed last?" asks Mo.
"The tower."
"Crazy."
"Yeah . . ."

He looks down. Away. Then back.

"You?"
"Grow grids."
"Right on. Certainly done my share of those."

Mo wants to know more about the tower. To hear about it firsthand, but it would be in poor taste to pry. Now's not the time. Not yet. Can't force it. Fighting the urge to ask if he's working on the trachea. She'd bet money he is but Rexen made her sign a non-disclosure. The riggers doing shift work in isolation. Given explicit instruction not to discuss it with anyone outside the parameters of work. Which seems to include everything outside the harness. Love to compare notes but it's not worth it. Never know who's listening.

WORK BRIEFING:

"Great first week. The work is getting done. Steady pace. No complaints. Today we start grafting. Grafts require time to heal so we need to get them started. Debridement—graft—debridement—graft. Alternating between the two each week as we go."

GRAFT:

It takes five minutes to graft the first puncture. John pulls the mesh from its cylinder. Stretches, staples, snips the mesh over the wound before spraying on the grafting solution until the mesh is no longer visible. Slow going at first but he's getting the hang of it. Moving from one to the next. Grafting 143 punctures in the first four hours of his shift.

Stretch. Staple. Snip. Spray. Next. Ren misses a marker and an alert goes off. Doubles back. Six hours in. Skin grafting what appears to be necrotic tissue. Slowly rotting. So how the hell does that work? What's the point? What's it matter? Following orders. Four hundred and eighty punctures sealed and grafted thus far. Once again, Ren is craving a goddamn cigarette.

Mo is in a mood. Trapped in this fucking hole eight hours a day and she can't listen to music while she works. Went with it at first but now she's pissed. Makes no difference for what they're doing. The sound cuts out during surface communications and M.A.P.S won't let you skip steps without approval. So what are they worried about? That she'll get distracted? By what? What's going to slow her down? Monkey work. More of the same. Nothing special. No reason for no music. Fucking bullshit. Fuck their NDA. Asking Ren. Gauge his response.

OFF-HOURS:

John stares at their family photo from the edge of his bed. Provide. He's the provider. What an honour. A blessing. More than enough. Must remember. Give thanks. Show gratitude. Nothing to fear. There is nothing to fear.

Walked in mid-scrap. Ren watching the cleanup crew kick up dust outside the viewing window. Still swinging on each other. No idea what set it off. The rest of the work detail watching them duke it out. Standing off to the side by a loader filled to the brim with dead fuglies they're culling and clearing to build the courtyard. In the distance he sees workers setting posts for the perimeter fence. Oblivious to the scrap that's taking place some fifty yards away. The fight ends up in the clinch followed by a hip toss and scramble on the ground. One of the combatants locks in a choke hold, squeezing the other guy unconscious when the rest of the crew runs in and separates them. Ren takes a sip his coffee. A little entertainment and the boys get to blow off some steam. No big deal. He takes a seat at the coach and scrolls through dispatches on his phone.

"Why no music?"

Ren looks up. It's Mo with a mini scowl. Hair up in a topknot. Furrowed brow. Wound tight. Arms crossed in a form-fitting black tracksuit. Can see her build. Fit. Fighting shape. Impressed.

"Work ordinance."
"Why, though?"
"Safety, I suppose."

Harness

"Bullshit."
"Keep us focussed on the job."
"It's not that complicated."
"Not yet."

Now they're talking. Mo ready to test her theory.

"When that happens, I'll turn my music off."

Ren puts his hands up in mock defense.

"Hey, it's not my call."
"You know what's distracting?"
"What?'
"An endless black void."

The trachea. Has to be. Ren scans the room. Just them.

"Clean. Mark. Measure."
"Stretch. Staple. Snip. Spray."
"Yeah its . . . it's something."
"You ever work a gig like this?"
"No. This one's . . . shall we say . . . unique."
"Music would help, right?"
"It would."
"I'm going to push Jim on it."
"Not his call. Safety guidelines for the job. We're handed to him."
"So who do I talk to?"
"Someone in health and safety. Rexen's legal department. Can't say. Just remember there's a lot of people not working right now."
"So, I'm replaced because I want to listen to music or a podcast while I'm stuck in the bowels of the beast or whatever the fuck that is."
"Not saying that but you've got to approach these things the right way."
"Obviously. I'm not going to be a cunt about it."
"Give it a shot, then."

"I will."

"Great."

"What's the first song you'd listen to?"

"Good question. Something to ponder."

DIAGNOSTICS (1 Month):

Blood pressure. Blood samples. Urine. Mandatory. Doctor Nadri checks on all John's vitals followed by a psychological assessment with staff counsellor Janice Gustavsson. John arrives at her office to find the door open. Knocks to announce himself. Janice looks up from her screen. Smile. Waves John in. Seems eager to see him. High energy.

"Hello, John, please come in."

The office filled with a variety of plants and a room containing a Lumen Capsule for colour bathing. Available to all with advanced booking. John directed to the couch. Takes a seat. Small talk to start. General pleasantries. Discuss family, onsite accommodations, etc. Fifteen minutes in, the evaluation takes a sudden shift to the job itself.

"So, John, tell me about the trachea."

Knows the name.

"What about our NDA?"

"Speak freely. This is a protected space. Nothing said here breaches the confidentiality agreement."

"What, uh . . . what do you want to know?"

"Anything. Everything. Share your thoughts. Feelings. Whatever it evokes."

"Umm . . . I, uh . . . I don't know."

"Is the work what you expected?"

"No, but I . . . my expectations have nothing to do with it."

"With what?"

"The job."

"How so?"

"They have no bearing on the work. What's required."

Harness

"Are the requirements being met?"
"Not for me to say. You'd have to ask Jim."

Ren considers the counsellor's question. Repeats it back to her.

"Do I feel safe and secure . . ."

Strange wording. Too wide. Too broad.

"Regarding the trachea, automation is a double-edged sword, right? Operating at that depth, that distance, requires precision instrumentation. The tensile load needs to be exact. If there's a glitch, a defect, or miscalculation, things can go upside down and sideways real fast. But you know . . . Inherent risk. It's right there in our contract. Why we get paid the big bucks."
"Understanding that, do you believe, based on your informed professional opinion, the work is being done in a manner that meets your metrics for safety?"
"So far, so good but I mean . . . this is a strange one."
"How so?"
"How so? Have you seen the fuckin' thing?"

The evaluation taking a sharp turn into the abstract. Mo fires back the same question.

"What does it represent to you?"
"I can't speak from your vantage point."
"You've got an imagination. Put yourself in my place. You're suspended thousands of feet underground, over an endless pit, inside a rotting flesh chute of unknown origin for unknown reasons. These are the realities of my work environment. So, you tell me—what does the trachea mean to you?"

TYRANT

Flipped the script. Caught her off guard. Calculating a response.

"I'm not being evaluated. It's your interpretation that matters."

"Why? What difference does it make? The work is the work. I'm doing the job that's been asked of me."

"We can move on. You're not required to answer the question."

"Are you given a list or do you come up with these questions on your own?"

"Let's move on. As you are aware, the amount of time it takes to lower you to your starting point then bring you back from your end point has to be calculated into the workday. As the project progresses, the window of work grows smaller. Adhering to your work contract regarding turnaround and overtime, what are your thoughts on creating temporary rest stations within the trachea to allow an interval of recovery, followed by the resumption of work from said area?"

"Honest answer?"

"Of course."

"It sounds awful and I'd want to renegotiate my contract."

"Duly noted."

WORK BRIEFING:

"The requested amendments in your contract have been ratified and we're ready to begin the next stage of work. Know that your professionalism thus far is greatly appreciated. This project, its undertaking, is unprecedented in a number of ways. We apply our expertise, knowledge, skill sets to the work but we're also learning as we go. Making the necessary adjustments. Pushing the boundaries of what's possible. Part of what makes this collaboration, this challenge, so special. Why we must continue to practice patience and steel our resolve. It's an arduous process at times, as you can attest. No denying it. Three months in . . . We're a quarter of the way there. Let's maintain our focus and see this thing through."

Harness

OVERNIGHT:

Trial run. In the hole for forty-eight hours. Six-hour work shifts with two-hour rest intervals. Operating at his overtime rate in hour one. Paid for every hour he's in the trachea, then recieveing a twelve hour flat rate when he's not. That's the agreement for working overnights. Give it a go, see what happens. John attaches his harness to hoist and lowers himself into the trachea. Takes two hours to reach the first marker. Can only go so fast. Three months in and they're doing overnights. How long can they keep this going? Once the drop time to reach the starting marker crosses a certain threshold it will no longer be viable work for human operators. Can't imagine anyone willing to stay in the trachea for over a week. Not sure he can last two days. The questions remain: How far down does it go? Are they willing to go? At some point, line loss will become an issue. The new conduit is incredible but there's a limit to all things. They can't afford a "glitch" at these depths. A true medical emergency would likely be fatal. Too far down. Hours to reach the surface. Stop. Just stop. John catches himself. Fixating on negative outcomes beyond his control. Do the job or don't. Finish the year. Finish the contract. Return to his family. How it's going to be.

Ren attaches the resting station to the ribbing by drilling diamond-tipped anchors into the bone. Eight points to secure and spread the web. Able to adjust the tension from each point but likes where it is. Can walk on the web but there's still some give. Ren disconnects from the back clasp, clipping into the chest clasp. Plugged in, he lets out enough slack to lie on his back. It's that or his stomach. Those are the options. Tethered at all times. Two hours' rest. First attempt in the bowels of the beast. Ren closes his eyes. Breathing through his nose. Slow. Measured. Relaxed. Home is where the heart is. He is here. He is home. Anywhere. All times.

Up. Down. Same view either way. As above so below. Lost the surface light long ago. Mo staring into black from her back. Not tired. Annoyed. Two hours of nothing. No music. Was sure they'd make an exception for the overnight. Something soothing during their rest intervals. Denied from on high. Neither Jim nor Jan could explain it. Beyond their jurisdiction. Nothing more to say on the matter. Now it's just her and her thoughts. No, thanks. Rather not. Money, remember the money. Making bank. Will be the most she's ever made by far. Game changer. Can buy her truck and then some. Four more contracts on par with this one and she's set. Bases covered. Everything else goes to retirement.

The pulse of the alarm wakes John from his fourth rest interval. The first stop he's slept straight through. Shut his eyes and was out like a light. Feels good. Refreshed.

"Good morning, ground control."

"Good morning, John."

"Switching plugs and we'll get started."

"Copy that."

John switches his line from front to back. Bumps up. Hovering just above the webbing, he removes the resting station. Packs it. Takes a piss and begins again. Clean. Mark. Measure. Drop. Clean. Mark. Drop . . .

Exhausted. Wired. Restless. Bored. Can't sleep. Not this time. Ren walks the webbing to the wall. Shines his light through a bowling-ball-sized puncture. About an arm's length to the outside. Bizarre how the depth, damage, and decay to the dermis varies at each site. One section of wall, of lining, looks like it was hit with buckshot and another like it was attacked by a tiger. Some sections have meat on them while others are threadbare strands of tissue between him and the void. What's he looking at? What's he looking into? Cavern? Cavity? Eats up the light. Snuffed out after twenty feet. Absorbed.

Harness

Not alone. She's not alone. Head lamp on. To her right. Seated against the wall. Legs crossed. Weeping. Rocking. Dad. Father. Face in hands. Looks up. Light reflected across the black mask. Face coated in crystals. Frozen in pain. Mouth open. Eyes covered. Sealed. Screaming into the next one. A dream. Awake. In danger. In the shadows from the shadows. Attacking from the edge. Closing in. Get up. Sit up. Glitching. Locked. Move. Stuck. Scalpel. Pop the scalpel. Can't. Closing in. Now. No no no—

Awake. Actually awake. Still buzzing. Sleep paralysis. Years since she had one. Now four in her lifetime. Unequivocally terrifying. A straight shot of fear. Same features each time. False awakenings. From one nightmare into the next. The last "wake-up" always involves the shadow figures lurking in the peripheral of wherever she's sleeping. Evil intentions. The shadow creeping in for the kill the second she registers its presence. An immediate undeniable threat that sends her into fits, spasms, as she tries to break the grip of paralysis. Overwhelmed, she cracks the dream. Wakes up for real. Mo checks the time. Thirty minutes before the alarm. Fuck that. Final shift of the overnight. Pack it up and get to work.

OFF-HOURS:

Two objectives. Write his family a letter and schedule a massage. His body bent out of shape from forty-eight hours in his harness but what really hurts is how much John misses his wife and child. Here now but he won't do it again. This will be the largest payment he's ever earned by a landslide and they'd have to double it for him to even consider returning. The isolation he can endure but he misses his family way too much. Lilly's laughter. Elroy's fixed interest on anything that grabs his attention, from the pages of his bedtime story to the bees in their garden. The look on his face. His focus. It's almost comedic. Makes him see things from a new angle. Another lens. Shared wonder. It aches how much he misses them. This job. The trachea. He will accept its blessing. The ability to earn. To provide. Complete his contract and return home. Home is where the heart is. Never has a statement rang so true. The further away, the stronger the pull. Too far. Too long. Lesson learned.

Something to loosen up would be nice. Soak up the sun rays and sip an ice-cold beer, or two, or three, or four. Decompress. Let the mind drift for a moment. Light inebriation. Subtle. Strum up a tune back in his room. That would be ideal but it's not in the cards. Dry planet in more ways than one. Sober living unless you've got a script for meds. Not so bad but also, at times, fuckin' sucks. Nice to have a courtyard. Outside space. The site still expanding. Increasing the scale of the operations. Adding water boxes. Installing another greenhouse. More options for recreation. Ren rounds the bend of the building. Passes the recently paved basketball court. Empty. Clear. Most workers at work. Grabs a ball from the rack. Feels good to bounce it off the ground. Between his legs. Takes a few shots. Makes thirty and moves on. Reaches the rock garden. Steps through the bamboo gates. Takes a seat on the bamboo bench. Admires the layout. A few large rocks strategically placed amongst gravel that's raked into patterns: ripple, stream, straight line, plant, vortices, water drop, waves. These lines, these patterns, have a calming effect. Structure. Order. Creation. A place for all things. Likes where it leads him. Called a Zen garden for a reason.

Weight room. Heavy bag. Endless pool. Mo switches from her one-piece to a black bikini. Hits the sundeck. Takes a sip from her bottle of lemon water and lays her towel down on the beach chair. Sits down. Leans back. Likes what she saw in the weight room. Cute guy skipping rope. Hitting the speed bag like a pro. Standing five-nine, maybe five-ten. Shaved head. Blue eyes. Bent nose. The bridge basically gone. Crushed. Cauliflower ear. Chipped tooth. Likes his look. Making a move next time she sees him. Has to. No idea when they cross paths again. Every department, team, worker on their own schedule. Met people at the start she's never seen again. Not leaving it to chance. Going for it. Getting bored and horny out here. Brought her vibrator but the real thing would be nice. Hopefully he's into it. Why wouldn't he be? Might have a girlfriend waiting patiently for him back home. Yeah, sure. See you in a year. Not even going to ask. Let him bring it up. Home is home. Here is now.

Surprise. John scrambling for a response. Yua, the beautiful Japanese woman he booked his massage with is not available but the big black guy is. Of course, he has no problem with anyone's skin pigment, it's more the "man" part. A massage is a personal thing. Personal space. Never been massaged by a man's hands and the idea of it makes him somewhat uncomfortable.

"No pressure, John. I'm only offering it as an option."
"Uh, yeah . . . I, uh, I was, uh . . ."
"All good, John. I get it. Whatever you're comfortable with. Just know if there's aches, pains, strains, or general muscle tension that's troubling you, I can help. I promise. I'm good at this."
"Yeah, I know, yeah, yes, of course."
"I'm Ellis, by the way."

Warm smile. Strong handshake. Athletic build. His musculature. His frame. Legs like a running back. Wonders if he played.

"Nice to meet you, Ellis."
"So, what would you prefer? Rebook with Yua or I can see you now."

John checks his watch for some reason. Stalling, fumbling, trying to make a decision. Why not? Who cares? Needs it. Neck and back painfully stiff. No need to suffer. Loosen up. The man's a professional.

"Yeah, you know, yeah . . . yeah, now works, sure."
"Great, let's head on back. Work out the kinks."

John follows Ellis down the hallway to the massage table.

"So change up. Get under the towel. I'm right outside the door. Holla at me and we'll get to work."

"Great. Sounds good."

Ellis closes the door. Now what? Conflicted. Does he keep his briefs on or not? Could offend him either way. No. Being silly. Everyone's adults here. Strip down. Get under the towel. Relax. Let the man work. No big deal.

Ren looks up from the courtyard. Perfect circle. Glowing white. The moon die cut like the sun. No craters or markings. Not a star to be seen. Strange considering there's little to no light pollution and zero cloud cover. Bizarre, but he's done trying to explain this place. Ren walks towards the ever-expanding perimeter. The fuglies culled, removed, pushed back. Sound buffers installed along the wall fence, but when he places his ear to it, Ren can still hear their song. The faint sound of snarling and screeching as they cannibalize each other on the outside. Fucked up. Strange setting. Has a knack for finding them. Didn't need drugs for this one although he'd gladly partake. Just a joint would be nice. A low-grade indica. Listen to music. Play music. Kick back and watch a movie. Munchies from the kitchen. Reminds him of the redhead. Part of the kitchen staff. Placing her in her forties. Saw her at the chow hall in her chef whites, seated at the far table, taking notes with a stern look on her face. Can tell she's got some curves under her kitchen garb. Sexy in her own way. Intense. Definitely piqued his interest but who's to say when he'll see her again. That's the thing about this place. You never know.

What luck. Mo finds her man watching cartoons in the rec room. Just her and him and some grunts playing foosball in the corner. Out of earshot. Perfect time to make a move but she's not so sure now. Looks different. Baggy hoodie, ripped jeans, but it's not what he's wearing. Bad posture. The way he's sitting. Leaning back on the couch but still hunched over. Hand on his lap. Neck out. Mouth open. Might be a mouth breather. Can understand with the broken nose, a deviated septum, but he looks sort of slack-jawed.

Harness

Somewhat vacant. Perplexed by what he's watching or a little too absorbed. Something onscreen makes him laugh and she sees the spark. Snaps back into focus. Normal laugh. Not retarded. Mo moves in. Stands behind the couch.

"What are we watching?"

He checks behind his shoulder to see who's asking. Turns back to his cartoon.

"Bog Fog."

Tentacled creatures dancing around a rusted oil drum with emerald flames lashing out from the open top. Mo takes a seat at the other end of the couch. Crosses her arms and legs.

"I'm bored."

Hoodie still up, he gives her a quick glance then it's back to the bog.

"Sorry, am I interrupting your show?"
"Nah, just something to watch."
"What's your name?"
"Cort."
"Hi, Cort. My name's Mo."
"Hey."
"Hay is for horses, grass is free."
"You breaking my balls?"

Asked still staring at his cartoon.

"Maybe. What do you do here?"
"Heavy equipment. Driving a hauler at the mine."
"Long hours?"
"Twelves. How bout you?"
"Rigging."
"Rigging what?"
"Whatever they ask me to."
"Okay."
"Saw you at the gym yesterday."
"Saw you too."
"Watched you working that speed bag."
"What about it?"

"Seem to know what you're doing."
"Should hope so."
"Noticed your ears."
"What about 'em?"
"You wrestle?"
"Used to."
"You fight?"
"Used to."
"Why'd you stop?"
"Wasn't paying my bills. Lost my last one."
"How bad?"
"Knockout."
"Lucky shot?"
"Nope. Was getting beaten pillar to post."
"That sucks."
"Sure does."

Mo twirls her hair. Considers her course of action. Best be direct before they're interrupted.

"You wanna play ping pong, maybe shuffleboard, when your show's over?"
"Which one? Can play right now."

Straight to it. Roll the dice.

"Or maybe we skip the games and do something else."
"Sounds good."
"Yeah?"
"You tell me."
"Your place or mine?"
"I'm in open barracks."
"Mine it is."

Mo leads the way. Across corridors, they reach her room. Stopped outside the door, she states her stipulation.

"If we do this, no drama. No bullshit."
"No problem."

Harness

Likes his answer. Lets him in.

Immediate rapport. In sync. Strong finish. Allows a minute for the afterglow and lets him know.

> "Nice work."
> "Takes two."
> "Happy to do my part . . . Having said that, it's time to go."

Cort smiles. Doffs his imaginary hat.

> "Understood."

Leaves her bed. Pulls on his pants and underwear. Easy. No attitude. Mo extends her appreciation.

> "That was fun. Thank you."
> "Much obliged."

Cort buckles his belt. Digits exchanged. Points of contact. No plans. No pressure.

John wakes up with the lights on. Checks the time. 4 a.m. Returned to his room after the massage and passed out. Slept right through dinner. Thirsty. Needs water. John sits up slowly. Tests his neck. Relief. The pain is gone. Full range of motion. Checks his arm, the tendinitis in his elbow, turns and twist it. Noticeable improvement. Hurt like heck when Ellis applied the pressure but it's much better now. Back. Shoulders. Hips. Unlocked them. Worked out the kinks. Crazy strength. Putty in his hands. Found where the pain is and kneaded it out. Intense, painful at times, but well worth it. What now? Wide awake. Take advantage. A swim to kickstart his metabolism, followed by rolled oats for breakfast. Practice his Mandarin. Promised himself he'd complete the course by the end of the year. Work on the mech model for a few hours. Walk the yard. Get some sun. Start work on the next module: How to Handle a Vortex Across a Pressure Boundary. Has been stalling with school. Still struggling to absorb the subject matter. Nowhere near an assessment. Must commit during his off hours. Made the investment. Follow through for the family. Earn his degree. An alternative to rigging. That's the idea. Less risk. Longer window of employment. Better pay. Closer to home. Patience. Persistence. That's the key.

Three months. Three songs. Might have an album by year's end. Or not. Ren's done forcing these things. If it's there, grab it. If not, oh well. Oh fucking well. Making money. Good money. For what, though? For what? The question that's been nagging at him. Early on it was evident. Food. Shelter. Survival. Then some lean years. Scarcity. One step forward. Ten back. Snakes and ladders. Opiates. Opioids. Scrapping it together when he was getting off the gear. Fucking brutal. Ren remembers being junk sick in a lift. Hiding in the bucket. Tucked into the rafters at the back of the building. Found a way. Rode it out. Recovered. Took some time. Traction. Tools. Savings. Hard lessons formed his foundation. Just in time. Dodged the rockslide. Stayed away from the shale. Spread like a wildfire when it hit the streets. A little ambition, attainable short-term goals, and some self-respect quelled his curiosity long enough to see the side effects. Some saw it as a sacred medicine. Others a good time. Either way, it ended in affliction. Biological slavery. By the time it arrived, he was done seeking outside salvation. Enough with the external stimulus. The answers arrive from within. Patience. Perseverance. Nothing lacking. No rush. Steadfast and forgiving of self. Already there. Here. Complete. A remarkable transformation in hindsight. Thought he was fucked. Boxed in. Broken. Cornered. Soon to be crushed. Now there's options. The earnings from this assignment ups the ante. He could actually make a move. Plant roots. Four to six more years on the same contract and he can contemplate retirement. Which is what? What's he doing? What's he leaving? Legacy. There's that word again. Was never applicable. Now it's on the table. Does he need a mini me? Is that the idea? Create the conduit. Another branch. Level up. Divine duty. Biological imperative. Has a dozen nieces and nephews. Does he really need his own kid? His family certainly thought so but gave up a while ago. Stopped pushing when he passed forty. Still in great shape, though. Far better condition than when he was in his thirties, for obvious reasons. Maybe that's the move. Find a willing participant. Plant a

Harness

seed. Watch it grow. Raise it right. Something beyond yourself. A tall order at his age. Any age. Is that the path? Man needs a mission. Purpose. Or they spiral in its absence. Makes sense but it's simply not how he operates. Driven but it's incremental. Shorts burst out of necessity. Skin in the game. Beholden to the system's financial prerequisites for survival. Otherwise, he'd gladly float gently down the stream. Observe. Reflect. Partake. Enjoy. Not how it works, though. The rocks shape the river. Resistance required. Let it flow.

Iced coffee in the courtyard. Waiting out the morning rush to take a shit. Hates having to use the communal washroom. Another fifteen and it's all clear. So is she. Can start the day. Light breakfast. Coconut kefir with raspberries, blueberries, and toasted pumpkin seeds. Mo allows a moment to digest, packs her bag, and hits the climbing wall for a few hours. One other person using it. A stocky Asian man with a scar running down the back of his skull to the top of his neck. A simple nod is all that's required. An acknowledgement of the other's presence. Strong climber for his size. Carries his weight well. Mo goes until her grip strength is gone. Arms cramping. Calls it. Back to her room. Change into bikini. Lemon cucumber water from the mini fridge. Towel over her shoulder. Slides on. Out the door. Runs into Ren kicking back on a beach chair. Hair down. Shades on. Sweating in the sun.

"Moseph, what's happening?"

Ren's impromptu combination of broseph and Mo.

"Getting some sun before I go back in the hole."
"Great idea."

Ren takes a slow sip of water.

"Enjoy the overnight?"
"I'll enjoy the money."
"How'd you sleep down there?"
"Like a baby."
"Really?"
"Fuck no."

"Strange setting to catch some shuteye."
"It's fucked down there."
"Ain't the place if you're claustrophobic."
"Ain't the place period."
"Imagine a face or an eyeball peering through a puncture."
"Stab it with the scalpel."
"Might set off a chain reaction."
"You ever reach out past the puncture?"
"No, thanks. Seen that movie."

Clocks two hours of focussed study on toroidal fields. Quick reset in the rock garden. John watches the old Russian rakes the gravel. Thin build. Shaved head. Long beard. Sad eyes. Custodian. Maintenance man. Not sure what his job title is. Can fix a leaky faucet or reset a malfunctioning access panel. During the evenings, he's usually driving the industrial floor scrubber around base. Watches him smooth the gravel to an even thickness with a fine-toothed metal rake, erasing old patterns before using a wide-toothed wooden rake to trace the new ones. A mesmerizing process. Precise. Effortless. A natural. Watched him build it but was it his idea? Might be the curator. Finishes one section, smooths out another, stops, turns to John, holds out the wooden rake. An offering.

"No. No, thank you. Thank you, though. Don't want to mess it up."
"The gravel?"
"Yeah."
"How you do this?"
"You've created such lovely lines, your patterns, I don't want to ruin the look. The, uh . . . the effect you've created."
"I leave. You rake."

The Russian leans the rake against the bamboo fencing. Gives a subtle bow to John before leaving.

Harness

Shooting hoops, Ren sees Sergei measuring and marking out a ten-foot by twenty-foot section of the courtyard. Tagging the corners with orange spray paint. Outside the lines is a bale of chicken wire, t-posts, tin snips, edger/trencher, and sledgehammer. Ren puts the ball back in the rack. Walks over to see what he's working on.

"What up, Sergei? We building a chicken coop?"
"Surprise. You see tomorrow."
"Working the next two days. Won't see it."
"You see after."
"We starting a petting zoo?"
"Petting zoo?"
"A little farm. Mini farm for kids. Rabbits. Sheep. Small animals. Maybe a llama."
"No. No llama. You see."
"I see."

Sergei fires up the trencher. Ren leaves him be.

Dread. Mo doesn't want to go back there. Definitely doesn't want to sleep there. Fuckin' nightmare. Tough luck. Too bad. Had an out and didn't take it. Could have stepped away when they switched to overnights. Within her rights. Had to change the contact. No longer beholden but she saw the money and doubled down. Committed. Now she needs to suck it up. So what if it's not the ideal work environment? Rarely is. The work is what matters. Task at hand. The system has safety on top of safety. Load limit isn't an issue. Neither is the weather. All self-contained. Needs to stop spiralling over preconceived calamities. Nerves. That's all. Nervous energy. Needs to hit the heavy bag.

OVERNIGHT:

Clean. Mark. Measure. Stop. Six hours in. Set up the rest station. Anchor the webbing. Switch plugs. Lie back. John can feel the keloid scar on the back of his head/neck pressing against his helmet. Can always feel it. Tightness. A tension. Doesn't limit movement but it's always there. The reminder. Working on the tower two years before its collapse. Long hours. Obscene. Pushed to exhaustion. Couldn't say no. Lilly was pregnant. Bills to pay. Piling up. Accrued interest. Took on too much too soon. Starts with a toothache. Nagging. Getting worse. Side of his jaw is swollen. Swollen. Gargles with salt water. Applies various salves. Oral gels. Ibuprofen. Not going away. Push through. Fight past. Pain starts to subside. Almost manageable or maybe his tolerance has gone up. Pulls another powershift. Wakes up in the middle of night. Nauseous. Spinning. Bucket by the bed. Pukes himself to sleep. Wakes up the next morning and everything's off. Extreme vertigo. Can't get out of bed. Half his body is paralyzed. Not responding. Limbs won't listen. Can't form his words. Every utterance mangled. A very pregnant Lilly appears in the doorway. Kneels down by the bedside. Can't understand a word she's saying. Gibberish. Like listening to a record in reverse. Completely scrambled. Paramedics arrive. Rushed to hospital. Suspected odontogenic infection. Administered empirical antibiotics. During imaging analyses, a one-centimetre by one-centimetre perforation of the right sphenoid bone is detected and the MRI showed a 1.3-centimetre by 1.8-centimetre capsulated regular mass in the right temporal lobe along with irregular edema. Diagnosed with a brain abscess of dental origin. Put under. Intubated. Undergoes abscess drainage through decompressive craniotomy and aspiration. Approximately eight millilitres of yellowish-brown pus was aspirated from the lesion. Put on postoperative intravenous antibiotic therapy until all symptoms subsided. After forty-eight hours, there was no bacterial growth from the pus culture. A week after undergoing decompressive craniotomy, his cracked upper right second molar, suspected to be the source of the infection, is extracted while under local anesthesia. Handed a two-month script for antibiotics and discharged from the hospital with neurological sequela. Damage to his central nervous system requiring a year of speech therapy and rehabilitation motor function to repair and restore what was lost. School and work on pause. Stalled. Suspended. Savings gone. Major setback. Baby born. Elroy. At home with his son for year one. Its own blessing. Help Lilly where he can. A joy watching Elroy awaken to world. No time, no place for self-pity. Progress. Provide. Don't let them down. Won't let them down.

Harness

Clean. Mark. Measure. Drop. Alert. Section flagged. Tore up. Like a dirty bomb went off inside. Ten thousand six hundred and seventy-four punctures. Straps the ribs. Sixteen diamond anchors. Eight points. Eight lines. Not much to clean. Ren can mesh over most of it. Takes a sip of Nor before popping the scalpel. The idea of a cigarette is still there, stopping for a smoke break, but the physical craving is gone. No longer nags at him. Cigarettes and booze. Last ones on the list. Truly sober for the first time in for-fucking-ever. Knows it's a dry jobsite but still counts. Does it? Knew in advance. Made the choice to be here. But could he abstain otherwise? Would he, is the real question. Was managing before he left. Trying to keep the alcohol in check. Functioning, as they say. Knew when he kicked heroin that he didn't want to dive into the bottle. Another road to hell. Al-Kuhl in Arabic. Translates to the "Body-eating spirit." Sneaks up on ya. From a glass of wine with a dinner to cracking cold ones every day after work with a couple pints at lunch. Had to check himself a few times. Could tell it was fucking with his sleep. Lowering the circadian rhythm. Corrosive. Felt more susceptible to lower impulses. Fear, anger, envy. All amplified. Underlying anxiety. Ratcheting up. Distorted. Getting worse. Needed a drink to normalize. Had to rein it in but Sabine still wanted to party. Wasn't going to stop her. Not how it works and she was already pulling away. Could feel it. Hurt. But they had their fun. Goddamn did they have some fun.

To the core. Cold. Fucking shaking. Teeth chattering. The trachea coated in layers of frost. Freezer burned. Further down. Colder still. Starting to sting. Burning Mo's extremities: ears, nose, feet, hands. Continues the descent. Getting worse. Going numb. Looks up. The conduit collecting ice. Can't continue. Calls it in. No response from ground control. Not waiting. Rise up. Nothing. The line is dead. Tries again. Nothing. Can't be. Not happening. Terror. Panic. Stop. Don't spiral. Concentrate. Switching systems. Manual ascension: Waist Prusik with a hollow block attachment and a climb heist on a double-length sling for her foot. Taking up slack. Alternating between the waist Prusik and foot sling. Sit. Stand. Adjust. Sit. Stand. Adjust.

Muscles losing heat. Contracting. Cramping. Too slow. Too cold. Too far down. Fucked. She's fucked. Can't be. Not like this. Gut-wrenching realization. Game over. No—Mo's eyes snap open. Another nightmare. Every damn time she closes her eyes down here. Again with thirty minutes left on the clock. Not happening. Lights on. Sit up. Warm up. Actually cold. Mind made her cold. Brought down her body temperature. How does that work? Get moving. Clasp to the back. Mo packs the rest station and starts her shift.

Strapped in. John drills the last anchor. Shocked the section was still hanging on. Dermis destroyed. Like it was attacked by a swarm of locusts. Almost translucent. Tattered cheesecloth. Defies logic that the rest of the trachea didn't detach. Ripped right off. The weight alone. John shines his arm light down the trachea, a light with an output of two hundred thousand lumens that can reach over eight thousand feet, and it's simply absorbed by the black. Nothing's changed. No end in sight. Does not make sense. The distance, length, weight, and decay of this rotting structure. It should have snapped apart. Dead hang. For how long? The spinal column somehow still holding together. What is it? Was it? This creature. Snake. Serpent. How long did it take to send a signal down the spinal cord? Never ends. How'd it function? Impossible to conceptualize the biological requirements. Its growth curve. Should not exist. How could it survive down here? In the absence? How did it generate that kind of mass? From what? Not right. None of this. Mind racing. Reeling. Starting to unspool. Elevated heart rate. Chest getting tight. Bring it in. Breathe. Physiological sigh. Double inhale, extended exhale. In through the nose. Fill the lungs to capacity, sneak in another inhale, a little more air at the end. Inflate the alveoli. Slow exhale. Offload the carbon dioxide. Repeat three times. Better. Slowing down. Centre. Back to centre. Let go—gain control. Clinging to questions he doesn't need to answer. Can't answer. The work. The work is getting done. Back to it.

Harness

Hundreds of feet. Ren still descending. Mind drifting. What if? What if he stopped, popped the scalpel, and sliced a section off? Hacked through the massive vertebrae. Disconnect. Sever. Let it fall. Watch what's left tumble into the void. Vanish out of existence. How's that play out? Fired? Charged? Arrested? Jailed? Who knows how far it escalates for him, but the project itself? What happens? What do they do? These lungs they referenced at the beginning, could they connect them at the cut or does this windpipe actually go somewhere? What's at the end? Where's the connection? The intersection? Why? For what? On and on it goes. Where it stops, nobody knows . . .

Flag on the play. Three in a row. Thirty-nine feet. Twenty-four straps. Six thousand four hundred and fifty-two punctures. Five hundred and forty-three requiring debridement. Kept her busy. Occupied. Now rest. Needs it. Mo lying in the centre of the web. Eyes closed. Sleep. No more nightmares. Two hours. All she's asking. Last one had her shook. The cold. That cold. Dredged things up again. To the surface. Ugly. Such an ugly ending. The regret still raw. Returned to the trailer. Sees the small mound of cocaine, white residue smeared across the coffee table. Dad's got company. Skinny woman with bad tattoos and a worse perm. Hair bleached. Fried. In her bra and panties on their couch. Snorts a line. Looks up. Sees Mo standing in the kitchen. Watching. Poor woman is mortified. Curls up. Hiding her face. Humiliated. Dad unfazed. Sitting in his underwear, smoking inside. Takes a drag, butts out in one of the many beer cans covering the coffee table. Didn't care or forgot she was flying home that morning from a visit with her mother. Carves himself another line. Snorts it.

"How's Mom?"

Brutal. Blatant disrespect. At a loss for words. He could stay with her so long as he was sober and looking for work. That was the deal. Their arrangement. Done with his bullshit. The self-sabotage. Won't participate. When she finds the words, they're final.

"Get out. Don't come back."

No objection. Nods. Concedes. Scrape his cocaine into a paper bindle while the woman, avoiding eye contact, puts her clothes back on. Everyone dressed. Dad pockets his pack of cigarettes and they're out the door. No parting words. No condition to drive but he gets behind the wheel of his truck. Backs out. Drives off. Doesn't want him to crash, kill someone, have it on her conscience. Struggle over calling the cops but she can't do it. Can't call him in. So she prays, prays that he doesn't hurt anyone. Pathetic. What it's come to? What she's left with? Next day. No news is good news. Not a clue where he went. Ended up. Couldn't care less as long as it's away from her. Out of sight. Out of mind. How it has to be. How it is. Months later. Temperature plummets. Extreme cold front stretching into the new year. The kind to catch your lungs, sting your skin. Wake up for work and he's parked in her driveway. Truck still running. Pulls on her boots, parka, toque. Steps outside. Sees him. Steadies herself. No need to check for a pulse but she does. Nothing. Turns off the ignition. He's gone. Empty vessel. Shell. Leaned back in the driver's seat, eyes half open. Glass pipe in his hand, on his lap. Black crystalline deposits on his skin, from his pores. Shale. Started smoking shale. Crusted yellow vomit around the mouth and neck. His complexion grey, white, waxen. Blue lips. Dad's dead. Matter of fact.

OFF-HOURS:

Back on solid ground. John lays out the yoga mat. Needs to address his anxiety. Getting worse. His psyche starting to reject the setting. Could feel his cortisol spiking on the last drop. Never wants to use the needle. An admission of defeat. If it gets so bad that forced sedation is required, he may as well quit. How could he go back? Nothing changes. Same location. Same stressors. Likely happen again. Needs to be proactive. Refocus on his breathwork and meditation. Increase his capacity for stress. Condition his nervous system. Can work on it like any other muscle. Build resistance. Strength. Practice. Fire up those fear receptors. Fight or flight. Find a way. Calm in the storm.

Harness

New addition to the dust bowl. A most welcome surprise. Amazing little creature. Adorable. Such character. Marches straight over to Ren. Neck out. Fearless. Looking right up at them.

"Ernest . . ." Ren repeating its name.

Sergei nods, smiling down at the baby tortoise. It's the first time Ren's seen him smile.

"What kind of tortoise?" asks Ren.
"Sulcata."

Sergei pulls out the hibiscus flower from his chest pocket, offering it to Ernest, who charges across the dirt and starts munching on the petal.

"Really going for it."
"Good appetite."
"What else do you feed him?"
"Grass, hay, shrubs, other edible flowers. Greens from kitchen like bok choy, watercress, escarole, parsley, turnip greens, green onions, red leaf, green leaf, or butter lettuce."
"Getting plenty of chlorophyll."

Sergei hands the hibiscus to Ren, who offers it to Ernest, who rushes in and resumes munching on his flower.

"Large enclosure for a little guy."
"Little now."
"How big?"
"Three feet length, hundred, hundred fifty, maybe two hundred pounds."
"No wonder he's mowing down. Little guy has some growing to do."

Ernest looks up at Ren. Pieces of pink hibiscus petal hanging off his mouth. The small tortoise bobs its head. A quick thank you, perhaps. Then it keeps chewing. Ren feels acknowledged. An honour. More than welcome.

"He's awesome."

TYRANT

Once Ernest has had his fill he wonders off in another direction. Kindred spirits.

Well past it. Why? Why's she still stuck on this? Plagued by the same old questions. Why didn't he knock? Was he too fucked up to stand? Was it a message? On purpose? Suicide? No note. Who knows—who cares. Dead is dead. Rest in peace and that's the end of it. What was she supposed to do? The guy had everything going for him. Loving wife. Healthy child. Thriving business. Summit Scaffold. Solid crew. Steady expansion. Bigger and bigger contracts. Would bring her to their jobsites with her little hard hat and lunch box. Have lunch with the boys. Loved it. Then he got high on his own success. Starts splurging. Buys the boat, jet ski, motorcycle, vacation home. Spending more time at the pub than he does at home. Fucking around on Mom. Showing up wasted. Starts slipping with work. Making mistakes. Snorting their earnings up his nose. Losing contracts and crew. Overextended. Stretched so thin there's nothing left to save. Pissed it all away. Not her problem. Shed her tears. Slayed her demons. Trying to. At some point you've got to get your act together. Quit fucking around. Stop staring at the ceiling. Mo sits up. Springs into action. Stuck in her head long enough. Packs her gym bag. Sweat it out. Hit the heavy bag. Unleash.

Delivery. John opens his mail packet. Presses play on the tablet. A slideshow of Lilly and Elroy, followed by pictures from the ultrasound, then a time lapse of blossoming rhododendrons. A girl. They're having a girl. Azalea. Agreed upon. A daughter. Incredible. Boy then girl. Brother. Sister. Just like that. Heart flooded with gratitude. A warm serenity. Strength. He's going to finish the job, get back home, and hold his daughter. It's as simple as that. God willing. Always. Of course. With humility. Now what? Was going to study. Will study. Right now, a walk in the sun. Bask in the moment if only for a moment. Blessed.

Harness

Four songs now. Working on five. Hands cramping. Ren gives his fingers a rest. Go visit his new buddy. Beholds a vision of the beautiful Yua inside the enclosure. Sundress and shorts. Kneeling down watching Ernest burrow into his sandbox. Needs to book another appointment with her. In the harness for forty-eight hours. Suspended the majority of the time. Arms extended. Makes the adjustments but there's odd angles. Aches and pain are adding up. How it goes. Ren announces himself, not wanting to barge in.

"He's something, ain't he?"

Yua turns. Smiles back. Warm. Welcoming.

"Our new arrival is quite active."
"Covers a lot of ground for a little guy."

Yua stands up. Ren enters the enclosure.

"Sergei was telling me Sulcatas can get as big two hundred pounds."
"Wow . . ."
"Yeah . . ."
"Can live upwards of seventy years."
"Think they'll be here that long?"
"Appears so. Keep expanding."
"How's your back?"
"Should book another appointment. Getting a little tight. Starting to wrench up. Shoulder too. Working on it with the tension bands but it gets a little wonky. Feels like there's an impingement or something"
"Book a time. We'll address both issues. If you're experiencing pain or discomfort, you don't want to prolong it."
"Preventive medicine."
"Exactly."
"I'll schedule an appointment today."
"Please do."
"On that note, I have a booking in ten minutes."

"Duty calls."

"It does. Bye, Ernest."

"You know his name?"

"It was in the announcements. Bio introduced Ernest with a species profile."

"Cool."

"Nice seeing you."

"Likewise."

With a wave, she's gone. Ernest stopped burrowing. Now looking up at him.

"I know, buddy. I know. She's married."

Meathead merc with the mullet hawk. Dark tan. Green eyes. Ripped physique. Shredded. Swole. More like a bodybuilder. That type of vascularity. Steroids for sure. Covered in tattoos. Standard fare: script, skulls, shield, spear, sword, various apex predators. Another aspiring Spartan. Nothing new. He made a move. Good enough. Bored. Mo brought him back. Nothing special. Out of sync. Pounding away. Performative. A little too intense. Sort of silly. Self-involved. God's gift. Got off but had to tune him out. Knows he'll brag to his buddies. Obviously. Oh well. Fuck them. Who cares. She does. Can't deny it. Sort of gross. Somewhat embarrassed. Minor regret. That's allowed. One time only but she'd like to hook up with Cort again. Better. Nicer. Chill. Just hang out but she hasn't seen him. What if he hears about it? They always do. Then what? Turned off? Angry? Disgusted? Fuck it. Fuck him too.

Eyes strained. Hard to focus. Checks the clock. John shuts it down. Spent the last six hours studying cycloid-spiral-space curves. Saves his work. Closes the application. Relax for the rest of the evening. Get his mind right for the next descent. Clean. Mark. Measure. Strap.

Harness

Yua tests Ren's range of motion and makes her assessment. Thirty minutes of corrective movements and stretching followed by a thirty-minute deep tissue massage. Feels markedly better afterwards. His back is loose with unobstructed movement of the shoulder. Incredible. Yua's skillset an asset for everyone in camp. With a heartfelt thanks, Ren returns to his room and plays guitar for the remainder of the evening. Closing in on five. Eight more make an album. Enjoying the experience. Invested. Inspired. Something to do.

Warm up. Skip. Speed bag. Heavy bag. Weights. Swim. Food: grilled chicken with tahini and broccolini on wild grain rice. That's it. Mo lays low for the rest of the evening. Out of sight. Out of mind. Watches tutorials on bike modifications for when she gets back. Has some ideas and the money to make them happen. Truck. Trailer. Bike. Hitch 'em up and hit the road. Everything dialed in. East to west. Cut loose. See what's out there.

Study break. New sign posted outside the enclosure stating Ernest's name, species, and visiting guidelines. Pretty simple. Don't feed him outside food or disturb him when he's sleeping. John sips green tea while watching the tiny tortoise burrow in his sandbox. Hard at work. Moving with purpose. A true delight. This little creature on a mission.

"Good morning."

A tall man enters the enclosure. At least six-five. Glasses. Lined face. Sunbaked. Stubble. Brown hair, cut short, thinning.

"See you've met our new recruit."
"Yes, a welcome addition."

John recognizes the man from the crew index. Head of the biology department.

"Glad to hear it. Lobbied for the little guy. Suitable climate. Community project slash pet."
"I appreciate his namesake. The polar explorer."

"Shackleton. Yes. Certainly possesses an inquisitive spirit. Always on the move."

The man appears to have a twitch. Reflexive squinting. Might be the sun or something in his eyes.

"My name's John."
"John, I'm Ed."

Firm handshake.

"What do you do, John?"
"Rigger."
"Ah, yes, the wheelhouse."
"You're involved in the project?"
"I was."
"What changed?"

Pronounced pause.

"I wanted to return to field work."
"Not to offend, but aside from the fuglies, it doesn't seem like there's a lot out there."
"Such a silly name."
"Is it official?"
"No, we have yet to settle that hotly contested debate. I call them quill pigs or quills. Regarding your initial question, although it appears the quills have exclusive rights to the region, we are currently tracking something substantial."
"Okay . . . well, you've piqued my curiosity."
"Between me, you, and the fence post, it's a massive quadruped. Heel to heel, it's thirty feet. Eighteen across. We've only found one track so far."
"No sightings?"
"Seismic captured some footage from a considerable distance. Pixelated. Shakey. Hard to get an accurate read but it does confirm the size."
"Exciting."
"Our team refers to it as the Landlord."

"Must feed on the fuglies."
"Scat analysis says yes."
"Must have an iron-plated mouth and stomach to eat those things."
"And strong digestive enzymes."
"Well, that's exciting. I hope we get to see it. At least some quality footage."
"As do I."
"Can I ask, referring to the wheelhouse, realizing there's a non-disclosure, but we've both been there, and you know . . . speaking broadly, peer to peer, what's your take? What is it?"

Mulling over his answer. Tensing up. Switching from excitement over the Landlord to dour contemplation.

"I can't . . . No. Not at liberty to discuss."

Shifts gears again, skipped over.

"But I do appreciate our conversation, however brief. I wanted to check in on Ernest. Active as ever. Now I must return to the team in preparation for our next excursion."
"Tracking?"
"Indeed."
"Good luck."
"To you as well."

Cards with the boys. Same crew from the start. Added a few players. Eight in total. Ideal. Bigger pot. Play with poker chips. Pay with tokens. The pot transferred to the winner's account. Couple of cowboys in the group. Ren bows out at the same time as his buddy Harris. Not burning a week's pay playing poker. Trachea time is something else. Expands. Contracts. Minutes last hours. Then it flips. Hours erased. Feels like minutes. The hard minutes hurt, though. Takes a toll. Charges interest. Accept the setting. That's the trick. Wish you were someplace else and it slowly gnaws away at you. Planned on shutting it down for the night but Harris extended the invite. Jackson Harris, another scary-looking merc with neck tats and a beard, who happens to be an avid wine drinker. Makes his own at home. Alcohol may be a restricted item but there's nothing in the code of conduct about brewing it on base. Prison hooch. That's what they're drinking. Did his research. Decided to give it a shot. Had a hookup in the kitchen. Grape juice, chopped fruit, sugar, yeast, all poured into an industrial trash bag, tied off the top, with a straw sticking out of it so the bag won't explode while giving off carbon dioxide. Removed his clothes from his closet, stashed the bag in there, and let it ferment in the dark for twenty-one days. Got a hold of some incense to cover up the scent. Ran the fan. None the wiser. Jackson fills their plastic cups. Hands one to Ren. Looks like wine. Smells like fresh, sweet grapes. Encouraging. Ren takes a sip. Sour, but certainly not terrible. Surprisingly dry. Definitely wine. No idea what the alcohol percentage is but it's in there. Copping a buzz off the first cup. Laughing at how they've lost their tolerance. Feeling tipsy off two. Jackson picks up his tablet.

"Saw some shit."

Scrolling through.

"Here it is."

Presses play on the video.

"I'm on patrol with seismic. Pushing it. Four days. Night watch. Night goggles. Zoom these motherfuckers way in. Those dots. They fuglies. Ain't nothing but pixels at this point. Now see this mass. That blur. Like a little hill but watch, just watch . . . See that? See 'em scatter? Shifted. Motherfucker moved. It's alive."
"How big? From that far out. How big is that?"
"Fuckin' huge. Like a three-storey building."
"Why didn't you go after it?"
"After it? Bruh . . . I'm working with seismic. We ain't on safari."

Harness

Mo sees him under an umbrella. Ren looks wrecked. Laid out on his beach chair, arms limp, with a bag of ice on his forehead. Decides to check in. Lays her towel down on the seat beside him and lathers on some suntan oil.

> "Headache?"
> "The worst."
> "Looking a little haggard."
> "Can you keep a secret?"
> "I'll try."
> "Hungover."
> "How?"
> "Prison hooch."
> "From where?"
> "Plead the fifth."
> "Worth it?"
> "Right now, no."

Ren pulls down his sunglasses. Looks at Mo. Squinting from the sun.

> "What?"

Mo takes a seat. Ren pulls up his shades.

> "Recalling our last discussion . . . I don't suppose there's any way you can show mercy on an old man and make a one-time exception. Might be my only hope for this headache."
> "Find strength in the suffering."
> "I might not make it."
> "Should we toss your body down the trach or feed it to the fuglies?"

REJECTION:

Six months in. 9,399 miles down. 49,626,905 feet below surface. The time it takes to reach the starting marker means the riggers must alternate work weeks. That's two weeks off between their next turn in the trachea. At least that's the plan until the skin grafts start changing colours from pink to red to purple, then brown, green, and eventually black. The level of decay varying with each graft. Full stop. The project at risk. Scrambling for a solution. Reverse course. Right back to the beginning. Fortify the structure. Every section. Strapping one level, ring, rib, to the next with thirteen feet between them, all the way down, while attaching time-release patches to any area of dermis they can get purchase on. A form of treatment. One applied every six sections. Starting at section six. No more overnights. Not yet. Working eight-hour shifts, seven days a week until told otherwise. Somewhat civilized. Back in their beds each night. A welcome change.

CHECK-IN:

Happens every few weeks or months. Random. No fixed time. Site supervisor Jim Dunn leaves a text or voice memo requesting a sit-down meeting in his office. Quick chat. Not a briefing. Open concept. Feedback and guidance. General inquiries. Never more than twenty minutes. John notices Jim has lost some weight. Tall man. Taller, at least. Six-foot-three, maybe four. Carried a substantial beer belly when they first met. Starting to slim down. Considers mentioning it. Doesn't want to be rude. The office is sparse. Clean. Digital drafting boards and tablets. Nothing to see. Displays turned off. Blank desk. John sips his coffee across in his recliner.

"How we doing, John?"
"No complaints."
"You never do. The skin graft was a setback but we'll get there."
"Paid by the hour."
"Exactly. Everything else good? How's the family?"
"Just received another transmission. All is well and the baby's on schedule."
"Excellent. Family first. You're a good man, John, and I won't take up any more of your time. Thanks for checking in."
"Thank you, sir."

Harness

Sitting across from the man once more. Likes Jim. No bullshit. Knows the job. Gets it done and will raise a glass with you when it's over (several in fact). Keeps his distance until then. Makes sense. Cross the finish line then celebrate. One of the few voices of reason on the tower. Should've bailed when he did. Disaster. The drugs took over after that one. Clawed his way back. No need to dredge it up at this point. Was a relief to hear Jim was running this site. Cool customer. Doesn't get rattled. No barking. Calmly checks the boxes. Sees it through.

"Renzetti, how the hell are ya?"
"Hanging in there."
"Yeah, you are."
"How you doing, boss?"
"The fuckin' skin graft being rejected was a setback but that's beyond us."
"I mean . . . to be expected? Appears we're grafting onto a carcass. At least what it looks like. And I'm assuming there's no circulation, which you know . . . might help."
"Beyond me."
"And what happens if we can't stop the spread and the skin, what's left of it, rots off?"
"Straps and ribs. Nothing but a bone necklace. Mind you, I have no idea what function it serves in the first place. So there's that."
"Still no clue on the grand design?"
"Nada."
"This whole project is need-to-know from the top on down. Nothing I need to stress over. No point. Get my marching orders and we make it happen."
"Glad you're at the helm on this one."
"Glad you answered the call."
"What are the lungs? Anything on that?"
"Nope. Everything in increments. Trickledown effect."
"Chinese water torture."

"Ha! Yeah . . . this one's mighty strange."
"Best guess?"
"You tell me. You're inside it. Slept in the fucking thing."
"Make a great garbage chute."
"By God, you might be onto something."

Mo's dealt with all kinds: hotheads, creeps, ball-washing ladder climbers. Not Jim, he's calm, cordial, in control. Not some ball-busting power tripper. So many aspiring alphas get a whiff of power and start puffing their chests. Not how it works. Jim's the man for a reason. Kind. Fair. Earned his stripes. Knows he's only as good as the crew he surrounds himself with and acts accordingly. Earned his place and subsequently their respect. Knows when to push back and protect his crew. Helped negotiate new terms in their agreement. Get them a raise. Pay them what they're worth. A lot of leads become company men and can't be bothered to engage disputes between their crew and the corporation. All about their earnings. Their title. The crew comes last. A replaceable commodity. Not Jim. He sees the big picture. Everyone eats. These check-ins are always appreciated. Let her know someone's looking out.

"Talk to me, Mo. How we doing?"
"Halfway there."
"Six months in. Still standing."
"Standing. Suspended. To-may-to, to-mah-to."
"The job's getting done."
"Is it?"
"We got a list and we're checking all the boxes."
"You're good, I'm good."
"Appreciated. Still bothers me I couldn't turn them around on the music. Told 'em it makes no damn sense. You're in there alone. You know the job. No danger to anyone. Automatic at this point. Why not let you guys listen to some music? We send you in there with a goddamn needle to prevent panic attacks but heaven forbid you listen to a little music as a welcome distraction? For the simple goddamn

pleasure of it? Wouldn't or couldn't explain it to me. Kept parroting policy. Weren't going to budge on it."
"Fuck 'em. Thank you for making the effort."
"Sorry I couldn't swing it for ya."
"All good. Over it."
"How you doing otherwise?"
"Same, same."
"No issues?"
"Nope."
"Then I won't take up anymore of your time."

CHECK-OUT:

Suicide. The biologist. Edmund Burrage. Sliced his wrists in his room. In memoriam posted to all accounts the next day with a subsequent statement from Rexen regarding occupational burnout with a list of warning signs, prevention strategies, and treatments. One week later Santiago Garza, a member of the security team, drives his APC miles outside the perimeter, steps out of the vehicle, puts his gun to the roof of his mouth, and pulls the trigger. The retrieval team reaches his coordinates an hour after the alert went out. By that point the fuglies have completely swarmed the body. The team has to machine-gun them off to access what's left. Neither suicide left a note. Grief counselling made available to all staff. Rumours circulated that Rexen might suspend operations for an official inquiry into the matter but production continues unabated.

INFERNO:

The well drilling into a high-pressure zone. Pierces the reservoir. Formation fluids flow into the wellbore and up the inside of the drill pipe, which causes the kick. Pressure-control system failure. The BOP valve affixed to the wellhead won't close. Mechanical barrier breakdown. Unable to shut in the well.

Influx. Roar. Blow out. Ejects the drill string. The explosive concussion kills seven oilmen near the rig. Oil spewing in all directions. Ignition during the emergency response. Either a spark from rocks being ejected or simply heat generated by friction. Combustion. Conflagration. The derrick evaporates. Melting casings. Heavy machinery writhes and twists into mangled forms as the fountainhead rains fire down on oil-soaked workmen and medics. Eighteen casualties in total. Four oilmen lose their hearing entirely. Catastrophic. Massive plumes of black smoke darken the sky as the control company attempts to extinguish the blaze. Water dousing isn't working. Running out of reserves. Explosives surrounded by fire retardant chemicals are placed within fifty-five-gallon drums wrapped with insulating material. A horizontal crane is used to bring the drum as close to the wellhead as possible. Upon detonation, the explosives create a shockwave that pushes the burning fuel and local atmospheric oxygen away from a well. Success. The flame removed but the blowout cannot be capped. Too much force. Relief wells are drilled to intersect the pocket in order to allow kill-weight fluids to be introduced at depth, slowing fluid entry into the wellbore and allowing capping to commence using brass tools so as not to strike sparks. By the time the well is sealed, the landscape is coated in thousands of barrels of oil.

DIAGNOSTICS (9 Months):

No viable circulatory system, at least by John's understanding, yet the treatment's working. The majority of the grafts somehow starting to heal. The tissue repairing itself. The patches likely introducing growth factors stimulating cell proliferation, wound healing, but not indicative of a functioning system. Surface level. For show. A short-term solution requiring long-term care. Still paid by the hour. Going back to overnights. Tomorrow. No choice. Too far down. Today it's another physical followed by a psychological evaluation. Doctor Nadri checks John's vitals. Draws a blood sample. Sends him down the hallway to Doctor Gustavsson. A noted difference in her energy. Subdued. Tired. Flat. Likely exhaustion responding to the emotional fallout of recent tragedies. John recognizing her role in the response.

Harness

"I imagine the last few months have been challenging for you."

Doesn't seem to register. Doctor Gustavsson looks up from her notes

"And you, John? How's your headspace these days?"
"Sombre. My heart goes out to the families of the deceased."
"Of course, and the work itself? That's going well?"
"Again, it's not for me to say, but I'm doing what's been asked of me to best of my abilities."
"Excellent."

Automated response. Doctor Gustavsson checks her notes for the fifth time in four minutes.

Dark days, indeed. The accident on the oil field triggering flashbacks from the tower. Ren's coworkers and friends crushed under the wreckage. Some unclipped and died from the fall. Others died waiting, some hanging in their harness off a partial collapse. Killed by suspension trauma or orthostatic intolerance. An effect that occurs when the human body is held upright without any movement for a period of time. Workers suspended in their safety harnesses for long periods suffer from blood pooling in the lower body. The onset of symptoms usually occurs after twenty minutes of free hanging: pallor, sweating, shortness of breath, blurred vision, dizziness, nausea, hypotension, and numbness of the legs. Eventually it leads to a central ischaemic response (also known as syncope or fainting). Fainting while remaining vertical increases the risk of death from cerebral hypoxia—death due to oxygen deprivation of the brain. Something Ren witnessed from the twisted ledge he was able to climb onto. No way to reach them. Completely helpless. Hearing their screams, coworkers crying out in agony before they blacked out, their limp bodies hanging from their harnesses. The horror of it. Had to stomp it down to function. Took its toll. Fucked him up. Well aware how a project with ostensibly unlimited funding can go sideways in a second. Workplace accident. Such an odd descriptor. Is what it is but still seems like a gross trivialization. The signs they post: "This jobsite has worked _____ number of days since time-loss accident." Right there in front of you. Time. Time is money. Just another number. How do they categorize the suicides? Do they count? How much time was lost? Two employees kill themselves within a week of each other and they send out a fucking pamphlet. God forbid they halt production for a fuckin' second. Fuck this job. Sent down a fuckin' wormhole. Two hundred and seventy-three days in and he still has no idea what he signed up for.

Unofficially official. Reconnected with Cort. Rattled over the recent series of events. Reached out. Upfront about her interlude with the meathead. He didn't bat an eye. Still wanted to hang out. Made a couple quips in jest but that was the end of it. No judgement. No pressure. So far so good. The sex is on point but for the first time in a long time she enjoys the hang-arounds too. Chilling. Laughing. Lounging. Easy to be around. Nice to look at. Quiet. Observant. Not closed off but hardly an open book. Been a few days since they've seen each other. Conflicting work schedules. Meeting up today. Soon. They start with sex then a stroll. Span some time before her physical and mental health assessment. Check in on Ernest. Watching him munch clover and shrubs from the garden bed. Keep walking the courtyard.

"Had you won your last fight would you have kept going?"
"Maybe."
"Did you like fighting?"
"Liked training. Gave me what I needed."
"What's that?"
"Purpose. Got me out."
"Of what?"

Cort makes his little growl noise. A little rumble noise in his throat. A grumble. Not sure he's aware he's doing it.

"Dark place."
"Go on."
"Smoking shale. Flaked out. Took over. Starting to crystallize. Could see it on my forearms. The sun would make it sparkle.

Harness

Run my hand across my arm and the deposits would flake off like glitter. Stopped eating. Stopped caring. Where I wanted to be."

"Which is where?"

"Never tried it?"

"No."

"I mean . . . I can attempt to describe it but you can't. Not really."

"Try. Your version."

"First off, you feel amazing. Like you can breathe again. Ya know . . . like you've been holding your breath this whole time and didn't know it. Been carrying this weight that's suddenly lifted. Feel it in your bones. Physically lighter. Then your vision changes . . . and it's . . . where it's hard to describe. You just glide through this construct like this cathedral or dark palace. And like you're here but you're not because it works as overlay. Like that style of animation. Roto . . . roto something . . . can't remember but there's like, you can see this grid and it shifts and shimmers and shows you things. This wave you're riding. This dance. I don't know. Communication. Communion. And it's effortless and you're like—this is it. This is where you're supposed to be and you don't want to leave the place. I didn't."

"What's the comedown feel like?"

"Gentle at first. Fades away. You're back where you were and you're grateful to be there. Filled with gratitude but it's fleeting. Ya know . . . matter of hours and it's gone. You're empty. Tapped out. Hollowed out. Bored. Bored like it's a terminal illness. Nothing entertains or engages. Want to sleep but you can't. Stagnant. Agitated. Annoyed. Obviously, the down, that crash, gets worse the more you do it. Every ask is an insurmountable obstacle. Brushing your teeth is too much. Fuckin' trapped. Take it for too long and the tremens kick in. Waking nightmares. Hallucinations. Puking out both ends. First time I tried to kick it I was writhing, crying, every cell screamed. Pumped me full of sedatives. Months of rehab. Sobriety. Shit don't work. Because I knew. Knew I wanted to go back. Stay there. Tried to. Wasting away. Dying. Dying for sure. Then I got jumped. Not sure why, was out there, you know, gliding when it happened. Got lumped up bad. Split open. Stomped. Still somehow walking around. Once the shale wore off, I saw myself in the mirror and it was . . . I was . . . abstract. Face was so swollen. Smeared in blood. Looked so fucked. Like a mutant. A busted grape. It wasn't me. Wasn't real. Can't be. Remember the ringing in my ears before I fainted. Wake up in hospital. Active withdrawal. Induced coma. Regain consciousness. Survived but I'm nauseous. Start tracing the stitches and staples in my face, my head, and it grounds me. This is real. I'm here. Pain as teacher. Rang up my old wrestling coach when I got out. Told him I wanted to fight for a living. Asked if he knew anyone and he set it up. That's it. There it is. Spilled my guts. Now ya know."

The most words he's said their entire, albeit brief, relationship. Mo is moved. Wants to take his hand. Cort stops. Looks back to the barracks.

"Coffee's kicking in. Gotta take a shit."

DOWN:

Onwards. No more doubling back. Clean. Mark. Measure. Mesh. Staple. Snip. Spray. Strap. Drop. All at once. As required. Complete each segment step by step. John confused as to why that wasn't the working procedure from the beginning. Endless descent, so what's the rush? Were they hoping to save on strapping? Doesn't make sense. Doesn't matter. Do the work. Stay focussed. Dialled in. Make it home to her. Azalea. Hold his baby girl. His daughter. Family. Feeling so far removed. It can be calculated but it's impossible to grasp. Don't dwell. Progress. Continue his studies. Practice his Mandarin. Starting to retain it. Something to hang his hat on.

Harness

Fear. The anger stemmed from fear. No place for it. No need. Be aware but not afraid. Serves no purpose. Corrosive. Exhausting. These are the facts. The suicides then the blowout. Sudden death. Back-to-back. Started spiralling. Ren lashed out at the counsellor, at Janice, when she asked if work was going well. Such an insipid, canned question in light of everything that transpired. Struck a nerve. Went on the attack. Told her their assessments are a fucking waste of time. Had nothing to do with their well-being. Formalities. The bigwigs at Rexen don't give a fuck. Insurance against liabilities. Intel. That's it. Digging up the dirt. Ammunition against litigation, whether it's a workplace accident, harassment, breach of contract, or wrongful termination. Every one of them disposable and easily replaced if they become an inconvenience. Including her. Just a fence. A firewall. Paid informant. Snitch. Instant regret when he ended his tirade. Could see her shock. Unfair. Apologized. Apology accepted. Understood. Everyone under pressure. In shock. Grieving. All have their own reactions whether they knew the deceased or not. Links his response to the tower. Suppressed memories. Emotion. PTSD. Caught in a series of errors, malfeasance, and misfeasance outside his control leading to catastrophe. Impossible to predict how and when that trauma might manifest. No surprise recent tragedies would evoke a response. Trigger the alarm that it was happening again. Fight, flight, freeze. Perhaps a combination of all three. That raw emotion. Can't deny it. Engage. Observe. Allow a moment to understand where it stems from. Participate. Process. Detach. Detach . . . What if he detached from his harness? How would that work out? Untethered to the world. Freefall in a limitless void. How long would it take to die?

For her own amusement. Entertain. Occupy. Mo talking to herself as she goes. Spoken word. Random rhymes. Veering into song.

"Graft. Strap. Next. Graft. Strap. Next. Never fucking ends. Graft. Strap. Next. Never fucking ends. The things we do for a paycheque. It's pretty fucking silly, really. Really? Yes. It's pretty fucking silly. **Clip. Snip. Spray.** All fucking day. So ya want to be a rigger, do ya? Want to rig a thing? If you want to be a rigger then you better learn to sing. To sling? To sing. To sing? To sling.

TYRANT

Singinyourhole.Singfromyourhole.Shitdownthehole.We'reinahole.Never endinghole.Thisishowweroll.Getbackinyourhole.Needtoknowyourrole."

Break. John sets the net. Sits down. Sips some Nor. Considers cavitation. The formation of an empty space within a solid object or body. Partial vacuums in a liquid by a swiftly moving solid body. Truncate the current and it creates a gap. Ether physics. Nature says no. Abhors a vacuum. Doesn't believe in empty space. Something's supposed to be there so existence collapses in on it. Cavitation. Pure potential is solid. We live in a bubble of infinite potential. Potential pours in. We are the potentiated. We live in space. That's the idea. Which is what? What's he reaching for? Grasping at? Says it out loud to the universe.

> "As it relates to the trachea . . . potential is saying this space is for something and I'm going to fill it. Okay . . . so what? What made this space? What cleared it? And subsequently, what's supposed to fill it?"

Crossed up. Confused. Doesn't have the capacity to compute the questions he's asking. It's right there, though. Needs rest. Restore his processing power. Be still. Patient. Revelation. Can sense it. Something's knocking at the door.

Settled in. Ren going through the motions. From graft to strap. Sealing punctures. From one to the next. Sets the line. Pops the scalpel. Staples the net. Easy. Using the tools available to him. That's the gist of it. Knows how to use things. Somethings. Simple things. That's it. An odd ponderance. Ultimately, he's of very little use. Doesn't produce anything of value. These things. They just show up. Night vision, for example. Through his visor, he can see full-spectrum colour in a pitch-black environment and it's totally taken for granted. Can parrot the concept behind the technology but has no clue how it was brought to fruition. Never mind that. The run-of-the-mill measuring tape is a minor miracle. Has a rough idea of how it functions: The

Harness

measuring blade hooks onto a soft metal strip almost as long as the blade itself. As the strip coils around the central hub, it turns into a spring that winds more tightly as the blade slides out. Release the lock and the spring recoils. The basic concept then you contemplate the manufacturing. Everything involved. How all the components come together to create this marvel. This wonderous little measuring device but it's a complete afterthought. Doesn't even register. Why would it? Riding waves to newfound shores. Entering new fields of space with frequency and vibrations. Transport. Call it transport. Going through this mind-bending trip where the nuts and bolts seem irrelevant but they're not. As essential as ever. Nothing exists without this other thing and on and on and here he is using things but what's he making? What can he provide? A song? His service? That don't count. No one needs him. Ask him to make a pencil and he'd have no idea where to start. These things just appear and we accept it. Shape takes form. Shape takes form . . . What the fuck does that even mean? Could use a drink. Really could. Speaking of shape and form, when he gets back to the surface, he's making a move on the redhead. Irene. Relaxed approach. Quick introduction. Subtle inquiry. See if there's something there. Three months left. Worth a shot. Something for the pleasure receptors. Dopamine rush. Imagine. All you can do down here.

 Fucking disgusting. Mo imagines taking the yellowed skin shavings from the trachea, slapping them between a Kaiser bun and serving it up on a plate for some unsuspecting customer. Some au jus to dip it in. Makes her retch. The most bizarre musings in her boredom. Endless repetition. Any monkey can do this. Ultimately every job a variation of the last one. Know the order and placement of things. Learn your tools. The hardware. Basic techniques. Again, it's repetition. The engineers do the math. Crunch the numbers. Create the installation. Eighty percent of it's automated. If the initial install won't work, find another way. Make the attempt. If there isn't one, send it back. A rigger needs to be comfortable working at heights, or in this case, lows but if they can spin a wrench that's a good start. Know five knots with names and you're halfway there. So much of the work is mechanized; you might never use them but they're good to know. Good to know . . . Mo shakes her head. Who the fuck is she talking to? Losing it. Adjusts the line. Pops the scalpel.

Needs a pita to collect the shavings. Fuckin' shawarma. Serve that up with some pickled turnips and garlic sauce. Makes herself retch again. Needs to stop. Be serious. Serious work. Paid professional. Mo starts singing, "Money money money money, moneyyy."

Stalled at the next section. Tingling in hands. The wrecked dermis has a disturbing porosity. Needs to mesh the whole thing. Nothing new but it's hard to look at. Something in the pattern. The pockmarks and punctures projecting an imperceivable threat. John feels a constriction in the chest. Heart racing. Palpitations. Starting to panic. Needs to sit down. Collect himself. Pulls on the stirrups like he's taken a shit. Suspended with his head between his legs. Going into shock. Flop sweats. Body buzzing. Trying to focus on his breathing. Slow it down. Inhale: one, two, three. Hold: one, two, three. Out: one, two, three. Repeat. Not working. Heart pounding. Bad. Getting worse. Can't catch his breath. Needs air. Oxygen. Not panic. No. Something's wrong. Under attack. Inquisition. Scripture. Verse. Voice. Projection. Possession.

"In my Father's house there are many rooms."

Pushing.

"In my Father's house there are many rooms."

Prodding.

"In my Father's house there are many rooms."

Demanding a response. John looks up at the torn tapestry. Hears the answer in the form of a question.

"Then whose room is this?"

Sinks in. Current shoots through his arms across his chest. Lighting storm in the back of his brain. The crown of his head going cold. Numb. Trembling. Losing control. Terror. Terrified. About to explode. Heart. Seizure. Stroke. No. Not now. Not here. Needle. Use the needle. Hands shaking. Losing his peripheral. Starting to tunnel. Closing in. John fumbles for then flips the clasp. Removes the syringe from its cartridge and slams the needle into his leg. Pushing down on the plunger, vomit explodes from his mouth, splashing off his face mask. Spits the puke from his mouth as the lights go out. Signal sent. John's unconscious body pulled to the surface.

Ren sent back two days early. Knows John worked the shift before him. Asked if everything's alright. Jim assured him John's fine. Wasn't feeling well so they pulled him out of there. Ren agreed to finish the shift. Work some overtime. Glad to hear John's fine but this section ain't. Tattered skin rag. Invisible parasites. Microscopic. Feeding. Always feeding. Ceaseless consumption at every level. This endless ongoing sacrifice. No wonder procreation is such a strong biological imperative. Needs something else to eat. Ren applies a three-sixty mesh to the section and moves the fuck on.

Of course. Wasn't nagging at her while she was working. Busy. Occupied. Moving. Now Mo's got the net out, time to rest, and the gears start grinding. Mo saw the date on the calendar. Knew she'd be down here. Built it up in her head all week. Psyched herself out. Spooked for no fuckin' reason. Can't shake the dread. This fucking dread. What the fuck is she expecting? Whatever. Sleep with the lights on. Sleep. That's the problem. Fucking nightmares. Never the place to be but today of all days . . . Just stop. Stop thinking about it. Why? What's she going to manifest? Dead babies falling from the sky? Fuck off. Nothing to fear. Made a mistake. Mistakes are made. Wanted the pill. A week too late. Waited too long. Denial. Now she needs the procedure. Reads the risks: incomplete abortion, infection, hemorrhaging, blood clots, future fertility issues. Makes the call. Takes the first day, first opening, they offer. Happens to coincide with her father's birthday. Sick joke. So be it. The appointment scheduled that afternoon but her boyfriend got blackout drunk the night before. Supposed to pick her up but isn't answering his phone. Freaking out. Has to happen. Wants it gone. Three-hour drive to the clinic. Supposed to leave now. Has to leave now. No licence. Not yet. Fifteen. Learner's. Just take it. Take the truck. Go. No. Might get pulled over.

Stopped. Clock is ticking. No money. Broke. Just enough for the operation. Fear. Fear to fury. Furious at her dumb-fuck boyfriend. Furious at herself for allowing this to happen. A moment. A mistake. Now there's this thing and it's real and she's trapped. Not like this. Can't have it. Won't. Not missing her appointment. Mom's away. Dad. Dad needs to drive her. Needs to know. Now. Fuck. He's going to lose it. Going to snap. Demand to know who did it. Who got her pregnant. Search and destroy. Won't be able to rein him in. Yes, she will. Strong. Calm. Direct. Has to happen. Still sleeping. So wake him up. Knocks on the door. Knocks again.

"Dad?"
"Yeah?"
"Can I open the door?"
"Yeah."

In bed, eyes closed, lying on his side. Arms and legs wrapped around the body pillow. Pill vials and beer empties on the bedside table. Half-smoked joint wedged between the beer tab.

"I need you to wake up."
"Why?"
"We need to go."

Eyes still closed.

"Go where?"
"I need you to drive me somewhere."
"Where?"
"It's a long drive. We need to go now."
"Where?"
"A clinic."

Eyes open.

"For what?"
"You need to drive me."
"For what?"
"Doesn't matter. Get dressed. We need to leave."

Harness

Dad sits up. Feet on the floor. Looks hungover. Is hungover. Wipes the sleep from his eyes.

"What is this? What's going on?"
"Got pregnant. Getting an abortion. Get angry with me later."
"What?"
"You heard me. Please, let's go. It's a long drive."
"Don't fuck with me, Mo. You're fucking serious?"
"Yes."
"Who? Who's the fucking piece of shit that got you pregnant?"
"Doesn't matter."
"Fuckin' rights it matters. Who is it? Where? Where the fuck is this guy?"
"Doesn't matter, doesn't help, doesn't change the situation."
"Does he know?"
"We need to go. I'll wait in the truck. Get dressed. Let's go."

Starts the truck. Sits in the passenger seat. Waits. Five minutes later, Dad leaves the house in jogging pants, hoodie, t-shirt. Dishevelled. Shaking his head. Smoking a cigarette. Takes the driver's seat. Cracks the window.

"What the fuck, Mo."
"I know. I know. I'm sorry."

Staring straight ahead. Another drag. Blows it out.

"Alright. Where we going?"

They get into it on the drive. Dad ramping up. Starting to rage. Threatening to turn around if she doesn't tell him who got her pregnant. Tells him. Repeats the name. Has no idea nor would he.

"How old? How old is this fucking guy?"
"Seventeen."
"Where? Where the fuck is he? Why isn't he here?"
"I don't know. Wasn't answering his phone."

"Sounds like a prize. Is he one of the cool kids? A bad boy? I've seen it. Seen the crowd you're hanging out with. Acting tough. Acting cool. You like the bad boys . . . well, how'd that work out? 'Cuz here we are. Here we are. Your dad's driving you to the abortion clinic. Young, dumb, having fun. No big deal, right? Fuck that. There's consequences, Mo. This fuckin' life. There're consequences."

Don't yell. Don't cry. Keep it together.

"No fucking shit. I fucked up. I apologize. Doing what needs to be done. That's it, okay? That's it."

Starting to crack. Catches it. Collects herself. Not a word for miles. Dad sparks another cigarette. Clears his throat.

"I'm sorry, Mo . . . It's on me. Failed. Failed as a father."
"Stop."
"Fuck that. I'm supposed to protect you. Got lazy. Negligent. Caught up at work. Distracted by the bullshit. Never took the time. You're at that age, on your way, a young woman—"
"It's not like I didn't know."
"You think you know but shit gets real, real fast."
"Like now. Like right now if you're looking for a textbook example."
"And that's where I dropped the ball. Sometimes a parent needs to break it down for ya. I didn't. Wasn't there. Negligent in my duties as a father and these are the consequences. Mine as much as yours. For that I'm sorry. Truly sorry."
"I'm sorry you're sorry."
"Forget that. This is what you want to do?"
"Yes."
"You're aware there's other options?"
"Not for me."
"No questions? Nothing you want to discuss?"
"Dad."
"What?"

"No."

"Fair enough."

Drive there. Drive back. The procedure takes three minutes. Fuckin' sucks. Literally and figuratively. Extremely uncomfortable. Invasive. Lightheaded after it's done. Nauseous. After an hour in the recovery room, she's ready to go. Relief ain't the word. Acceptance. Loss. That was a loss. Ashamed. Embarrassed. Fuck anyone who tells her otherwise. Curled up. Cramping during the drive. Barely a word spoken. Return home. Walk through the door. Exhausted. Heads to her room. He calls her back. Arms open. Big hug. That's when she breaks. Buries her head in his chest. Lets it all go. Sorry. So sorry. Sorry she did that. Happy birthday.

CHAOS:

A battery of tests rules out a heart condition or stroke. Panic attack. That's the diagnosis. John meets all the criteria but it's hard to accept. Overwhelming an understatement. The attack itself, his physical response, so pronounced it's difficult to process. Completely hijacked his operating system. An astonishing, albeit terrifying at the time, example of the mind-body connection. Impossible to deny. Needs to ensure it doesn't become a panic disorder. Trauma over trauma. Breathing techniques used to alleviate anxiety don't always apply to panic attacks. In fact, they can work against you. Amplifying the attack by sending the signal you're under attack. Fear from fear. Wires crossed. You override the response through acceptance. Lean into it. Acknowledge the indicators: palpitations, tightening, tingling, numbness, temperature fluctuations, rapid breathing. Of course they're uncomfortable, alarming if you don't understand their origin, just know that you are safe. Your body is doing what it's supposed to. Explore the reaction. Be inquisitive. A natural response. The sympathetic nervous system adjusting to a perceived threat but there's nothing to fear. That's the key. Allowing it to happen makes the correction. Rescinds the signal. Breaking the feedback loop and restoring order. John doing his part by practising breathing techniques that purposefully activate the acute stress response in order to increase his tolerance. About to be put it into practice. Returning to the trachea. Saddle up for another descent.

Back on solid ground. Sunlight. Ren sees her in the hallway. Heading towards him. About to pass. Now. No idea when he'll see her next. Makes his move. Shoots his shot.

"Kudos to the chef."

"Thank you."

Flicker of a smile as she glides right past him. Head back down. She's always on a mission or maybe she doesn't want strangers stopping her in hallways. Throws caution to the wind.

"It's the other way."

Slows her down. Looks back.

"It's the other way."

She stops.

"What's the other way?"

"My introduction."

Perplexed and slightly annoyed.

"My improvised attempt to make you stop so I can say hi."

"Okay."

Her eyebrow raised. Cautious. Still confused.

"Hello."

"Hi."

"My name's Ren."

"Irene."

"Our head chef."

"Executive."

"Either way, I'm big fan of your work. Of all the base camps I've been to, the food here is the best."

"Thank you. Working with what's provided."

"And you and the kitchen staff are doing a heck of a job."

"Thanks."

Harness

"I work in the rigging department, in case you're worried I wandered in off the streets."

"Okay . . ."

"There's three months left on my contract and it would make my year if you met me for a cup of coffee."

"Appreciate the inquiry but I'm seeing somebody."

"Understood . . . Well, thanks for stopping."

"Yeah, good luck the rest of the way."

"Likewise."

Ren pats his chest above the heart. Watches her go. Shot down. Seeing somebody. Sure. Maybe. Maybe not. Either way, Irene's not interested. On to the next one and he may be out options at this point. Only a handful of women to choose from onsite. Two of them taken. Make that three. Seems Mo's linked to the kid with the cauliflower ears. Good for them. Had his chance. Blew it. An age gap but they shared a moment. Playful flirtations. Potential hookup. Hesitated. Took too long and it was gone. Went direct and she pressed pause. Platonic. Said she "could use a friend out here." No need to complicate things. Of course. Coworkers. Colleagues. Keeps things above board. Pardon the interruption. Standing down. Gets a laugh. Back to being friends. Better for it. No ulterior motives or agenda. Always a friendly face. Shoulder to cry on, need be. Back to our regularly scheduled programming.

Mo's happy. She's happy. That's the word. Feels nice. Not anxious or agitated. Life doesn't feel like such a fuckin' chore. Looking forward. Cort finishes his shift in four hours. Enjoying their evenings together. Start at the gym, then sex, separate showers, reunite for dinner, games in the rec room, cards or chess back in her bedroom. Maybe a movie. Sleep. Often together but sometimes she sends him back to the barracks. Needs her space. Not often. Likes having him around. Comfortable. She's comfortable. How crazy is that?

Head back. John stands on the platform with outstretched arms. Deep breath through the nose on the inhale. Slow exhale. Strong. Safe. Committed. Plugs in. Drops down. Hours to the last marker. How long can they keep this going? Soon they'll be doing seven-day shifts. Staying overnight. Day one and seven just for travel. Where do they go from there? Two weeks in the trachea? A month? How long can people last in here? Total isolation in a nightmare setting. They'd have to change their policy regarding outside software. Need to allow music, podcasts, game apps, some kind of distraction in the off-hours. Work. Sip Nor. Sleep (if you can). Repeat. Daunting. Draining. For what? Already struck oil. Mining minerals. Huge payloads. What's this about? Where's it going? Home. He's going home. Under three months now. All that matters. Stop asking questions that don't apply. Dwelling on things outside his control. Drive himself crazy. Already did. Something snapped.

Card night. Another early exit. More hooch. Harris tops his cup. Ren setting himself a three-cup limit. Two and he's tipsy.

"I went for it."
"And?"
"Denied."
"Reason?"
"Seeing someone."
"Who?"
"Not me."

Knock at the door.

"Da fuck?"

Harris stashes the mason jar of wine back in his closet. Checks the peephole. Opens the door.

"We got it, man. Got the footage. You've got ta see this shit."

Keith from recon. Ren raises his cup in greeting. Keith remains standing in the doorway.

"Boys, we need the big screen."

Harness

Sweet spot. Pleasure pulse. Rocks off. Release. Mo sighs in satisfaction. Cort gets it done. Nothing fancy. Takes the time. Makes the effort. A few instances where she couldn't get there but he wasn't weird about it, which is always appreciated. Became an issue with an old boyfriend. Making her orgasm became an imperative. Needed the validation. Felt like a failure otherwise. Started deflecting. Blaming. Accusing. Simple solution. Broke up with him. The climax is not the prerequisite for sex. Not for her. Doesn't need to blast off every time but it's certainly nice basking in the afterglow. Cool down. Catching their breath. Checks in with Cort staring up at the ceiling.

"Still want to hang out?"
"Sure."
"You're not sick of me yet?"
"No."
"Getting there?"
"No."
"Are you my boyfriend?"
"Sure."
"Are you sure?"
"Yes."

Officially official. May as well. More and more. Likes this guy. Really does.

Doesn't want to get caught off guard again but the reality is, John can't remember. Not really. Partial blackout. Blank spots. Embarrassed when he came around. Confused. When did he break? What was it? Understanding panic doesn't require a trigger but something set him off. Rapid onset. Suddenly overwhelmed. A rough idea but John can't pinpoint the moment. There was a pronounced disturbance but it's hard to define. Creating doubt. Instigating fear. John recalibrates, realizing this is the wrong approach. Fine now. Composed. Present. Aware. This is work. Nothing more. John drills another strap. Lines up the next. Takes the strap off the string. Anchors it in. Next. Simple. No pressure. Paid by the hour. Paid well at that. This is good.

He is grateful. Earning a living. A life for the wife and kids. All for them. That's it. Never trapped. They set him free.

Mo calls her shot.

"Eight-ball corner pocket."

Sinks it. Cort shakes his head, can't help but crack a smile.

"Double or nothing."
"Rack 'em up."

He fills the rack. Places the cue ball on the dot. Chalks the cue. Breaks. Sinks the fifteen and four. Continues with stripes. Setting his aim on twelve when Keith, Ren, and Randall enter the rec room. Keith waves them over to the TV.

"Everyone in. Gather around."

Keith links the projector.

"Footage from our last scout. I'm taking a nap in the AFV."

The video starts in black.

Audio: "I felt that. I felt that . . . "

Keith's voice followed by a deafening roar. Guttural. Piercing.

Audio: "Fuck youuuuu, that was loud."

Night vision kicks in. Illuminates a field of fuglies in a feeding frenzy.

Keith leans towards the screen as the footage plays out.

"Wait for it. Wait . . ."

The beast glides into frame. A floating set of serrated teeth and yellow eyes. Jet-black body on a black backdrop with no trees, hills, or stars to offer contrast. Scarcely a silhouette. Mo has to squint to see the outline. Then it begins. Like the night grew claws. The beast spikes, stabs, slashes, and scoops the quills into its mouth. Chomping one after another.

Harness

Audio: "There it is. There it is. The Landlord."

The camera zooms into a blazing yellow eye. Vertical pupils like a housecat. Tilts towards its teeth. Blood-stained, sabre-like incisors. Grinding quilled chunks of flesh filled between massive molars.

Audio: "Christ almighty, would you look at that . . ."

Keith inverts the image with a negative filter. Cyan bloodbath. The beast glowing white. Yellow eyes now electric blue. Big as a four-storey building with cat-like movement. Fluid. Sudden. Precise. On its toes with heels positioned halfway up its legs. Its skin smooth as marble. Some sections appear plated like an exoskeleton. Armour. Horn above its nose. Hooks back. The crown of its head a carapace with a fan-shaped frill, scooped like an upside-down shoehorn, almost ornamental. Filter removed. Back to black. Tracking mode. Highlights its contours in red. Mo watches the display of carnage in awe. A stunning amalgamation of form and movement. This crazed yet seamless combination of a panther and a rhinoceros beetle. Tilts its head to the sky. Takes notice. The rover goes in reverse. Spins around. Shifting gears. Acceleration. Plowing through patches of fuglies with puncture-proof airless tires. Keith presses pause.

> "Wildlife warned us. Compared their tracking data to our projected coordinates. Said we might see it. Well, there ya go. There ya fucking go. Saw it through the same lens I did. Not sure it knew we were there but when that thing started sniffing the air, I sure as shit wasn't waiting around to find out."

Moving along nicely. Steady pace. Not as many punctures. Mostly strapping. Making good progress. John corrects himself. Laughs at the notion. How does one measure progress in the current context? More of the same. Plug away. Complete the contract. One day at a time. Divides the eighty-eight hours underground into four twenty-two-hour shifts. Halfway through this one. Time spent either way, but it gives him perspective. Breaks things up a bit. Relieved he's managed to keep it together thus far. Confident he'll finish his shift without occurrence. Had some doubts. Don't know until you're in it. Taught to recognize the automatic physiological reactions of the flight or fight response but there's no guarantee he can control it. That's the catch. He can't cling to composure. Has to surrender control to find it. What's that look like, though? For how long? How bad? Can he work through it? Does he have the motor skills? The cognitive awareness? He'll try and if he can't, he can't. No rush. Can take a minute if needed. Completed three sections in less than two hours. Not going to tap out now. No way he's leaving that much money on the table.

Ren wakes up hungry. Rare occurrence. Usually takes a minute for his appetite to kick in. Partial hangover. Needs grease, fat, sugar. Chugs some water. Heads to the chow hall. Goes for the English breakfast option: sausage, back bacon, eggs, seared tomatoes, mushrooms, fried toast, beans. Can only finish half the plate. Takes his coffee on the road. Still thinking about the movie monster. The fact that beast is wandering around out there. Fucking insane. The Landlord. Thought there was just snarling sand urchins and a hole in the ground. Guess not. What else is there? Are there others beasts? Does it have a mate? Offspring? Male? Female? How old is it? Where's it go? Find shelter? Exposed to the elements all day? The questions continue. Can't put it down. How much ground does it cover in a day? Always moving like a shark or does it rest and digest between feedings? What's it thinking? Level of intelligence? Perception? How long's it been here? What's it seen? Green? A single solitary blade of grass? Scorched earth. Stuck on this prison planet. We find it and fuck off. Bring our toys in. Our tools. Extract what's available and move on. No big deal. Next. Ren enters Ernest's enclosure. His favourite tortoise still in one of its hides. A simple structure comprised of a concrete tile across concrete blocks to provide shade, with a misting system in the opposite corner. Ren scoops a wilted piece of red lettuce out of the pond. There's a stillness to the day. Something. Can't explain it. Same sounds. A truck backing into a loading bay. Can hear the construction. Drilling in the distance. Something being sawed. Like any other day. Staff, crew, still going about their business. Starting work. Leaving work. What's different? Nothing.

Harness

Start inquiring. Make arrangements. That's the mission. If possible, Mo wants to accompany a field team on one of her off days or try to extend her stay for a viewing. Find a way. Talked late into the night about the Landlord. Charged up. That's the crown jewel. Like seeing a dragon in the flesh. May be the last of its kind. Curious how Rexen will handle the new discovery. Their charter says observe without interference but that's lip service. It's all a commodity. Import. Export. Proprietary rights. Land claims. Everything under the sun legally speaking. Will they tranq, tag, and track? Draw samples? Administer an injection of foreign compounds, having no idea how it will react? Or do they seize and capture? Wouldn't be surprised if they brought it back. Another novelty. Stuff in a zoo. String together a bullshit story surrounding its capture. Why it was necessary for its benefit, preservation, survival. Rake it in with some spin. That's assuming they don't kill the creature first. If it attacks the base or a work site, they'll blast it if they're out of options. Big as a building but has no chance against their weaponry. Harris convinced the flat terrain and lack of foliage ensures that scenario never plays out. Artillery would see it coming from miles away. Arrange intervention. Push back. Scare it off with sonic weaponry, tactical lights, or tranquilize and relocate if need be. Asked Keith to send her the footage. Wouldn't. Couldn't. Not yet. Doesn't matter. She's going to see it before she goes. In the flesh. That's the mission. First-hand experience. Snag some photos and video of her own. The Landlord. That's the image for the tour. Tattoo or t-shirt. Likely both.

Dead asleep. Voice in the dark. Calling his name. Once. Twice. Intercom. Headset. Answer.

"Hello?"
"Hey, John, we need to pull you out of there."
"Why?"
"Precautionary measure."
"In relation to what?"
"The situation is being assessed but it's best we get you out of there."

"Copy."

"Leave the net. We'll grab it later."

"Copy. Switching plugs."

Stands up. Switches his lanyard from front to back.

"Line up. Returning to ground."

"Roger that."

John begins his ascent.

"What's the issue, Stan?"

"Erring on the side of caution. Jim gave us the exit order."

"Can I speak to him?"

"Offsite at the moment."

"Copy."

Reaching top speed. Spinal column flickering past. Surprise turn of events. Early exit and it's not on him. Some indication as to why would be appreciated but it doesn't really matter. Nothing he can do from down here. Now what? Hours to the top. Ponder what awaits. What's the emergency? Likely the point. Trying to avoid one. Trusts Jim's judgment implicitly. So what's the concern? Something's off. So long as that line is still running smoothly, which it is. Prayer. No panic. Prayer. Pray for safe passage. Reach the surface. Feet on the ground.

An hour later still no word. At least the line's moving. Going up. All that matters. Feeling a hint of motion sickness, scanning colour options, when he's suddenly shot up and out. Slammed against the ribcage. Freefall. No. Not like this. Recoil. Snapped back. Suspended. Dead hang. Dark blue. Switches back to night vision. Heart pumping from a full shot of adrenaline. Needs to act. On what? If the line's compromised, grab a hold of something else. John rocks his body. Kicks his legs. Gathering motions. Swings to the side. Grabs a strap. Feet resting on a rib. The weight of the line pulling him back. With one hand he slings to a strap and connects it to a carabiner clip on his sternal attachment point. Leans back. Legs shaking. Carrying all weight.

"Ground control, please respond."

Harness

Nothing. Waiting. Waiting for word. Communications could be out. Heart still racing. What's happening? Happened? Now? Next? Cool it. Calm down. Strapped in. Secure. Clearly the line got caught. Somehow snagged. Jammed up. How? Why? Where's the pinch point and how much stress is it under? Listen. If the line breaks, he can't be attached to it. Squeeze the wall and pray it doesn't catch him on the way down. Remain attached for now. Hope they get comms back on. If the line snaps, he'll hear it. Twist the disconnect. Pull in. Squeeze the strap. Go small.

Thirty minutes in. Legs are burning. Like a prolonged wall sit. On fire from taking all the weight. Needs to adjust position. Slide the sling down the strap so he can squat down for a minute. Pulls himself in, starts letting out some slack when he hears the shot. SNAP. TWANG. John hits the quick release. Pops the plug. Squeezes the strap. Stomach, chest, face shield up against it. Eyes closed. Seconds later. Screams past. Echoes down. Silence. Lost the line. Lost the line. Inconceivable. Thousands of miles down. Nowhere near the surface. So far removed it's an abstraction. Can't be true. Impossible to deny. These are the facts. Panic is not an option. The needle won't save him now. Needs to remain alert. Aware. Spared. He was spared. A story. This is a story. Another chapter. Wait for response. Rescue. Hang tight. Hold on.

Into range. On security's radar. Blip. Dot. Speck. In the distance, drawing closer until it comes into view. Wildlife brought in to aid in the assessment. Describes its gait. Direct registering. Each hind paw directly in the print of the corresponding fore paw. Charting a direct path towards them. Approaching the installation. Artillery, a wall of mobile weapons, instructed to meet it halfway and tranquilize the target. The Landlord on its way with a relaxed approach, at leisure until it sights them, lowers its head just below shoulder height, and shifts into a trot. Closing ground, it switches to a canter, then a run. The order goes out. Fire when ready. Full sprint. Only a single paw touches the ground at any one time. Massive strides. Erasing the distance. Shot fired. Ducked. Deflected off the frill. Starts shuttering. Skipping frames. Switching angles. There one second, gone the next. Impossible to track. On them. Over them. Flips the convoy upside down and sideways.

Crushing armoured fighting vehicles like beer cans. Mashed under its paws. Hooked, scooped, and tossed by its horn. Smashed by its tail. Splintered. Peeling off. Retreat. Too slow. Squashed. The wail of defence sirens fills the air. The inquiry is upon them and it's angry.

Shooting hoops. Something to do. Now sirens. Ordered to return inside over the loudspeaker. Mess hall. Emergency meeting place. They see it coming. Flickering in and out of sight. Until it slows down upon approach. Holds form. There it is. The Landlord. Ren and Mo take it in. Recording the moment with their phones. Miles away but close enough. Ren zooms out. Wide shot. Can see the fence is barely up to its knees.

"Mo, let's go."

Ignores him.

"Mo, you've seen it. Got the shot."

Holding her ground.

"Quit fucking around. We've got to get inside. Let's go."

Mo stops recording. Mesmerized. The Landlord's shadow reaching the fence. Sees them. Sees her. Supernatural. Can feel its presence. The pull. Polarity. Female. Crackling with energy. Charged. Everything alive. Arriving at base, the beast simply steps over the fence.

"Mo, let's fucking go!"

Snaps out of it. Moves towards the door. Won't turn her back. Eyes forward. On it. Step inside. Behind the glass. Stops. Pulls out her phone. Resumes recording. Ren right behind her. Siren still blaring. Without a passing glance, the Landlord whips its tail, obliterates the loudspeakers, crouching down as it approaches the door. Its face filling the frame. Blocking the light. Turns its head. Pans left. Eyes to giant eye. Bright yellow framed in black. Specks of gold. The beast chuffs. Fogs the glass. Ren behind her.

"Too close. Might blow the glass out."

Harness

Said under his breath. Trying to keep quiet. Mo stops recording. Slowly steps away as security rushes in, guns raised, filling the foyer. Forcing her down the hallway towards the mess hall. Blocking her view of the entrance. Outside movement. Light shines through the glass. Mo registers the moment before the doors explode.

RESOLVE:

Two options. Wait for rescue or start climbing. John makes some quick calculations. Rough estimate. Enough Nor to last three weeks. Minimum four weeks to climb to the surface. With no idea what's taking place up there, time is of the essence. Start climbing while he can. While he has the capacity. God willing the rescue team picks him up along the way but what if they assume there's nothing to rescue? Nonsense. Not how it works. Comms have been cut off but their sensors still work. Multiple options. Bio-radar, thermal imaging, and his beacon's on. They know. They can see him unless ground control's been destroyed. Has it? How? For the line to fail like that is almost incomprehensible. Multiple safeties in place. Factored in. Would have to be an atypical combination of human error and mechanical failure. That or an outside event: natural disaster, explosion, collision. All three. Who knows. Here now. It's on him. Find a way out. A way home. The strapping will be his rope, rib to rib, all the way up. Can't use a GriGri, won't get around the strap. What'll it be? Waist Prusik with a hollow block attachment and a climb heist on a double-length sling for his foot. Will have to reattach and adjust for each section. Going to be a painful process. John looks up. Following the spinal column as it fades out of sight. The enormity of the challenge sinks in. Impossible. Impossible climb. Doesn't have the physical reserves. Insurmountable. Panic setting in. Feeling trapped. Buried. John steps away from the emotion. Bears witness. Allows it to wash over him. Accepts his circumstance. Slow going. Patience. Be not afraid. Do not despair. John secures his foot sling with a Prusik around the strap. Takes up the slack. Sitting on the waist Prusik, he stands up on the climb heist. Pull up on the waist Prusik. Repeats until he reaches the next set of ribs, attaches safeties, reconnects, continues. All he can do.

TYRANT

Twisted metal. Splintered wood. Shattered glass. The instillation in ruins. Exposed. Tore the place apart. Ripped back the roof. Not done. Landlord on the prowl. Picking them off at will. Caught running for cover. Stomped. Chomped. Torn in two. The beast found food. Something new. How many until it's full? Not slowing down. People hiding amongst the debris. Sniffed out. Dragged out. Skewered between six-foot incisors. Mashed between molars. Gulp. Gone. Consumed. Still not satiated. Mo and Ren hiding under the climbing wall that's collapsed into an A-frame. Listening. Can hear the crying, the screams as it sifts through the wreckage for something else to eat. Mo knows they can't stay there. Then where? Whispers to Ren.

> "The wheelhouse. Gotta go for it. Sitting ducks if we stay here. Get low. Down the trachea."

Interrupted by another round of gunfire. What's left of the security battalion still engaged. Hear the roar. Pain. Something got through. Broke the skin. Distracted. Recognize the opportunity. Go. Ren and Mo scramble through the rubble. No clear path. Dead ends. Around obstacles. Find an opening. Collapsed wall to the outside. Stopped in their tracks as the beast flickers past, limping, leaking blood from a damaged hind leg, pursued by an AFV. They move forward. Peek around the corner. The AFV jams on the brakes. Sudden stop. A man they recognize as base commander Abram Kral steps out armed with an RPG. Covered in dust and blood, he takes aims and fires. The grenade hits the other hind leg. Exploding into its hock. The beast bellows. Drops. Turns. Drags itself towards the base commander on its forelegs. Abram tosses the RPG aside, reaches into the AFV, and pulls out a sniper rifle. He waits on the wounded animal. Within twenty yard he takes aim—fires. Its eyeball explodes. Pink mist. Kill shot. Feel the ground shake when it falls. Walking through a cloud of dust, Commander Kral kneels before his kill. Head lowered in prayer. Ren and Mo step out into the open. In the distance, smoke rises from the wheelhouse.

Harness

Flipped AFVs and APCs. Tossed. Crushed. Blood stains the sand. Guts. Entrails. Strewn about. Continue. Ren and Mo arrive on site. Inside the wheelhouse. Ripped through another roof. Systems smashed. Smoldering. Scrapped. Aerial lifts on their side. Tipped over. Trachea open. Hoist split in half. Tangled line. Snapped. John. Gone. They lost him. All that's implied. Sinks in. Stunned. In shock. Staggered. Searching for a response as they stumble through the wreckage. Control boards obliterated. Grim discovery. Jim Dunn in a broken heap beside indented electrical panels. Shattered. Somehow still hanging on. Blood bubbling out his mouth and nose. Choked for air. Gurgling. Massive internal injuries. Not going to make it. Matter of minutes. They sit down beside him. Jim looking up. Out. Past. Soon he stops struggling. Falls still. Mo closes his eyes. Ren reins it in. Breaks the silence.

"John may have detached in advance. Had warning. Hooked onto a rib or strap."

Extinguish the fire then salvage what's required. Find a functioning forklift in the warehouse. Clear all obstacles, wreckage, debris for an unobstructed path to the trachea. Collect a combination of climbing gear and accessories. Manual override. They forklift massive spools of rope still on their pins from the warehouse to a giant winch system anchored into the floor. Emergency backup for a system failure. Can't run a line from the hoist or roof. Straight shot from the wall. It's decided Ren will do the drop while Mo operates the line release. Not wearing the suit. Standard harness with night vision goggles. Communicating via long-range walkies. Ren ties in, secures a rope roller with concrete anchors, then applies the edge protector. All set. Strapped with a camel pack of Nor equating to roughly three weeks of food provisions and a portaledge, Ren runs the rope to the rim of the trachea and leans back.

"Alright, Moseph. Let's do this."

Mo turns the crank. Letting out the line as Ren descends into the trachea. Four feet between him and the wall. Enough of an overhang that he doesn't catch against it but can still reach the ribbing.

Depleted. Drained. Everything hurts. Hands cramping. Ripped blisters. Raw. John looks up. Nothing's changed. No light. Feels like he's been climbing for days. Didn't make a dent. Where are they? Where's the rescue response? Should have reached him by now. Sent a signal. Something. Anything. What if the entire base was erased by a weather event? Weather, which hasn't changed since their arrival. Escalating heat throughout the day. Steep drop at night. Eerily consistent. Abnormal. No seasons. No change. Maybe they've been in the eye of the storm this entire time. Perhaps a sudden swing in temperature triggered a massive tornado that wiped them off the map. Obliterated. Survivors scrounging for food and shelter. Who responds to that? If the instillation was annihilated, does transport have the ability to bring them back? They arrived here somehow. Started somewhere. Can do it again. What's the process? No one knows. Not really. The inner workings of the transport department are a mystery. It's a hyper-specialized field by design. Dead-end reductionism. John knows transport workers who readily admit it's impossible to understand the system as a whole. Rigorous security protocol and counterintelligence. Surveillance. Deception. Loyalty tests. Smoke and mirrors to conceal the source. Each branch, by and large, operating in isolation. Tightly controlled exchanges of information. Restricted to three points of contact. A secret that can't be deciphered.

Damn near a day now. The rope winch so much slower. Set speed. Yelling John's name every hundred feet. Nothing but the void. Starting to fuck with his head. How far does he take this? Until the last set of strapping? Has to take the time loss into account on the return. Spirit starting to drop. Serious doubt. Had the right idea but that doesn't change the outcome. John is likely gone. Can't imagine. Won't. Change subjects. Shift topics. Stop soon. Secure the portaledge to the strapping. Sleep on it.

Cort had no idea. At the mine during the attack. Kept working. Informed end of shift. Security handed back their phones and he saw her messages.

Unable to leave. All remaining transport vehicles commandeered by security. Held at site until the battalion completed a damage assessment. Finally brought back to base camp. Now a disaster area. Triage. Search, rescue, recovery. Cort operating one of the excavators. Carefully clearing debris. A path to access to the injured, the dead, and aid in the retrieval of salvageable essential goods. Creating space for clearing stations and temporary sleeping quarters. Awake over twenty-four hours. Finally, another driver takes over. Cort sneaks off site. Arrives at the wheelhouse with pillows and blankets. Covers Jim's body with the spare blanket. When Ren signs out for sleep it's time to rest. Pillows down. Mo and Cort side by side. One blanket under them, one over. Walkie on when Ren's ready to go. Hard floor. Lying on their backs. Fade out fast before they're blasted by light. Both shielding their eyes. Trying to gain their bearings.

"This is a restricted zone. I need names and pass cards."

Only outlines. Mo squinting to see who's behind the light.

"The entire installation was destroyed and you're asking for ID?"
"One has no relation to the other. Same rules apply."
"I work here. I work the wheelhouse. I'm one of the riggers. The hoist line snapped while another rigger, John Choi, was working the trachea."
"Names and pass cards."
"You fucking serious?"

No response.

"Start by aiming your light away from my eyes so I can see who the fuck I'm talking to."

The light redirected off to the side. Faces take form. Soldiers. Security battalion. The base commander holding the light. Square jaw. Strong chin. Crew cut. Clean. No visible tattoos. Average height. Muscular build. Natural frame. Unlike Meathead who's posing hard behind him with two other grunts she recognizes but has never met. A wiry brown guy, maybe South Indian, with burn scars across the right side of his face. The second looks Samoan.

Massive man, six-foot-six, three hundred pounds. Black hair with a Zeus beard. Burly. Barrel chest.

"My name is Margot Medlam. Who am I speaking to?"
"Base commander Abram Kral."
"Abram, the rope running from this winch system into that hole is connected to rigger Ernesto Renzetti, who's searching for our colleague John Choi. John was suspended inside it when our hoist was destroyed."
"You're running the winch?"
"I am. Corresponding over two-way radio. Agreed to rest. When Renzetti wakes up, we'll continue the search."
"Jim's Dunn's your department head."
"Jim's dead. His body's under the blanket by those electrical panels."

Mo pointing in the general direction. Abram doesn't bat an eye.

"Is there any indication John's alive?"
"We're hoping he was alerted to the threat and secured himself to the structure, the strapping, before his line snapped."
"That's a whole lot of hope."

Silence. Stone-faced. Not playing these games. Wait him out. Abram checks the time.

"At twenty-two hundred hours, we're pulling Renzetti out of there."

Directs his attention to Cort.

"You, sir, I saw you operating the excavator. What's your name?"
"Cort Gwitt."
"Cort, you can't be here. Go get some rest back at basecamp."
"Would just as soon stay here. Catch a few hours shuteye then continue cleanup."
"Not an option."

Harness

"Look around ya, man. What playbook you running off?"
"We remain subject to the Code of Service."

Mo intervenes before it escalates. Kneels in front of Cort with her back to Kral.

"Not worth it. I'll be fine. We'll be fine. Leave it. Just go."

Delirious. Can't rest. Not really. No sleep. No way to take the weight off. Falling apart. Starting to hallucinate. Walls are shifting. Seeing faces. Shadows. Streaks. Stains in the tissue. Needs a break. A bed. A bath. Brush his teeth. Imagine. Imagine being anywhere else. Why here? How'd this happen? Family. Family first. Food on the table. Providers provide. Past tense. Present tension. Pain. Under constant strain. Body. Vessel. Host. How much can it host? Endure. Resist. Resistance. Ohm. Aum. Home. Source. See how it sounds. Knees bent. Back straight. Waist sling takes the weight. Arms slack by his side. Starting with the "A," holding the "U" a little longer, and then ending the exhale on the "M."

"Auuuum . . . Auuuum . . . Auuuum . . ."

Half-formed images. Storylines starting to coalesce when he hears her voice through static.

"Ren."

Once more.

"Ren."

Keys the walkie.

"Mo."
"Sorry to wake you. Status update. Security battalion says they're pulling you out of there at twenty-two hundred hours."

Relief. Be lying if he said otherwise. Lights on. Checks the time. Only been an hour. Not wasting another.

"Copy. Give me a moment to pack up the portaledge and we'll get going."

Ren makes sure everything's in place. Secured. Attached. Steps out onto the rib. Takes his time collapsing and packing the hanging cot. Tighten the slack. Suspended by the line. Feet against the rib. Final push. Pray for a miracle before he's relieved of duty. Nothing to lose. Be direct. Say it. Straight to source. Whoever, whatever is listening.

"Dear lord, creator, creation, if John's alive, if he's down here, somehow hanging on, let us find him. Please let us find him. Guide the way. Grant us strength. Amen and everything else."

Ren keys the walkie.

"Alright, Mo, we're good to go."

Jim's body removed. Two guards posted at the wheelhouse. Officers Lakmal and Miller a.k.a. Meathead. Anyone else but him. Lakmal still on patrol. Taking too fucking long. Mo works the winch with her back turned to Miller. Can feel his eyeballs on her.

"So why you giving me the cold shoulder?"

Of course. Of course he can't keep his mouth shut.

"You don't need to be here."
"Not my call."

Doesn't care enough to continue the line of conversation.

"You look angry . . . tense."

Not taking the bait.

"Would a quick shag help?"

"Shut the fuck up. One more word and I'm calling Commander Kral to write you up."

"She said, he said. Just trying to strike up some conversation. Offer my services. Wasn't sure if your new boyfriend with the fucked-up ears was getting the job done."

"Buddy . . . are you that fuckin' broken? Must be hell inside your head. To be that insecure."

"Good enough to stick my cock in you."

"Seek help, dude. Seriously. I might be mad if you weren't so pathetic."

"Cause you're acting like a cunt and—"

Hears footsteps. Miller pipes down. Lakmal returns from patrol.

"Uh oh . . . looks like I walked into a lover's quarrel."

Mo shoots daggers in his direction.

"You fucking serious?"

"Nah, just trying ta keep things light. Break the tension."

Blood boiling. Locks the crank. Keys her walkie.

"Ren."

"Mo."

"Need to pause for five minutes."

"You good?"

"We're good. Back in five."

"Copy."

Adrenaline pumping. Shaking. Don't show it. Don't give them the satisfaction. Calm. Collected. Mo pulls up the crew contact list on her phone. Scrolls through departments. Finds it. Calling Commander Kral. Four rings for an answer.

"Commander Kral speaking."

"It's Margot Medlam at the wheelhouse. Your boys are acting cute and I don't appreciate it. Not my vibe. You need to replace them now."

Miller talking shit while Mo works the winch. Enraged she ratted on him. Chirping until they hear the APC pull up outside. Lakmal and Miller stand at attention when Commander Kral enters with two replacement officers. Harris and Vera. She likes Harris. Never met Vera. Not officially. Lean little Latin dude with a scorpion tattooed on the side of his skull. Seen him in passing. Usually running laps in the courtyard wearing a weighted vest. Mo continues letting out line as Commander Kral steps forward.

"Hold the work."
"Why?"
"Explain the situation. What was said?"
"Doesn't matter, just keep them away from me."
"It does matter. It's why we're here."

Mo locks the crank, keys Ren.

"Ren."
"Mo."
"Five more minutes."
"What's going on?"
"Five minutes. All good. Explain later."
"Copy."

Mo directs her attention to Commander Kral.

"I'm running the line on a high-angle rescue operation and these two want to start a conversation."
"What else?"
"You need more?"

Commander Kral stares back with a straight face. Unnerving. Can't tell what registers. Impossible to read. Turns his attention to Lakmal and Miller.

"What else?"

They both look away. To the side. Down. Neither can hold eye contact. Commander Kral approaches Miller. Stops. Arm's length away. Standing directly in front of him.

"What else?"

Miller stumbles and stammers out a response.

"Nothing . . . we, uh . . . was just making small talk . . . like a misunderstanding."

Kral sweeps his legs out with a clothesline to the chest. Pulls a pistol from his holster and points it at his head.

"What else?"

Insane overreaction but the other mercs don't bat an eye. Mo in shock. Miller on his back. Eyes wide. Hands up in surrender.

"I don't know . . . I don't . . . I . . . sorry. I'm sorry."
"Our comrades have been killed. Our brothers. Our sisters. Those that survived, that can help, are currently engaged in relief efforts. Counting the dead. Tending to the wounded. And you're in here fucking around. Harassing the woman who's trying to rescue her colleague. Tell me why I don't waste you?"
"I fucked up. Fucked up. Mistake. Made a—"

Kral steps in, gun raised. Posturing. Has to be. No way. There's no way.

"Mistake? You didn't know what you were doing?"

Miller's lip trembling.

"It was . . . no . . . yeah . . . Error . . . error in judgement."

Kral pulls back on the gun hammer. No. Too much. Mo steps in. Speaks up.

"Stop. Please stop. This is not that situation. No need to pull a weapon. No one needs to die."

Still locked on Miller.

"What did he say to you?"
"He made—"

The words get caught. Mo clears her throat.

"Made like a stupid overture. Rude. It was rude. Idiotic. All of that . . . but this is not . . . this is not a warranted response. Let's just please take a breath and walk it back."

Impassive. No clue what's getting through. Miller pleading for mercy.

"I am sorry. Sorry to Margot. Sorry to everyone here. I was out of order."

Kral stone cold. Fixed stance. Aim. Mo feels sick. What has she done? This maniac about to squeeze the trigger.

"Commander, please don't shoot me. I'll make amends. Make things right. I will. I promise."

Kral considers. Nods to Miller.

"And this is not your own doing; it is the gift of God."

Holsters the pistol.

John destroyed. In denial. Keep going. That was the mantra. Simple. Now he can't and it's complicated. Tore his hamstring pushing off the climb heist. Severe strain. Grade two without a doubt. Possibly three. Full rupture. Felt like he took it off the bone. Blinding. Like a bomb went off. Incapacitated. Excruciating pain. Can't push off the other leg. Can't. Can't do it. Leg needs to immobilize. Shock wearing off. Drained. Defeated. Completely spent. No closer to the surface. Not really. No light. No rescue. Despair. He's going to die here and doesn't know how.

Sign of life. Sound. Signal. Something. Has to happen. Hours on the clock. Winding down. Ren's voice hoarse from yelling John's name. Ren speaks to the source once more.

"If that man is alive, let us find him. Today's the day."

Harness

Hail Mary pass. Has to ask. Be a fool not to. Spoken to the universe now straight to him.

"Let's go, John. Let's go . . ."

Another attempt. Has to. Sickening jolt of pain. Gasps. Grasps the strap. Stuck. He's stuck. That's it. The anguish of it all. For what? Money. Family. Family without a father. Big man. Provider. What are you providing now? Nothing. Failed. Took the bait. Debt now—pay later: house, truck, van, tools, school. Building a better life. Family deserves it. Check all the boxes. Meet every metric. Standardized success. Status. Big city dreams. Schemes. Where the work is. Had to be a homeowner. Doesn't own a home. Owns a mortgage. A mortgage they won't be able to pay without him. Right back to the bank. Big shot. Big man. Well, here you are, right where they want you. In a hole running on empty. Pride. Ego. Hubris. Survived the tower and stepped right into another trap. Convinced if the effort was there his faith would guide him. Confident a strong work ethic could take them to the promised land. Generational wealth. Lay the foundation. Him and his wife looking out from their front porch at their grandkids playing in the grass. Tried to make it happen. Failed. May God protect them. Forgive his pride, envy, all of it. At the end. How? How does he do this? How does the soul separate from the host? The spirit leave its vessel? Not going to starve. Takes too long. Needless suffering. Remove his helmet and hang himself. Suicide. Not there yet. Never. Hold on. Pain is teacher. Teaching what? That he loves his family beyond measure? That he'd surrender everything for them? Already knew that. Knows love. Is love. Shot through with gratitude. Gutted in grief. For the first time in forever, John weeps.

Ren checks the time. Under an hour. Whispers creeping in. Getting louder. Doubt. Defeat. John's gone. Lost his lifeline. These are the facts. Cable snapped. Freefall. Too awful to consider. Then don't. Still time on the clock. Every minute, every second, counts. On the cusp. Getting closer.

TYRANT

Gotta believe. Forty-five minutes for a miracle. Divine agency. Out of the dark and into the light. Now and then. All we ask. Let it happen. Why not. Lead us back.

Leaning back on his waist Prusik. One foot resting on the rib. Bad leg dangling in the air. All his weight transferred to his good leg. Lactic acid building up. Burning. Staring at a festering skin graft bordered by the waxen dermis. Another infection. Nonsense. Total fucking nonsense. Going to die in this hell hole. Simmering anger. Every error whirling around. Boiling up. Rage. It wants you to scream. This thing. This fucking thing feeding off him. Don't give in. Don't give it the satisfaction. Silence. Well, guess what . . . it eats that too. John lifts his visor. Illumination off. Swallowed by darkness. Breathes in the cool damp air. Releases a scream, a howl, that turns into a roar.

Something. That was something. Muffled sound. Barely audible. Ears piqued. Waiting for more. Nothing. Ren fills his lung. Yells down. Back. Awaits response. Nothing. Knows he heard something. Ren fires his laser down the hole.

John looks up. Sees the light. Green line. Laser. Life. Yells. Screams. Voice breaks. Shot. Gone. Remembers he has his own laser. Arm up. Point and shoot.

Fires right past Ren. Between him and the wall. Inches away. Flickers back. Recognition. Rush. Pure exhilaration.

"Johnny boy! On our way, buddy! We're on our way!"

Harness

Twenty-two hundred hours. Harris breaks the silence. Lets her know.

"We've got to call it, Mo."

Acknowledged. Resigned. On cue—Ren through the walkie.

"Let there be light. A laser line just shot right past me."

Mo looks to Harris. Not asking but the answer is obvious. Harris confirms.

"Go get him."

White light. Likely a head lamp. Speed of descent barely perceptible but inching closer. Visor down. Into view. Ren to the rescue. Communicating over the walkie. Can hear the countdown.

"Fifty . . . Forty . . . Thirty . . . Twenty . . . Ten . . . Five . . ."

Slows to a stop.

"Touchdown."

Eye to eye.

"John. "
"Ren."
"Let's get the fuck outta here."

TANK

Matthew 13:47: "Again, the Kingdom of Heaven is like a dragnet, that was cast into the sea, and gathered some fish of every kind, which, when it was filled, they drew up on the beach. They sat down and gathered the good into containers, but the bad they threw away. So will it be at the end of the age. The angels will come forth, and separate the wicked from among the righteous, and will cast them into the furnace of fire. There will be the weeping and the gnashing of teeth."

To whom it may concern,

I've been working with an outreach program for the community of Morden, another bankrupt district abandoned by the state. We do basic health and wellness checks for the most vulnerable in the area, providing food, water, clothing, and toiletries to those in need. My motives are by no means altruistic. I'm currently in recovery for drug and alcohol abuse. Helping others helps me. It interrupts my pattern of addiction and gives my time purpose.

While meeting the people of Morden and hearing their stories, I became aware of an urban legend many locals claim to be true. A story your periodical might want to investigate. I believe the subject and tone is in line with your content and something your readership would find compelling. It certainly piqued my interest, which led to me recording interviews with residents willing to speak on the matter. Most did not want to be on camera. They're suspicious of outsiders, concerned the information they provide will somehow be used against them. In the end it was easier to capture audio files (available upon request). I've transcribed and included eight of these conversations for you to gauge your interest on, changing the names of those that don't want to be identified. I preface each exchange with a brief summary of the subject and setting.

Onto the interviews:

Eddie, thirty-eight years old, was born and raised in Morden. Like many locals, he could not afford to leave as the situation went from bad to worse. He worked as a general labourer at the steel mill before it closed. After he was laid off, Eddie added crack cocaine to his daily consumption of pain pills and alcohol. Now it's his primary addiction. He collects scrap metal and returns empties for money. Stealing when necessary. Problem being there's not much left to steal in Morden, with limited options for sale. Eddie hawks his stolen goods to the only pawn shop in town for pennies on the dollar.

I interview Eddie under a tarp he's tied to four pieces of rebar jutting out from the cracked concrete of two corner walls. These walls are all that remain standing amidst a pile of rubble from a collapsed warehouse outlet. This is where Eddie lives. He has his tent and a makeshift fire pit built from the rubble to cook on. Eddie's on the comedown. His spirits are low and it's unlikely he would have spoken with me had I not brought food provisions.

IN: What do you know about the fish?

EDDIE: There's nothing to know.

When did you first hear about it?

In the womb.

Can you explain what you mean by that?

Always there, was, and will be.

I'm not sure I understand.

Just is. Next question.

What's the aquarium?

A trap.

Trap meaning trap house.

Smoke crack, shoot smack in this town, ya end up there eventually.

I've heard the building was originally a church.

Gutted and stripped right down to the wall beams.

Tank

Did you ever attend service when it was a functioning church?

Few times as a kid. Better when I could buy crack.

Where was the fish?

Basement.

And you saw it?

(Eddie nods.)

What'd you see?

(Pause.)

The fish was there before the building. Before us.

How's that possible?

Done. Don't want to talk about this no more.

Charlie, forty-two years old, moved to Morden when he was five. His mother dropped him off with his grandmother, then disappeared. Charlie never knew his father. Until the reset, he had steady work with a landscaping company. The business went under, and it was a string of temporary gigs and side hustles until he started working full-time at the aquarium.

I interview Charlie in the parking lot of a shuttered grocery story. With no cloud cover, we drive around to the shaded side of the building. Charlie unstraps a pair of fold-out lawn chairs for us to sit on from the roof rack of a rusted white minivan. The van doubles as his vehicle and place of residence.

IN: Let's talk about the aquarium.

CHARLIE: Had its own orbit. Place was crawling.

In what way?

Dope fiends. Crackheads. Tweakers.

I heard it was originally a church.

Yup.

Did you ever go to a service?

TYRANT

Nope.

How'd the Dace set start?

Not for me to say.

Were they local? Obviously, they recruited from the area.

Not for me to say.

What about the fish?

What about it?

Did you know it was there?

No.

When do you find out?

When I start working.

With Dace.

Correct.

How's that happen?

Submitted a resumé with a cover letter.

(Charlie sells it. Leaves me hanging.)

You're joking, right?

Connections. Know people. Meet people. Signed up cause I was sick of treading water. Every job part-time. Piecemeal. Day shift. Night shift. Don't matter. Debt keeps piling on. Dragging ya down. So what the fuck you going to do? Sell drugs, that's what. Work the tank one night, make more money than a week of mowing lawns and stocking shelves.

What kind of work is it?

Production. Assembly-line shit. Behind a steel-plated door with armed guards posted outside.

Do you meet the fish on your first day?

Nah, man. Ain't like an official introduction.

Tank

But you know it's there.

You hear about it.

How?

Just happens.

How does it happen?

Like mentioned in passing.

In what way?

Look, man, it's not, like, actively talked about.

It's just there.

Pretty much.

When do you see it? How does that work?

Fish need feeding. Chumming the water. Cousin Isaac handed me a slop bucket filled with scraps from the butcher's but we fed it all kinds of shit: roadkill, raccoon, possum, rat, dead birds.

Where's the fish kept?

Basement. Back of the basement. Had its own room.

Can you describe the room?

Industrial kitchen. Everything tore out of there. Can see exposed connections for the appliances. Cracked tiles. No windows. Tube lighting. Half of them burnt out.

Where's the fish?

Tank. Middle of the room. No stand or nothing. Right there on the floor.

What are the dimensions of the tank?

Say, like . . . the length and width of a king-size bed.

How high? What's the depth?

I'm six-two and the top of the tank was the base of my neck.

Let's talk about what's inside the tank.

Fuck if I know.

You know it's a fish.

Parts of one.

Explain.

Water's filthy. Fucking stank. Cloudy grey-green colour. Filters all fucked up. Mold growing up the sides of the tank. Can't see it. Can't see through. At a distance like there's nothing there. Second you step in the room it starts thrashing. Smashing up against the glass. Water spilling over. Lights flickering. Buzzing. You empty that bucket and best stand back. Fucking chaos. Can't believe it did't crack that shit.

So, you never really saw the fish.

Catching glimpses. Like snapshots. Was all kinds of fucked up.

Could you guess at what kind of species it might be?

Ain't no marine biologist but I never seen shit like that. The fuckin' teeth on this thing. Smush its ugly face against the glass. Mean-ass underbite with these dirty blades jutting out every direction. Swipe around see its fins, tattered tail with these spikes. These black-tipped spines. Nasty business, man. Scars on its skin. Scales missing. Ragged-looking creature.

How big was it?

Too big for its tank. Stuck in that gangrene gutter water. No wonder it was ready to kill a motherfucker. I'm shaking my head like . . . how the fuck this thing get here?

Any ideas?

Not a clue.

Why is there no footage of the fish?

Policy.

Why?

Tank

Exodus 20:4

I'm not familiar.

Was spray painted on the kitchen.

What's it mean?

«Thou shalt not make unto thee any graven image.»

Is that general policy or specific to the fish?

We at work. Put the phone away.

But the fish was there before Dace arrived. It came with the place.

True.

Then there has to be something. Footage somewhere.

Maybe. Maybe not. Might a been scrubbed.

Why would anyone care? What's it matter?

Break your brain trying to make sense of this one.

Did the fish have a primary caretaker or was it a shared responsibility?

Shared responsibility? Nah, man. Neither. Fed when we fed it. Not like a set schedule or nothing. Somehow survived.

Did it have a name?

Like a pet?

Yeah.

Fish. Fish in the basement.

Remy, sixty-four years old, was born and raised in Westhill, a wealthy suburb an hour's drive outside of Morden. He remained there as an adult, raising his own family while working as a real estate lawyer. During a booze-soaked weekend at the cottage, he crashed his jet-ski into a partially submerged rock formation, snapping both wrists and breaking his collarbone. During his subsequent treatment (multiple surgeries) and recovery, Remy developed an opioid addiction. Between the pain pills, alcohol, and a tanking economy, Remy lost his house and destroyed his marriage. As the descent continued, he switched from a steady diet of oxycodone and Percocet to heroin because it was cheaper (and apparently better for his liver). I spoke with Remy on the rooftop of a shuttered car dealership he was squatting in with several others.

IN: How were you introduced to the aquarium?

REMY: Had a client that was interested in purchasing the property.

Was it still a functioning church at the time?

Nope. It was a dilapidated drug den filled with squatters.

What did your client plan to do with the property?

Tear it down. Sit and wait. He thought the market had bottomed out. Could only go up. Thought wrong. Not a lull. This was a depression. Convinced him to stay away from the property, not realizing I'd soon be sucked into its vortex.

How'd that happen?

Vice. Weakness. Indulgence. Addiction. Whatever you want to call it. Would park my BMW several blocks away and send someone in to cop for me.

How's that work?

Incentive. One for me, one for you. Staying in my car where there's a gun in the glove box. Worked for a while but inevitably I get ripped off. Send this woman to score and she doesn't come back. Fuck it. Go straight to the source. Park right there in front of the church. March up those steps. Go straight inside where guys with guns meet me at the door. Group of them parked inside the vestibule. No issues, though. Place my order. Grab and go. How I roll until my car's repoed. Total tailspin at that point. Taking the bus to church now. Shooting smack right there on the dais. Strange setting but no one would fuck with you. Not really. I'll give them that. Dace crew always had someone posted in a pew at the back. Fuck around, start shit, and they'd cut you off.

How'd you learn about the fish?

My first mass, as it were. Tie up on site, shoot it, seconds later this junkie, Jed, with his mouth full of rotten teeth, says, "Welcome to the tank." On the nod now. In and out. Rolling dream. See this old head Larry blasting a crack rock. Singed beard. Burnt fingers. Sucking in that sweet smoke. After a slow exhale he does a little shimmy shake and announces to the room: "Ladies and gentlemen, welcome to another night at the aquarium." I'm like, what is this? What am I missing here? Understanding there's a twisted gallows humour attached to the pain of end-game addiction. I imagine they're referencing the observational freakshow quality of the church. Not yet realizing the structure actually houses this monstrous mythological fish.

When do you find that out?

Deidre. This woman was cracked before the crack. Crazy. Truly certifiable. Violence at the drop of a dime. Feral. Would fly off the fucking handle. Anything could set her off but Deidre knew to be on her best behaviour at the aquarium. So one day I step out of the nave—

What's the nave?

The area of the church where parishioners, members of the church, sit or stand. Then there's the sanctuary, which is in front of the nave. The sanctuary is the area with the altar, the tabernacle, pulpit, and choir loft, if there is one.

How do you know all this?

I was an altar boy in another life. In this instance, the nave and the sanctuary are where people would blast off and shoot smack. Leave that area and you're stepping into this hallway that goes from the vestibule to the staircase at the back. Along the way, down that hall, there's offices and rooms used for Sunday school, daycare, whatever . . . The first room, which I believe was a coat check or some kind of concession, is now the exchange.

What's that?

What it sounds like. Where drugs are exchanged for money. On this day, I step out of the nave into the vestibule. Still in a stupor, I see Deidre losing it outside the exchange. She's flapping her arms, screaming at Keon, who's security. Watch her lean backs and spit in his face. No hesitation, he drops her with an overhand right. Grabs a fistful of her hair and starts dragging her down the hallway to the back staircase. Says she's going for a swim. Fish food. Deidre hears this and starts screeching, kicking her legs, fucking flailing. Basically going into convulsions. Begging forgiveness, "Please, no, please, no,

God, no, help me, God, help me!" Keon crouches down, cranks her neck by her hair, and tells her to get the fuck out. Never come back. "I promise, promise, promise," she keeps repeating. He lets go. Booting her in the ass as she runs away. Deidre faceplants. Scrambles to her feet and scurries out the door. And that's how I first heard about the fish.

Did you ever see it?

The back stairwell and basement were employees only but there was one guard who let you sneak a peek. You had to ask nicely and it helped if you had food to feed it. Case in point, we're in the middle of another power outage. Two weeks without electricity. My buddy Bob had a stack of these cheap minute steaks that expired. Meat's turned grey. Stinks. He's going to toss 'em so I take them to the tank. Get a good look at this thing. Guards wave me past. Down the stairs into the basement. Walk through the mess hall through a set of double doors into darkness. Pitch black. Fumble for the lights. Flip on the overhead fluorescents. Some of the tubes are burnt out, some smashed, others flickering. All the appliances have been removed. Everything cleared out so your eyes are pulled towards this monolith in the middle of the room. A giant six-by-six tank filled with cloudy, grey-green wastewater. At first glance, there's nothing in the tank. Still. Stagnant. Until I step forward, then it's chaos. The fish rams its head against the glass. Starts thrashing around the tank. Water sloshing over the sides. Collect myself. Creep forward. Can't make out the fish in its entirety. Catching a glimpse. What I see is damaged and diseased. Cloudy eye. Tattered tail and fins. Mouth rot: all chewed up in the corners. Scales missing and broken. Fish was covered in fungal infections. God knows how many parasites it was infested with. No clue how it survived in those conditions. The water filter was useless. Covered in calcium deposits.

How many times did you view the fish?

That was it. Once was enough. Tossed in those minute steaks and left. The water was putrid.

Have you seen the church since it burnt down?

Charred remains. Nothing to see.

The tank is gone.

Claimed by the flames.

No. There's nothing there. If you explore the aftermath, you'll see there's significant smoke damage but the kitchen's still standing. Not sure how it was preserved. Possibly because it was built below ground. Insulated by the concrete foundation. Maybe the metal doors or tiling. Who knows. Point being, the structure's intact yet there's no evidence of the tank. No melted glass or plastic from the filter. There should be something. Some kind of impression or remnant. Unless it was removed in advance.

Then it was removed.

By who?

You tell me.

How do you think the fire started?

Combustion.

From what?

I could guess. Does it matter?

Why did Dace stop operating out of the church?

Look around you, man. Everything's boarded up. No power. No running water. No nothing. Can't get blood from a stone. Can't return empties when people can't afford beer. Collecting scraps of scrap metal. Running out of shit to steal. Nothing to serve. Nowhere to work. You need some semblance of an economy to sell drugs. Especially at the volume they were moving. Drug trafficking don't work on a barter system. Not at that scale. So they shut it down. Supply and demand don't mean a thing when there's nothing to exchange. Forget the bottom rung. Morden ain't even on the ladder at this point.

What does the fish represent to you?

Words won't do it.

Try.

Not today.

Deidre, forty-two, was born and raised in Morden. She owned a hair salon but could no longer afford the rent after a series of financial setbacks she'd rather not share. After shutting down the salon, she worked several years as a waitress and store clerk at various retail outlets. Deidre worked two, sometimes three jobs to make ends meet as a single mother. Cocaine and opioids helped her get through the work week until they didn't. A significant portion of her paycheque going towards them, she now needed a side hustle. That hustle was prostitution, which paid better than either of her other jobs. Along the way, cocaine turned to crack and crystal meth. Heroin became a reasonable substitute for the pain pills. She'll take whatever's available. Up or down, does not matter. Deidre doesn't discriminate when it comes to drugs, stating, "Beggars can't be choosers and it's a miracle I've lasted this long." Our interview takes place inside Laser Quest, an abandoned arcade and laser tag park located near the strip mall where she ran her hair salon. Laser Quest was now Deidre's new place of residence. Always on the move in more ways than one, stating, "I hate standing still. Need ta stay busy." We speak near the entrance before a mirrored wall that's cracked and dusty. Deidre uses available light from the front windows, cutting the frayed bleached ends of her hair with a child's paper scissors that are bright green and shaped like an alligator.

DEIDRE: I'm cutting this shit off. Going back to my natural hair colour.

IN: Brunette?

My eight-inch roots give that away? I'd shave my fucking head if I had a pair of clippers.

Deidre, I know there's trauma attached to it but what can you tell me about the aquarium?

Trauma attached to everything at this point.

Fair enough.

What's that fucking term? Den of iniquity. Was a real den of iniquity.

Why was it called the aquarium?

Tank or church. No one called it the aquarium.

Why those names?

Tank

Church 'cause it was church. Tank cause there's a goddamn fish, in a goddamn tank, in the goddamn basement, that could fuel your fucking nightmares for a lifetime.

Did you ever see it?

They almost fed me to the fucking thing.

Who?

Dace.

Why?

'Cause I called them out on their bullshit.

And they threatened you with the fish.

Not just a threat. Started dragging me towards the tank but I fucking lost it. No one's turning me into fish food. Couldn't constrain me. Broke free. Ran out. Never looked back.

But you saw it.

Not then. Never got me down those stairs.

When did you see it?

Was there before those assholes took over. Saw some sick fuck smackhead toss a cat in the tank for a laugh.

The cat was alive?

Sure was. Same guy had his throat sliced with a box cutter when he was on the nod later that night.

Dead?

Fed to the fish.

Who killed him?

Ha! Next question.

Do you know how the fish got there?

Heard some stories. None worth repeating.

They don't need to be true.

The fish is a gate.

How so?

Entrance and exit.

Like a portal?

Exactly.

To what?

Hell.

How would that work?

How the fuck should I know?

Anyone ever jump in to find out?

They've been thrown in.

Alive?

Hand to God.

Can you cite a specific example?

Two of 'em. Saw Dace drag a guy downstairs one night. Brought him in from outside. Was beaten within an inch of his life. Eyes swelled shut. Leaking blood. Lumped him up so bad his own mother wouldn't recognize him. No idea what he did. Never saw him again. Another time a new recruit on the exchange recognized this old head as one of his mom's ex-boyfriends. Guess this guy used to beat them. Surprise, surprise. I'm smoking a rock when the kid storms in and stomps him out. Again, they drag this bloody heap downstairs, never to return.

I've heard overdoses ended up in the tank.

If nobody spoke for 'em.

Any names?

You going to notify their families?

I can try.

Bunkie, Jolene, and Grubs. Rattled off three for ya.

Any last names?

Just what they went by. So good luck with that.

Do you know how the fire started?

The church burning?

Yeah.

Don't know. Don't care.

The fish was removed in advance.

Wouldn't know. Banned before the fire.

Why were you banned?

Gotta give respect to get respect from me. And we'll leave it at that.

Did you burn the church down?

Dace was done. Couldn't give a shit.

You were born and raised in Morden.

Unfortunately.

Alive when the tank was a church.

Sure was.

Ever attend a service?

Ha! Sundays were for football. Daddy wasn't taking us to no church. But here's one for ya—Ava Anne Montgomery. God rest her soul. Was a nurse who started getting high on her own supply. Somewhere along the way she ended up at the aquarium. Where we met. By this point, Ava's in her seventies. No joke. Well-preserved. Heroin can do that if it don't kill ya first. Anyhow, Ava was a lovely woman. Kind. Soft-spoken. Happened to be there the day she died. Stopped by the exchange. Took her medicine. Nodded off. Never woke up from. Clean up comes in and I throw my body over her. Ain't no way they're feeding her to that fish. Get 'em to back off and a group of us carried Ava Anne to a nearby park. Leaned her up against the oak tree. Folded her arms on her lap. Looking as peaceful as can be when I called the medics to come get her. This was a week before they suspended emergency services to the area. I bring up Ava because she's a story worth sharing and happened to be member of the church when it was a church. Recall she brought up the priest. Father Brack. Name stuck with me. Ava's mother ran the prayer group, which was held in the basement. Father Brack was supposed to join them that day. Said her mom stepped away then came back in for her. Brings Ava to the stairwell where Father Brack's passed out on the, what the fuck you call it, the platform between stairs?

Landing?

That's it. Brack's passed out on the middle landing. Leaned against the wall. Head split open. Blood running down his face. Soaked in sweat. One of his sleeves is rolled up, and here's the kicker . . . he's got fucking track marks on his arm. Ava can't see it for what it is, not at that age, but knows there's a problem. Leaves an impression. She has to hold a cold compress on his neck while her mom wipes away the blood and disinfects the head wound.

What a scene . . .

Another interesting tidbit about Father Brack. He was a soldier. A war veteran that worked in intelligence before joining the priesthood.

Intelligence?

A spy! A spook! The guy was a fucking spook! Can you believe that shit?

Hell of a resume.

And a fucking dope fiend to boot!

How do you know this?

I don't. Ava told me.

Did she tell you why the church closed?

Property lost its value and the congregation had no money for the collection plate.

Tank

Where are locals buying their drugs now?

Couple small pockets of production. They do drive-bys like an ice cream truck.

Any plans to leave Morden?

Where? How? Don't have a say in the matter.

Anything else you like to add?

Said too much already, hahahahahah.

Niesha, twenty-two, has lived in Morden her entire life. Going into in grade 10, her high school closed from lack of funding and never reopened. Niesha is pregnant. Mike, her boyfriend and the father of her child, died in the church fire.

I interview Niesha on the bleachers overlooking the scorched grass of her shuttered high school's football field. Niesha and her uncle Anton live in a shelter they made under the bleachers with the means available to them. The walls are made from scraps of plywood, tin, and tarp that have been fastened onto the bleacher supports with plumbers' strap and rope. They each have their own room and air mattress, sharing a common area complete with couch, recliner, and coffee table. Further down the bleachers, suspended to an upright, is a bladder-bag shower. This area is walled off with dollar store shower curtains suspended on yellow nylon rope tied to the uprights. On the opposite side of the field, under the opposing bleachers, they have two tarped-off sections with honey bucket toilets they dump down a storm drain. Their toilet paper and trash are disposed of in the school's industrial dumpster that's approaching capacity.

Before the bleachers, Niesha and her uncle lived in several abandoned homes but there were always encroachments and disturbances they could not look past. One night, out of options and energy, after another eviction (of sorts), they set up camp under the bleachers and have yet to leave.

Recently, they dug up the front lawn of the high school, planting a variety of seeds Anton had squirreled away for a vegetable patch. The patch has the potential to provide cucumbers, tomatoes, sweet potatoes, squash, and green beans but it won't happen without rain. The recent drought alert is nothing more than a statement of fact. It does not help their garden. It does not help them.

IN: Church, tank, aquarium. What did you call it?

NIESHA: Don't know. Just was. Tank, I guess.

When did you discover the place?

Didn't discover nothing. Just there. Lived at 681.

The housing block at the end of the street?

Dace chopped outta there until they took over the church.

How?

Don't know. Claimed it. Dace set up shop and you could see the lineup from my window. Zombos, scratchers, bed bugs. What we called 'em as kids.

Where are your parents now?

Dead. Mom overdosed. Dad got shot.

Where's your sister?

Couldn't tell you. Took off after the church burning.

How'd you end up at the tank?

Boyfriend. Smoked crack. Crack to smack.

When did you learn about the fish?

I didn't learn nothing about the fish.

When were you made aware of its existence?

Kid. Was a kid.

How'd you hear about it?

Just there. Just know.

Did you know they were feeding it people who had overdosed?

Can't speak to that.

You never heard that?

Never saw it.

Did you ever see the fish?

Barely.

Can you describe the encounter?

On the nod but we moving. Step into the hallway. Mike's holding my hand. Go left instead of right. Past the workers. Pay no mind. Keep going. Down the stairs. Cross this empty space to the back. And it feels like . . . feels like we drifting. Through the doors. Stop. No windows. Pitch black. Flip the switch. Fish kicks off. Fuck that. Ain't going no closer. Staying right there at the door. Mike fucking wit it. Flicking the lights on and off. Fish going crazy. Fierce.

What did it look like?
A blur. Seeing scales. Teeth. Tail.
What do you feel? What's the impression?
Fear.
You feel threatened?
Fish was fittin' to smash through the glass.
Where do you think it came from? How'd it get there?

No clue.
I heard a crazy concept—that fish is a gate into another dimension.
Some teleportation shit?
Not sure how it worked.
Nah.
You don't believe the fish was a portal into other dimensions?
When it dream, maybe. How it take us, though?
Your guess is as good as mine.
It don't. Trapped like us.
You feel trapped?
Not like I was.
What changed?

(Niesha pats her pregnant belly.)
Found out. Stopped using. Not that second but I stopped. Saved me from the fire.
Considering your circumstances, did you consider having an abortion?
I did.
Why'd you decide against it?
Hope where there was none. Right or wrong.
Did Mike's family ever reach out to you?
What family?
How do you feel about the future?
What future? We here now.

Kadeem, twenty-seven years old, moved to Morden with his mother when most were trying to leave. Kadeem had just turned eleven. His uncle Isaac found his mom work at the church where she prepped and packed product for sale. Kadeem and his mother now live in a trailer home purchased for pennies on the dollar at the river's edge. Kadeem supplies me with a fishing rod and we bait our hooks using night crawlers collected the night before. My phone records our conversation as we cast into the water.

IN: Can you eat the fish from this river?

KADEEM: I wouldn't. All kinds of industry leaching in. Tributaries are toxic.

When you first moved to Morden, where'd you stay?

Uncle Isaac's. Auntie watched me and my cousins while Mom worked. I turn twelve and it's time to earn. Isaac takes me to the tank. Janitor slash errand boy. Gloved up. Steel toes. Taking out bins of used needles. Wiping blood off the walls. Pouring sawdust on the puke. Soaks it up so you can sweep it up. From there I worked the back rooms: production, processing, packing. Go from there to guard duty. Counting house the ultimate upgrade. Running the machines. Banding bills.

Why were they called Dace crew?

Uncle told me it meant "of the nobility" but it's a double meaning 'cause a dace is also a type of fish, like a river minnow. Idea being we small fish but together own the pond.

What about the big fish? The one in the basement.

Was like . . . what's the word . . . amalgamation. Was an amalgamation of a grouper, an anglerfish, and a payara, like some river monster shit. Always shifting, though. Could never get a clear shot at it. Never lock it in.

And the fish is located in the kitchen, which connects to the mess hall.

Correct.

Aside from the chancel and nave, the mess hall is the biggest room in the building.

What the chancel and nave?

The main part of the church where everyone sits.

Shooting gallery.

Tank

Yeah.

So, what's the question?

From what I've heard the mess hall was kept empty. My question is why?

Why not?

Thought Dace could use the space?

Guess not.

Next question. I know it was never changed but the water would evaporate eventually. How did the tank not dry up?

Top it off when we had to.

When was that?

When it came to mind. Bro, we working a trap. Forget a fish.

Fair enough. Why is there no footage? Not a single photo or video of the fish.

Was on my old phone.

What about Exodus 20:4?

What about it?

"You shall not make for yourself an image in the form of anything in heaven above or on the earth beneath or in the waters below."

I shall. I did.

Where's your old phone?

Gone.

Where?

Out the window.

How?

She tossed it.

115

Who?

My ex.

The footage wasn't backed up onto a cloud drive?

Nah. But you can't see shit. Filthy water. Murky murk. And the fish go ballistic the second you bring your phone out. Stir shit up.

Sounds like it goes ballistic the second you step inside the room.

It'll calm down if you give it a minute.

Will it?

Got a story for you.

Let's hear it.

One day I ate mushrooms and spoke to the fish.

There's an idea.

First time and only time I took them. Friend puts a pile in my palm. Force 'em back. Playing videogames waiting for them to kick in. Feeling heavy. Bloated. Burping. Dragging me down. Can't stop yawning. Splash some cold water on my face. Check the mirror and I'm fucked. Dilated pupils. Fuckin' saucers. Walls start breathing and shit. Had me shook. Have to leave. Bug out to the park. Trees are moving, twisting, winding, waving. They're alive. I mean, I know they're alive, but they're like—

Alive alive.

Exactly. And I just . . . it keeps escalating. Feeling the fear. About to lose my mind. Fall to my knees. Start praying. The second I relinquish control, it's like . . . serenity is too strong a word. Acceptance. Now I'm in the pocket. Everything aligned. Walking the streets. Taking it in. Trippin'. Heaven in hell. Vice versa. Who's to say. Either way, I'm entertained. In awe of everything. Walking past these wounded souls. See their strength in the suffering. Dignity in the decay. The destruction. Decide I need to see the fish. That's my mission. Belly of the beast. Going from scene to scene. All the sudden I'm there. Cross the mess hall to the kitchen. Step through those double doors. Hit by the stench. The rot. About to turn on the lights. Leave it. Standing

Tank

there in the dark. Waiting for a response. Nothing. Still water. Think it might be dead. Smells dead but know it ain't. Can feel its presence. Its power. Tell the fish I'm turning on the lights. Flip the switch and it goes ballistic. Hostile territory. Take a breath. Find my centre. Move towards it. Press my hands against the glass. Fish starts smashing into it. Shaking the tank. Rage. It's ready to die. All that anger with no place to go. Start talking. Telling it to relax. Chill. Just chill. Close my eyes. Trying to calm the waters. Peace be upon you. That's what I hear. What I say. Peace be upon you. Peace be upon you. And then it stops. The thrashing stops. Goes quiet. Open my eyes and it's right there—this giant, cataract-covered fish eye. Staring through the fog straight at me. Let it know. I'm here to pay respect. To commiserate with this wretched creature in our fallen kingdom. Show it my back. Slow turn. Lean against the glass. Slide to the ground. Sitting in the spillover. The stink. Shared space. Old world. Old god. There's this hum. A current in my core. Don't ask me to explain. All I can do is listen.

YETI

Had a dream that stuck with me. Two realities folding into one. The dawn of a new world. Pioneers establishing their settlements. Bearing witness to random moments of toil, turmoil, and misery. The early settlers strive and starve to establish themselves on this new frontier. Sunken faces. Hollowed eyes. Skin covered in dirt and grime. Streaked with ash. Dried blood and dead bugs smeared across skin covered in a sheen of sweat from hard labour. Men possessed. Driven. Captured. See them stake their claim. Clearing land. Chopping trees. Digging trenches. Slinging buckets of water as they build a well. Sow this soil. Raise that fence. Lift these walls. Cleaning muskets. Patching sails. Continue. Maintain. They will establish themselves and rule this land come hell or high water. Work themselves to exhaustion. Tired. Spent. Starved. Blood boils. Grudges formed. Some simmer. Others bubble over. Limits reached and breached. The steady rhythm of work interrupted by sporadic outbursts of violence.

In the old world. Eternal. See the beast that crosses cultures. Spanning time. Mythos. Known by several names: Wendigo, Yeti, Sasquatch, Bigfoot. Multiple interpretations of the same idea—a massive, hairy creature, walking upright, that lives in the woods.

I see two of them. Mother and child. Their faces resembling that of the three-toed sloth with similar eye markings. Their fur/hair is roughly the same length and close in texture but slightly softer. Their hands are more akin to the paws of a gorilla: five fingers, opposable thumbs, thickly padded palms. As for their feet, they lived up to their namesake with a massive footprint. The bone structure akin to a human, albeit covered in way more hair. Big foot, yes, but in proportion with the rest of the Yeti's giant frame. The mother stands over seven feet tall and must weigh somewhere between eight and nine hundred pounds. The young Yeti's stature is close to that of a full-grown chimp, around a metre and a half in height, weighing around two hundred pounds.

My first glimpse of the Yetis is a scene of absolute serenity. Mother and child grazing in a forest clearing. Tall grass surrounded by large trees. Shielded. Embrace. The Yetis move with such grace and ease, the child never wandering too far from mother. In sync with their environment. Unity. The mother a hulking figure, showing great love and tenderness towards her child. Watch her slowly wave a stick in front of him. The young one transfixed. Following the stick closely with his eyes. When he reaches out for it, mother releases the stick to him. Their physicality gentle. A tender touch. Patient. Content.

I can't say for certain if the Yetis are herbivores. They may well be omnivores but I only see them eating plants. Grazing on grass, flowers, leaves. One mannerism I see performed several times is what I'd call sky offerings. Every so often, while ripping fists full of tall grass from the ground, the Yetis pause, holding the grass up to the sky with outstretched arms for several moments. Seems like a symbolic gesture or offering to the universe before they stuff the grass into their mouths.

Now the infant Yeti is almost fully grown. Still several feet shorter than his mother but his frame has filled out. Seems emboldened. There's an efficiency of movement. Confidence in his stride. Venturing further and further away from his mother. Stopping at a large, moss-covered log at least forty yards away from her. Curious, the young Yeti lifts the log, checking underneath when his mother stands up and walks away. Disappearing into the dense growth of forest without looking back. When the young Yeti turns his head towards her, she is gone.

Another break. Leaping forward to the next reveal.

Young Yeti fully grown. Crouching down on a sandy cliff jutting out from the emerald foliage. Watch him raise fists full of sand to the sky. Held towards the sun, he lets the sand run out through the cracks between his fingers. Resplendent light casting his fur in a golden hue as he radiates love and gratitude for the world he inhabits. Enchanted by the spirit and its ways.

Yeti

Without warning, worlds collide. There is war. The glory wiped out by wrath. Grace usurped by ignorance and greed. The Yeti tied down with thick rope to a massive upright post. Stood beside other captives tied to their stakes. Emaciated men smeared with tar. Eyes wide. Some closed. The oppressors stare back with stone faces. Lined up shoulder to shoulder fifteen feet away. Broken beings dressed in rags. See the orange glow behind the wall. A gaunt man with vacant brown eyes and greasy black curls parts the crowd, carrying a flaming cone of birch bark fuelled by dried grass and leaves. Stepping forward, he holds the torch to kindling gathered under a captive's feet. The fire rips upwards, engulfing the prisoner in flames. Screams choked by smoke. Skin turns black as eyes roll back. The executioner works from left to right. One at a time. Standing at the centre stake, he looks up at the Yeti. Sets the blaze. Watching it burn. The Yeti can't understand this betrayal. Where does the pain come from and why? Bellows in anguish. The fire searing fur and flesh. No. Not right. The Yeti howls. Surging adrenaline. Rocking its head back then forward. Flexing arms, chest, shoulders, and back. Rope loosens. Allowing an inch of movement. Keeps rocking. Gathering momentum. With another flex, it snaps the ropes. Launches a fiery headbutt at the executioner. Caves his face. Crushed. Yeti rips away the ropes. His captors scatter as he charges into the forest. A massive body of flames streaking through the woods towards the shore. Yeti launches himself off a stone overhang into the water. Fully submerged for one long, drawn-out moment before he breaks the surface. Arms slapping down on the water. Heaving for air. Yeti swims to shore. Staggers through the reeds. Steam rising from his charred skin in the chill of night. Yeti collapses onto the muddy shore. Body scorched. Nerve centre cooked. He will not live through this. He hurts. He suffers. He wants to know why. What did he do? Tired. So tired. Needs to sleep. Hopefully then the answers will arrive.

DAMAGE DEPOSIT

Ten years. Three apartments. A one-bedroom every time. All they can reasonably afford. The first was a refurbished attic in a poorly insulated house. It was a sauna during the summer. During a heat wave, they'd take cold showers in their t-shirts and underwear then go to bed wearing them still sopping wet. An hour later, they'd be bone dry. When the temperature swung the other way, it was an icebox. In the grip of winter, they could never get warm. Always a chill. They'd have to layer clothes inside their apartment. Frost would gather around the inside of the windows and the bathroom tiles were ice to the touch. They'd keep their electric heaters blasting through the night. Mercifully, they didn't have to pay for hydro.

There was also the issue of parking. Not allowed access to the driveway, they had to pay for street permits, and were required to switch their vehicles from one side of the street to the other mid-month. The date changing depending on the month. The meter maids eager to nail you with a parking ticket if you didn't. Rex waking up to the yellow slip under his windshield wiper more than once. Adding to the frustration of their parking situation was the fact that paying for a street permit did not guarantee you a parking space. After a snowstorm, when half the available spots were buried by waist-high mounds of ice and snow, they'd have to park wherever they found an opening. Often on side streets several blocks away, where again they'd run the risk of a parking ticket.

After the owner sold the house, their next stop was a grimy apartment block/tower that charged twenty-two hundred dollars a month, utilities not included, plus a hundred dollars a month for underground parking. This place brought a new host of stressors. During peak hours, the elevators were always full, stopping at every floor. It would take ten minutes to reach the underground parking. They also dealt with a succession of noisy neighbours. Many of the tenants were on disability, with substance abuse issues. A significant portion were newly landed immigrants on subsidy programs. Empty bottles, nitrous canisters, needles, and cigarette butts littered the hallway and parking lot. People had their cars broken into but it was the bedbugs that broke them. An ongoing problem the building management seemingly refused to acknowledge or resolve.

The next stop, their current residence, is a basement apartment in a triplex they rent for twenty-five hundred dollars a month, hydro not included. They share a small parking lot with the neighbouring triplex, a mirror image of their triplex. At first, any issues with their apartment are small ones. Newly renovated. Never finished. There are no handles on the kitchen cupboards. No doorknobs on the closets. No plates on the electrical outlets and no outlet in the bathroom. Rita has to run her hair dryer off an extension cord plugged into the kitchen outlet. All minor grievances. They're fine with the building. It's the superintendent they have a problem with.

His name is Jeb. An ex-con with a faded neck tattoo, rotten teeth, Bic'd bald head, long goatee, and ever-present wraparound sunglasses. Jeb served time for assault and drug possession before he got sober and turned his life around. Information he shared freely when Rex offered him a beer the night they moved in. Claiming ten years since he's had a drop of alcohol.

Jeb lives on the third floor of the neighbouring triplex, where he posts watch in a fold-out chair parked on the front steps. That's his spot. Day or night. Rain, sun, or snow. Vape mod in hand with a baseball bat by his side. Blowing giant clouds of chemically synthesized flavours, cotton candy and watermelon being two of his favourites. The scent wafting into any open windows. Jeb a constant presence the other tenants can't avoid. From inside the building, they can hear him coughing and clearing his throat. Posted up like a gnarled old guard dog waiting for something to bark at. Whether it's a delivery driver parking in front of the driveway, people dropping dog shit bags in "his trashcans" or the neighbours shovelling snow against "his buildings"; buildings in fact owned by Jeb's former trial lawyer.

That's how he got the job. A form of work placement. These aren't Jeb's buildings. That's the delusion. Mop the stairwell, clean the laundry room, roll out the garbage, shovel the snow, trim the hedges, mow the measly patch of

Damage Deposit

grass out front: These are his duties. Simple tasks he begrudgingly performs with a scowl on his face. The second a tenant brings up any issue relating to building maintenance, Jeb deflects the blame back on them. When the building's washing machine broke, he accused the tenants of overloading it. When they started seeing cockroaches, he told them to stop leaving food out. When the building's two garbage cans, already overflowing with trash, were tipped over by raccoons it was because the tenants didn't close the lids.

Each month, Jeb imposes another rule. Deciding he's tired of cleaning the stairwell, he posts a notice that each tenant is now required to remove their shoes when they enter the building. Sick of shovelling snow, he posts a notice that tenants are now responsible for shovelling their own parking spots, with specific instruction not to use the "building shovel." Deciding that he needs more storage space, he posts a notice that bikes can no longer be kept in the laundry room. He fills half the laundry room with boxes of his own personal possessions (including his bike) the following week.

Anything or anyone that undermines his authority breeds resentment. Induces rage. Giant hissy fits. That winter, when an unidentified tenant had the temerity to turn up the thermostat in the laundry room because the building (the triplex Jeb didn't live in) was cold, Jeb went ballistic. Screaming. Yelling. Slamming doors. The next morning, there was a notice under every door threatening immediate eviction should this act of insubordination happen again.

Another meltdown occurred over the side-door entrance into the building being left open. A side door with a rotten wood frame, no strike plate, and chewed-up door jamb, which caused the latch to pop open on its own. Jeb's solution: tape a piece of paper on the door with "CLOSE SIDE DOOR!!!" angrily scrawled in Sharpie. Of course, the door popped open the next day and Jeb blamed it on clueless tenants who couldn't follow simple instructions. So infuriated by this blatant disrespect, he kicked the door hard enough to crack its glass viewing window. Instead of getting that fixed, he boarded up the entire door with plywood, drilling the entrance shut so it no longer functioned as an emergency exit, completely ignoring or oblivious to fire code.

The latest flare-up occurred when Rex mentioned to Jeb that the smell of sewage was permeating from the laundry basin into their basement apartment. Jeb, immediately on the defensive, fired back with, "I hope you didn't break a pipe. You guys can't be flushing fuckin' tampons and wet wipes down there." Rex assuring him they didn't. Suggesting the pipe may have cracked or backed up over the winter. Jeb snorting, retorting with, "Oh, so you're a plumber now?" Rex replying, "No, and neither are you. So please bring one in and get it fixed." Jeb responded by telling Rex to "Fuck off!" before storming off down the street to who knows where. A tirade of profanities following in his wake.

Unacceptable response. The situation had to be addressed. That night, Rita and Rex discussed their options. Somehow, they needed to circumnavigate Jeb and call their landlord. Problem being they didn't have his number and it was unlikely they'd get it from Jeb. A closely guarded secret. They recalled him screaming at a former tenant in the driveway who had the nerve to request the owner's number. Jeb let everyone within earshot know that all building-related matters went through him. The owner didn't have time for their bullshit. The following week, Jeb served the tenant and his family (wife and kid) an eviction notice for fire code violations. They'd burnt something in their stove and unplugged their fire alarm while airing out their apartment. When Jeb smelled smoke in the stairwell, he banged on their door. When they opened it, he saw the unplugged detector. That was all the justification he needed, announcing it was immediate grounds for eviction.

Going online and looking further into the matter, there were other means to acquire the landlord's number. They could go through the city, or it might be as simple as calling 411. But then what? Jeb would likely spin some bullshit story against them. And in the unlikely event he was fired, there was no telling what a vindictive personality like that might do. In the end, they decided to wipe their hands, cut their losses, and start looking for a new place.

They were respectful tenants who paid their rent on time. They didn't need this shit in their lives but the clock was ticking. The pressure was on to find a new place before the first of the month. What overpriced, underwhelming living unit will they cram themselves into next? The application process alone was exhausting: bank statements, T4s, reference letters, photocopies of social security numbers and driver licences. Fingers crossed if they do a credit check. The fact they were dealing with this shit into their late thirties was beyond frustrating. Demoralizing, a more apt description. Still scraping by. No savings. No space or solitude. It put pressure on their relationship.

Damage Deposit

Could feel the strain. When they're fighting, when it's bad, they're always in one another's way. Start getting snippy. Taking shots. The bickering builds to a boiling point and the gloves come off. Low blows. Attacking each other's sore spots. Their shame. Hostile vibrations. Waves of contempt. Nowhere to hide. Closed in. Confined. Living room, bathroom, bedroom. These are their options. Pushed to their breaking point, ready to call it quits before cooler minds prevail. Each taking a backwards step. Compromise and heartfelt apologies bringing them back to centre. They know it's not the case but sometimes it feels like the essential ingredient to a happy relationship is square footage. A luxury they can't afford. Long walks or a drink at the bar become essential coping mechanisms.

This is their dilemma. If they stay in the city, space will always be an issue. Yet the cost of living there makes it exceedingly difficult to save for something else. Rural properties and rent aren't getting any cheaper. Costs skyrocketing everywhere. It's quite the conundrum. All they know is now. And now they need to move.

The next morning, Rex hits the road with knots in his stomach. Hates it. Fucking hates having to move again but they need to cut their losses. The situation's devolved to the point where it feels dangerous. Jeb escalating things. Acting unhinged. Rex stamping down his own anger. Wanting to strangle Jeb for the stress he's caused them. Miserable wretch. Fucking bully stuck on his bullshit little power trip. Total nonsense. Rex knows he needs to let it go. Distracting. Draining. He's glad to get away. Let things cool down. This is a good gig. Simple. Two-week job driving throughout the province, swapping out light ballasts in various office buildings and storefronts, temporary work through a friend of a friend. Twenty dollars an hour paid under the table. Hopefully Rita has some leads on a new place when he gets back.

His phone is plugged into the outlet in an empty office cubicle. Rex receives the text while standing on a ladder. Arms raised, he detaches the old ballast from the ceiling. Brings it to the ground and checks the text from Rita:

> We're moving. I found the place. Trust me. Took the day off work. Packing boxes right now.

A job well done. Work lined up for next month. More ballasts. Rex exits the highway with his window down. AC not working. Conked out during last week's heat wave. He can feel the humidity. Muggy. Dense. It has to break. To rain. The sky starts spitting when he reaches the exit. Rex is meeting Rita at their new address, having no idea what to expect. She wants to surprise him. At the first traffic light he receives her text:

> Pick up beer. :)

Already planned on it.

He gets another text waiting in line, beer under his arm:

> When you get here, park in the driveway. I took the garage.

Driveway . . . garage . . . sounds like she's describing a house. Must be. Fifteen minutes away now. The area looks bleak. Desolate streets between massive housing blocks. Oppressive concrete towers housing those living on the margins. Outposts. Somewhere to stack the working class. He assumed they'd end up there again. Five minutes from his destination, the scenery shifts. A river appears. Peeking out behind, between, the drab buildings and business fronts. Five minutes from the address and grey gives way to green. He enters the river valley. Residential now. Removed from the heavy traffic and congestion. What remains of the natural landscape warrants respect. Trees. Trails. Paths. Peace of mind. He turns the volume down. Drives slowly. Hears the rain. The sound of the wind rustling through the leaves. He's at a stop light when the sky opens up. From drizzle to downpour. Rex turns the wipers to their highest setting in order to see. After the intersection, the road takes a gradual incline. At the top of the hill, he hooks a left into a pocket neighbourhood resting above the ravine. Arrives at the address. An old house. Three stories with a wide front porch. Rain pelts the shingles. Water streams off the veranda, pouring through rusted eaves troughing. As instructed, Rex parks in the driveway. How? How did she find this place and how many tenants are they sharing it with? Rex grabs the beer from the back of the truck and rushes up the front steps. Sheltered from the rain, he sees the exterior paint, white for the siding, black for the window trim, is flaking off, revealing the grey wood underneath. Front door left open, Rex heads inside.

Standing on stripped pinewood flooring, Rex looks up in awe of the spacious dimensions. Devoid of any furniture, it feels like a great hall or chamber. The ceiling rests thirty feet high. If not higher. Pressure cracks branch out from the corners. Likely from the foundation shifting over time. Straight ahead of him is a wide wooden staircase that winds left. A wood banister spans the second floor, which overlooks the living room. A living room with an old brick fireplace. Rex walks the ground floor. Goes through a wide threshold into the kitchen, which opens into a dining room and circles back into the living room.

Multiple rooms. Bathrooms. Still no furniture. Still no Rita. He finally finds Rita on the third floor working a mop and bucket across a room large enough to house all their possessions. EarPods in, wearing cutoff jean shorts and a tank top with her hair tied back in a bandana. She looks up. See him. Smiles. Takes out her EarPods and points to a set of French doors by the windows.

"Look! Our new bedroom comes with a balcony."

Her face flushed. Beaming.

"Where's everybody else?"
"Who?"
"The other tenants?"
"Just you and me, babe."
"Bullshit."
"For the same rent. Twenty-five hundred dollars a month, hydro not included."
"Impossible. You're fucking with me."
"We got lucky."
"No. There's no way. This is a two-million-dollar property."
"Minimum, and we're moving in tomorrow."
"How? How did find you this place?"
"Pass me a beer and I'll tell you."

Rex puts the bag of beer down. Reaches in. Tosses Rita a tall boy before grabbing one for himself. Rita cracks her beer. Takes a swig.

"Had a landscaping gig across the street during the heat alert. There was a moving truck parked in front of this house. Two movers. One looked Native. Black hair. Ponytail. Grim reaper tattoo on his forearm. The other was this big, burly, bearded white dude. Had a sweat stain on his beer gut that looked like a Rorschach test."

Rita opens the patio door. They step outside. Torrents of water rush down the street into the storm drains.

"So, they're loading the moving truck while this little old lady, leaning on her walking cane, is standing on the lawn watching them. Sun blasting down on her. I'm planting begonias in the sweltering heat when she faints. I run across the street to help. Kneel down beside her. The movers see what's happening. Put down the giant dresser they're carrying and rush over. The woman's unresponsive. Eyes fluttering. Arms shaking. I'm convinced she's having a stroke or seizure. I tell the movers I'm calling the 911. Somehow, she hears this. Starts making noises, mumbling, trying to talk, to communicate."

Rita snaps her fingers.

"Eyes open. She grabs my wrist. 'No. No ambulance.' Starts squeezing, I'm shocked by her strength. I agree not to. Not yet. But we need to bring her inside out of the sun. The movers help her up. Walk her into the house. Bring her to the sofa and she waves them away. 'Keep working. Keep working. I'm fine. Time is money.' She's got this thick Eastern Bloc accent."

Rita sips her beer.

"The movers look confused. Not sure what to do. I tell them not to worry, I'll watch her. They go back to loading the truck and I bring her a glass of water and a damp cloth that I hold to the back of her neck. After a few sips of water and the cold compress, I can see she's feeling better. She thanks me. Asks for my name. I tell her. She says, 'You have nice face, Rita. I'm Nyura. Nyura Marchenko.'"

"Marchenko. Is that Russian?"

Damage Deposit

"She's from Ukraine. Her husband bought this home ten years after they immigrated."

"Where's he?"

"Dead. Then the discussion shifted to the house. I mentioned the stained-glass windows in the kitchen. How much I liked them. That's what started it."

"Where's she now?"

"Assisted living facility. The house was going on the market."

"Exactly. Start the bidding war. What are we doing here?"

"She made me an offer. I accepted."

"What offer?"

"Wait . . . so I grab an orange from my truck, thinking she could use the sugar. I peel it. She only wants half. I hand it to her. She thanks me. Eats a slice. Asks where I live. I tell her. She nods. Continues eating the orange. When the orange is gone, she asks, 'How much? How much for house?' I tell her, two, maybe three million. She asks, 'Where you live now? How much you pay?' I explain we rent. She wants to know how much. I tell her. She pauses. Thinks it over. Announces—'Okay. You pay same. Live here.'"

"No way . . . delirious. Suffering sunstroke."

"Which is why I repeat it back to her: 'Mrs. Marchenko, if you're willing to rent your home to me and my boyfriend for twenty-five hundred dollars a month, I gladly accept' to which she replies, 'You have dog?' No. No dog. 'You buy dog. Dog bark. Neighbour complains. Your problem. Not mine. Old house. Needs work. Maybe problems. You fix. Not me. I'm done.'"

"Insane."

"I know."

The first beer goes down fast. Rex grabs another.

"What about her family? There's no way they agree to this."

"'There's no family past granddaughter.'"

"Where's her granddaughter?"

"'She's gone.'"

"Gone where?"
"She didn't elaborate."
"What about payment? Paperwork?"
"I wrote her a cheque that day."
"No lease? Nothing?"
"'No time for this. Pay by month. Simple.'"
"You cut her a cheque. She hands you the keys."
"Once the truck is loaded, I drive her to the bank so she deposits the cheque. Then I drop her off at the retirement home. We shake hands. Done deal. "
"What about the begonias?"
"I came back and finished the job."
"This can't last. You know that, right?"
"If we get the boot, so be it."
"Okay . . . just don't get attached to this place."
"Let's just appreciate it for what it is."
"What it is a fucking miracle."
"Praise the lord."
"Amen."

There's a break in the storm. The rain subsides.

"You ready for the tour?"
"Lead the way."

They close the balcony behind them. Rita opens the door to the master bathroom.

"Look at this pedestal sink."
"Impressive."
"It's wider than our last two sinks combined. No more excuses. I don't want to find hair or shaving cream along the outside edges."
"Now that I've got room to work, everything goes down the drain."
"Check out our new bathtub."

Rita pulls back the curtains on the oval shower rod, revealing a large claw-foot tub. In their first apartment, the attic, there was no bathtub, just a stand-up shower. The next two apartments had economy-sized bathtubs that functioned but didn't have the size, volume, or curvature for a proper soak.

"Break out the bubble bath and play me some whale music.
That's the bathtub I've been waiting for."

They move downstairs to the second floor. Rita takes two rights at the bottom of the staircase into a room with a twelve-foot ceiling. Grey wood plank flooring and large double-hung windows open to the front yard. A cool breeze flows through the room.

"This could be your studio."

Rita beams back at him. What a beauty. She knew. She knows. His connection to the room, to the space, is immediate. He feels the charge. Let this be real. What a blessing it would be. Won't squander this opportunity. No chance. Committing to the canvas.

"What do you think?"
"I'm not worthy."
"Make it so."
"Yeah . . . that's the plan."

He looks to Rita. Still together. Still standing. The last five years hit them hard: Rita's mother was diagnosed with pancreatic cancer and passed away after enduring multiple rounds of chemotherapy and radiation treatment. Within that time span, Rex's dad died from a heart attack after decades of alcohol abuse. The couple processing their grief while struggling to stay afloat, stumbling from one financial stress test to the next. There were savage winters and stilted summers. So much fear. Doubt. Dread. Aggravation and anxiety. Now, maybe, finally some peace of mind. A little breathing room.

They step back into the hallway. There's a door to their left near the next flight of stairs. They enter the sun porch, a large room filled with light despite the overcast sky. Rex views the expansive backyard. The grass is a foot high. Full of weeds and wildflowers, surrounded by high hedges. Past the hedges, an unobstructed view of the horizon.

"Look at that . . ."
"You like?"
"How is this real? We have a backyard now . . ."

"And it comes with a kiln."

Rita points out the brick kiln in the left corner of the yard.

"I can stop looking for work and start making ashtrays for a living."

"So long as you find time to mow all that grass."

"Leave it. We've got the enchanted forest back here."

"I'm fine with it but we need to mow the front. Keep peace with the neighbours."

"Business in the front. Party in the back."

"Exactly."

"Did they leave the lawnmower?"

"There's one in the garden shed, along with a rake, shovel, and hedge trimmers."

"What about a wheelbarrow?"

"There's a wheelbarrow."

"Garden hose? Sprinkler?"

"All our lawn care needs are covered. You know what else I found?"

"Tell me."

"A croquet set."

"It's official. We own the summer."

"We're missing one crucial ingredient."

"What's that?"

"A barbeque."

"Charcoal grill with an offset smoker."

"The hibachi will do for now while we save for an upgrade."

"Smoked ribs. How good would that be?"

"I'm hungry."

"Me too."

"Grab something on the way. We need to get back to Wilshire so I can finish packing."

The rain has stopped. Smoke rises from the barrel curling out from under the canopy. The cook pulls the jerk chicken off the grill and chops it with a cleaver. Serves it to them with rice and beans covered in oxtail gravy and

Damage Deposit

a side of coleslaw. Ready to eat, Rex drops the tailgate on his pickup truck to use as a table. They eat standing. The chicken is perfectly cooked. Full of flavour. The oxtail gravy taking it to another level. All is well. The sun has set; streetlights shine in the dark, electrical current casting halos through the mist. The world hums. Brimming with potential. Clarity. Colour. A universe in accordance. The miracle restored.

The rain returns the next morning. Light drizzle. Everything is boxed, bagged, and ready to move. Rex picks up the U-Haul while Rita waits at the triplex with friends and family she's convinced to help with the move. The recruits include her sister Gale, brother-in-law Evan, and another couple, Blake and Carol.

When Rex gets back with the U-Haul, he parks it on the street by the end of the driveway, sure not to block the entrance. Of course, Jeb is posted in his chair on the front steps. Blowing clouds. Bat by his side. Sunglasses on in spite of the rain. Rex nods. Not a word said between them.

Before they start loading the truck, Rita goes over the game plan. It will take two runs. Boxes, bags, and bikes first. She reminds everyone to ignore Jeb if he tries baiting them into a confrontation. Rex knows the comment's directed towards him.

Jeb, frozen scowl on his face, monitors the move from his chair without a word. Rex is ten feet from the cube truck carrying a heavy box of books when the bottom drops out over a mud puddle filling a pothole in the driveway. Jeb snorts. Giggling with glee. Rex takes a breath, trying to maintain his composure. Rita, seeing the situation unfold, rushes in with another box. Ignoring Jeb's sniggering, they pick up the books, shake off the dripping water, load them into the new box, then the U-Haul.

Cube truck full, everyone drives over to the house, unloads the boxes, then returns to the apartment for the furniture: sofa, bed, dressers, desks, chairs, cabinet, coffee table, TV stand. Jeb whistles to Rex through his teeth. Informs him he's taken photos of the stairwell and doorways. If there's any damage he'll know. Watching intently every time another item is carried outside. Moving with caution, they manage to empty the apartment without leaving a nick or scratch. That's it. They're outta there. Rita leaves first and the other cars follow.

Rex closes the back of the U-Haul, walks to the edge of the driveway, and tosses his apartment keys into the same puddle the books fell into. Jeb rushes forward, unleashing a torrent of profanities. Flicking his cigarette at Rex's chest. Rex brushes the ash off his t-shirt and walks around to the driver's side of the U-Haul while Jeb follows him, hurling insults and threats of violence. Unfazed, Rex climbs inside the truck and closes the door. Jeb spits on the window and boots the door with the bottom of his foot, hitting it with such force he bounces back. Falling into the middle of the road. Rex calmly turns on the windshield wipers, beeps the horn, and drives off, middle finger raised.

Breaks in the cloud cover. Sun peeking through. Spinning gold through the trees. Everyone waiting on the front porch. Rex backs into the driveway. Steps out. Sees Jeb left a sizeable dent in the door. Whatever. Charge it to the credit card. Was worth it watching him fall on his ass. Good riddance to bad news. Rex opens up the back of the truck and pulls out the ramp.

Back of the truck. Best for last. Blake and Rex lift one last piece of furniture, an oak dresser, up the stairs to the third floor, catching their breath at each landing. Finally reaching the master bedroom, they bend their knees and gently place the dresser down.

"That's it, that's all. Thank you everyone. Beer's in the fridge."

Before Rex drops off the cube truck, Evan suggests he try pulling the dent out of the door with a toilet plunger. He receives a round of applause when it actually works. The trip takes thirty minutes there and back, including a stop to top off the gas tank. No extra charges or penalties. When he returns, everyone is gathered in the sunroom. Grey and gold hues. Soft ambient lighting. Evan exhales a cloud of smoke from a lit joint and hands it to Gale, who takes a haul and turns to Rex.

"That's quite a view, mister."
"I know."
"And there's a kiln in your backyard."
"I know."
"A kiln . . ."
"Should I sign you up for my ceramics workshop?"
"No, but if I ever need a bag of charcoal, I know who to call."

Damage Deposit

Gale passes Rex the joint. He takes several hits and tries handing it off to Carol, who refrains. Rex waves the joint in front of Blake, who's eyeing the threshold of the sunroom.

"Definitely an extension."

Blake takes the joint.

"Way back when, wealthy homeowners built sun porches to treat tuberculosis."

Evan is still staring out the window.

"What's behind the hedges?"

Rex replies.

"Nothing. It drops into the ravine."

Evan, forgetting the rotation order, hands the joint back to Gale who in turn offers it to Rita. Normally, she'd decline. Today, on this special occasion, she accepts.

"You guys need to host a backyard barbeque. Set off some fireworks."
"We need a barbeque first."
"Big green egg," chimes in Carol.
"Love to, but they're fuckin' expensive."
"Have a pig roast. There's enough real estate back there. Dig out a trench."
"Discover where the bodies are buried."
"That took a dark turn."
"Find a femur for the dog to chew on."
"Oh yeah, we're getting a dog."
"What kind?"
"A mutt from the rescue."
"We're going to wait a couple months first. Make sure this is real."

Late afternoon. Still gathered in the sun porch. Dark storm clouds rolling in. Distant thunder. Intermittent lightning. Sitting on the floor. Still plenty of beer left. Carol kindly agrees to be the designated driver when a blinding white flash illuminates the room, followed by a deafening crack of thunder that rattles the house.

> "Goddamn! That sounded like it was in the living room."
> "Jesus . . . that was loud."
> "Getting spooky."
> "Getting hungry."
> "I'll place the order."

Watching lightning branch across the ashen sky. Each thunder crash successively louder. Conversation continues while Rita collects the leftover pizza into one box. Brings it downstairs. Returning with a bottle of wine. Pours two glasses. One for her and one for Gale, who makes a suggestion.

> "Sufficiently stoned, it occurs to me that we should perform a séance and introduce ourselves to your new abode."

On cue, the power goes out as a black cloud snuffs out whatever sunlight was getting through. Eyebrows raise around the room. Rita signs off on her sister's plan.

> "I'll break out the candles. Set the mood."

Weather on display. Active. Alive. Sun flares through darkness. Bursts. Breaks. Peaks between waves of the storm. The group gathered in a circle. Glowing candles in the centre. Gale, barely concealing her smile, sits legs crossed in the lotus position.

> "We thank you, ghosts. Our gracious hosts. Please pardon the intrusion."

Punctuated by a chill that runs up Rex's spine.

> "We ask that you accept Rex and Rita into your home. Let us use this opportunity to establish some ground rules. Parameters with honest intentions. Hoping to avoid future conflict."

Creeping up. Closing in. Rex does a shoulder check. Nothing but the house.

Damage Deposit

"Let us engage in an open dialogue with the spirit of understanding."

Wrong. Rex feels the discordance. It wants them to stop. Stop this mockery.

"We are ready to listen. Let your voice be heard and—"

A guttural high-pitched scream rips through like a compound fracture. Inside the house. Outside the room. Blake faints. Carol cries. Rita clutches Gale. The colour drained from Evan's face. Rex stands up. Pulse pounding. Looks to Rita. Arm around her sister. Eyes wide in terror. At a loss, waiting for his direction.

"I know. I know. I know . . ."

He does not. Mind reeling. Rex flinching from another piercing scream.

"Okay . . . okay . . . Let's leave. We should leave."

Down the stairs. Out the door. Down the stairs. Out the door. That's the mantra. The others trailing behind him across the interior balcony. Reaches the stairs. Stops. Scans the room with his hand on the banister. Something. Something there. Soft beams of silver across hardwood floor. Catches a glimpse. Time ceases. Suspended. Still. There. In the corner. A baby. Ten months to a year. The child crawls into the light. Translucent skin. Looks up with blank red eyes. Its tiny mouth agape. A vacant vessel waiting for reply. Without response, it crawls in a circle back to its corner. Away from the light. Ghost baby. A hacky horror movie prop. Except it's real. Registers. Rex at a loss. Words scrambled, stacked, swept away. One remains: acceptance. Let it go. You cannot stay. All must exit. Down the stairs—out the door.

MULLIGAN

What a relief to finally concede defeat.

"Any preferences?"

"I'd like to work alone."

Seymour receives a posting with Reverie. Warehouse work in a shuttered steel mill repurposed as a storage facility for cancelled Atman accounts. All spillover from another facility.

Pressure. Needs to piss. Seymour installs and catalogues one more file before bringing the lift down. Takes a leak into the grimy washbasin tucked out of view from the security cameras.

Sun still high in the sky. He's waiting outside the loading bay for the truck to arrive with more transfers. Maybe a quarter of the cancelled accounts are voluntary. Likely less. The vast majority couldn't keep up with the payments so they're sent to lower-tier facilities to collect dust. Reverie could clear the drives and repurpose them for new accounts but they don't. Stored for safekeeping. Some kind of collateral. Management tried to keep things quiet but news leaked out. Reverie is now in litigation against former account holders demanding their drives be erased. The company filed counter suits against the class action. Claiming it's in the contract. Per usual, the devil is in the details. A far larger controversy is Reverie's use of proxies and the black market that's arisen from it. All this standing in stark contrast to the awe and adulation of the technology's inception.

Investors swooned when Armin Tull introduced the Atman. Memories mapped and stored. Brought back through Samsara, a subscription software sold as the ultimate life insurance for those that can afford it. Money moved.

Mergers made. Reverie immediately acquired by Rexen for a record-shattering sum, which then assimilated Guest Works, Apogee, Axiom, and Monstrance in rapid succession to corner the market. Shareholders celebrated once more when Reverie announced an interface option between their Tyaga console and the Atman. The biological vessel no longer required to choose your own adventure. Still gotta pay for it, though. Still gotta pay. Something Seymour knows all too well.

Lost everything to Tyaga. Cleaned him out. Kicked him off. Account suspended for missed payments. Reality a cruel comedown. Homeless. Hungry. Alone. Ashamed. The E.O.L. program an option but involved too much paperwork. Couldn't afford a gun to blow his brains out so he started looking for the right place to hang the rope, eventually deciding an opioid overdose in the privacy of his tent was the way to go. Respiratory depression into death. A day's labour enough to make the purchase.

He was at the agency when the doors opened. Sent to a residential construction site to help dig the trench for a large retaining wall. Didn't mind the job. Simple. Shovelling dirt. Pushing wheelbarrows. Problem being he was malnourished and weak. Shaky ground. Struggled to finish the morning. Slept through lunch. Somehow made it through the day. Paid out. Enough to make the purchase and pay for one last meal with a couple of pints as an added bonus.

Recalls standing there waiting for the bus. Arms spent. Legs shot. Back locking up. Takes a seat on the stone ledge of someone's front lawn. Lays back on the grass. Needs a second to stretch out and rest his legs. Feels the warmth of the sun. Hears the birds chirping. Completely passed out when the bus zooms past him. Wakes him up. Not mad. Nowhere to go. Not really. Catch the next one. Hears a meow. Turns to it. Sees the cat parked on the lawn behind him. A grey tabby with aqua green eyes. Says hello and it marches over. Tail up with a slight curve at the top. The cat leans into him. Rubbing its cheek against his arm. Starts purring. He pets it from head to back. The cat looping around for more. Does a few rounds before it hops onto the sidewalk and continues down the street.

A brief encounter but that was the moment. Brought him back. He's honoured by the acknowledgement of this curious cat. It reminded him of what was lost - gratitude. An appreciation for life's tender mercies. These minor miracles. Was so consumed by his own supercharged simulation that he developed a disdain for life itself. How could it compete? He was banging supermodels on yachts one sequence then snowboarding through the Swiss Alps the next. Seamless transitions. Switching gears from pro-surfer to cage-fighting champion. Fully realized in vivid detail. Creating his own cast of family, friends, and lovers.

All else paled in comparison. Every engagement outside of Tyaga was an act of aggravation. Mindless drudgery. Wasted time better spent sequencing. His quality of life outside the system in sharp decline. Hardly eating. Rarely sleeping. Ignoring his health while resenting the fact death would one day end his interaction with Tyaga. Cursing the destruction of realities, he'd rendered and realized. Completely oblivious to his own delusion. Had him hooked. Couldn't stop. The system hijacking his dopamine receptors. Seizing his central nervous system. Forget his actual family and friends. Fuck work. Ignore obligations. Relinquish responsibility.

All he wanted to do was spin sequences. His finances forced him out. He was fired from a series of job. Evicted from his dwellings. Into the streets. Exposed. Exposed to violence. Filled with fear. Endless indignities. Humiliations. Useless. Pathetic. Paralyzed by a crippling self-loathing.

His encounter with the cat restored a semblance of self-worth with a sliver of wonder and a glimmer of hope. That moment carrying enough charge to continue.

From one season into the next. Cigarette smoke clings to clothes in a different way in the cold. Overpowering. Less like smoke, more a cloying, buttery rot. Hard to describe. On an empty stomach, it makes Seymour want to retch. Stuck with it now. Standing shoulder to shoulder with the huddled mass shuffling forward towards the train platform. He suspects it's the destitute old man standing ten feet ahead of him. Blackened fingers with long, nicotine-stained nails. Likely has a pocket full of discarded cigarette butts. Is what it is. One either suffers through the misery of public transit or pays the obscene tolls to grind through guaranteed gridlock. Constant road closures cripple the flow of traffic. Impossible to avoid the bottlenecks unless you have money to charter a private helicopter service. That's life for those who require the city for sustenance. So be it. Learning to let go. No one's forcing him to stay. There's always the labour camps. He can leave any time. Here for now and that's enough.

Seymour returns to his coffin. Developers call them iso-pods. Enclosed single-sized beds. Thousands of soundproof units stacked on top of each other. Daily, weekly, or monthly rentals available. It's all he can afford outside the barracks. Sacrificing square footage for solitude. Surrendering headroom for headspace. Standing five-foot-ten, he still needs to bend his neck while kneeling in the coffin. A recessed thirty-by-thirty-by-twenty shelf holds his possessions: clothes, phone, toiletries. For food, he keeps canned or dry snacks. There's no kitchen in his building. No common area either. There's the iso-pods and communal washrooms. That's it. The building has a strict no-guest policy, which has not been an issue for Seymour thus far.

Total darkness. Arm asleep. Rolls over. Blood rushing back. Pins and needles. Needs to pee. Seymour turns on the light. Slips into his slides and opens the hatch. The hall is clear. He climbs down and makes his way to the washroom.

Squinting from the harsh overhead lights, he sees the young man standing in front of the mirror in his boxers. Gaunt, ghastly pale, with a patchy shaved head. The young man leans against the sink. Looks down. Throws his head back and slams it into the mirror. Smashing glass. Stumbling backwards. Blood pulses and pours from a deep gash in his forehead. The young man teeters on his feet. Blood leaking into his eyes. Dripping off his nose. Chin. Running down his neck. Seymour snaps out of it. Steps forwards. Insists the young man sit down. Holds his elbow to provide stability as he helps him to the ground.

"Going to get help. Grab a towel for the cut. Stay there. Stay here. Be right back."

Seymour alerts security to call an ambulance. Runs to his pod. Grabs a clean towel. Rushes back. The young man slouched against the wall. Blood now smeared across his chest and stomach. Seymour kneels down beside him. Presses the towel into the open wound, applying pressure to slow the bleeding.

"Hold still, man . . . relax. Help's on the way."

Mulligan

Police arrive with the medics. Seymour removes the towel. Steps aside. Blood bubbles out of the wound, running into the young man's mouth. The cops ask his name. He spits blood onto the floor. They ask again.

"Mark."

Seymour washes the blood from his hands. Takes a piss. Washes his hands again. Before he can leave, one of the officers pulls him aside for a statement. Not much to say. Offers what he can.

> "Woke up. Had to piss. Saw him staring at the mirror before he smashed his head into it."
> "Do you know him?"
> "No. First time I've seen him."

Disturbed. Unable to sleep. Seymour says a prayer of peace for the young man.

Pay upgrade. Trained and transferred to the tombs, fortified columns filled with active Atman accounts. Each column buried miles into the ground while reaching thousands of feet above the surface. Giant forum tubes that continue expanding upwards with the ability to stack one section, level, ring on top of the next. The files are stored inside the walls of these colossal cylinders. Deposited by the warehouse teams using swing stages.

Day one. Graveyard shift. Seymour enters at ground level. Walks the hallway to the construction hoist that takes him to the floor. Each flash, slash, speck of light another account. Billions of lives. Memories mapped, sorted, and stored. The hoist hits the floor. Rock bottom. Seymour steps out of the cage into the cylinder. Looks up from the inner circle at the blinking lights tunnelling towards a black dot sky. Dizzying heights. Seymour staggers back. The size and scale of the Atman throws off his equilibrium. Spiralling at the sight of it. Overwhelmed and his supervisor sees it.

> "Breathe, Seymour. Focus on your breathing. Clear your mind. Lie down if you need to."

These are the instructions. Agoraphobia, claustrophobia, and sudden vertigo are normal reactions for new recruits. No amount of off-site training can prepare one for the epicentre. New hires are given twenty minutes to lower their heart rate and re-establish continuity or be dismissed. Seymour takes ten. Settles in. Past the panic, drenched in sweat, he returns to his feet. Cognizant. Coherent. Aware.

Able to answer their questions, he's given the green light. Seymour loads the cases of new accounts into the swing-stage. Attaches his lanyard to the rope grab on his safety line and begins the ascent. Their assignment, his job, is depositing new accounts while collecting those requested for download. A sorter and stacker of lives lived. Memory banks. His own file is in there somewhere, blinking on and off with the rest of them. Seymour declined Samsara but the account was mandatory. First presented to him as a signing bonus or benefit, he soon found out it was a condition of employment. Let 'em have it. There for the paycheque. Nothing and nobody can claim his soul.

Winter firmly entrenched. The city buried in sleet and snow. Wind tunnels whipping Seymour with ice pellets on the way to work. He approaches the intersection. Hears the mashing of horns. Traffic stopped in each direction. In the middle of the road stands Mark. His hair has grown out since their initial encounter. Spiked, jagged, black. He did not look well then and is noticeably worse now. Rail thin. Tattered hoodie hanging off his shoulder blades. Torn jeans held up above his waist with a shoelace borrowed from one of his steel-toe boots. The tongue flapping open. Boot filled with snow. The shivering young man locked in a trance. Vacant expression. Staring out into nothing. Commuters now screaming for him to get off the road. Seymour intervenes. Hurries over with his hands out to traffic. Motioning for calm. Patience. Sees the serrated scar split down the middle of Mark's forehead. Lips looks blue. Likely hypothermic.

"Mark, we've got to move, buddy."

Sunken green eyes turn towards him. Seymour registers a dull flicker of recognition.

"Let's go get warm. Grab some food."

Seymour waves him forward.

"Can't stay here, man. Blocking traffic. Gotta keep it moving."

Something clicks. Mark follows.

Warmth. Seated in the teahouse. Corner booth. The shivering has subsided. Mark's lips are split. Chapped and peeling but no longer blue. Not a word since they sat down. Still staring at the table. Ten minutes now. Seymour sips his tea. Starts thing off.

"Where you living these days?"

Long pause. Seymour searching for the next question when the answer arrives.

"Under the ice."

Seymour rolls with it.

"What's that like?"
"Cold."
"How'd you end up there?"
"Transporting tailings from the mine. Convoy saw cracks in the ice. Too late."

Samsara. Has to be. Seymour tops off their teacups. Prompts him to continue.

"Too late for what?"
"Black outside the windows. Ice water filling the cab. Smash the glass. Rushes in. Gasp. Catch my breath. Fighting for the surface. Too far down. Currents pulling me away. Cold stabbing every cell. Completely numb. Done . . . I'm done. About to break. Kick. Thrash. Crack. Drag water into my lungs."

Mark clears his throat. Continues.

"The divers find my body that morning. Everything's intact. Well preserved. Ideal interruption. Reverie pulls my file. Go back to work. Last a week. Leave my truck on the side of the road and start walking."

Mark runs his middle finger across the scar on his forehead. Closes his eyes.

"Mark?"

"Yeah . . ."

"You described your death like you were there."

No answer.

"How long between upload and interruption?"

Still tracing his scar.

"Sixty-seven days."

"Why'd you take so long to upload?"

"Lazy . . . nothing I needed to remember."

"What made you bank the last one?"

Mark opens his eyes. Puts his hand down.

"Vacation. Real one. Good buzz going. Sun, sand, splashing around in the waves. Big blue sky. Flock of Macaws — bright red — flies overhead into the jungle. Just the sight of them . . . That setting. Made it. Made this happen. Put in the work. Picked the place. Showed up."

"Beauty."

"Yeah."

"What now?"

Mark looks out the window. Giant flakes of wet snow melting against the glass.

"Winter."

PROPOGATION

Ten minutes into the drive home and Stan is already seething. A tipped-over semi-trailer forces a detour through an area of the industrial park he's unfamiliar with. That's when he sees it. A small house with a rusted-out pickup truck parked in the driveway. A place of residence inside the gargantuan industrial park. Impossible. Like a mirage. Right across the road from the garment factory under the shadow of the Rexen chemical plant. Exposed roof. Missing shingles. Boarded-up windows. Most of the paint stripped off its exterior, replaced by a thick layer of industrial soot. In a serious state of disrepair but it's there. He's looking at it. How has it not been demolished? Stan wants to drive in for a closer look but Rexen's perimeter fence runs directly across the end of the driveway, cutting the house off from the road.

Stan pulls off to the shoulder of the road and flips on his hazards. Walking out of the storm ditch, he hops the waist-high chain-link fence crossing the field of scorched grass towards the house. All four tires on the rusted pickup are flat. Sections of house siding are torn off, exposing blackened insulation. The front steps leading up to the porch are broken and rotted through. Stan tries peeking through the windows that aren't boarded up but can't see past the film and grime. Circling the house, he sees the backyard strewn with piles of trash. Garbage bags stacked ten feet high. Excluding a narrow pathway to the door, the back porch is crammed full of empty beer and wine bottles. Convinced the house is abandoned, he knocks anyway. After several knocks with no answer, Stan turns the door handle and it opens.

"Hello? Anyone home?"

No reply. He steps inside. The kitchen is relatively clean, ignoring the dirty stack of dishes with flies buzzing around it. Moving into the living room, he sees a velvet painting of a black bull standing in the foreground of a bombed cityscape with a neon-green mushroom cloud rising from its ashes. The painting is positioned above a floral-patterned couch. The rest of the walls are bare. The couch and coffee table the only pieces of furniture. Moving upstairs. All doors are closed. Stan knocks on what he suspects is the upstairs bathroom. No answer. He twists the handle. Unlocked. Opening the door, he immediately slams it shut on the morbid snapshot. The image burned into his psyche. Stan gathers himself. Decides to take another look. Stare it down. The corpse is in a state of active decay well into the putrefaction stage. Bacteria are breaking down tissue and cells. The bathtub is filled with whatever sludge had been dispelled from the body, now green with rot. Blowflies buzzing all around. Maggots secreting digestive enzymes. Tearing tissue with their mouth hooks. The swelling of tissues around the neck and face causes the old man's tongue to protrude from his mouth. A final mocking gesture. Had it not been for his olfactory handicap, Stan would have instantly caught the waft of death. What he imagines to be a mix of shit, rotting meat, and rancid fat. All tinged with an underlying sweetness triggering a revulsion that would have turned him away the second he stepped inside the house. Too late now. The damage is done. Then it occurs to him he found this place for a reason. Meant to be but he has to make it happen. Somehow. Someway.

Stan hears the air brakes from outside; another Rexen rig turning right. The rumble of the trucks and the chemical plant undeniably loud at that proximity but Stan will not be dissuaded. Earplugs. Sound baffling. Whatever. The house is within walking distance of work. All that matters. End of discussion. Now he needs to find out who's in line to inherit the property. Stan opens the door to one of the other rooms upstairs. Appears to be an office. The deceased's computer an archaic system covered in a layer of dust. Still on but requires a password. Stan turns it off and continues searching the house. Retrieves stacks of legal documents, utility bills, and a family photo album stuffed with old Christmas and birthday cards. He loads all of it into the back of his car and begins the gruelling transit back to his accommodations. An hour into his drive, he alerts emergency dispatch to the presence of the body.

With the seized documents and online sleuthing, Stan is able to piece together a picture. The deceased's name is Reginald Darling. Eighty-six years

Propogation

old at the time of his passing. Before retiring, Reginald worked as a systems analyst with various institutes and agencies. His deceased brother Elliot Darling was an otologist. His deceased sister Dedra Darling a math teacher. Dedra's daughter Alex is Reginald's only living relative. The sole heir to his estate. Regarding the house, when the district was officially re-zoned for industry, Reginald refused to accept a settlement for relocation. He would not sign over his property rights to Rexen. Everyone else took the money. It was an impoverished area with a high crime rate and limited services already overrun with factories and warehouses. Between the noise, traffic, and air pollution, the only reason to stay was not having the money to leave. Reginald was the exception. Steadfast in his resolve. It was his land. His home. He wasn't leaving, successfully defending himself in court against every city ordinance brought about to evict him. Throughout the legal process, Rexen continued to expand their perimeter. Purchasing the entry road to Reginald's house as an alternative entrance into the chemical plant, erecting the chain-link fence to block his access to the road. They also purchased the surrounding land so he couldn't build a new road. Reginald was boxed in. He tried to fight this in court but the judge was in Rexen's pocket and ruled against him, claiming Rexen had purchased the road from the city and were within their rights.

Knowing the backstory, Stan contacts Reginald's niece Alex through a social network, claiming to be a friend offering his condolences. After exchanging civilities, he inquires about her plans for the departed's house. Alex informs him her real estate agent is negotiating a sale with Rexen. Stan feigns disgust. Disappointment. How could she consider selling to them? Has she forgotten Reginald's history with Rexen? Is she aware? Alex confesses to not being well versed regarding her uncle. Never met the man. Reginald was a shut-in who isolated himself from the family. Calls were made but never returned. Stan takes the opportunity to inform. Alex acknowledges her uncle's battle to keep his home while insisting she has no other options. No one else is going to purchase the property. It's too small for commercial property and no one wants to live between smokestacks. Stan recognizes her dilemma, realizing Rexen has all the leverage and will likely make a lowball offer. Seeing his opportunity, Stan makes Alex promise to allow him to submit a counteroffer after Rexen submits their bid.

Two weeks later, Stan gets the call he's been waiting for. As expected, Rexen presented a nothing offer, having all the negotiating power. Alex, having fired her real estate agent, wants to sell to Stan directly on the condition he keep the house as a place of residence. Fuck Rexen. After agreeing on a down payment, the sale is made. Steal of a deal.

He discards the mattress from the master bedroom but keeps the rest of the furniture. Stan smashes the claw-foot bathtub into manageable pieces for carry while workers drag bags of trash across the driveway to the junk removal truck parked at the shoulder of the road with its emergency lights on. They need to move fast before Rexen security removes them from the road.

Frost on the inside of the rattling windows. A draft in every corner of the house. Stan feels the cold kitchen tiles through his socks as he sips a cup of silver tea (boiled water to warm the core). With five years until retirement, he refuses to invest in repairs or renovations. Bought a new bathtub and that's it. Done. Everything else goes into his savings. He can suffer minor discomforts until his work release. They all pale in comparison to the four hours of soul-crushing traffic he used to suffer on his daily commute to and from work. Now it's no more than a fifteen-minute walk to the power plant.

Stan dumps his silver tea down the sink. Packs a bottle of Norgesta. Bundles up and steps outside. Seven p.m. and it's already dark out. Hopping the fence, he turns right, facing a cruel headwind as he trudges through the snow. Sticking to the shoulder as giant tractor trailers roar past him.

Stan scrapes the ice and snow off his car. Because he can't drive onto his property, he keeps it parked at work. The power plant is always open should he need it. After signing in with security, Stan changes at his locker then drives a forklift to his station, where it's considerably warmer around the tanks. The humidity comparable to a botanical garden. Nasal hairs defrosting, he wipes his runny nose on his sleeve and checks the readings. With the numbers where they should be, Stan grabs the goad, a fifteen-foot rubber staff, and walks to the edge of the tank where he finds Berta with her mouth sticking out of the water. Being an obligate air-breather, she must rise to the surface every ten minutes, gulping air into her mouth, before sinking back to the bottom. Stan waits for Berta to finish drawing oxygen before prodding her with the goad to trigger an electrical discharge. On average, each response

Propogation

carries thirty thousand volts. Berta gets the goad every thirty minutes. In a twelve-hour shift, Berta produces thirty thousand volts of electricity, in a day three hundred and sixty thousand volts, in a year 262,800,000 volts. Each tank has massive conductors, which transfer the charge to storage cells, feeding power to a super grid, with a high-voltage DC switch. The power corps has thirty tanks and thirty eels currently supplying eight billion gigawatts of power a year. There are plans to install thirty more tanks within the decade to meet the power demands of industry and city expansion.

The eels, which are technically genetically modified fish of the genus Electrophorus, have an average life expectancy of fifteen years. The power corps maintains a nursery of them ready to replace sick, dead, or dying production eels at a moment's notice. The transfer and integration can be completed in under an hour. Berta is fourteen years old. Stan was there the day she was brought over from the nursery and has worked her station his entire tenure. He received the posting after months of training, earning the highest test scores in the class by committing the entire system to memory. To his mind, it wasn't that complicated: converters, conductors, circuits, load, supply. Learn it. Earn it. Retire.

Held up in traffic. Delayed. Diverted. Stalled. Stan in a foul mood when Olivia lets him into the building. Taking the elevator to her studio unit. Bedroom, bathroom, kitchen, all sharing the same two-hundred-square-foot space. A stand-up shower in her kitchen with the toilet stowed away in a cramped wall compartment by the front entrance. Her apartment has one window. A half bubble, something for a submarine, built into the wall behind the foldout bed that doubles as a couch. Olivia propped up by a stack of pillows. Sipping cheap wine from a bottle she's halfway through. Still dressed in the same patient gown she left the hospital in. Stan reaches into his jacket and tosses her a vial of pills.

> "Nice to you see you dressed for the occasion."
> "Pay more money, I'll make more effort."
> "Take the gown off. Let me have a look at you."

Ignoring his request, she washes back a couple of pills with a slug of wine.

> "Seriously, I'm going to be sleeping in one of those coffin units soon."

"Or an actual coffin."

"Fuck off."

"You're the one who chose a degree in advertising media management."

"I'm charging more for these visits unless you want me taking on other clients."

"Other clients? Really, that's interesting. The first time we did this you wept with shame, now you want to expand the business."

"Trying to keep up with the cost of living."

"Try cutting back on the booze."

"Job requirement."

"Taking on new clients is a short-term fix. You're in your forties now. The cracks are showing. That body ain't what it used to be. Soon you won't be able to give it away."

Olivia clears her throat.

"Stan . . . I know you're cursed with a small dick but why don't you fix your teeth?"

"By the time I had the money to fix them, I realized I could just pay for pussy. When a woman's desperate enough, it's amazing how she'll demean herself."

Olivia yawns, rolling her eyes.

"Would you get the fuck out of my apartment already?"

"Sure, but I'll have to take those pills back."

She whips the vial at his head. It explodes against the wall, scattering pills throughout the apartment. Stan crushes one under his boot before leaving.

The chubby Filipino desk attendant at the massage parlour is wearing a zebra-print robe. There's a pause before she looks up from filing her nails.

"Hi, how are ya?"

"Good. Who's available right now?"

"I am."

"There's a girl I have in mind but I forget her name."

Propogation

"Mia, Missy, Jenna, Ellie, Jade, Sierra, Nina. That's who's working right now."

"Can you bring them out so I can take a look?"

"Nina and Jade are with clients right now but I can bring out the other girls."

"Thanks."

The attendant disappears down the hallway. Stan turns his attention towards the tropical aquarium that used to be the centrepiece of the lobby. A thick layer of algae is growing over the glass, spreading out from the corners. Two gobies hover around lifeless coral at the back. A dead dottyback floats upside down by the filter. Years ago, there were clown fish, triggerfish, tangs, royal grammas, and a peppermint shrimp. Back when the glass was clean. Now everything's dead or dying. When the girls return to the lobby, he's gone.

A wasted excursion to the godforsaken city. Stuck slogging back through traffic, Stan passes the twenty-four-hour diner at the edge of the highway. There was a time when a slice of apple pie and a scoop of ice cream would provide some consolation. Before that fucking meathead fucked his shit up. Stan had just turned thirty and was working as a commercial electrician. Already a journeyman, the company forced him to take on an apprentice. Some garlic knot named Giovanni that went by Gio. Big kid. Used to be a bouncer at a strip club. Simple math sailed right over his head. Stan was convinced Gio had dyslexia and ADD. Constantly inverting the numbers and unable to follow basic instructions. Kept repeating the same mistakes. Stan finally put him on notice. Figure it out or find another line of work. Didn't help. The errors continued piling up. Losing time, losing money on each job. Stan had to remove Gio from any real responsibility. Fetching tools, carrying ladders, and going on coffee runs was all he could be trusted with. The kid was dead weight. Had to go. Stan addressed the situation with their supervisor, Frank Cuttino, who explained the circumstance of Giovanni's employment.

"My niece is pregnant. Gio's the father. That's the situation. I'm trying to help her out. We give him another month."

The next day at work, Stan tells Gio to grab the tools and ladder but he refuses. Frustrations boiling over.

"I'm sick of doing bitch work."
"I can't trust you with anything else."
"Fuck this shit. You're a fucking asshole!"
"Why should I be punished because you shot a load in Frank's niece?"

Gio drops his tool belt. Fists clenched.

"Keep talking shit. I'll knock you the fuck out."
"You're going to fight me now? You're going to attack your journeyman?"
"Fuck you."
"Wow . . . you are special."

Stan wakes up covered in blood and sawdust with one of the HVAC guys kneeling beside him. Head pounding. Face throbbing. Feels sick. Concussed. Cops called. Gio gone. Ambulance on its way. X-rays confirm the obvious: broken nose and orbital bones. Weeks later, he still can't taste his food. Subsequently diagnosed with anosmia: the inability to perceive odours. The doctors hope it's a temporary affliction from the inflammation of the nasal mucosa. When the condition persists, it's blamed on cranial nerve damage to the temporal lobe. Eating is now a joyless experience. Smell and taste inextricably linked. Without his olfaction, it's all tasteless mush. Ingestion just another chore. Done with solids, Stan switches to Norgesta, the dirt-cheap meal replacement that kept millions of refugees alive during the initial exodus. The algae formula tastes like lawnmower mulch infused with French vanilla. Flavour no longer a concern, Norgesta is an expedient and economical method of nutrient and caloric intake.

Back to work. Berta hovering idly at the bottom of the tank. Heavy cataracts render her essentially blind. The pits in her face work as receivers for her radar system used to navigate her surroundings and locate prey. This super-sized electric eel with hundreds of millions of flattened electrocytes connected in series. Low-voltage EODs emitted by the Sachs's organ associated with electro-location. High-voltage EODs are emitted by the Hunter's organ during predatory attacks. Stan understands the mechanics, its function, but what the hell is she thinking? Most likely nothing. Living on low-grade impulse: hunger, air, disturbance. Reacting to immediate need or

Propogation

threat. Being nocturnal, Berta's notably less active during the day with lower EOD emission. Stan once again wonders whether she slips into a staggered dream state while resting. What would that be? What would it look like with no internal narrative or concept of self? The real question being why he's suddenly giving such consideration to this damned fish. Stan walks the ramp to the top of the tank and grabs the prod.

Slipping and stumbling over ice, he curses the endless winter. The lonely moan and incessant whine of the wind. The crunch of grey snow and gravel under feet. Sick of it. Everything aggravates. Three months left but it feels like an eternity. Craving warmth from the sun. Brought to the brink by this miserable season. On his birthday weekend, he deserves a reprieve.

Stan walks past the suspended waterfall, checking in with reception. The lounge is filled with expensive suits and short skirts. The Diadem Hotel is where old and new money can mingle together with an emphasis on discretion and a premium on privacy. It's a place where the upper echelon can conspire while indulging their privilege. Stan does not belong, yet here he is, sipping his club soda at the bar. Enjoying the carbonation as he scans for the room for high-end escorts. Willing to pay a premium on his birthday. From across the bar, Stan catches an alluring smile from a fetching young woman in a glittery silver dress. She holds eye contact while stirring her drink. Sending the signal. Clearly there for work. Stan raises his glass, ready to buy her drink and initiate the transaction.

"Stanley Grindle, what are you doing here?!"

Interruption. The voice raises his hackles. Stan turns to face that same shit-eating grin. Chase Young, the bully who took such pleasure torturing Stan, now stands before him in a tailored suit with platinum cufflinks. They haven't seen each other since high school. Through some cruel twist of fate, they are brought together on his birthday.

"That's a face I hoped I'd never see again."

Chase gleefully laughs at the comment. Patting Stan on the back.

"C'mon, Stan, we're old acquaintances. Can I buy you a drink?"

"Can I toss it in your face?"

This elicits a cackle from Chase.

"Suppose I deserve that. You married? Kids?"
"No."
"How about work? What do you do?"
"Spare me the small talk. You don't give a shit and neither do I."

There was a time when he couldn't address Chase without stuttering and stammering from fear of further humiliations. Now he's in control. Nothing left. Not really. He'll dictate the terms of their conversation.

"Such vitriol. I get it. I do. I owe you an apology."
"You're forgiven. Now fuck off."
"Hear me out. I saw you eyeing that escort. Lydia does good work but if you want next level, let me introduce you to the sirens."
"You're a pimp now?"
"International diplomat."
"So, you're the whore."

This garners another guffaw from Chase. No surprise the bully who pissed in his shampoo bottle, snuck frozen dog shit into his book bag, flicked gum into his hair, pantsed him in front of the girls' soccer team, and turned the few friends he had against him now holds rank in the highest levels of government.

"Seriously. How many dicks you have to suck for that job?"
"Don't hate. I'm offering you the experience of a lifetime to make amends."
"Cut the bullshit. What are you selling?"
"Transcendent bliss."

They take the elevator to the fourteenth floor. Chase leads the way. Walking the hallway, a door opens just ahead of them. A dapper gentleman with a square jaw and silver hair leaves the room in a dishevelled suit. Chase turns down an intersecting hallway where they stop just around the corner,

Propogation

waiting for the conversation to finish between said gentleman and whoever remains inside the bedroom.

> "Thank you, Artie. Thank you. I mean it. I'm floating right now. Cloud nine. Needed that. The lawsuits, the divorce, everything . . . I was ready to kill someone or jump out a fucking window."
>
> "Well, we certainly don't want that. I'm glad the service was beneficial."
>
> "Beneficial? I was having a full-fledged breakdown."
>
> "Once again, we're happy to provide assistance."
>
> "Thank you again Artie. Truly."
>
> "It's what we do, Bill. Until next time."

Stan and Chase wait until Bill passes them in the hall then proceed towards the room he appeared from. Chase knocks on the door. A peculiar-looking character answers. Short. Maybe five feet tall with a hunched-over posture and round belly. Bald, with a messy fringe of grey hair around the sides. His thick-framed glasses have lenses that make his eyes look tiny. Like a mole. Completing his look is a poorly fitted, oversized, carnation-pink suit with giant lapels and shoulder pads. The mole man steps aside, waving them into the room and closing the door behind them. They move into the living room area, where introductions are made.

> "Artie, thanks for seeing us on such short notice. This is Stan Grindle, an old friend of mine."

Artie greets Stan with short bow.

> "Mr. Grindle, nice to meet you."

Stan nods. Chase pats him on the back.

> "Everything's taken care of. Hope this clears the karmic slate. Enjoy the ride, Stano."

In the corner of the room is a large rectangular object hidden under black velvet cloth. The object, what appears to be an aquarium, rests on a rolling countertop. Ten feet away is a pink leather recliner matching Artie's suit. Beside the chair is a tripod mic stand with a microphone attached to the boom arm. In the far corner of the room is a swivelling office chair parked in front of an antiquated mixing console and a radio mic. A series of wires run from the input/output channels, across the floor, plugging into the back of whatever's concealed under the velvet.

"Please take a seat."

Artie motions to the pink recliner. Stan sits down. Artie adjusts the stand so the mic's positioned near Stan's face. Next, he opens the headphones, places them over Stan's ears, and returns to his seat behind the mixing board. Wearing his own bulky white headphones, Artie turns the system on and speaks into the radio mic.

"Okay, Stan, bear with me while I set the levels."

Stan rips off his headphones.

"This is a joke, right? A prank? What the fuck is this?"

Artie removes his headphones.

"My apologies, I falsely assumed you'd been briefed on the process."

"The sirens. You're supposed to introduce me to the sirens. Where the fuck are they? When does that happen?"

"A symbiotic link is forged with the sirens through auditory transmission. This connection stimulates intense pleasure reactions across a distributed system of brain regions. Subcortical: nucleus accumbens, ventral pallidum. And cortical: orbitofrontal cortex and anterior cingulate cortex.

"No, thanks."

Stan hangs his headphones on the tripod and stands up.

"Sir, please sit down. I've complicated matters. It's very simple. I cue you with a series of music notes and you hum them back into your microphone. That's all that's required for unequivocal euphoria."

Stan hesitates as he looks towards the door.

"What the fuck is wrong with me . . ."

Propogation

Stan grudgingly sits back down.

"Fuck it. I surrender. Let's see what happens."

Artie plays a succession of music notes that Stan hums back, working his way through various scales.

"Okay, Stan. That's the final octave. We'll stop there. Now you're going to hear a series of three beeps that will cue the sirens' response. Lean back and enjoy the ride."

Call and return. It starts with a whisper. A tease. Cooing murmurs weaving into harmonic frequencies lapping onto shore. Play. Shimmer. Shine. Swirl. Slide. Soar. Launched through the air. Flying. Gliding. All so effortless. Drift. Roll. Delightful descent. Welcome embrace. Soothing adorations. Easing into warm pleasure pulse. A slow surge hinting towards infinity. Then the prize. A rapturous release. Sustained into serenity. Weightless. Floating. The volume fades with a gentle goodbye.

"Hello, Stan, welcome back. You may remove your headphones."

Eyes open. Stan panics, realizing he's ejaculated in his pants.

"How long? How long was I gone for?"
"Ten minutes. That's how long your interaction lasted."
"Wow . . . okay . . . yeah . . . okay . . . I should go."
"Stan, relax, you're safe. There's no rush. Enjoy the afterglow."

Stan hangs his headphones and stands up.

"Yeah . . . I don't know . . ."
"There's fifteen minutes before the next appointment. Take a moment, collect yourself."
"Okay . . . yeah . . . no . . . I need to go."
"Then I'll offer you our card."
Artie holds out a business card. Stan snags it on his way out the door. Waiting for the elevator, he gives it a glance: ghost white, pink cursive, with gold bordering. The card reads "Harmony: Piano Tuning and Repair."

Showering in the dark. Listening to the water hit the walls. Unwrapping the soap carries an agreeable charge. Fresh towels like a gift from heaven. Lying in bed, Stan feels his breath. Inhale. Exhale. Alive. Premium comfort. Stan grabs the remote and turns on the projector. Selects "Nature Clips." He could never excuse the cost but can't deny the breathtaking imagery. The 3D renderings are incredible. Truly breathtaking. Watches a lion take down a wildebeest, a bear battle a pack of wolves. A bald eagle soars over his bed, then dives down, talons out, ripping a salmon out of the water, and it's all happening in the middle of his room.

Scanning channels, Stan stops. Transfixed by a cartoon, an animated feature about a girl, her ghost, and a mange-ridden donkey. They travel over haunted landscapes, from one city ruin to the next, trying to reach the river. The design and detail are awe-inspiring. When they reach the end of their journey, ready to cross the river, Stan is fighting back tears.

Show's over. He turns the projector off. The room is dead quiet, sound-proof design blocking any noise from the hallway and neighbouring rooms. Strangers gathered in temporary residence. Divergent realities under one roof. Numerous storylines and personal dramas playing out behind closed doors. Hidden worlds given room numbers and key cards. Separate quarters. Same cleaning staff. Registered guests and their reasons. From one stranger to the next.

Cold morning light stabs his eyes. Cutting through the fog. Morning wood. Full bladder. Stan takes a leak and closes the blinds. Returning to bed, he turns on the projector, checking the pay channels. Picks a porn star. There she is. A private show. Stripping off her clothes. Like she's there in the flesh. Hits pause. Able to view her from every angle. He adjusts the image to his liking. On all fours. Directly over him on the bed. Her spectacular breasts inches from his face. Press play.

Showered and dressed with an hour until checkout. Stan plays Fractals, flipping, dragging, dropping increasingly complex fractals out of the air. Everything in its place until the game reaches terminal velocity. The space disappears, you run out of options, and it all comes crashing down.

Stan returns his key card and walks to the complimentary water station. One water dispenser has thin slices of cucumbers floating in it, the other

Propogation

lemon, subtle infusions of flavour lost on Stan. Simply a matter of hydration for him. Not ready to go home. Not yet. He reclines on a couch in the lobby as it slowly circles the waterfall.

Caught between the buildings. Head down, braced against a wind tunnel, Stan reaches the frozen park. Spots the hotdog stand. Sun, rain, or snow it's still working the same corner. He recalls that summer. Decades past. A kid. Ten or twelve. Standing in the sweltering heat. They were starving from the wait. He holds their place in a line that wraps around the entire park, leading to the natural history museum on the other side. Dad brings back food. A hotdog with mustard and onion. Quality street meat. You can tell by the snap of the skin. Paired with an ice-cold orange soda. A divine rush of carbonated sugar cleansing the palate for another bite. The sun setting. People stroll by into evening as they wait to see Bigfoot. A mother and her two children captured, "rescued,"' the preferred term. Likely the last of their kind. Had to be relocated. Necessary for survival. Their environment under climate threat. Wildfires. That region now a massive property development. Just another land grab disguised as crisis. How soon they forget. Stan doesn't. No, he does not.

This was the moment. The big unveiling. The public had known about the Sasquatch for two years but the beast is kept hidden during the legal battle over guardianship. Various factions making claims. A major source of contention, sparking a bidding war that generated more hype around the discovery. Everyone weighed in on the subject: lawyers, scientists, landowners, politicians, celebrities, and advocacy groups. A ruling finally arrived with an official statement for the public: "Everyone has a vested concern for the well-being of these animals. They're no one's property. The right decisions have to be made regarding their well-being. Sharing is the solution."

They'd go on tour. A travelling exhibit. From one museum to the next. Immediately they're the biggest draws the museums have ever seen. Gift shops smash sales records with Sasquatch merchandise. Father and son wait two hours for a ten-minute viewing. How long it takes for the conveyor belt to circle around the enclosure. When the moment arrives, they find the bipedal ape sitting at the base of a fake redwood tree. The young ones nestled by their mother's side as she stares forlornly at the ground. When a bale of shrubs and grass is lowered into the enclosure, she stands up, striding over to it. A hushed gasp ripples through the gathering. She's massive, at least eight feet tall. Feeling the magnitude of the moment, Stan looks at his father to gauge his reaction.

"Wow . . . Wow . . ."

The young Sasquatch follow their mother, who crouches down by the bale. Ripping off handfuls of shrubs and raising them to the sky. Holding them there for moment before munching on the vegetation. The young Sasquatch mimic the action. They repeat this ritual several times as they eat.

"Dad, why are they doing that?"
"Unreal . . ."

Offering or acknowledgement. Maybe both. Perhaps neither. Exiting through the gift shop, his dad buys him a t-shirt, fridge magnets, and a mug for Mom.

Aged and empty. There are cobwebs in the highest corners of the museum. The exhibit still has the circulating conveyor belt but there's no one there to usher you off it now. No need. The novelty wore off long ago. Today, he's the exhibit's lone patron. Koyah, named after the moon, is the only Bigfoot left. His mother and sister have since passed. Both had black skin, black hair. Koyah was born with a colour variation. His creased skin chalk white, his grey fur peppered and streaked black. The Sasquatch is sitting under the same fake redwood tree, its paint faded and scratched. He stares at the ground like his mother. A defeated expression. Slowly circling the outside of the glass, Stan studies Koyah's face. Each line written from loss. During his second lap around the enclosure, Koyah looks up. Locking eyes with Stan, but he knows this is impossible. One-way glass. The Sasquatch is staring at its own reflection. Yet the beast turns his head. Tracking Stan's movement on the conveyor belt. The eyes don't lie. Accusatory. Koyah is not impressed. It's hard to interpret his look any other way. Projections of a hatred. Disdain from under that pronounced brow. Koyah holds his stare until the conveyor belt brings Stan around the back of the tree. Stan expects it to meet him on the other side, but Koyah has gone back to staring at the ground. On his third pass around the outside, the bale of leaves and grass is lowered into the enclosure.

Propogation

Koyah strides over to it. Rips off a handful and chews it down. Not once does he raise his arm to the sky.

Back at the power plant. Stan waits in his car for a group of coworkers to return inside from smoking so he won't have to acknowledge them. When the last one leaves, he removes the key from the ignition and starts walking. Sticking to the shoulder of the road, crossing from one to the next, he approaches his house. Slogging through the storm ditch's thigh-high snow, he shuffles over the field of ice towards his front door. Eye on the ice before he's blinded by the flash. The concussion hits him square to the chest. Knocking him off his feet. Ruptured eardrums. Vacant screams. Stan spinning. Reeling. Nimbostratus clouds lit up by the fire roaring below. Dripping steel. Crashing orange. Flashing green.

Property rights revoked under the guise of public safety. The plant explosion was caused by a faulty valve leak. Stan's forced backed into the city. Seeking reparation. One injunction after another. Rexen refuses to settle. Trying to bury the suit. Stall tactics. Bleed him dry. If a ruling doesn't go their way, they file an appeal until it does. They have the resources to drag the case out indefinitely. Stan's lawyers agree to defer payment, hoping for a percentage of the settlement. Tracking their hours, every meeting, every phone call. Forget compensation. There will be nothing left after legal fees.

His ruptured eardrum has long since healed. Hearing restored, now every waking minute in his new dwelling is spent with earplugs in. There was less noise pollution in the industrial park. Far less grating. His upstairs neighbours with their incessant stomping. Their dog's nails clacking against the floor. Their dreadful music like two robots arguing. Worse yet, the moaning, grunting, and squeaking of their bed frame at night. He hears all of it. Every cough, laugh, sneeze. And there's no escape. Summer brings its own aggravations. Stan loathes these hip young families infesting the area. Better when it was a slum. Sidewalks taken over by battalions of baby strollers carrying their precious cargo in stylish clothing ensembles. All these proud parents informed. In tune. Aware. Ambassadors of culture. So original. Unique. Annoying. He's forced to pay exorbitantly inflated rent because these fools are buying starter homes at ten times their actual value. They've learned nothing from the correction. Debt slaves eagerly accepting the next offer. Access. Easy credit. Rushing right back into luxuries and status. Convinced they're special. This time's different. There won't be another crash. The system can be trusted. Fools. Fucking peasants. Stan imagines another outcome where he's asleep in bed during the explosion. Death without dread. Instantaneous. Done. Over. Gone.

The chum block slides off the forks and sinks to the bottom of the tank, clouding the waters as it erodes. Berta's not eating today, but she still gets the prod. He'll notify the care team regarding her lack of appetite, something they'll have to address if it persists. For now, voltage readings are consistent. During break, Stan ponders the weekend between swigs of Norgesta. Maybe he'll buy a high-end projector. It would be so easy. To hell with the rest of it. Just let go; let them feed you their content. Infinite channels, incalculable variations. Forget what you know, you've found your filter to the universe. That's entertainment.

Subjected to his daily torture. Driving back from work. Stuck at the bottleneck. One massive clogged artery. Stan's ready to kill. The city planners should be put before a firing a squad. It doesn't matter how many times the city is destroyed and resurrected; they will fuck it up again. Rest assured. Grinding through the trap, seething, when he receives a phone call. Not recognizing the number, he refuses to answer. Waits for the voicemail then plays it over the speakers:

> "Hello, Mr. Grindell. My name is Emma Reid, I'm a personal assistant for Lloyd Blitzstein. Your grandfather requested I call and extend an invitation for you to join us this Thanksgiving weekend at his ocean view estate. He'll pay for your travel expenses and a room will be waiting for you. Please contact me at this number if there's any possibility you can make it. I'd be happy to make the travel arrangements for you."

Lloyd Blitzstein is Stan's great-great-grandfather. Lloyd's son Rahm was father to Leib who was father to Stan's mother Miriam. Lloyd outlived both son and grandson. Rahm was killed in a motorcycle accident. Leib died from a drug overdose. Stan has encountered Lloyd twice in his life. Stan was six years old when he first met his great-grandfather. Lloyd stopped by for a

Propogation

surprise visit during Christmas vacation. In the middle of dinner, Miriam screamed for him to get out of their house. As a teenager, Stan learned about the Blitzstein family fortune. Hoping he might be entitled to a portion of it somewhere down the road, Stan tried to broker a peace between his parents and Lloyd. In order to mend fences, he had to understand how they broke in the first place. He received a measured response from his father.

> "The Blitzsteins have produced generations of bankers. That's their racket but Lloyd wasn't interested in the world of finance. He wanted to drive race cars. Then he lost his legs in a crash and quit the circuit. After that, he pursued a series of failed business ventures with the family fortune. One more spectacular than the next. Lloyd became a pariah and was excommunicated. They gave him an allowance but that was the extent of their relationship. Then he lost the arm in a sailing accident. Another scandal. I bring this up because Lloyd is quick to pass judgment on those who don't share his viewpoints. I believe this traces back to his own insecurities."

That's when Stan's mother weighed in on the discussion.

> "Lloyd is a fucking asshole. End of story."

Stan didn't see Lloyd again until Miriam's funeral. He arrived with a woman half his age. Something you'd drag out of a strip club. A bottle blonde with giant fake tits on display. Lloyd kept his sunglasses on the entire time. Not saying a word to anyone, he left while Stan's father delivered the eulogy.

Thirty-five thousand feet in the air with no legroom and folds of fat spilling over his arm rests. Stan calculates the odds of getting sandwiched between the two fattest passengers on the airplane. Wishing he could wager on which one will drop dead of a heart attack first. For once, he's thankful for his broken nose. Spared the smell of body odour wafting off the two sweat hogs they've parked beside him. Then there's the baby. Even with the volume cranked in his headphones he can still hear it crying from three rows back. What's wrong, baby? Are your ears popping? You're hungry? Did you shit yourself? All of the above? Tell us. Tell us what it will take to shut you up. Oh, that's right . . . you can't talk. So maybe international travel at such a tender age wasn't such a great idea. All good, baby, you don't pick your parents. Hopefully you don't become them.

Blasted by the heat and humidity, Stan steps off the plane into another atmosphere. Walking through arrivals, he spots his driver holding a sign with his name on it. A lanky black man sucking on a lollipop. Dressed in flip-flops and bright orange board shorts with a white t-shirt that's draped around his neck. Stan places him between forty and sixty years old. Hard to tell with the blacks.

"Stan Grindle?"
"That's me."

The man nods. Takes his bag. Turns, revealing a smiling jack-o-lantern face on the seat of his shorts. Heading for the exit, he waves for Stan to follow. They cross the road into the parking lot. Tossing his lollipop, ruby-red fractals of hardened corn syrup shatter across the asphalt. His ride is an old work van with powder-blue paint peeling off the exterior. The vehicle rigged with rusted bio-fuel modifiers. The man opens the passenger side door. Nods for Stan to get in.

The air cools the closer they get to the water. Halfway through a joint, the driver offers it to Stan, who declines. Doesn't smoke. Hates weed. Makes him paranoid. Content having his hand out the window. Riding the air currents while enjoying the musical selection. Subdued instrumentals but the energy is there. Feels like they're on a mission. Winding up the mountain without a word spoken. They finally arrive at the front gates. Stan turns to the driver.

"Do you know Lloyd?"
"Grandpa's a fucking freak."

The gates open to the courtyard. A young blonde woman with delicate features and a perfectly toned body stands at the entrance of the house in tank top and panties.

"Thanks for the ride."

The driver ignores him, focussed on the woman. Stan steps out of the van with his travel bag. The driver's hand shoots out with an orange business card

Propogation

as bright as his board shorts. Stan reaches through the window and takes the card with nothing but a phone number stamped on it in bold black print.

> "Now you know where to find it."
> "Find what?"
> "You tell me."

The driver nods to the woman and peels out of the courtyard. Stan approaches the girl at the door, who appears to be a natural blonde.

> "Hello, I'm Emma. Mr. Blitzstein apologizes for not being awake to greet you."
> "Not a problem. I know it's late."
> "I'll bring you to your room."

She leads the way up the stairs. Her perfect posterior accentuated by hip-hugging panties. Mesmerized by its motion, Stan misplaces his step and trips on the staircase. Getting his hands out just in time to break the fall.

> "Are you alright?"

Pushing off from the stairs, Stan quickly pops up.

> "I'm fine. Too much wine on the plane ride, I guess."
> "Oh . . . well, there's water by your bedside and ibuprofen in the medicine cabinet."
> "It was a joke. I don't drink."
> "Okay . . . um, yeah. That's good, I guess."

Emma continues up the stairs to the third storey, where they arrive at his room: ocean view, balcony, queen-sized bed, ensuite bathroom, and a premium projector system. The wall panels cast a warm welcoming glow.

> "I hope the room meets your requirements."
> "Above and beyond."
> "Fantastic. In that case, I'll be seeing you in the morning."
> "You live here, then?"
> "Yes. Mr. Blitzstein provides me a room. My own room. Goodnight, Mr. Grindle."

TYRANT

Waking without an alarm is its own reward. Stan steps onto the balcony in his boxers and takes in the breathtaking panorama. Sunrise casts a dazzling array of colours over the coast. Two hundred feet below him the ocean crashes against the rocky shore.

Feeling refreshed from his shower, Stan throws on a pair of shorts and a t-shirt and slides into his flip flops. Not having to bundle up for the cold feels like the ultimate luxury. Rested. Renewed. Stan mixes some Norgesta, shakes it up, chugs it back, and washes out the bottle. Ready to begin his day. Downstairs, he finds Emma sitting at the kitchen table in front of her laptop with a fruit smoothie. Looking beautiful in a white sundress with a splash of flower petals patterned onto it.

"Mornin'"

Emma looks up from her laptop.

> "Good morning. Lilani can make you some breakfast if you'd like."

Stan notices another beautiful young woman, brown skin, black hair, washing down the kitchen counter.

> "No, thank you. I have specific diet requirements."

Then a roar from upstairs.

> "Laura, get yeerrr fucking hands out of there! You've had enough!"

Stan flinches from the unexpected outburst.

> "Nikki, grab me my legs!"

Emma takes a sip of her smoothie.

> "Mr. Blitzstein's awake."

Lloyd loudly clears his throat as he makes his way downstairs. Stan feels tension in his chest. Stress. He has no idea what to expect but it sounds angry. Lloyd turns the corner and there it is—on full display.

> "Loni, I need coffee, grapefruit, and a hardboiled egg."

Propogation

No housecoat. Completely naked. A horror show of sagging skin and knotted veins. The nightmare hangs limp between shiny black prosthetic legs. Stan can see the scarring from a series of botched enlargement procedures. Layers of tissue stapled, stitched, and grafted together. A patchwork of epidermis with approximating skin tone. Grandpa's Franken-phallus large enough to club a baby seal. Emma and Lilani seem completely unfazed by Lloyd's nudity. Emma continues typing on her laptop while Lilani sets the water to boil and retrieves a grapefruit from the fridge. Grandpa scratches under his distended scrotum.

"Stanley, nice to see you."

With a bowlegged walk, Lloyd's grotesquerie swings and slaps against the inside of his prosthetic legs as he approaches Stan with his hand held out. The same hand he scratched his sack with.

"I'm glad you could make it."

Stan reminds himself he's here for the money. Here to secure a potential inheritance. That's the mission. Fighting back his aversion, he shakes Grandpa's hand.

"Thanks for the invite, and the plane ticket, of course."
"Nonsense. It's been far too long, Stanley. We're overdue for a visit. I'll shoulder the blame on that one."

Lloyd steps onto the balcony, arches his back, and stretches his arms to the sky. Bringing them back down, hands on his waist, he starts doing hip gyrations.

"Have you had breakfast?"
"I ate." "Good 'cause you'll need the energy for the gym this morning. See if you can keep up with Grandpa."

Lloyd drives fast. Obnoxiously fast. The car is a marvel of engineering. Locked to the road. Taking corners at the drop of the dime. When they hit a stretch of open road, Stan is pinned against his seat from the acceleration. Grandpa yelling in his ear.

"I've got weights, elliptical, spin bike, swimming pool, everything I need for a workout is back at home. And Dash, my trainer, makes house calls but I like going to the gym. There's some nice trim there. It motivates me."

Lloyd's gym attire consists of a purple, skintight, sleeveless dry-fit shirt tucked into white track pants pulled up past his belly button. Skulking around the exercise machines, Stan watches from the sidelines as Dash, with his blonde topknot, blue eyes, cleft chin, and Spartan's physique, puts Lloyd through his program.

"Jack it up, Lloyd! You got this! All you, buddy! All you!"

Lloyd grunts, growls, and strains his way through each exercise as Dash shouts for more. It's quite the performance. Lloyd screaming, snarling, farting during a crooked bench press. His prosthetic arm lifts the weight, while his feeble flesh arm dips down until Dash has to take over, lifting the weight onto the rack.

"Nice work, Lloyd! All you! You're earning it today, buddy!"

Stan cringes. Lloyd making an absolute spectacle of himself but no one else seems to notice. Beautiful women wander across the gym with their earphones in. All wearing variations of the same gym gear: yoga pants or booty shorts with midriff tank tops. Hard nipples and camel toes on full display. Selfies between sets. It's the middle of the day. Don't they have jobs? Are they all on vacation? A trophy blonde with a perfect tan and exquisite pair of surgically enhanced breasts strides past him to the pulldown machine trailed by a camera man. Then it dawns on him. This is their job. Posting thirst traps. Getting clicks while they keep the trophy polished.

"What are you staring at?"

Lloyd slaps him hard across the back.

"That's Jenny, I'll call her over."
"Please don't."
"Pussy. I'm going to hit the heavy bag with Dash, then we'll cool off with some laps in the pool."

Holding the heavy bag, Dash yells out combinations. Lloyd's awkward little jabs from his frail flesh arm barely make a dent. The bag doesn't move.

Propogation

Then he twists his hips and delivers a right cross with his prosthetic arm that almost folds the bag in half.

"Nice, Lloyd! Almost broke my shoulder with that one."

Propelled by his prosthetic legs, Lloyd laps Stan several times in the pool. Splashing water in his face as he motors past him.

Back in the change room, Lloyd places one foot on the bench as he towels off. His mangled phallus hangs at Stan's eye level.

"Not much of an athlete, are you?"
"No. I was never compelled by sports."
"You're one of those guys. No talent. No interest."
"I guess so."
"Quit pouting. I'm just breaking your balls. When we get home, I'll introduce you to the girls and we'll go for a boat ride."

The girls. Nikki and Laura. Stan places them in their thirties. One bottle blonde. One brunette. Big fake tits. Both lying topless by the pool. Working on their tans while lazily snacking on fruit plates Lilani prepared for them. Each wearing sunglasses that take up half their face.

"Girls, this is my grandson, Stanley."

Lizards. Neither one moves an inch from their spot in the sun. Unwilling to even tilt their head in his direction.

"Hi, Stanley."

A forced greeting. Spoken in unison. Bored annoyance with a hint of contempt. Lloyd leering down at them.

"Look at those tits . . . spectacular, aren't they?"

Stan hesitates. Unsure how to reply.

"Speak up, Stan, I can't hear you."
"They're nice."
"Nice? That's all you've got?"
"They're perfect."

"Damn well should be. I paid enough for them."
"Perfection has its price."
"Shaved box. No bush. Just the way I like it."

Oblivious or used to it. Lloyd's comments garner no reaction from the girls.

"Girls, turn over for me, will you?"

This elicits a begrudging sigh as the girls drop the back of their lounge chairs and flip onto their stomachs. Both with Brazilian butt lifts.

"Ass all day. Look at those haunches. The shape. The contour. Paid for the implants but I make them work for it. Insist. They're in the gym four times a week doing squats, lunges, deadlifts, step-ups, hip rises. Trained them well. They used to think not eating was a substitute for exercise. Now they're thick, toned, and tanned. Something I can sink my teeth into."

Stan has no idea how to respond. Wants to change the subject but Lloyd keeps going.

"I know they're rolling their eyes under those sunglasses right now. They like to complain, pretend I'm some kind of slave driver but I treat my girls well. They know that. The problem is they're lazy. If they had an ounce of initiative, I wouldn't have to harp on them about the importance of exercise. These girls want to be objectified but they've got earn it."

The sun glints off Nikki's ass cheeks, glistening from the tanning oil. Stan imagines Lloyd's cadaver-cock prying them open, its scaly head plunging down. Nikki's eyes bulging, gripping her chair, stilted scream. Grandpa misinterpreting acute pain for pleasure. Or not, maybe he's well aware of how much it hurts and that's the point.

Switch scenes. The girls still topless. Now basking in the sun at the bow of the yacht. Lloyd pilots the ship in his captain's hat with gold-framed aviators and a pair of powder-blue Speedos stretched over his coiled bulge. Everything

Propogation

from the sagging skin on his mole-covered back to the tufts of wiry hair growing out his ears carries a level of revulsion.

"You're not a family man, are you, Stanley?"
"No, I live alone."
"And you're alright with that?"
"I am."
"You like women though, right?"
"Yes."
"But you don't want to live with them?"
"If the right one came along."
"Don't bother. They're always the right one until they're not. Pussy on demand, that's how I like it."
"Must get expensive."
"Less than a divorce."
"True."
"You want kids?"
"No."
"What's the plan, then?"
"Save for retirement."
"And what's that look like?"
"Live someplace warm. Travel once a year."
"Sounds attainable. You like your job?"
"It could be worse."
"So no, then."
"It's relatively painless with reasonable compensation but the transit is a source of misery."
"A goddamn nightmare, most cities. Fucking gridlock. Need to hire an air charter service. Private helicopter to get anywhere in a reasonable amount of time."
"Above my pay grade."

Lloyd holds course towards the horizon.

"Why does man still sail dead oceans?"
"We like floating, I guess."

"Sure, you can scrape the floor for sea urchins. Drag a net full of jellies but that's about it. But I remember a time when you might catch a fish out here. That's how fucking old I am. Now if you want to see a shark, you go to the mall."

Lloyd slows the engine down to a crawl, turns the engine off, and lets it drift.

"Blood sugar is starting to drop. Let's do lunch."

Stan follows Lloyd down the stairs into the kitchen. Lilani is sitting at the dining table reading a tattered paperback. She tucks it back into her handbag and stands up to greet them. Lloyd ignores her. Grabs two beers from the fridge and tries handing one to Stan.

"No, thanks. I don't drink."
"Why?"
"I prefer sobriety."
"Yeah, I can tell. Loni, whip us up some fish tacos, will you."
"None for me, thank you."
"What now? You don't like fish?"

Lloyd cracks his beer.

"I'm not hungry."
"You seasick?"
"No appetite."
"You better have one when Loni cooks up that turkey."
"I should have mentioned this earlier but I don't eat solid foods."
"What the fuck does that mean?"
"It's an unpleasant experience for me."
"Are you fucking kidding me? What's unpleasant about a juicy fuckin' steak or a goddamn cheeseburger?"
"There's no point. They'd be wasted on me. I can't taste them."
"Why the hell not?"
"Car accident."

Propogation

Stan doesn't feel like recapping the assault.

> "Head trauma. Lost my sense of smell. It's neurological."
> "The doctors can't fix that shit?"
> "I'm sure they could, given enough time and money."
> "So, what the hell do you eat?"
> "Norgesta."
> "Peasant food. Christ . . . no wonder you look so miserable."

Back on shore, they disembark from the yacht. Stan stumbles down the dock. It feels likes the ocean is still under him.

> "Watch out, ladies, somebody's still got their sea legs!"

Lloyd slaps Stan on the back with his prosthetic arm, almost knocking him over.

> "Cheer up, Stano! Loni's cousins are coming over to give me a massage but I'm willing to share."

Aolani is the younger of the sisters by at least ten years. Beautiful build. Smooth skin. Tanned, toned legs. Must surf. Stan can see the muscle tone in her arms and back. Her sister Malulani is a thick woman. Wide hips. Broad cheekbones. Deep brown eyes. They both offer smiles but there's a rigidness to their demeanour. It's clear they're there to work, wasting no time setting up their massage tables on the balcony. As soon as they're set up, Lloyd drops his robe, sits down on the table, detaches his legs, and hands them to Aolani, who sets them aside. With his prosthetic arm removed, Lloyd leans on his flesh arm until Aolani gets her hand behind his shoulders and gently lays him down on the table. Once she rolls him over, Lloyd shifts his weight, leaning on his elbow so Aolani can pull his mangled member out from underneath his stomach. It sticks out from his torso like a tail with his distended scrotum draped over it. Aolani covers Grandpa's waist with a towel.

Stan decides to keep his shorts on while Malulani works on him. Shocked by the strength in her hands. The way she digs in, applying pressure to his muscle tissue. Painful at first but he can feel the tension melting away. He can't recall the last time anyone exerted this much effort on his behalf. When the message is over, Malulani gently notifies Stan by whispering in his ear, "All done, sir." Stan takes a moment. Slowly sits up and opens his eyes. Ten feet away, Lloyd continues moaning while Aolani kneads his stumps with oil. Now on his back. His Franken-phallus in full tumescence. The white towel hanging from it like a windless sail. Malulani gives a curt nod to her sister. It's time to pack up.

> "Alright, Mr. Blitzstein. I hope you enjoyed the massage."
> "Always do, Lani."

With all his limbs reattached, Lloyd tosses the towel, stands up, and stretches out, still half erect.

> "Like a new man. That's how you work the kinks out."

They move inside while the sisters pack their tables.

> "Back in a bit, Stano. I'm going help the girls with
> their homework."

Lloyd gives Stan a wink and marches into the living room where the girls are watching celebrity projections. Another A-lister answering who they're wearing as they walk the red carpet.

> "Alright, girls, let's go."

Lloyd waves them upstairs. The girls sigh, turning off the projector.

Late evening. Stan gently sways in the poolside hammock. The night sky lit up with stars. Lloyd steps onto the deck dressed head to toe in white.

> "It doesn't get better than this, Stano. Put in the work and
> you can move mountains."

Full of shit. Fucking delusional. Stan can't hold his tongue any longer.

> "Without your family allowance, you'd be dead and buried."

Lloyd's tongue flicks in and out of his mouth.

> "What the fuck did you just say?"
> "C'mon, Lloyd, get real."
> "Bullshit! I built this life. Earned it."
> "Lloyd . . . I know your story."
> "You don't know shit, ya fuckin' loser. Fuckin' pussy. And it
> doesn't make a goddamn difference where the money comes

Propogation

> from. I'll be burying my cock in fresh trim until the sun burns out!"
> "Your cock? That's what you call it? Chop that thing off and toss it back in the jar of formaldehyde you stole it from."

Lloyd shakes his head and gnashes his teeth

> "I'm your grandfather . . . You show some goddamn respect!"
> "Leib was my grandfather."
> "Leib was a fucking junkie. His music softer than his spine."
> "He never took their money."

Stan sees Emma, Lilani, and the girls watching from the other side of the glass.

> "Oh, yes, he did. His wife, your sad-sack grandmother, went to me for a handout because that piece of shit was too busy sticking a needle in his arm to pay the bills. Fuck him. Just another tortured artist. Useless. His family suffered so he could feed his ego."
> "Nice of you to share your allowance."

Fists clenched. Nostrils flared. Lloyd looks ready to charge. Stan knows one punch from that prosthetic arm would shatter his jaw.

> "What am I doing here, Lloyd? Don't give me this bullshit about Thanksgiving."

Lloyd smashes his fist through the patio table.

> "Get the fuck out of my house!"

Emma insists Stan wait in his room until the driver arrives. Downstairs, Lloyd continues to snarl and bark over Stan's insolence. When the driver arrives, Emma, Lilani, and the girls form a wall in front of Lloyd so Stan can pass by.

> "Your mother took it to your dad with a strap-on!"
> "Fuck you, ya fucking loser. Still collecting birthday candles. Have some dignity and die already."

TYRANT

Lloyd charges Stan, who turns for the door, slamming it behind him as he beelines it to the blue van parked in the courtyard. The driver with a burning joint dangling from his mouth.

"I told you Grandpa was a freak."
"Go. Just go."

The driver spins his tires in reverse.

Heading to a hotel. Ocean breeze. To hell with these rich old cunts and their endless indulgence. Get the fuck out of the way and make room for the rest of us. Stan still buzzing from the adrenaline when his phone rings.

"Hello . . ."
"He wants your blood."
"Emma?"
"It's literal. Bone marrow too. Last month, a bomb planted by Kingdom destroyed the life-extension clinic carrying Mr. Blitzstein's account, which held stem cells from your mother's umbilical cord. When life extension became a feasible service, Mr. Blitzstein was too old. His stem cells were useless. Your grandmother was desperate for money at the time."
"How the fuck do you know all this?"
"Mr. Blitzstein is desperate to get back on the program but he needs a new supply. A new source. Although not ideal, given your age, you are his best option for a genetic match."
"When did he plan on mentioning this?"
"He wasn't. You were going to be administered a sedative during turkey dinner. Once you were unconscious, the medical team would arrive and take what they needed. You'd wake up and return home without knowing the difference. Your diet was a wrinkle we didn't foresee but there was always a contingency plan."
"What was that?"
"I was going to stab you with a needle."
"What the fuck? Why not ask? "
"His concern was extortion."
"Extortion?"

Propogation

"I'm diverting you from your route. No hotel. The driver's taking you directly to the airport. I'm sending you the new flight information."

"Fuck that. Fuck Lloyd. I have two nights left. Vacation starts now."

"Mr. Grindle, men with guns are looking for you."

"Then I need to call the police."

"That's who I'm referring to. They're on his payroll."

"Why the warning? What's your angle?"

"I'm in line to inherit his fortune."

"Is that what he told you?"

"I was there when his lawyer drew up the document. Lloyd was very emotional that night. I'd saved his life during dinner. He was choking on a piece of steak fat. I gave him the Heimlich maneuver."

In and out of traffic. Cutting through alleyways. Sticking to side roads. Then the highway. Finally arriving at the airport. Sweating bullets, Stan clears customs. An hour later, he's in the air. Four connecting flights before the final descent. Sayonara, Lloyd. Stan gives him three months. No way he lasts past six at his absurdly advanced age. Without treatment, the rate of decline will accelerate exponentially towards its inevitable conclusion. Stan imagines Lloyd wasting away. Clinging to life support with an ICU setup in his bedroom. Surrounded by a team of nurses and doctors trying to stave off death one more day, one more hour, while the girls flip listlessly through glossy fashion magazines by the pool.

Wake to winter. Back to work. The tank is empty. Berta dead and gone. He arrived at work one morning and found her floating upside down. Arrangements made. Stan facilitates the arrival of another eel. Textbook transfer. Prod the beast. Accept the charge. All systems go. From one chum block to the next. Today assimilated by tomorrow.

The traffic is killing him. Not just a euphemism. It's twisting his soul and hardening his arteries. Heart attack. Stroke. Cancer. What's it going to be? Exasperation. Anger. Rage. Stabbing headache as he idles on the overpass.

Heater cranked. Still cold. Staring at rows of vehicles stretching into the frozen horizon as far as he can see. A pale sun rises.

Punch in. Punch out. Thirty-six minutes until the end of his shift. The headache persists. Too much coffee. Not enough sleep. Slouched over in his chair, Stan massages his temples, trying to alleviate the pressure.

Outside, it's still snowing. Sore throat. His mouth feels phlegmy. Tries to spit and it catches on the collar of his jacket. Stan wipes it off with his glove and grabs the ice scraper from the trunk of his car.

Grinding through gridlock. Cursing every minute of it. Stan pulls into his parking garage three hours after leaving work. His headache now blinding. He leaves the lights off in his apartment. Lying down in bed, he curls up in the fetal position. Presses his palms into his eye sockets, trying to alleviate the pressure. It's a pulsing, crushing pain, with no end in sight. After an hour, it still hasn't subsided. Something's wrong. Desperate for relief, he digs through his wallet and finds the card and places the call.

"Hello, you've reached Harmony: piano tuning and repair."

He recognizes the voice as Artie's.

"I need to see the sirens."
"May I ask who's speaking?"
"Stan Grindle."
"Sorry, Mr. Grindle. They're in a refractory period. We're not taking appointments until next month."
"Please . . . if there's any way. I'm in serious pain. A fucking migraine . . . a brain tumour . . . I don't know but I'm desperate."
"I suggest you see a doctor."
"Fuck that. Need something stronger."
"Mr. Grendel . . . it sounds like you're in a bad way, so I'll make the exception just this once."
"Thank you, Artie. Thank you."
"The address is 606 Crescent Street."

Propogation

The driver notifies him they've arrived. Still battling a pulsing headache, Stan opens his eyes and takes out his wallet. The small house is a relic from the past squeezed in between two giant cubist structures. Mechanized mansions. Stan walks the cracked pathway. A narrow-shovelled strip through the snow to the front door. The roof is new on the house but that's about it. Paint is peeling off the siding. Dirty window awnings weighed down by the snow. His arrival sets off a series of squawks and barks from inside. Artie opens the door dressed in baggy brown slacks and a tan turtleneck sweater. There's a hole in one of his black socks right between the middle and ring toe. A gnarled-looking bulldog stands guard by his feet, while a blue macaw flares its wings and hisses behind them.

> "Thaddeus! Kratos! Be quiet! Excuse them, they're not used to guests. Please come in. Keep your shoes on."

Shelves of dusty books line the walls of the living room, with more books stacked in piles on the floor. Stan follows Artie through the kitchen, where a dishwasher from another era chugs and churns. Artie grabs a flashlight from the kitchen drawer and opens the door to the basement, blocking the bulldog by gently nudging him back with his foot.

> "No, boy. We won't be long. Guard the front door."

Kratos flies onto the kitchen counter, perching by the sink. His wings still flared. Shifting from one foot to the other. Artie turns on the flashlight, making his way down the darkened staircase.

> "Please close the door behind you."

Stan closes it. The noise from the dishwasher drops off as the narrow staircase creaks with each step. Reaching the cracked concrete foundation, Stan's eyes are drawn to a collection of glowing blue petri dishes. Artie walks past them, turning on selected lamps, illuminating multiple terrariums scattered around the room resting on shelves, dressers, and the floor. Each light reveals more. Every wall, including the ceiling, has been painted with black sound sealant. At the back of the basement, there's a mattress with ruffled bedsheets on the floor. In the opposite corner, the mixing board and siren tank still draped in black velvet.

"You sleep down here?"

"I've always slept in the basement. Keeps me cool in the summer."

Artie rolls out the pink recliner from a storage area beside the washer and dryer.

"Please take a seat."

Stan lies back in the recliner, massaging his temples.

"How much will this cost me?"

"We can discuss that afterwards. I can see you're in active pain so let's see if it offers you any relief."

"Ballpark."

"Free. This one's free."

"No. I'll pay. I'll pay. Just need an idea on the price point."

"Like I said, this one's free. I hope it helps."

"Thank you, sir. Thank you."

Artie moves behind ground control. Makes the necessary adjustments. Tweaking levels. Turning dials.

"Alright, Mr. Grindle, headphones on."

"Please, call me Stan."

"Alright, Stan, same as last time. I'll cue you with a music note and you hum it back into the microphone."

Stan goes through the scales.

"Okay, we've got what we need. Once again, you're going to hear three beeps to cue the response—"

"Wait . . . wait . . . before we go can I see them?"

The question hangs in the air.

"Some things are best left to the imagination."

"No. Not for me. Do you mind? Is that possible?"

Artie takes a moment to consider the request. Nods. Removes his headphones and proceeds to turn off each lamp until they're left in complete darkness.

Propogation

"Alright, Mr. Grindle, are you ready for the grand reveal?"
"As I'll ever be."

Artie pulls back the curtain. Glowing pink floating in black. A complex network of veins and nerves endings. They push off the glass with their tendrils, slowly rotating around each other.

"Wow . . . that's . . . Where did you find them?"
"Arctic expedition. I scraped their remains off the ice and cultivated them in my basement."
"What do you feed them?"
"A customized spray solution, which they absorb through their skin along with specific sound vibrations that stimulate cellular replication."
"Are there others?"
"None that I'm aware of."
"Why do you keep them behind the curtains?"
"They're sensitive to light. Shall we proceed?"
"Yes. Of course. Thank you."
"Very well, then."

Artie covers the sirens and turns on a lamp beside ground control.

"Three beeps will cue their response. Lean back and enjoy the ride."

The sirens seek. See. Tangled knots. Kinked cords. Twisted tension. Blinded and bonded. From restriction to release. Thaw. Melt. Whisper. Giggle. Roll. Shimmer. Shine. Swoosh . . . Soar. Shuttering horizons. Project. Ascend . . . Eject. Piercing pain. The sirens are screaming. Shrieking. Shattered as the needle stabs the stomach. Blood rushes the chamber. Extraction. Men in black ski masks rush up the stairs. Spent shell casings. Artie on the floor. Face down. Dead. Four exit wounds out the back. Dog whining by his side. Parrot squawking from the stairs. Glass fragments on a blood-soaked rug. Brain matter. Sirens silenced.

Dragging himself up the stairs when emergency response arrives. Stan answers every question then answers them again. Lloyd's responsible for this. Knows he sent them. Artie an innocent bystander. He explains the entire backstory to the investigating officers. They ask he not contact Mr. Blitzstein unless directed otherwise.

Sick leave. The first of his tenure. Incapacitated. Blinds drawn. Bedridden. He should be dead. Dead like Artie. Bullet in the head. Grandpa got his precious fucking stem cells. Why spare his life? Why leave loose ends? A contingency plan? Is he worried the lab might get torched again? Bullshit. The answer arrives via text. A selfie of Lloyd with four bikini-clad young women, surrounding him in his hot-top with the caption:

> Meet the new recruits! Not one a day over twenty-five! Feeling like I could live another hundred years! By the way, I had to fire Emma. Treacherous cunt.

To gloat. The piece of shit kept him alive to gloat.

Four weeks later. The sirens still screaming. Won't stop. His phone flashing in the dark. Another text alert. It's Emma:

> Lloyd's dead. Drive-by shooting on his way to the gym.

Who the hell knows. Stan doesn't bother replying.

Over a month now. His health continuing to deteriorate. System starving. Living on sips of water. Stagnation is taking its toll. Stan's lower back ratchet-tight. Suddenly, violent cramping seizes both legs. Feels likes his hamstrings are about to snap. Grunting and growling through the pain. Forced to his feet. Desperate to get the blood flowing. Screaming as he shuffles forward to his dresser, leaning against it until, mercifully, the cramping subsides.

Showered and dressed, Stan sits on the edge of his bed. The alarm on his phone goes off and he smashes it against the wall. Five minutes after forcing back a bottle of Norgesta for breakfast, he rushes to the toilet and pukes it out. Thirty minutes into his commute to work, traffic slows to a crawl then grinds to a halt. Trapped. Choked. Immobilized by anger, Stan turns on the radio. Traffic and news: construction closures, election analysis, market reports, more lies, then a blurb about a dead Sasquatch. Koyah has left his cage. Confirmation.

Employee parking. Dark skies cover the gold between the grid. Stan waits for the sun to slip below the horizon. Not stopping at his locker, he drives the

Propogation

forklift straight to his station. The eel hovers idly at the bottom of the tank. No name for it yet. No need. Stan walks up the ramp and steps to the edge. The refraction from the overhead lights distort the image below. Stan steps over. He feels the water stir underneath him. Any second now—

QUICK SLICE

The wolves chase down the deer
Exhausted, it falls
The wolves tear in
When does the deer go numb?
Where does it go?
Watch the eyes
When it's done
The starving children swarm the carcass to feed on what's left
Wrapping scraps of meat in dusty bandanas
something for later
We leave
They follow
Tracking us
These children are dangerous
They do work for evil men in order to survive
The little girl with cloudy eyes
Damage
or
defect
Either way
Partially blind
Carrying her mother's mummified head in a tote bag
So it goes
From the woods
into the streets
A seamless transition

TYRANT

At the margins
they continue to gather
Desperate
Damned
The impoverished smell an opportunity
We are not welcome
We are prey until proven otherwise
Moving on
I'm not here to negotiate for their acceptance
Stay if you want
I'm not
Keep walking
Up the road I ask for directions
Nothing down there
but you can grab a slice by the brewery
near the piers
A pop-up cafeteria of sorts
welded into a sea can
serving steaming trays of pizza
Gooey cheese
glistening grease
on
quality dough
Sun out
The staff happy to see me
Ready to serve
Two slices with a cold can of Coke
Deal
Ham and pineapple
Pepperoni and mushroom
Five dollars in my pocket
More than enough

THE TWINS

Bullet points. Harbin has an inkling of how it works, a rough outline, but ultimately no idea. First, they find the pulse. Initiation. The twins, acting as scouts, are strapped into separate spheres that map their biometry while acting as transceivers for energy forms. Once situated inside their respective spheres, the twins receive a target controlled intravenous infusion (tciv) of hallucinogenic plant alkaloids. Because this patented chemical composite has no subjective tolerance, pharmacokinetic modelling can predict the absorption, distribution, metabolism, and excretion of the drug over time, thus allowing transport to dictate the depth and duration of the experience. The drug designed to perturb the brain, melting formed patterns of the cortical mosaic, obliterating the scout's reality, allowing them to receive and inform the construction of alternate world models.

When the infusion is administered, the spheres are submerged into the black water contained in the monolithic natatorium. Then the giant swimming pool is inundated with energy transfers propagated through multiple waveguides collectively known as the organ. The water is the membrane/medium/messenger/map. From there, transport waits for a ping—any disturbance in the medium that registers with the twins. That ping is a signal. This isolated signal has a sound. The sound has a vibration. The vibration imprints on the membrane. Visible sound through cymatics. Resonant frequencies on display.

Symbols. Signs. Direction. Every vibrating molecule of sound contains all the information that exists in the trillions of other molecules in the sound wave. The wave is also a bubble, blip, dot, monad. Dots on the membrane reveal the field. Extreme geometrical patterns. Floating mandalas. Gating information. Guidance. Coding. Markers made and mapped.

Full circle. Frequency reveals form. That form has a frequency. Frequency equals location. Locate the frequency—create the form. Once transport knows the coordinates, they need to pierce the veil. Access to extract. A barrier to entry which only the mirror twins can cross. Tuning forks which act as anchors. A recognized resonance. Each twin possessing a cast/mold/cavity of the other's tuning fork. One goes. The other stays.

No injection needed. Lowered back down into the dark water. It's timber and tone. Call and response. Corollary chambers. Beacons. Create the connection. Secure the link. Shared breath. Conjoined realities.

Trade route established. The floodgates open and the dark water flows into the second pool where a third sphere is introduced. Contained in the third sphere is a wave rendering of the structure or body that needs to be shipped. Its physical form contained in the ever-expanding hull. As the dark water flows, circulating between the two pools, one twin reads the rendering and communicates it to the other. Conception equals perception. Vice versa. Eventually a transport base is built on the other side and structures/bodies can be sent back.

That's A.L.L (Arrive. Location. Link). Those ready to make the leap are assured the technology is securely rooted in hard science. Having no idea their foray into the unknown is entirely dependent on source. Fallible human resource. The tech does not exist without the twins. Their extra-sensory perception an essential component that's intangible. Not many would make the leap of faith knowing their safe transport was dependant on transceivers compromised of flesh and bone.

Once again, it's all about perception. The twins possessing retro cognition, access to what ancient Indian texts called the "Akashic records." Knowledge of the hidden or distant through superphysical faculty. A hyperdimensional heritage. Living testaments to the non-local nature of human consciousness. Granted the ability to discern what 99.9 percent of the populace cannot. At least in their lifetime. Of course, there are other gifted relations—siblings, twins, mirror twins, in fact—but none has shown the proven potential of Sky and Pearl.

Upon their retirement from active duty, the institute intends to introduce them to other participants of the program, hoping they can teach or transfer their gift. Somehow expediate/awaken/amplify the abilities of the

The Twins

others. This could, of course, be wishful thinking but that is the intention. Right now, the priority is Pearl's health. She has exhaustion. Blurred vision. Headaches. Presenting symptoms but nothing conclusive.

The twins' intrinsic value to the institute means their biometrics are closely monitored. Any issues or concerns are immediately addressed. Pearl and Sky are the anchors and access to Rexen's most difficult and distant fields of exploration. Per usual, and in perpetuity, there is work to be done. Make hay while the sun shines. In this case, the sun is represented by the twins, who are approaching seventy. Considering their age, there's a driving imperative to breach the veil and extract what's available with the time available. Therein lies the rub.

As biological beings, there are limitations to what their physical forms can carry. The current field, their focus for a decade, has caused them both considerable strain. Pushed to their breaking point to find it. The initiation an ordeal for both. The disturbance a traumatic discovery. Cortisol levels off the charts. Shell-shocked when they brought them back. Tremors, confusion, nightmares, impaired sight and hearing. Both twins completely dysregulated. Painful to witness. It took months of biofeedback therapy and psychotherapy before they could return to work and secure the connection. Treatments continuing over the course of the project with Pearl's condition deteriorating in recent months. A most pressing concern.

There have been talks of suspending transport on the project and the logistics involved. The operation already beset by recent tragedies. Two staff suicides within a week of each other. Followed by a blowout at one of the drilling sites, resulting in eighteen casualties amongst the injured. To suspend transport now would add considerable distress to a demoralized workforce. Coupled with the fact that those outside the inner sanctum will have no idea why, which inevitably leads to wild speculation. An official statement is currently being conceived and drafted in the event it's needed.

Cued up. Harbin views the video. Played back. Barely perceptible. A shudder. Twitching. Then still. Sky wakes from her sleep. Wails in pain. Wounded. Knows her sister's gone without looking. Crosses the room. Crawls into bed with her. Rocking. Weeping. Pearl dead. Suffered a stroke in her sleep. Sky inconsolable. Closed off. Shut down.

TYRANT

Weeks removed. Sky refusing to communicate. Stopped eating. Harbin can see the anger simmering in her grief. Won't look at them. Distant glare. Tears still streaming down her face. Leaking. Must tread lightly. So much at risk and she holds all the cards. Access to other realities, entire planes of existence lost should she refuse to participate. Right now, it's a rescue mission. Field 0-1259 is the priority. People first, then the product. Early test trials proved in some instances the viewer could connect to a location (once mapped) without a transmitting agent.

Possible but nothing of this magnitude. Conjuring a field from a mind-boggling distance/depth on her own likely too much to ask. If that won't work, they'll try installing another agent at either end, hoping Sky's willing and able to work with them. Failure a horrifying prospect. To permanently lose the connection would be devastating. Thousands of workers trapped on site. Their bodies in this realm locked in the hull. Warehoused with a vast armoury of supplies, weapons, and machinery. They can pull their inventory, the hardware, from the hull but the people won't work. Sentient beings get cooked. Fries their wiring. The fracture sends their nervous system into chaos. Signals misfire, splinter, until it shorts out. Cardiac arrest. Seizures. Death. Unavoidable at this point. Consciousness requires a connection, a conduit, to be reintroduced. The vessel can't handle the disruption. Rexen has managed to contain the news for now but in a matter of weeks another wave of workers is scheduled to return after completion of contract. Family members ready to welcome them home after a yearlong absence.

Today. Harbin wakes up rested. Make it happen. Running out of time. Almost a month without communications, with scheduled arrivals end of week. If command has managed to keep it quiet, they won't be able to much longer. People are going to demand answers when it's time to go back. They can only stall for so long. How do they quell the dissent? The panic? What's that look like? Harbin goes over his presentation, his pitch, during the drive into work. Must plead, persuade, beg Sky to get back in her sphere. She can't leave them there. Not an option. Needs to snap out of it. A massive ask, all things considered.

Born seventeen minutes apart. Sky the older sister. Doting and fiercely protective of Pearl from their formative years onwards. Consoled her during

The Twins

periods of crippling depression and reined her in during manic outbursts. Sky the steady hand, as it were. Pearl, in turn, providing her unique blend of sweetness and humour with a streak of mischief. Flights of fancy that were endlessly entertaining for Sky. Always an eager participant, as children, in the next play or project. A wonder to watch their interactions. Finishing each other's sentences aloud, then continuing their conversation in private with thought transference. Seamlessly going back and forth. In some instances, you could understand the switch, why they'd keep certain subjects confidential; other times, it seemed completely arbitrary, as though unaware they were doing it. Unconcerned about communicating out loud or "in person." So why not pick a lane? One of many mysteries regarding the mirror twins.

They were in the corporation's custody since age six. Agents scouring key sectors with directives from R&D when the twins were discovered by happenstance. Grandmother had purchased another mountain range (river valley included) and a security battalion was tasked with removing vagrant sects from said mountains. Evicting them from the coniferous forest where they found the malnourished twins, living on dirt floors, under tarp and tree with their mother, who was sick with fever and in no condition to relocate. Each twin possessing the striking feature of different coloured eyes. Blue—brown. Brown—blue. Mirrored heterochromia. Reflections. Carrying over to the cowlicks on the back of their heads. Inversed. Running clockwise on one, counterclockwise on the other. This trait continuing with gestures and movements. One twin right-handed, the other left-handed. The entire battalion was struck by the curiosity.

Commander Dacey Glatt, in charge of carrying out the eviction order, empathized with the family's plight and made the decision to bring them back to base, where the mother could be treated by private medical staff and her twins attended to until she was capable of providing care. The other itinerants were flushed out and rounded up to be brought by bus to the drop site, an abandoned air hangar, for state officials to process. The twins and their mother to travel with Commander Glatt in his armoured personnel carrier.

In transit, Glatt's insight on the situation changes when Sky remarks that Pearl is sick. Looking back from the front passenger seat, he sees the little girl is looking green. Her mother is sleeping. Glatt instructs the driver to pull over and notifies the rest of the convoy to continue without.

TYRANT

Parked on the side of the road, tractor trailers roaring by, Staff Sargent Ty Percy helps Pearl out of the APC. Walking her away from the road to the guardrail. Seconds later, Sky announces, "Snake," from inside the APC. Glatt again looks back from the passenger seat. Sees no snake or anything resembling a snake in the vehicle. With deadpan delivery, Sky then reports, "Weak words."

The commander is confused, having no idea what any of this is in reference to, when Pearl and Sargent Percy return to the APC. Percy confirms Pearl threw up but is feeling much better, with brief mention of a garter snake that slithered past his boot by the guardrail. Giving him a good jump. When asked by Commander Glatt if he used "weak words" in response to being startled, Sargent Percy admits Pearl may have heard some profanities.

The successful eviction and coinciding discovery are communicated to Grandmother, who's flown in from her yacht to meet the twins. Aware of the anomaly, she plans to test it for herself. Promising the twins they'll see their mother as soon as she's better. In the meantime, Grandmother suggest they play a game. A guessing game to win a prize. The prize being two pocket-sized animatrons. If they can guess what the tiny spheres, intricately etched in gold and silver, turn into, they get to keep them. The twins are intrigued. Both agree.

The game goes as follows: One twin stands in the corner wearing a blindfold while the other watches the sphere reveal its form. The blindfolded twin then has to guess what it is. Each takes a turn. Both twins have to guess correctly to win.

Sky goes first. Stands in the corner. Grandmother ties her blindfold. Turns to Pearl, standing in the opposite corner, and rolls the sphere across the floor towards her. The sphere pops open, revealing a dancing skeleton. Pearl watches transfixed while the skeleton shakes it bones before curling up. Grandmother asks Sky for her answer. Slight pause.

"Dancing skeleton."

Grandmother removes the blindfold. Correct. Applauds. The sisters switch corners. Pearl up next. Grandmother ties her blindfold and rolls the sphere to Sky. The animatron unlocks into a praying mantis, rocking back and forth

The Twins

with its front legs raised, ready for battle, before tucking back into a sphere. Grandmother asks Pearl for her answer. Pearl hesitates before answering.

"Angry insect."

Sky jumps in to clarify.

"Praying mantis."

Grandmother laughs.

"Close enough."

Another round of applause. Everyone a winner.

Attached to the institute. Embedded in limestone cliffs. The twins' living quarters an impressive space. Open concept. Fifteen thousand square feet with high ceilings. The kitchen and bathroom are insular mobile units that can be moved by remote or forklift, if need be. Mobile VR walls create space within the space. The structural walls painted pastel yellow, adorned with artwork: paintings, signs, symbols, maps, tribal and native masks collected over the years. Their beds are at opposite ends of the room beside the window with the panoramic view of the river canyon. Each bed surrounded by a cluster of dressers, cabinets, display cases and stands containing clothing, books, artifacts, and oddities. Collections of comic books, postage stamps, seashells, snail shells, fishing lures, crystals, stones, mounted insects, petrified wood, animal skulls, bones, bird feathers, match books, and old automatons. Most of which have been removed. Walls now bare. Sky on suicide watch. Administered feedings. Nor forced down her throat through a feeding tube.

No permission. No choice. Harbin overrides the lock with an emergency access code. Gains entry. Sky still in bed, staring blankly out the window. The creek, twisting and turning as it makes its way through the bedrock layer to the window's focal point—a cascading waterfall dropping down from a height of forty metres. Crystal clear in the fall with a light shade of turquoise during the summer months. As young girls, the twins talked aloud to the waterfalls. Had a name for it. Foss. Affectionately called Fossy. Active imaginations, childhood games, or a genuine communion. One never knows with the twins.

Harbin breaks the ice.

"Good morning, Sky."

Ignored.

"I imagine you know why I'm here."

Allows a moment. Continues.

"Pearl's death is a profound loss. None of us can speak to your pain, but there's the unavoidable and urgent matter of field Twelve-Five-Nine. Thousands of workers are trapped onsite. Many of them expecting to return home at the end of the week. Families eagerly awaiting their arrival after a yearlong absence. To deny that, to break our contract, would cause a considerable amount of distress for everyone involved."

Sky still staring out the window. Yet to acknowledge his presence.

"Liability waivers. Assuming they signed them."

Rattled by her cold-blooded response.

"My concern is not for the company. That's not what this is about. It's the personnel. The people and their families. Almost a month without communications. Completely cut off. No idea what's happening. What's their reaction going to be when they find out they're not going home? It's hard to quantify the concern, the panic, that will cause."
"Rexen should have brought them back when it had the chance. You knew she was unwell."
"Unwell, yes, but it was not—"

Harbin takes a beat. Collects himself.

"Her death took everyone by surprise."
"You knew what was at risk and continued to ignore the warnings."
"You say 'you' as though it was my decision?"
"Speaking broadly. The company. The collective. I know your word carries no weight in these matters."

The Twins

Distracted through dinner. Reading to the kids on autopilot. Tucks them into bed. Time with the wife. Watch fail videos. Easy entertainment. Lights out. Can't sleep. Sky's comment still stings. Cut him open. Can feel her disdain. Not his choice. Can't select your bloodline. A child when his mother died. Killed in a plane crash. His father a fuckup. Coward. Started smoking shale. Junkie addict. Shell of a human being. Hidden away. Out of view. Brother Harrod the chosen one. Illuminated. Broken. Both. Handpicked by Grandmother. Lucy's heir apparent. Different dimensions of psychopathy. Equally ruthless. Cold. Calculated. Each with their own method of attack. Harrod has you on your heels immediately. Feel the chill when he steps in the room. Attacks with surgical precision. No time wasted. Lucy displays warmth, conveys empathy, makes one feel special before chopping their head off. All business but not in the way most imagine. Money is meaningless at this stage. Transcended those trappings long ago. All about assets. Currency. Conduction. The transfer—capture—crystallization of energy in all forms. Relentless consumption.

What Sky said is true. He has no say in such matters. Errand boy. Messenger. Mascot at meet-and-greets. Intermediary for the twins his true assignment. Which lands him somewhere between chaperone, corrections officer, and paid informant. Was conflicted at first. Harboured resentment. Felt like a fraud. Not a real job. Handout. Grandmother placating him. Insisting it's an essential role. The twins a critical component of power. Transport the crown jewel of the corporation. Can't trust anyone else with such responsibility. Not sure the twins would allow it. Handpicked for the position. She could see it when he was a child. How much joy he brought them. The way they laughed. Smiled. Acting as surrogate mothers, sisters, aunts. They'd read to him. Watch movies together. Make meals. Draw. Paint. Arts and crafts. When he was hurt, they'd heal him. Lift his spirits. The twins folded into the family. Taken on vacation. An integral part of his childhood. In many ways, the best part. Felt safe around them. Protected. Connected. Loved their walks through the wildlife. Camping. Blissfully unaware there was always a security perimeter around them. Control. Which brings it back around. Lucy. Harrod. They make the decisions. Difficult ones. Excruciating. Knows his role and accepts it. What they do. What they've done. To reside over this entity. This egregore. Impossible to convey what they're beholden to. Now and then he gets a glimpse, insight into its internal operations, and has to look away. Deny. Distract. Has his own family. Daughter. Son. Wife. For that bond, for this life, he's eternally grateful. It's how he came to terms with his placement inside the company. Acceptance. As long as his loved ones are provided for, he can find peace. He doesn't require external validation, and employment outside of Rexen isn't an option. Not really. Everything kept in house. If he chose to strike out on his own, to separate from the establishment, their response, what that looks like, is another discussion entirely.

Arrives at work. Hoping for good news but there's none to be had. The other scouts can't find field 0-1259. Unable to key the coordinates. Sky remains their only hope and that's still a stretch. Odds are she can't do it without Pearl. Together it was taxing. Took its toll. The full extent they may never know. Has to try, though. Too many lives lost without. Unbearable tragedy. She won't allow it. Knows she won't. Sky is hurt. Healing. Let her regain strength and there's a remote chance she can restore the link. Ready to adopt a shift in strategy. Time. This will take time and everyone needs to come to terms with that. His heart goes out to the families awaiting arrival but it's not something they can force.

Harbin parks the buggy outside her room. Enters the emergency access code. Sky hasn't moved. How it looks. Still staring out the window. Defeated. Detached. Broken. Resigned. All of the above. Missing something. What is it? What's the word? Not anger. Knows that's there. What's he looking at? Move on. Focus. Makes his presentation. Plead his case.

"Morning, Sky."

Not a passing glance.

> "I wanted to apologize for the way we've approached things. Obviously, the recovery of Twelve-Five-Nine is a pressing concern for the company but it's not something we can force."
> "Like the gruel that was forced down my throat."
> "I assure you that's the last thing anyone wanted to do. You hadn't eaten in weeks. Muscle wasting was setting in. All your charts were off and getting worse. Was for your own well-being. We had to intervene."

The Twins

"You didn't have to do anything."

Making it personal. Won't take the bait.

"Maybe a change of scenery is the right idea. Take a trip to one of the islands. White sand, blue water, soak up the sun. Time to heal. Recharge."

"Then what?"

"We don't need to answer that right now."

"I do."

"Full transparency, I'm hoping you'll return to work. Help us re-establish Twelve-Five-Nine. Secure the link long enough to rescue the workers. Bring them home to their families."

"Then what?"

"That's the imperative. Our primary focus."

"Then what?"

"You tell me."

"Retirement. Release. Dissolve the conservatorship. Transfer the trust into my control. Full autonomy. I want nothing to do with you and your ilk."

Outright rejection. Decades denied. His childhood. The twins helped raise him. Roles reversed. Became their caretaker. Ambassador. Tried to address every concern. Caught in the middle of an impossible situation. Now Sky blames him for Pearl's death. Not right. Not fair. He tried. Told them she needed a break. Insisted. Overruled. Ignored. Now he's being punished. The blame more than he can bear. Awful. Pronounced depression. Pulled down. Cried when Pearl died. Wept. Gutted by the loss. "You and your ilk?" What's that mean? Family. They're family. Can't end like this.

Chain of command. Into the tomb. Harbin's term for Harrod's office. Sees him standing behind the tablets. Dark brown hair slicked back, with a pronounced widow's peak. Tall. Lean. High cheekbones. Alabaster skin. Dark circles under dark brown eyes. Near black. Plugged in. Fed. Composing from a palette of data points. Isolating. Integrating. Analyzing all outcomes before the list goes out. A set of instructions. Targets of opportunity: mergers and acquisitions. Followed by redundancies. Where to trim the fat. Remove dead weight. Cutback. Lay off. Dismiss.

"What's required."

Dry delivery. Question, statement, greeting rolled into one.

"Sky is willing to enter the sphere and attempt to reconnect with Twelve-Five-Nine."
"Great."

Harrod swiping and scanning tablets. Yet to make eye contact.

"On the condition we guarantee her release."
"Release from what?"
"From our custody, from her contract, with full control of their trust."
"Into what?"
"The world. A life outside the institute."
"No. She's a danger to herself and others."
"Then we've lost Twelve-Five-Nine."
"Nothing's lost."
"You know what I mean. The link is lost. We're locked out."

Harrod scrolling through data. Harbin waiting for response. Continues.

"What are we doing? What are we telling the families?"
"I'll draft something up. Unforeseen tragedy . . . great loss . . . time of pain . . . sacrifice will not be forgotten . . . Rexen stands by the families in their time of need . . . full support . . . furthermore . . . something something, et cetera. We suspend production. Cut our losses. Recalibrate. Go back when another set of scouts can secure the link. Found it once. We'll find it again. Recently acquired another pair of mirror twins, brother and sister, that's very promising. Their metrics are off the charts. We'll be integrating them into the program in short order. Based on our projections, ten years is a realistic time frame. Lines up with the development curve."
"So, our staff, workers, personnel, people, people with families, spend a decade in the hull trapped on that fucking dust bowl."

The Twins

"Terraforming. Not the original intention but the infrastructure is there. So's the ability. The base hosting a vast array of skillsets. Barring unforeseen circumstance, the likelihood of survival is quite good."

"If there's a chance to bring them back now, it's what we need to do."

"We don't accept ultimatums."

"We just implement and enforce them."

"Correct."

"How are we explaining this to the families without disclosing transport operations?"

"Well, we can't. Patented. Protected. State security."

"So, what are we saying happened to them?"

"Gone. Lost."

"But nothing's lost, right?"

"They are. As far as their families are concerned. Regarding why . . . let's say . . . mechanical failure of some sort. A breach. Possible sabotage. Integrate it with another narrative. Pin it on resistance groups, perhaps. Point being, there's options."

"To be clear, we're telling the families their loved ones are dead."

"Lost. In good conscience . . . full transparency . . . likelihood of recovery . . . suspending rescue operations . . . roll it out in stages."

"String them along."

"A month or two. Gauge response. Pivot where we need to."

"Bring Sky back. Let her work. Let her go."

"She has no leverage. We're not a charity."

"We're liable to the workers and their families."

"They signed waivers."

"Morally."

Harrod turns away from the tablets. Directs his attention to Harbin. Amused.

"Free will. They can fight us in court."

"Where we crush them with our armada of lawyers funded by an inexhaustible reserve."

"Now you're getting it."

"You're fucked."

"I'm family"

"Fuck you."

"We'll negotiate a settlement. Each family will receive more than any one employee could earn in their career span."

"The money doesn't matter."

"Never has."

"You know what I mean. The pain and suffering—"

"And we'll eat that too. Step off your soapbox, I've seen where you live. What the uninitiated imprints on us does not matter. Let them lap up their tragedy. Victims. They love that role. An easy out."

"Brother . . ."

"Yes."

"What . . . what are we doing? What's the point?"

Harrod locks in.

"That's the point. There is none. Eat. The whole system is parasitic. Inverted. Constantly chewing up and spitting out energy. An endless cycle of torture and pleasure from the intake and expelling of energy. Understand?"

"No."

"That's why you're weak. Erase your empathy. When compassion and conscience are killed, we can devour, swell, expand."

"I . . . what do I say to that?"

"Nothing. Indulge. Enjoy."

"Harrod."

"Yes."

"I'm going to Grandmother on this."

"Of course you are."

Touchdown. Harbin boards Abraxas, an amalgamation of a mega yacht and battleship. The massive dreadnought built for pleasure but ready for war.

The Twins

Over a thousand crew members operating at the behest of Grandmother. Lucy Menk. Wide-brimmed straw sunhat with a black ribbon and Wayfarer shades. Approaching in her motorized wheelchair from outside the safe zone of the heliport. Took to the chair recently. On regenerative therapy for decades until she decided to stop. Allowing the encroachment of age while preparing Harrod for succession. One could argue he already runs the company, but Lucy still holds the crown, rarely intervening in its operation, but her word is final. In that, there's no debate. Over a year since Harbin last saw her. Skin looks thinner. Drier. More cross-hatching. Wrinkles. Age spots. A few strands of black hair but mostly grey now. Lucy smiles. Pearly whites. Bleached.

"Welcome aboard. How's my grandson?"
"I'm well."

Harbin leans in and gives her a hug. Can feel her spine, the sharp ridge of her scapula through her sweater. Controlled withdrawal but it's happening so fast. Might not seem so pronounced if he saw her every day. When Lucy announced her intentions to the family five years ago, she simply stated it was time and would happen "at a civilized pace." Slowly weaning herself off her injections. Said if she went cold turkey she wouldn't last the night, then burst out laughing, stating, "You have to laugh, don't you? How could you not?" with no need to clarify it was on the next order of business.

Cold beer, wagyu steak and snow crab with grilled vegetables for dinner. Grandmother has yet to mention the twins or Twelve-Five-Nine. Harbin tried to initiate the conversation earlier but she shut it down: "Later, dear, let's keep it light for dinner." They talk about the grandkids, their interests and development. Lucy questions when Harrod and his wife will start a family and why they haven't already done so. Then it drifts into the political arena and media. Lucy laughs at various caricatures they've selected and presented.

"Blatantly absurd. Amazed it still works. So painfully transparent. Like they want to be lied to. Something to complain about. Obfuscate their own responsibility while we serve up another scapegoat."

The serving staff clears their plates and Grandmother pulls a joint out from her arm rest.

"Shall we?"

Stoned. Very stoned. Uncomfortably so. Lucy seemingly unfazed. Wide awake. Wants to show him something. Lets her lead the way while he follows in the golf cart. Her chair can move faster than he can walk. Faster than he can run, for that matter. Pivots on a dime. Interfacing with the human motor cortex. Further than he remembered. The boat just keeps going. Abraxas designed to accept attachments, additions, extension. Grandma racing across the deck to the extension when the monolith comes into view. Black cube. Neon-red outline. Five minutes to reach the bow, or is it the stern? Not sure. Stars blazing bright. Clusters. Sound of the water rushing past. The giant giftbox at least fifty feet in height. Grandma outside of it. Parks the cart. On the approach, a door slides open. Seamless. Gone. Can't see the mechanism. One door leads to another. Down a short hallway. The last door drops into the floor, revealing the gift anchored onto a turntable. Slowly turning counterclockwise. Tip of the spear. A four-fletch broad arrow twisting into an inverted vortex. Like a drill bit carved from a giant chunk of bone. Buffed and polished with an iridescent shine. Edge to rounded edge, it's maybe thirty feet in diameter. Matched in height. Harbin stands back. Overawed by the object. Staggered. Grandmother answers before he asks.

"The Godhead."

Has a name. Now he needs the story.

> "From where? Who made this?"
> "Twelve-Five-Nine"
> "We found this?"
> "On arrival. Sticking out of the ground. Lopped the serpent's head off and brought it back. Cleaned and preserved. The crown of our accomplishments."

As he circles the skull, it feels as though it's shifting. Amorphous. The ridge resembling the bow of a boat. Cresting back like the nose of a hognose snake. A serrated scoop with three extended points. Spike, claw, shovel. All in one. Blunt but sharp. Searching for its eye sockets. Where's the mouth? Can't see a jaw. Grandmother pauses the rotation with a small remote that looks

The Twins

like a piece of black quartz. She drives under one of the arches at the base of the skull, stopping at the centre point, and turns to him.

"If you're searching for its eye sockets, they're under here."

Harbin steps inside the skull. Grandmother continues.

"We added recessed lighting. Tucked into the cavities. Those are the sockets. Housing an internal guidance system. Sensory detection of some sort. That's the understanding. Best guess, if we're being honest."

The ambient sound amplified. Multiple frequencies. Like stepping into a seashell. Soft roar. Sacred space. Cathedral. Cathode. Feels connected. Charged. Looking up at the complex channels and compartments configured in bone. Uplighting casting shadows on the contours. Six egg-shaped chambers shaped into the carapace. Glowing gold.

"No jawbone? Where's its mouth?"
"Doesn't have one."
"How does it eat?"
"Absorption."
"Of what?"
"Sound. Vibration."
"How?"
"Would you accept 'We're working on it'?"
"Of course . . . I'm just . . ."
"Amazed."
"Yeah."
"You can feel it?"
"I think so . . ."
"Grounded. Centred. Charged. Runs through your core."
"Yeah."
"The resonance carries through. That's the thread. Have you ever set foot in an anechoic chamber?"
"No."
"Do you know what it is?"
"A soundproof room."

"Designed to achieve complete silence by preventing the reflection of sound from the room boundaries. So quiet that after a short period of time, an inhabitant would be able to hear their heartbeat, their bones grinding, creaking. Eventually they'd lose their balance because the absolute lack of reverberation sabotages your spatial awareness. Whereas this space is the anchor. The anchor and the altar."

"Tuned in."

"Exactly!"

Grandmother claps her hand in delight. Holds them.

"Now let us discuss what brought you here."

Lucy leaves the skull. Parks by the fireplace. Harbin takes a seat on the sectional. The flickering flames cast shadows on Grandmother's face. Snake tongues.

"Now what's this about the twins and Twelve-Five-Nine?"

"Twin. Sky's our only shot at re-establishing the link. We've secured other fields with other scouts but this one's different. I can't say how these things are measured but let's just say it's too far."

"Whatever the case, she's refusing to do her job."

"Is that how you see it?"

"How else? She's paid a considerable sum to perform her duties as required."

"Her sister just died and—"

"As we do. I've treated the twins as though they were my own. Afforded them every luxury available to me."

"Except for their autonomy. Independence."

"That's not something you can grant or bestow upon a person."

"It is when you're their captor."

"Substitute captor with caretaker. Guardian. I pulled them out of despair and provided them with a life most dream of. Access. Privilege. They never went without."

"They weren't allowed to leave."

The Twins

"They had plenty of adventures on their own."

"Under your watch."

"Those two would have been eaten alive had we not found them. Their gift is a curse without the support structures we put in place. They simply do not have the coping mechanism to integrate within the social framework. They would have been preyed upon. Drug-addled and destitute. Would likely have committed suicide."

"You can't make that claim."

"I just did."

"Then what now? You don't believe Sky can survive on her own?"

"I do not."

"Then we failed them."

"There are forces you aren't aware of. She'd be in constant danger. Furthermore, she'd be a danger to herself."

"You don't know that."

"Set loose, Sky would be exposed to realities she could not compute. Far too much noise. Overwhelmed and undone. We provided the filter. She'd unravel otherwise."

"Then we help her integrate. Provide support. Create the framework for a structured release."

"Sky's welcome to leave. Show her the door. She'll be in breach of contract but that's fine. We'll freeze her trust so she can truly stand on her own."

"They've unlocked untold fortunes for you. Allowed us to seize wealth and resources we didn't know existed. Pushed them to their absolute limit in doing so. Pearl died. She died so we wouldn't slow down production."

"We don't know that."

"I do. I saw it. Watched her deteriorate and did nothing."

"You voiced your concern."

"And continued to drive her to a job that was killing her. Saw it sap her strength. Sat her in the sphere. Clipped her in. Have to stay on schedule, though, right?"

"Try providing for your family on your own, without our funding, if you're so ashamed. Then you can learn what it means to pick your poison."

Skewered. Swallows it down. Take his medicine. Not wrong. Not what he's here for.

"Twelve-Five-Nine. What are we doing?"

"It will be back online soon enough."

"'Soon enough' is not a unit of time we can present to the workers' families."

"Which is why I agree with Harrod. We must cut to the chase. Come clean, as it were. They're lost. Gone. Never to be found. A painful misfortune. Mishap. Mechanical malfunction combined with human error. The rarest of probabilities. An infinitesimal cross-section of occurrence. Couldn't repeat it if you tried. Almost as though it was meant to be. When a new crop of scouts rediscovers Twelve-Five-Nine, hopefully there's some survivors. A miracle to be had. Just in time for Christmas. Who knows. It might be the twins' progeny that make the discovery."

Twist in his stomach. Of course. Of course she would.

"You had their eggs harvested."

Question. Statement.

"Would be foolish not to. You must insure your investment. Unfortunately, none of their offspring have inherited their mothers' gift. We've tried a number of combinations to no avail. At first, we fertilized their eggs with the sperm of male viewers, hoping it would insure, if not amplify, their abilities. No luck. All duds. Subsequent variations were men without the 'gift' who possessed high intelligence, acuity, acumen. Then athletic specimens. Physically gifted. Followed by men with a bit of both. Then we tried the middle ground. Joe average. Below average results. Went so far as to fertilize their eggs with the sperm of a high-functioning schizophrenic. Still

> waiting to see how that one plays out. Early indicators aren't promising. Perhaps they'll manifest post puberty. A process of trial and error."
>
> "What do you . . . Where are they?"
>
> "Another institute. Foster care, of sorts. Some released into the general populace when there's nothing doing. Cut off but we still keep tabs. Tracked."
>
> "How much do they know?"
>
> "They know what we tell them. Ultimately, the program has been a disappointment but who's to say in this grand experiment we call life."
>
> "While Sky sits in her room."
>
> "If she's chosen to retire, we'll likely have to move her offsite. A slight downgrade from what they're accustomed to but still comfortable. Your title will be dissolved unless you want to shepherd the next set."

The matter closed. Sinks in. Total failure. Turns to the flame.

> "No right . . . We have no right—"
>
> "Honey, must you be so dramatic? I see you're suffering. I do. I know you mean well. I understand your intention. Unfortunately, it's a matter of perception and your perception is off."

Grandmother rotates her chair to face the Godhead.

> "Let us consider the dot, the line, and the circle. The dot is the most primitive and fundamental symbol. Draw a circle around the dot and you've created the symbol of the Godhead. The Godhead represents the portal of creation. Of light. In man, the spirit is represented by the dot. Conscious activity or intelligence depicted by the line. The circle a symbolic and literal interpretation of the infinite all. Consciousness belongs to the sphere of the dot. Activity to the sphere of the circle. The centre and the circumference thus blended in the connecting line. The circle is the symbol of body and body is the limit of the radius. The radius is

action. The power of the mind pouring out of the substance of consciousness."

No clue where this is going.

"The primordial symbols of the dot, line, and circle are set forth in the three spheres of Christian theology. The dot is symbolic of heaven, the line of earth, and the circle of hell. The Fall of Man is the descent down the ladder from the dot to the circumference. The resurrection and redemption of man is his return from the circumference to the dot. In Chaldaic Hebrew, the dot is the Yod, a symbol of the seed. A comma with a twisting tail representing the germ of the spirit. From the seed growing in the earth comes the sprig—the line. The line is growth. The motion of the dot. The sun is the monad of life. The great dot. Each of its rays a line. Its own active principle in manifestation. Do you know the astronomical symbol of the sun?"

Doesn't care.

"Is it a dot in a circle?"

Deadpan delivery. Lucy continues unabated.

"Indeed it is. The dot, moving away from the self, projects the line; the line becomes the radius of an imaginary circle, and this circle is the circumference of the powers of the central dot. Every sun has a periphery where its rays end, every human life a periphery where its influence ceases, every human mind a margin beyond which it cannot function, and every human heart a boundary beyond which it cannot feel."

No clue how any of this connects to the matter at hand.

"Somewhere there is a limit to the scope of awareness. The circle is the symbol of this limit. It is the symbol of the vanishing point of central energy. The dot is the first illusion of the self, the first limitation of space, life localized as a centre of power. The blank paper is life unlimited. The dot must sometime be erased because nothing but the blank paper is eternal."

"What's the takeaway?"

"The bird fights its way out of the egg. The egg is the world. Whoever will be born must destroy a world."

Futile. Any excuse to justify their actions. Ensure their order.

"When the impediments to personal power acquisition are removed, then devouring the life energies of other beings becomes easy. I grow strong as they become weak. I am capable of this because I do not experience their pain. I am numb to it. Initiated. You were spared. Which is why I'd suggest you appreciate your place in the hierarchy and leave it at that."

"Accept evil."

"Eat or die. It unites us all. 'Genesis 3:22: And the Lord God said, 'Behold, the man is become as one of us, to know good and evil: and now, lest he put forth his hand, and take also of the tree of life, and eat, and live forever.' Some may take that as a warning, others a challenge."

Lucy lifts her hand to the Godhead. Another trophy on display.

Harbin pours himself a drink in his cabin. Planned to spend the night and fly out in the morning. Regrets it now. Wants to leave. Home. Pilots likely sleeping. Considers waking them. Best leave them be. Steps onto the balcony. Stars above. Water below. Black. Rushing past. Another world under there. Alien. Hop the rail and it's over. Gone. How's that work? Treading water as the beast ship pulls away. Watch it recede into the night. How long before the sharks find him? Pulled under. Picked apart. Maybe not. Maybe hypothermia sets in first. Exhaustion. Looking up at the stars before his lungs fill with water. Spasms of pain, then peace. Out of body. His view expanding. Able to see in all directions as he watches himself sink. At what point does the spirit surrender? Let go? What's that feel like and where's it go? Harbin takes it another direction. Plucked out of the water by a rescue team. Pictures it. Scooped up. Dropped on deck. Looking like a drowned rat. Coughing up water when Grandmother wheels out. Shakes her head. Rolls her eyes. "Silly boy. Did I say you could die?" Harbin takes a sip of whiskey. Shakes his head.

"Oh, Grandmother . . . you evil witch."

Lucy gave the green light. Must have. Harbin watches the press release on the flight back. Harrod holding court at podium. Two days out from the scheduled arrivals of 0-1259. Pre-emptive. Appears shaken yet poised. Somber. Reverent. Has them on the hook. Eating out of his hand. Total performance. Insane how he can turn it off and on. Anything for the agenda. His brother the psychopath presented to the public as mystery man genius. The playboy philanthropist. Business savant and begrudging leader. Reluctant heir to the Menk family fortune. All so contrived but the press and public continue to lap it up. Everyone playing their role in this silly little script. Used and abused. A never-ending consolidation scheme. Anything excused for another acquisition. Rexen keeps it moving. Leads the way. Progress. Innovation. Accountability. These are the tenets. Total bullshit. Can't make things right but he can correct the course for his children. Starts now. Today. The bearer of bad news. No deflections. Nothing to hedge. Own it.

No pass code required. Sky out of bed. Facing the falls. Standing in tree pose dressed in a hooded black jogging suit. Harbin stops at the centre of the room.

> "I spoke to Harrod and Lucy. They won't release the trust. You're to remain under conservatorship so long as they deem you a danger to yourself and others."

Sky relaxes the pose. Switches legs. Holds. Responds

> "There're two letters on my bedside desk. I wrote them in crayon because my pens and pencils were taken away. Please deliver them in person to ensure they're received."

Harbin picks up the letters. The names are written in Sky's handwriting.

Vultures circling outside his office window. Something dead or dying below the canopy. Harbin takes a seat behind his desk. Stares at the unsealed envelopes. Did she forget or didn't bother? Were they left open for a reason? Is

The Twins

he supposed to look? Is that the idea? Going to. Has to. Wants to know what's being said. Communicated. Starts with Harrod's letter. Unfolds the page:

"Spare the rod spoil the child." —Lucy the light bringer

That's it. Entirely plausible but not something he's ever heard Grandmother say. If so, he can't recall, and what's Harrod supposed to take away from that? Harbin checks Lucy's letter:

Your suffering will soon be over. Happy birthday.

How? Nobody knows when Grandmother was born. Many have guessed but none can say with certainty. Seemingly stripped from the public record. Her closely guarded secret. Lucy claiming it's no one's business but her own. That she can't be bothered with all the "fussing." Moreover, Sky didn't specify the date. Kept things cryptic. Could easily be viewed as a veiled threat. Lucy Menk is decidedly the wrong person to provoke. Sky is clearly making a statement but Harbin can't decipher the intent. Not for him to decide, just deliver.

Home early. Helping the kids prepare for their piano recital. Elena excited for tomorrow's public performance while Owen's acting like it's a death sentence. Seriously distressed. Hunched over in front of the piano. Stomach in knots. Feeling sick so they take a break. Harbin talks Owen through it. The recital doesn't matter. He's allowed to make mistakes. As a father, he's just proud to watch him play. To see him take the stage. Accept the challenge. Nothing to be embarrassed or nervous about. Seems to help. Owen returns to the piano. Continues practice. The moment jostles the memory. Connects. Early on. Children. Harrod always sick. Alone. Isolated. Ear infections. Stomach issues. Frail. Tired. Scared. Shy. This day. That moment. An exception. He was maybe eight. Harrod eleven. Having fun. Hanging with the twins. Head outside. Hide and seek. Tag. Everything changes when Harrod checks his phone. Lost track of time. Missed his math tutorial. Had his phone set to silent during violin lessons. Forgot to switch it off. Should have set an alarm. Missed calls from Grandmother. Harrod starts hyperventilating. Has to sit down. Looks clammy. Washed out. Lies back. Feeling sick. Going to puke. Pearl sits down on the floor beside Harrod. Back straight. Legs crossed. Guided breathing. Assures him he's alright. Everything's fine. Eyes closed, she holds her hands out. Hovering just above his stomach. Searching. Sensing. Struck. Eyes open. Aghast.

"Harrod..."

Spoken softly. Harrod not answering. Eyes closed. Still struggling.

"Harrod..."

Louder. He looks up at her.

"What happened?"

Harrod turns away. Staring at the ceiling.

"What did they do?"

Pearl asks again.

"What did she do?"

Harrod springs up. Storms off. Stayed away from the twins from that point forward. From him too, if he's being honest. Harbin notices the hourglass has emptied out. Commends the kids for a strong practice. Allowed an hour of TV then it's time to brush their teeth and get ready for bed.

No appetite. Cup of coffee while Laura makes the kids breakfast. Drives them to school on his way to work. Harrod on site. Sees his car. Harbin heads to the tomb. Finds Harrod conducting behind the tablets. Can't look away from the screen. Scanning. Tracking. Searching for deficiencies. The company can run itself and he still can't get enough.

"Have a letter for you."
"From who?"
"Sky."
"Why?"
"Why what?"
"What's she writing me for?"
"Didn't say."
"What's this about?"
"I don't know."

The Twins

Harrod turns to Harbin. Shooting daggers. Trying to shake him down. Get a read.

"She asked me to bring it you so here I am."

Harrod goes back to the screen.

"Put it down on the desk."

Straight to voicemail. Left a message. Sent a text. All he can do is wait. Over a week now but not without precedent, Grandmother going dark at times. Ceasing all communication. Could last a couple days or a couple months. Rarely offers an explanation. Simply returns. He wonders if this one has anything to do with the current news cycle. 0-1259 in heavy rotation, flashing the faces of lost crew members. Interviews with bereaved or emboldened family members. Some asking for prayers. Others justice. Multiple takes. Guest panels. In-depth analysis on wave transport technology and Rexen's workplace safety record. All red herrings. Redirects. New exposés on the Menk family dynasty. Dirt. Scandal. Adulation. More fodder for the masses. Watching the aerial footage capturing the smoldering wreckage from his mother's plane crash. Rumours she was murdered. An orchestrated "accident" because she threatened to leave his father over supposed infidelities. Wanted her piece of the family fortune. Ready to expose their inner workings. None of which can be corroborated aside from the fact Grandmother never liked his mom. He knows this because his dad told him so in a drunken stupor. Peasant blood. Cart girl at the golf course. Where they met. He was forty-two. She was twenty-two. Got her pregnant. Kept it a secret until it was too late. Public knowledge. Grandmother forced a paternity test. Harrod was his. Harbin soon followed. The family, their advisors, tried to make it work. To shape, mold, guide his mother in her new social standing, but she failed to conform. Could not grasp the reality of their situation. The non-negotiables. Knew she'd never go without yet refused to concede control on family matters outside her jurisdiction. Bred resentment. Became combative. Had to be contained. Harbin demanding clarification. Brushed aside as his father stumbled off to his bedroom. When the subject was revisited the next morning, his father poured himself a drink to steady his shaking hand and explained it was the wrong choice of wording. He meant acknowledged. Addressed. Marriage counselling as an example. Attempt reconciliation.

Nothing nefarious. Not lying about Grandmother though. Harbin knows that much. Lucy never spoke his mother's name. Not once. As though she did not exist. And in the midst of this thought, his phone rings. Grandmother on the call display. Turns off the TV.

"Hello."

"What's this nonsense about a letter."

"Exactly what I said. Sky handed me a letter she wants me to deliver to you in person."

"Why in person?"

"Ensure you received it."

"And you're the only one who could accomplish such a task?"

"Apparently."

"Did she mention what this letter was about?"

"No."

"Well, I'm still aboard Abraxas. Send it with one of our couriers."

"I can't."

"You can."

"I promised I'd deliver it in person."

"Why does that matter?"

"I gave my word."

A mocking cackle from Grandmother.

"I may just burn this letter sight unseen."

"That's your prerogative."

"Any mention of what it pertains to?"

"No."

"Then we'll do this right now. Switch to video so I can see this letter."

"You want me to open it?"

"No, I just want to admire the envelope."

"How do you want to do this?"

"How? Hold the letter up to the damn screen for me to read."

The Twins

Harbin switches to video-call. Props his phone against his coffee cup. Grandmother glaring back in her reading glasses.

"The letter wasn't sealed?"
"No."
"Did you read it?"
"No."
"Liar. Go ahead and read it to me, then."

Harbin unfolds the letter. Reads without emotion.

"Your suffering will soon be over. Happy birthday."
"It's not my birthday."
"That's the letter."

Harbin holds the letter up to the phone. Lucy waves it away. Can see she's rattled. Jaw clenched. Twitching. Searching for a reply.

"Nonsense and it's not my birthday."

Grandmother removes her reading glasses. Rubs her eyes, pinching the bridge of her nose.

"She's clearly suffering some kind of psychotic break after the loss of her sister."
"Shall I send you the letter?"
"No. Burn it. Trash it. Don't care. Now if you'll excuse me, I have more pressing matters I must attend to."
"Like what?"

Lucy switches from flustered to focussed. Pursed lips. Eyes burning a hole through the screen. All her ire now directed at him. Still a terrifying figure in her old age—however old that may be. Vicious. Visceral. The daemon host. Can see it simmering just below the surface. Like there's another entity ready to reach through the phone and rip his throat out. That's the feeling. Harbin tries not to flinch. Hold his ground. He's seen decorated war generals squirm and wither under her chastising gaze. The sustained pause is strategic. Designed to make him flail, stutter, stammer something out to end the awkward silence. Games. These stupid games. Harbin remembers to breathe. Focus on the breath. Grandmother continues to press.

"You seem emboldened."

"How so?"

Send it right back.

"Brave, are we?"

"Tired."

"Cheeky. Very cheeky."

"Anything else?"

Still staring. Hasn't blinked.

"Alright, Grandma, good talk, speak soon."

Ends the call. Hung up on her. He hung up on her. Adrenaline charging through his veins. You don't do that. You don't hang up on Grandmother. She remembers every slight. Every challenge. Needs to brace himself for her retaliation. Escalation. Should not have done that. Fuck it. Run. Run it off. Sneakers on.

Two days removed. No response. Makes it worse. On edge. Building dread. Reminds himself it doesn't matter. All is well. What's the worst that could happen? Written out of the will or fired? Excommunicated? He has his own money. Enough to last lifetimes. They'll survive. They'll thrive. What if she finds a way to freeze his funds? Cease them? Why? Why on earth would she do that? Family. They're family and he's done nothing wrong. It's on him. He's distorting the issue. Non-issue. Nothing there. Sure she's over it. No. . . . no, she's not. How far would she take it? What's she planning? Awful. Exhausted. Making this worse. Death sentence? Would she kill him? Poisoned. Suicided. Insane. That's insane. Not going to kill her grandchild because he hung up on her.

Not just that. The letter. That letter hit hard. Dug in. Never seen her react like that. Wounded. For a split second, she looked scared. Overture. Aggression. Act of war. What if she thinks he's aligned with Sky? Silly. He's being silly. No, he's not. The paranoia runs deep. How she took hold. Never stops. Secure. Control. Remove. Acquire. An endless consolidation scheme. Operating at levels he can't conceive of. Crossing into the occult. Harrod her successor. Harbin spared. Everything outside the agenda, their grand design, is pretense. Family a formality. A prop. She'd have him killed in an instant

The Twins

if she viewed him as a threat. Wouldn't hesitate. What's he going to do? Nothing. He won't see it coming. Has to stop. He will drive himself insane. Knows he can't compete so why take the bait? Won't go down that path. Sees it now. Picked apart until there's nothing left. The vessel vacated. Consumed. Possessed. All so gross. Wash it off. Reset. Sauna and an ice plunge before the kids get back from school. Be present for them for their piano recital.

Encore. Harbin in the moment. A miracle. Two of them. Owen and Elena. His children sitting at the same piano playing a duet of Pachelbel's Canon in D. Laura squeezes his hand. His wife. His life. Companion. Watching their two children playing in perfect sync. Appears effortless but he's watched them work. Paid off. Proud. Perfect. Sustained applause. All the kids come out. Standing ovation. All being recorded. Send this one to Grandmother. A peace offering. Break the ice. Let it melt. New beginnings. Connection. They're family and that means something. Has to. He needs to speak with Harrod. See him outside the tomb. Go for dinner, better yet, make dinner. Barbeque and beers. It'll be great. Let him know he's there. Offer support. Soften the edges. Something might get through. Find another way to operate. Born into this but that doesn't mean they can't make it better for all involved. Enough with the exploitation. This absurd advantage is not what they're here for. Their bloodline crushed the competition long ago. Now it's time to lead the way. Compassion. Cooperation. Charity. Give and it shall be given unto you. A higher calling. Has to be. Can't let your possessions or title own you. At some point, you have to surrender.

As the lights come up, Harbin checks his phone out of habit. Feels a flutter of panic when he sees a text alert from Larry Haber, their chief legal officer. Is this it? Lucy sticking the knife in his side. Harbin checks the text.

"Please call me a soon as you can. This is an urgent matter."

Not now. Why now? Harbin feels his stomach twisting. Tension through his neck.

"What's wrong?"

Laura sees it.

"Nothing. Not sure. Let's congratulate the kids then I need a minute to make a call."

TYRANT

He's not letting this, whatever this is, take away from their moment. Harbin piles on the praise. Shoulder squeeze. Pat on the back. Lets his kids know how great they were. Proof that hard work pays off. They took a risk performing in front of an audience. Now the reward. Respect for a job well done and a late-night pass. Two-hour push past their bedtime. Pizza, dessert, movie, videogames, whatever . . . have some fun. Elena beaming. Owen somewhat bashful, cracks a smile. Mingle with the other families for a few minutes before he steps away. Leave them with Laura so he can make the call outside. Outside edge of the parking lot. Under the elm trees. Waiting. Sure it's going to voicemail. On the fifth ring, Larry answers.

"Hi, Harbin."
"Larry." "There's no proper way to present this so I'm just going to say it. Are you sitting down?"
"I'm fine. Let's hear it."
"Harrod killed your grandmother."
"What?"
"Harrod killed your grandmother. He's being held on Abraxas until the authorities arrive. Someone on staff, some hero, alerted them before I could properly assess the situation. I'm in the air on my way now. Securing details as I go."

Heard it the first time. Had to ask. Has to know.

"How? I mean, how'd he kill her?"
"Bludgeoned with a baseball bat."

Sky. Those letters. Somehow, those letters. The seed. Sequence. Trigger. Set things off. What does he say? How to respond? Has to be there. Needs to be there. His brother. Still his brother.

"Stall them. Try to stall them. I want to see Harrod before they take him into custody."
"That's not how this works."
"Pay them. Just pay them. They can wait. It can wait. On a boat in the middle of the ocean. No one knows the difference."

The Twins

"That's not a call I can make. The Coast Guard's on their way. Likely there before I arrive."
"Do I get on a plane? What do I do? Where am I going?"
"Wait for word. Once he's booked and processed, I'll contact with all the pertinent information."
"What did he say? Have you spoken to him?"
"He's not talking."

Families filtering out of the concert hall. He moves further away into the woods.

"How? How'd it happen? He just shows up with a baseball and splits her skull open?"
"That's my understanding of it. They taxied him to her on a cart with the bat resting on his lap. No one on staff thinks he's going to use it to kill his grandmother. Happened fast. Did not hesitate. In and out in under a minute. Trying to get back on the cart to board the helo but he's covered in blood."
"Where were they? What part of the boat?"
"I'm not sure there's an official name for it. Staff call it the cube or the block. No one is allowed access unless authorized by Lucy."
"How'd they get in?
"Her CSO has an access code in case of emergency. When Harrod stepped out splattered in blood, they used it. Found Mrs. Menk. Ugly . . . it was ugly.

End of the line. Sacrificed before the altar. Killed under the crown.

"Brace yourself, Harbin. I know the Menks own key media outlets but you don't own them all. When the story breaks, they're going to swarm. Can't contain this one. Too late. Already out."

The queen is dead. The prince is done, so's his first-born son. Who's next? He is. By default. Can't be. They won't allow it. Who's «they»? The board members, shareholders, Grandmother. Harbin has no idea how she structured her estate but he hears the whispers. His ego inflating. Craving.

Could it be? Is he the king in waiting? About to be crowned? Feels the rush. Exhilarating. Elevating. Needs to bring it down. Dial it back. Setting himself up for the inevitable disappointment. Never imagined he'd reign over Rexen. Head of the table. Run the show. So don't. Not his world and his brother's in a bad way. Needs to be his focus. Priority. Protect Harrod. Harbin suddenly nauseous. Salivary glands opening. Starting to water. Sick. Going to be sick.

"Larry, I need a minute. Please, uh . . . please keep me posted as things regress."

Catches the gaffe the second he says it.

"Progress, sorry, either way, yeah, you know . . ."
"I know and will keep you informed."
"Thank you, Larry. Thank you."

Harbin ends the call and pukes onto an ostrich fern.

Buzzing. Beer fridge. One after another. Two in the morning. Family asleep. Let Laura know. Dealt with the kids. Gave him some space. Kept them distracted while he paced in the game room. Random updates. Harrod arrested. In custody. Being held for a bail hearing. Larry convinced he'll be denied. Considered a flight risk. No idea what to do with himself. Nervous energy. Should have worked out. Gone for a swim. Needed a drink. Took a pill. Sedative. Taking hold. Sinking in. Starting to fade. On the couch. Nodding off. Crossing over. Brought back by the ringtone. Collect call. Automated introduction from the institution. Harrod on the line. Granted three phone calls. Larry said he might get one. Harbin didn't think he'd be one of them. Accepts the charge.

"Harbin."
"Yes."
"I smashed the circle."
"Okay."
"Broke it with the baseball bat Dad bought me before he left."
"Didn't know you kept that."
"I inherited the T-ball set."
"That's right."

The Twins

Not sure where to take it. Everything pours into the silence. Words can't convey. Spilling over. Don't cry. Keep it together.

"We're free, brother. I can feel it."

Harrod's voice. His tone. At peace or in shock? Give it to him. Have to.

"Good. Good to hear."

Checks the time. Three thirty-three on the dot. He can see the numbers. Had to check. Confirmation. Old trick. Can't remember where. Maybe the twins. If you can see the numbers, you know you're awake.

"Now you know."
"Harrod."
"Yeah."
"I love you, brother."
"Love you too."

Crack of thunder. Flash of lightning. Harbin wakes up to multiple missed calls and texts. Numbers and names. Scans through. Some he knows, others he doesn't. Checking voicemail. Listen. Delete. Listen. Delete. Repeat. Keeps one from a homicide detective. Follow up. Call back later. Representatives from legal, PR, and security. Friends and friends of family. Cold calls from outside media, random shareholders—how'd they get his number? Another breach. Shouldn't happen. Wouldn't happen. Not to Harrod. Grandmother would gut someone if they leaked her contact. No more. He needs to own this. Phone off. Swim to clear the cobwebs. Breakfast. Coffee. Suit up. Step out. Start with her. Everything else can wait.

Sky's gone. Where? They don't know. Who let her out? They did. Harbin presses Sky's security detail for more information.

"When? When did you let her out?"
"Yesterday."
"We didn't know."
"Didn't know what?"
"Harrod. He gave us clearance."
"When?"
"Early morning."

"What did he say?"

"That Sky was free to leave. To stand down. No shadow."

"And who told her?"

"He did. Announced it over the intercom."

"What'd he say?

"'You can go now.'"

"That's it?"

"That's it."

"What'd she do?"

"She left. Was sitting at the edge of her bed with a carry-on suitcase already packed."

"Any indication where she's going?"

"No . . . Do you want us to track her?"

"No."

"Is she coming back?"

"Probably not."

"So, she's gone?"

"Well, she's not here."

"There's a letter. Sky left a letter on her bedside table."

"For who?"

"You."

Enter the room. Cross the floor. Waiting with his name on it. Setup. Trap. Intended to destroy the entire family. Well-deserved. A breath before the waterfall. What will be disclosed? Demanded. Harbin's hands shaking as he unfolds the letter:

Idreamtofaboywhoscrapedhiskneesanddustedoutthedirt.Unkempthair andwildeyes.Hesawourdogandsmiled.Hersmile.Sweetness.Honestengine. Here's to delayed arrivals. May we find what we're looking for.

Relief. Harbin still standing. Spared.

Scheduled meeting with the executors for a reading of Lucy's last will and testament. As expected, Harrod was to replace Lucy as majority shareholder. Thus, negated by the "Forfeiture Rule" or more fearsome-sounding "Slayer Rule," which clearly states that when a person commits a crime that results in another person's death, the transgressor is precluded from receiving any

The Twins

inheritance from the deceased's estate. The asset then goes to the next person according to the terms of the will or other estate-planning documents. Per the will, Harbin is next. The executors notified by Harrod's legal team that they intend to challenge the rule pending a conviction. Trust lawyers responding that while a criminal conviction requires proof beyond a reasonable doubt, the slayer rule applies to civil law, not criminal law, so the petitioner must only prove the murder by a preponderance of the evidence. Hence, even a slayer who is acquitted of the crime of murder can lose the inheritance by the civil court running the estate. Harrod's team claims due process. Insisting there are extenuating circumstances pertaining to the case that will be revealed during the trial. Contested. Disputed. Stalled.

Spectacle. All media salivating over the spectacle, scandal, and slaughter of Lucy Menk by one of her own. Heir to the throne. Harrod. The dark prince. Stuck in their binaries. Savant or spoiled brat? Visionary or fraud? Now murderer. Morbid curiosity. Meme. "HAD IT ALL AND CRUSHED HER SKULL"—an actual headline. Scavengers scrounging through their wreckage. Searching for clues. Breaking news. Expert panels. Insights. Opinions. Mrs. Menk once anointed the most powerful person on the planet by the same media outlets now feasting on her corpse. Watching the elite unravel. Destroy themselves. That's the ticket. Twelve-Five-Nine buried the second the news hit. The workers and their families an afterthought. The implosion of a dynasty far more interesting. Harbin turns it off. Task at hand: Lucy's obituary. He was presented with an initial draft written by her publicist. Cause of death complicates the matter. Asked to review. Some sections highlighted with notes. Starting at the top of the page. The big reveal. Lucy's birthdate matching her date of death, tagged with a note: "How do we handle this?" Sky called her shot. Of course she did. For how long? How long did she have that ace up her sleeve? That letter a loaded gun. Set him off with a sentence. Insane. Sky. Pearl. Those twins. Something else. Sacred ground. Harbin replies to the note. "Leave it . . . just leave it."

BROTHER WOLF

Temperature dropping. Fall into winter. Howling wind pushing dead leaves across the parking lot behind Sutherland's Drugs. The dishevelled, emaciated man dry heaving beside the dumpster. A patch of white hair on the back of his head and serrated keloid scarring down the back of his neck. A large raven perched on the edge of the waste bin cawing in his ear. Kal and Carrie watch the scene play out from the warmth of their truck.

"Poor bastard."

Vomit splattering onto the concrete and his mud-covered boots.

"Rough way to start the day."
"You recognize him?" asks Carrie.
"No, but he was passed out in front of the post office last week."

The stranger wipes the vomit from his scraggly beard and staggers away.

"New addition."
"Guess so."

Kal pulls out of the parking lot. Turns right on Franklin Avenue. Home in ten.

Either his new credit card went missing during delivery or was accidentally tossed in the trash with junk mail. Tried to buy an old industrial drafting table online. Steal of a deal. An easy resale but plans on keeping it. Perfect for that empty corner in his office. Beautiful piece. Adjustable. Original green metal base and weight mechanism. Rich patina wood top with pencil tray. Drafting tools and Toledo drafting stool included. Placed the purchase. Card declined. Expired. Has to pick up the new one at his local branch for security purposes. The bank he's been with his entire life requires more information for verification.

Kal parks in front of the bank. Sees the stranger sitting on a bench across the street, wearing the same clothes as last week, with a jar of pickled eggs between his legs. Once again in the company of ravens. The biggest one perched atop the back support. Three others hopping along the ground in front of him. In a daze, oblivious to the raven squawking in his ear, the stranger twists open the lid. Without removing his glove, he reaches into the jar and grabs an egg. Kal watches the bedraggled man stuff the egg into his sunken face. Chewing it with a distant, forlorn expression. He sees there's more scarring across his face. Wonders what happened. Where this man came from. How he ended up at this bench on Range Street eating pickled eggs. It occurs to him the man is probably asking himself the same question.

Two pieces of identification: driver's and gun licence. New card. Same PIN. The stranger has moved on and so have the ravens.

Kal and Carrie are at the accountant's going over their corporate tax returns. Fifteen years ago, he bought a sea can to store their stuff during a home renovation. One year later, he purchased ten more, renting them out as storage lockers. The majority of their customers are transient workers employed at the diamond mine where Kal worked as a blast mining technician. Five years since his retirement, he now owns forty sea cans and the yard he parks them in (a lot behind their house). An ideal business for residual income. Low overhead. Minimum maintenance. People come and go but the lockers never stay empty for long. Most of the year there's a waiting list. They currently have one container available because the renter stopped paying and won't answer his phone. Sent an official notice with no response. Cleared out the container. His possessions: power tools, snowboard, mountain bike, pieces of furniture, will be held for another month, maybe two, before they're sold or given away.

Beauty day. Blue sky. Sun shining. Kal heading home after winterizing the cabin. Arrives as Carrie's prepping their plates. Rack of lamb with roasted carrots and potatoes. Seated at the table for dinner, Carrie shares a story from earlier in the day. With a window of good weather, she met up with her daughter Kira and two-year-old granddaughter Hannah to walk the Frame Lake Trail. Carrie bringing along their Rottweiler Gemma.

"I'm walking Gemma. Hannah is bundled up against Gemma in the baby carrier. All is well. On the trail for twenty minutes when Gemma stops in her tracks. I'm trying to pull her along but she ain't moving. Staring into the woods. Starts huffing. Nothing there but a couple of ravens in a tree. Then we hear rustling in the woods. Branches snapping. Gemma snarling now, showing her teeth, when the guy we saw puking in the parking lot pops out of the brush and steps onto the trail twenty feet in front of us."

"Pickled eggs."

"What?"

"Never mind, keep going."

"So Gemma lunges after him. I'm leaning back with both hands on the leash and she's still inching me forward. Gnashing her teeth but the guy's oblivious. Total daze. A giant Rottie in full attack mode and he doesn't bat an eye. Just gives us a slow nod and continues down the trail. Meanwhile, my heart is racing."

"I've never seen her like that."

"Me neither. Had her hackles up until he was out of view."

With Carrie at work, Kal breaks out the sketch pad. Does some cross-hatching on a pen and ink drawing of their old pug, Buddy, standing proudly at the bow of their boat. Six years since they said goodbye. Bought him when they first met. The drawing is a surprise for Carrie, who's always encouraging Kal to pursue his artistic talent. Was looking for something to do. Found the old photo and decided to draw it.

Downtown. Dropping the illustration off for framing. Again with the ravens. Two of them playing tug-of-war with a filthy piece of blood-stained gauze. The stranger sits on the front steps of the old library. Splashing a bottle of hydrogen peroxide over mangled fingertips. Festering, filthy, encrusted in blood from the top knuckle up. Looks like his nails were ripped off. Scabbing over. Kal has questions. Not that he's asking.

Going with a white matte in a dark-grey burl wood frame. Ready for pickup in two days' time. The stranger still on the steps. Wrapping his finger-tips in fresh gauze. One of the ravens hopping along the hood of Kal's truck with a tattered piece of old gauze dangling from its mouth. The raven caws at him. Drops the bloodied gauze on the hood. Kal turns the ignition and the raven flies away. He considers telling the stranger to get his garbage off the truck but can't be bothered. The man's lost in a trance, wrapping his wounds. Nothing personal. Better to avoid the interaction altogether. Drive away. Kal hits the airport loop. Presses down on the pedal and the soiled gauze flies off into the ditch.

Back home. Lunch with Carrie. Butternut squash soup and a turkey sandwich.

"Must have owed some money."
"I don't what that guy's deal is but it's disturbing. He just looks so—"
"Haunted."

Driving down to meet the motivated seller of a twenty-six-foot hydraulic tilt deck trailer. Can use the trailer to haul his twenty-foot sea cans. Kal pulls down the sun visor. He was getting a direct hit. Soon arrives at the address. The trailer is parked in the driveway with the seller waiting outside. The air cold and crisp. Quick introductions, then an inspection of the trailer. The hydraulics function properly with a smooth tilt. There's no damage to the body-hitch. the coupler connecting to the hitch. The beds in good condition and the wheels have plenty of tread on them. Done deal.

Kal drives back down 49th with the trailer in tow. A sight to see as he approaches the RCMP station. At least a hundred ravens lining the roof ledge. He slows down as the stranger appears from the other side of the building. Standing on the sidewalk in piss-stained pants. Likely just released from the drunk tank. His face freshly busted and bruised. Several options as to why: The man either took a beating before they brought him in, when they brought him in, during his stay, or all of the above. On cue, a raven swoops down from the ledge, landing on a parking meter by the stranger. Starts cawing for his attention.

Kal is working the grill. Ready to plate the steaks. Carrie brought back some T-bones from the butcher. Green beans and baked potato side. Red wine. Everything at the table. Carrie tops off their glasses.

"A collection of crows is a murder but what's a group of ravens?"

Brother Wolf

"A flock. Might just be a flock."

Kal checks his phone. Reads the results.

"'Collective nouns for a group of ravens include rave, treachery, unkindness, and conspiracy. In practice, most people use the more generic flock.'"

"An unkindness?"

"'An unkindness is one of the names given to the jet-black birds with the dubious reputation. There is speculation as to the origin of the term, with some suggesting it draws on the creature's symbolic association with witches and death.'"

"I mostly associate them with tearing through the trash."

"A little messy but they've got personality."

"I don't consider their personality when I'm pressure washing their shit off my truck."

Retirement secured. No mortgage, car loans, or credit card debt. Insurance and utilities automated. Birthdays: grandkids, nephews, nieces entered into digital calendars for notification. Backed up by a personalized calendar comprised of family photos that Carrie printed out. There's nothing that needs to be done. Not really. By every conceivable measure, they've made it. Set before seventy. Carrie's done the math. They could live to a hundred off their savings alone and still have money in the bank. Both her children, now parents themselves, have high-paying jobs with benefits. Each will receive a lucrative inheritance when the time comes. Beyond their own needs, barring calamity, their family's future is set as well. He and Carrie are in the bonus rounds. So why this low-level depression? Most days, he'll scroll through his phone during that first cup of coffee. Today, he stares at the black void outside their windows. No plans. No need. The days used to burn by now they just disappear. Killing the clock. Get to the end of another one. Where's the gratitude? They have everything they need. What else does he want? An event . . . something real. Beyond the rinse and repeat narratives they're pushing in the news. Violent weather would do the trick. A surge. A storm. Blow down the dead wood. Peel back the shingles. If it's not anchored in place, send it flying. Ignore the cost. Dismiss the damage. If only for a moment, enjoy the show.

In the garage prepping their sleds for another season. Kal starts by removing the belt cover and giving the clutch a wash. Blows out any belt dust with compressed air. Uses a Scotch-Brite pad and parts cleaner on the sheaves. After the belt, he checks the battery. Tightens the spark plugs. Scans the track for any tears or missing lugs. Tests the tension with a twenty-dollar gauge. Inspects the hyfax wear line, idler wheels, bearings, suspension, carbide inserts, and grease Zerks, spraying them with low-temp grease. Continues down the checklist. Making sure the riser is in line with the steering post. Checking the ski stance. Testing chaincase tension. Looking for leaks. Topping off fluids. Ending it with a once-over of spray cleaner polish. All sorted. Sleds ready for winter. Washes up. Now what? Phone starts ringing. Sees it's his old buddy Lenny Badger. Worked at the mine together. He lives in Fort Providence now. Kal hears from him once in a blue moon.

"Badger."
"In town butchering up some moose meat."
"You see Carrie?"
"Told me to call you."
"Okay . . ."
"Says she's worried."
"About what?"
"Says your belly's getting big sitting around all day."
"Big when I was working."
"Suppose you're right. Mine too."
"Then there's nothing to worry about."
"Guess not."
"How's Jimmy?"
"He's a tank. How's Gemma?"
"Good. Coat's looking great."
"You keeping her on that raw food diet?"
"Yes, sir."
"Good man."
"Jimmy with you?"
"Of course."
"Swing on by for a visit."
"Might have to."
"Beer's in the fridge."
"Even better."

Gemma lies beside Badger on the couch while Jimmy sniffs around the house. Gemma and Jimmy from the same litter. Kal hands Badger a beer. Takes a seat across from "the big Cree with the bowlegs," as Lenny's referred to himself on occasion. A kind soul with enough mischief to keep things interesting. Also a skilled hunter that gives most of the meat away to friends and family. Kal and Carrie have filled their freezer several times with caribou, moose, bear, and bison he's brought them over the years. Not an avid hunter himself, Kal will join Badger on a hunt if invited. A rare opportunity to see his friend. Always in awe of Badger's tracking ability and intuition. The man carries a wealth of knowledge based on experience. Generations of his family running trap lines up North.

"Kal Koskinen . . ." Badger cracks his beer and leans back with his arm up on the couch. "Tell me how this life of leisure and luxury is treating you."

"Just fine."

"When's Carrie going to cash out and sell the butcher shop?"

"Tried. Snowdrift wanted to buy it before their accounts were frozen for a forensic audit."

"The conman."

"Big spender diverted millions into shell corporations owned by him and his wife."

"Everyone acting shocked but why would the council hire that fraud in the first place?"

"Maybe they read his book."

"What book?"

Kal pulls it up on his phone. "Available online through Amazon—**6 Mega Hacks for Power and Influence** by Manesh Pradeep."

"Only six?" chirps Badger.

Kal reads the author bio and synopsis. "'Mr. Pradeep is an acclaimed and award-winning career executive, entrepreneur, industrialist, and philanthropist who champions the wronged and disadvantaged Indigenous people of Northern Canada.'"

"What a hero."

Kal continues, "'This book will teach you how to get your way with others and take what you want from life.'"

Badger scoffs. "Take what you want until they seize all your assets. Including that purple Porsche he whips around in."

"Had 'em fooled, though."

"Sure did."

"How does that happen?"

"Lazy leadership. No oversight. Bribes. Blackmail. Both."

Badger shrugs his shoulders. Sips his beer. "Something switched. A lot of people are out of alignment. Whole system's sick. Corrupted by design."

"We going to see a reckoning?"

"Dead wood going to burn. Nothing we need to worry about."

Done sniffing around, Jimmy flops down on the floor with a satisfied sigh.

Badger looks down at his dog.

"See . . . Jimmy ain't stressing it."

"What's he weigh now?"

"One forty."

"Big boy but he's not overweight."

"Lean and not so mean."

Kal feels the conversation switching gears. Considers a subject that's been on his mind and how he might segue into it. Not sure if he should, though. Would have been an awful scene to come across. They haven't spoken since, aside from a brief text exchange; Kal checking in, offering assurance, support. To go there now might dampen the conversation. Darken their visit. Best let Badger bring it up. Seems odd to ignore, though. Kal decides to be direct.

"We can skip the conversation but—"

"The bear attack."

"Yeah."

Out fishing in late August, Badger discovered three mutilated bodies on the shore of the Mackenzie River near Fort Providence. The bodies later identified as Aksel Damgaard, Lise Jorgensen, and Christoffer Lund. Eco-tourists from Denmark travelling the Mackenzie River Delta.

"Gonna need another beer for this one."

Kal grabs them two more beers from the fridge. Badger slams back the one he's sipping on.

"So, I'm out on the water. Taking some casts. Catch a few pickerel. Floating downstream . . . See their tents. Bright red. Yellow. Straight away, I sense something's off. Can't say why, just this eerie kinda feeling. Like a stillness to it . . . Go in for a closer look. See the bone splinters. Their ribs. Pull up on shore . . . Bad scene. One, two, three bodies. Raven's picking away at what's left."

"Can't imagine coming across that kind of, I don't know . . ."

"Carnage. Why I gotta remind myself that ain't them. What I saw. Nothing there. Long gone. Spirit continues. Wake from one dream into the next. What keeps fucking with me is the story itself."

"How do you mean?"

"Newspaper says 'bear attack' in big bold letters. Bear found. Bear killed. That sums it up, right?"

"Yes?"

"Well, my buddy Bill Bernier was one of the wildlife officers brought in to track it down. Bill found a bear but it wasn't the one they shot. This bear was already dead. An old grizzly. Gutted and gored with its throat ripped out ten kilometres from the campsite."

"Damn . . ."

"Didn't read that in the paper, did you?"

"Left that part out."

"Bill made sure it was in the case report but apparently that small detail wasn't 'pertinent' to the story. Editorial decision. Told me they didn't want to cause confusion. Said one bear had nothing to do with the other. Pushed back, and what's the word they used . . . superfluous. Said it was superfluous information."

"Big words. Did you read the report?"

"Yeah."

"And they must have found human remains in the bear they shot."

"The necropsy said human bone fragments were prevalent but too small for gross identification."

"So that's the bear."

"Guess so."

"You don't believe the report?"

"Didn't say that."

"Did the report have an answer for what killed Bill's bear?"

"Tooth wear suggested it was an old bear. They suspect it died of natural causes and was scavenged by other predators in the area."

"Seems like a reasonable assessment."

"The officers shot and killed a two-hundred-pound black bear."

"Yeah . . ."

"A black bear."

"Three unarmed humans are light work for any full-sized bear."

"They wasted two canisters of bear spray on it."

"That's why you carry a gun for back-up."

"Bear spray is effective ninety-eight percent of the time."

"And the two percent of the—"

"There was another can left in the tent so why didn't they use it?"

"Cut off . . . Bear sees movement. Threatens to charge."

"Wait your turn while you watch your friends get ripped apart?"

"Maybe one of them went for it. Maybe that's what got them killed."

"RCMP found their flipped canoe stuck in the reeds six kilometres downstream."

"Same deal. Someone tried to get away. Tip the canoe getting in. Bear drags 'em back on shore."

"And it eats them all in one sitting? There was no cache. A black bear would cover its prey with leaves, needles, dirt, trash, whatever's in the area. Those bodies were left right out in the open."

"Do we know the duration? A hungry bear going into fall, it might—"

"No way. A large deer will keep a bear fed for several days and that's comparable to the combined weight of three adult humans."

"But how much of that is edible?"

"Damn near all of it for a bear."

"Fair enough."

"Internet says a typical adult human will yield around seventy-five pounds of edible meat. With a comparable caloric intake per pound to deer meat. Human is six-fifty and deer's around seven hundred."

"But there's evidence in the area, right? Bear scat? Prints?"

"Compromised by the rain. One print I could make. Bear at a glance. Five toes. Five claws. Pad. Different though . . . Narrow. Longer and it landed different."

"Affected by the rain. Distorted."

"Yeah. . ."

"Well, it wasn't a wolf."

"No."

"What else?"

"Guess we gotta go with bear."

Headache. Hungover. When Carrie came back, they cracked a couple of bottles of wine and kept it going. Engaged all matters of discussion with plenty of laughs peppered in between. Fairly polluted by the time they shut it down. Badger crashing in the guest bedroom. Gone before they woke up. Who knows when Kal will see him next. Maybe a meet up at their cabin over the holidays. For now, Kal needs to get some food in him. Went to bed on an empty stomach. Rookie mistake. Kal chugs back a glass of water, defrosts a frozen baguette, and reheats some beef stew; grass-fed with bacon drippings, carrot, potato, and butternut squash. When it's ready, he ladles himself a bowl and brings it to the table. Tearing off a small chunk of baguette, he lathers it in butter. About to dunk his bread in the broth when the phone rings. Doesn't recognize the number. Not answering. Let them leave a message or call back later. Phone keeps ringing. Reconsiders. Might be an inquiry about storage. Easier to answer.

"Hello?"

"This the number for Great Slave Storage?"

"It is."

"I'd like to rent one of your sea cans."

The caller has some kind of speech impediment. Can hear a lisp. The slurring of words. Might be drunk.

"I have a twenty-footer available."

"I need it for next week. That's it."

"Well, we charge by the month but I'll roll next week into November if you're still interested."

Paying in cash. There within the hour but doesn't have a cell phone. No way to call when he arrives. Kal waiting for a knock at the door. Scrolling through vacation destinations with Gemma on the couch beside him. Wants to break up the winter. Bunkered down through the last two. Spent most of the time at the cabin. Loves it there but they're due for a vacation. A beachfront getaway from February to the end of March would be ideal. Considering Belize, Barbados, and Costa Rica. Checking prices. Can hear the dogs from neighbouring kennels acting up. Not unusual for the area but when Gemma barks back, he takes notice. She usually ignores it.

"Gemma, quiet."

She starts huffing. Another bark. Springs from the couch. Slides across the floor. Scrambling towards the back door. Kal follows. Gemma whining to be let outside. Kal peeks through the window into the storage yard. Of course. Of course it's him. Stranger danger. Had to be.

His name is Jake Lunn. Up close, Kal gets a good look at the jagged scarring on his neck and pockmarked face. Some serious lacerations. Like he went through a windshield or was attacked by a dog. That aside, the man's in rough shape. Sunken blue eyes. Face sucked in. Kal can see his orbital bones outlined under the skin. Cratered mouth disappearing into gnarled beard. Missing teeth. That's the speech impediment. No tongue-to-tooth contact. Can't shape the sounds of certain letters. Arrived with nothing but the rent. Cash in hand. Month's rent plus the deposit. Ravens still flying in. At least fifty of them. Landing on the sea cans. Lining up along the top of the chain-link fence behind the barbed wire. Cawing. Shitting. Doing as they do. Kennel dogs howling. Gemma barking behind the door. Kal hands Jake the contract. Spots a piece of frayed gauze sticking out the end of the Jake's black Isotoner glove as he signs the contract without reading it.

"So there's no confusion, you're paid from now until the end of November."

Kal hands him a copy of the contract. Grabs a padlock from his lock bucket.

"I'm making this clear now because I've got no way to get ahold of you. December's rent needs to be paid December first. If we don't receive that payment in thirty days, you're in default. Your items will be removed and auctioned. Prohibited storage items are obvious: no hazardous materials, flammable or combustible items, no drugs, no food, no living things, be it animals, plants, or people. Aside from that, you have twenty-four-seven access to your lockup. The code to get into the yard is on the back of the contract. If for whatever reason the fence doesn't open, or you forget the code, just give me a call."

"Understood. Thank you."

"Thank you for your business."

Snow-covered road. Passing rusting vehicles and machinery covered in a crystallized layer of frost. Coldest day of the year thus far. Placed the call to Bruno's ten minutes ago. Comfort food. Pizza for pickup. Kal checks the fuel gauge. Low on gas. Stop at the station. Grab some candy for the trick-or-treaters while he's at it. Halloween on Sunday. Maybe a handful of chocolate bars. Not a lot of kids in the area. Kam Lake is mostly comprised of industrial and commercial operators with business-owner residences. Some owners, especially kennel operators, have caretakers living onsite in trailers or attached suites. The caretakers protect the property from thieves and animal predators. Kal knows a few of them. Some with children that will most likely circle another neighbourhood for Halloween, but there's still a slim chance they stop by. Best have some candy in case.

He approaches the Esso station in front of Mac's, formally Winks, formally Red Rooster. The pump station canopy and building lined wing to wing with ravens. Jake sitting on the cold concrete beside the pay phone with a raven perched on it. His back against the brick wall of the building. Head hung between his legs. Arms resting on his knees. Kal fills the tank and pays inside. Jacket pockets stuffed with chocolate bars, he leaves the store, stopping to check on Jake.

"Jake?"

No answer. Just the cawing raven.

"Hey, buddy, you alright?"

Eyes closed. Head still hung between his legs. Skin looks grey.

"You awake, Jake?"

Slight head bob. Kal can't tell if it's a reflex or response.

"You can't be falling asleep outside. Not tonight. Way too cold."

Nothing.

"Jake, you've got to say something. You've got to get up or I'm calling an ambulance."

One more time.

"Jake, wake up, buddy."

Claps in his ear.
"No . . ." A response.
"Yes."
"No ambulance."

Jake lifts his head, resting it against the brick wall.

"Don't . . . Just a little weak . . . Tired."
"Maybe it's your blood sugar? You want a chocolate bar?"
"No . . . can't keep nothing down."
"So let's get you to the hospital. Have you checked out."

Jake takes a deep breath through his nose. Struggles to stand up. Still leaning against the wall.

"Was on the phone . . . Little dizzy. Needed a moment. Better now."
"You sure?"
"I'm good. I'm good."
"You're looking a little shaky there, man."
"I'm fine. Fine. Feeling better . . ."

Jake staggers forward, slips on a patch of ice, crashes to the ground. The ravens start squawking.

"I'm good . . . I'm good. Didn't see the ice under snow."

Kal helps him up as he struggles to stand.

"I know but I can't leave you out here, man. Either I bring you to the hospital or the medics meet us here."

Brother Wolf

Jake sighs. Resigned to it.

"It's no big deal. We're five minutes from the hospital," assures Kal.

En route to Stanton Territorial Hospital. Rounding Franklin Avenue onto Old Airport Road. Jake squirming in his seat. Fumbling for the window control.

"You going to puke? You need me to crack the window?"

Jake nods. Kal lowers the window. Jake sticks his head out. Pukes. Falls back in his seat. Kal leaves the window down for some fresh air.

Emergency entrance parking. Kal helps Jake out of the truck. Holding an arm to keep him steady as they walk through the sliding doors. Brings him to an empty seat. Four other people in the lobby waiting for care. A burly white man with a broken nose, wearing a well-worn, brightly coloured snowmobile jacket and pale denim blue jeans. Eyes swollen shut. Head tilted back. His Hooters t-shirt covered in blood. Across from him, a sombre-looking old Inuit man wearing an oxygen mask in a wheelchair. Seated in the far corner, a young white kid with a tear-lined face. Still in his hockey gear. One winter boot on. The other off. Judging by the swelling, his ankle is broken. The kid's mother filling out intake forms. Kal joins her at the reception desk. The receptionist, still typing into the computer, doesn't look up from the screen.

"How can I help you?"

"I brought in the gentleman seated over there. Not sure what's going on. Very weak. Vomiting."

"Are you a friend or relative?"

"Neither. Found him sitting on the ground outside Mac's. Said he was feeling dizzy. Had to help him up."

"Okay, sir, please have him fill out this admission form."

Jake has no identification, address, or phone number. Unable to provide an emergency contact. Kal puts his name down and submits the form to reception. Done what he can do. Lets Jake know before leaving.

"Alright, man, you're checked in."

"Thank you."

"Not a problem. Hopefully you're not waiting too long."

Jake nods. Kal exits the ER. Drives to Bruno's Pizza to pick up his order.

Waiting for his return, Carrie sticks her head out the front door, sees Kal pressure washing his truck in their driveway.

"What are you doing?"
"Pressure washing the puke off my truck."
"Whose puke?"
"Grab the pizza. I'll explain inside."

Pizza reheating in the oven. Carrie fills the dog bowl with meat scraps and offal at the kitchen counter.

"Let's hear it."
"Yeah . . . bit of a detour."
"Where?"
"The hospital."
"Why?"
"Not for me."
"Who?"

Carrie places the bowl back in its tray. Gives the okay to Gemma, who scarfs her food back.

"Raven Mad Daze."
"No way . . ."
"Stopped for gas. He was slumped over outside Mac's."
"Wasted?"
"Don't know . . . either way, he was messed up. Didn't want me to call an ambulance so I drove him to the hospital."
"The puke."
"At least he got it out the window."
"Ravens?"
"Wing to wing."

Kal's phone starts ringing. Checks the call display. Answers.

"Hello . . ."
"Kal?"
"Yes."

"I'm calling from Stanton hospital. You're listed as the emergency contact for Jake Lunn."

"I brought him in but I don't know the guy."

"Oh . . . he has you as his contact."

"I helped him fill out his intake form. Couldn't give me a name for his emergency contact so I put mine down."

"Alright, well, he left the hospital before we could do an assessment."

"I don't know . . . He was in bad shape when I brought him in and temperature's dropping."

"I'll notify the RCMP. Ask them to keep an eye out."

"Sounds like a plan."

Can't find a movie. More content than ever with less to watch. Everything a watered-down version of something else. Digitized. No weight, depth, or dimension. Same candy-gloss finish. Flat. Fake. Oversaturated. The grain and grit are gone. An hour of YouTube compilations with an introduction to aquascaping then it's off to bed. Staring at the ceiling. Anxious. Low-level dread. Imagining a knock at their door the second he falls asleep. Gemma going ballistic. Jake outside. Unannounced. Not something Kal wants to deal with.

Cobwebs and a "Happy Halloween" banner across their window. Glowing pumpkin on the front steps. Trick or treat. Officially open for business. One family stops by. Greg Gaudreau (mechanic/caretaker at a neighbouring auto shop) brings his two boys and little girl. All wearing winter jackets over the costumes. One boy is dressed as Spiderman. His brother, face painted green, is the Incredible Hulk. Their little sister a skeleton. Kal gives them a handful of chocolate bars. Engaging in a bit of their own mischief, he and Carrie split a ten-milligram gummy procured from her son Caden. To honour the evening, they pass out on the couch watching Lon Chaney's **The Wolf Man**.

Days removed. Kal takes down the banner, clears the cotton cobwebs, and tosses the rotting pumpkin in the wastebin. Never heard back from the hospital. Did they find Jake? Is he dead? What's the word? Where's his family? His friends? Is anyone asking about him? Does anyone care? Kal considers calling the hospital for a follow-up. No. Not his problem. Sure he's fine, relatively speaking. If not, what's he going to do? Nothing and he knows it.

Jolted awake by the bark. High alert. Gemma howling. Not just her. Pandemonium. Every dog in the area set off. Clashing against the clamour of ravens. He's here. Has to be. Kal checks the cameras on his phone. No one there but the yard is filled with ravens. Every shipping container covered in them. Kal grabs the twelve gauge. Goes outside. The flock still flying in. Moon blazing bright. Gemma rushes the yard. Ravens scatter. Regroup. Gemma barking, snarling, snapping at the sea can. The one Jake rented—BOOM! The noise is from the inside the can. Then a howl that makes his blood run cold. Everything falls silent. Then chaos. Gnashing teeth. Clashing. Clawing. Scraping metal. The beast wants out of its cage. BOOM. Slamming into the sea can. Against the door. Kal takes a breath to compose himself. BOOM. No way it breaks the locking bars and padlock. Not going anywhere. Trapped.

"What the fuck is in there?"

Kal turns, sees Carrie standing beside him with her hunting rifle.

"Nothing I'm letting out."

Three squad cars. Then six. Their house, their lot, cordoned off. Access roads blocked. The conspiracy of ravens is deafening and the dogs won't stop. That includes the K9 unit. Rolling howls, yelps, relentless barking. Guttural growls from inside the sea can. Snarling and snapping. BOOM. The cops waiting for the trapped animal to exhaust itself. A sustained pause. BOOM. It appears they might be waiting awhile.

Kal uploads footage from the security camera onto his computer for Critical Incident Commander Scott Arbour. Sorting through clips, he finds what they're looking for. A thumbnail of Jake entering the yard. Not alone. Accompanied by a tall Native man in a mesh trucker cap with a gin blossom nose and wispy moustache. Part of the paper-bag crew usually parked outside the post office. Kal presses play on the clip. Watches the two men enter the yard and open the sea can. There's a brief exchange before Jake hugs the man then turns to face the open can. There's a pause, maybe a prayer, before he steps inside. His friend closes the door behind him, locks the latch, leaves the yard. Commander Arbour shaking his head at the paused video.

"There's something else in there with him."

Kal's not sure. "Is there?"

"Well, it's not Mr. Lunn making those noises."

"You sure about that . . . ?"

"Meaning what?"

"Seems to me Jake is what we'd call a werewolf. Certainly sounds like it."

Four a.m. The din of dogs and ravens now functioning as background noise. The beast still snarling. Dragging its claws across the COR-TEN steel as it paces back and forth. The cage stays closed. Commander's orders.

Morning light. Local news teams posted outside the yard. People on their way to work. The radio reporting a disturbance. Carrie receives a concerned call from her daughter. Tells Kira a black bear broke into the yard but she's not buying it. Each answer elicits another question. Carrie comes clean. Nothing to hide. A man locked himself in a sea can. No idea why. More questions. Out of answers.

The ravens fly away. Dogs done barking. The pacing has stopped. Not a sound from the sea can. Awaiting word. Commander Arbour bangs on the side of the sea can to incite a response. No reaction. Perfectly still.

"Alright, bring in the bolt cutters."

Officers in tactical gear and body armour form a line in front of the sea can. One officer holding a pair of bolt cutters. Each waiting for instruction.

"Officer Wright, remove the lock and wait for my command."

Officer Wright cuts the padlock. Removes it from the eyehole. Waits.

"As you open the door, I want you to fall back behind it for protection."

Commander Arbour then directs his attention to the row of officers standing in lined formation.

"Stand in ready position but hold your fire unless that thing lunges at us."

The officers draw their guns.

"I repeat—hold your fire unless attacked."

The moment has arrived.

"Alright. Let's open her up."

Ready for the reveal. Kal and Carrie watching from the window. Gemma with her paws on the sill. Holding their breath as the doors open . . . Nothing. No monster jumps out. Officers move in. All clear. The commander waves over the paramedics. Kal and Carrie unable to see inside the can from their vantage point.

"I need to know what's in there."

"Might be a body."

The medics are inside the sea can for less than a minute. One medic conferring with the commander while the other returns to the ambulance.

"I'm taking a look."

"No, you're not."

Kal ignores her. Heads for the door. Carrie chasing after him.

"Leave it!"

Down the stairs. Past the collection of cops sipping coffee. A direct line towards the shipping container.

"Kal!" Carrie yelling from the back steps.

Didn't close the door. Gemma racing past Kal into the container. Sets things off. Cops yelling for Kal to stop. Keeps going. Phone light on, illuminating the can. Gemma whining. Sniffing around a mangled mass of twisted limbs and blood-matted fur. Coarse black hair. Patches missing. Pallid skin. Skeletal fingers stretched and curled. Bones as claws through burst fingertips. Malformed. Half formed. Snapped, splayed, and splintered. Finds a face. Framed in fur. Blue eyes open. Jake Lunn. Aghast. Frozen in time. Didn't make it back. Halfway there. Heart attack or stroke. Gums distended from his mouth. Teeth erupted from his gums. Sharp. Jutted. Jagged. Stained in blood. The scale of suffering this man endured beyond comprehension. Hand on Kal's arm. Feels the grip. Turns to see the livid commander. His yelling muted. Muffled. Kal in shock. Snaps out of it. Pulls back his arm, breaking the commander's grip. Done talking. Calls for Gemma, who follows. Carrie trying to get past a row of officers. Kal blows past them. Carrie by his side.

"Stop right there!"

Ignoring the commander's orders, they continue towards the house. Seen enough. Had enough. Locks the door behind them. Moves to the living room. Closes the blinds. Sits down on the couch. Carrie still standing.

"What did you see in there?"

Supervised quarantine. Police posted outside their property. Lawyers called. Warrants issued. Items seized: phones, computers, cameras. Their property. The occurrence covered up by a bogus press release. Police claiming they were responding to an armed and barricaded adult male. Stating no one was injured and the man was taken into custody without incident thanks to the work of the crisis negotiation team. Complete fabrication. Kal and Carrie with no idea how this ends. Waiting on the contract. Some sort of NDA to sign that will coincide with their release.

Day six, the cavalry arrives. A motorcade of black SUVS pulls up outside the house. The goon squad, dressed in matte-black designer tactical, step out of their vehicles. Leading the pack is a squat man sporting a thick black moustache and military cut. Built like a brick shithouse with wide shoulders, thick neck, and traps up to his ears. Gemma starts barking. Carrie brings her to the bedroom. The squad leader nods to the plainclothes police officers parked in their driveway. Kal meets him at the front door. Looks down. At least two feet taller than the man.

"Who are you with?" Kal not in the mood for small talk.

A smirk from Mister Moustache.

"A good afternoon to you too."
"What department? Who are you with?"

The man removes his tactical glasses. Tucks them in the chest pocket.

"Not your concern."
"Talk to my lawyer."

Kal attempts to close the door but they bulldoze through. The entourage steering Kal into the living room.

"Take a seat on the couch," orders Mister Moustache.
Turning to Carrie when she appears from the bedroom.

"Ma'am . . ."

"Who the fuck are you?" she fires back.

"My name is Frank."

"Well, Frank, you want to tell me what the fuck you and your goons are doing here?"

Frank amused. Turns to Kal.

"She's a feisty one."

Carrie not having it.

"Fuck off. We're not talking to anyone without our lawyer."

"See, that's the problem. There seems to be a general misunderstanding surrounding your situation. We're here to offer clarification."

Carrie looks to Kal, who communicates a look of "let's get this over with" before taking a seat on the couch. At a loss, she begrudgingly joins him.

"Grab me a chair." Frank directs his men to the chairs at the kitchen table.

They place a chair in front of him. Frank sits down. Leans in.

"What you witnessed November third is a matter of international security. The normal standards and practices no longer apply. We're here to guide you through this process and see you safely to the other side."

"Get the fuck out of our house," snaps Carrie

Frank smiles. Waits a beat.

"Or what? You're going to call the cops?"

"Fuck you. You have no right—"

"Stop, just let him get through his spiel." Carrie cut off by Kal. Biting her tongue as Frank continues.

"Here's the deal . . . the events of November third are outside your jurisdiction. Meaning they're outside your understanding. Meaning they're a fucking blank spot in your memory."

"Talk to our lawyer," repeats Kal.

Frank doubles down. "Erased. Gone. Stricken from the record. This includes everything up to and until your release from quarantine."

Kal holds his ground. "Once again, who do you represent? What agency?"

"An aggression you can't comprehend. I'm advising you to keep it that way."

Frank cracks his knuckles. Carrie rattled. A mix of fury and fear. Kal sees the tears welling up in her eyes. Needs to get these goons out of their house. Speaking in circles.

"Yeah."
"Yeah what?"
"Saw nothing. Say nothing."

Frank grins. Turns to his team.

"Then our work here is done."

Kal and Carrie swept the house for surveillance bugs and spy cameras during their first day of quarantine. Nothing found. Thirty days since their release from house arrest and they continue checking to no avail. Doesn't mean they're not there. Can't trust their phones or computers. Added security software but they have to assume anyone can listen to or read both. That aside, Kal's gut instinct tells him active surveillance has ended. A bit of breathing room. No longer being followed when they go out. At least not in such a painfully obvious manner; the same vehicles following them with drivers he's never seen around town. Led them on a few wild goose chases, partially out of frustration, partially for his own amusement. Left the house, circled the airport loop through town, right back to their driveway.

Kal once again checks his truck for hidden cameras and tracking devices. Nothing found. He asks Carrie to join him for a walk with Gemma along the Frame Lake Trail. She agrees, despite the fact it's minus thirty with snow flurries. Both understanding if you're going to live in a northern climate, it's best to embrace it. Dressed for the weather, they drive to the Ruth Inch Memorial Pool, which overlooks Frame Lake. From the parking lot, it's easy access to the trail system. At a safe distance from the truck, Kal asks Carrie for directions.

"What part of the trail were you on when you saw Jake with Kira?"
"Where you enter the trail from Albatross Court. Just past it."

During summer, the trail showcases the flora and fauna of its subarctic environment: fireweed, foxtail barley, wild rose bushes, creeping juniper, paper birch, jack pine, and black spruce trees can all be seen along the way. The geology of the area also on display. Pink granite veins crosscutting dark volcanic rock. Shifting into white and grey the higher you climb. Most rocks covered in black, grey, or green lichen. Now it's all under ice and snow.

Kal and Carrie go off trail into the section of woods Jake appeared from. Trudging through knee-deep snow. Gemma off leash. Bounding past them. Chasing away a cluster of cooing ptarmigans as they continue uphill. Taking a break at the top. Kal scanning the wooded area. Able to see into the backyards of surrounding homes. Eyes trained for anything out of place. Kal spots a branch sticking out from a lower tier of rocks forty feet away. Moving closer to the ledge, he sees the makeshift shelter. They climb down to its level. Look at a lean-to that's roughly eight feet long, five feet wide, and six feet high. The roof/wall is comprised of layers of logs and branches tied together with paracord. The smaller branches interwoven. At the entrance, a tiny fire pit circled in stones. The inside of the shelter partially covered by snow drift. Kal ducks down into the lean-to. The shelter floor is lined with spruce tree branches. On top of that, a blue foam camping mat and a sleeping bag. Tucked in the corner, a duffel bag and drawstring backpack. Kal checks the contents of the bags: toilet paper, a box of Red Bird matches, three lighters, a lock blade, fork, spoon, can opener, two tins of pea soup, one can of baked beans, a frozen jar of pickled eggs, crumpled porn rags, dirty clothes, a dry bag, and a Pelican case. Inside the case, an SLR camera. Kal tries turning on the camera but the battery is dead. He checks the dry bag. Finds a spiral-ringed notebook with a pen hooked through the rings. Starts flipping through the notebook. Reads the scrawl. Searching for a sign, it appears he's found the story.

Camera charged. Packed in its case. Cup of coffee after a good night's rest. Before leaving, Kal does another sweep of the truck for spy cameras and tracking devices. Nothing found, he drives to the Bristol monument. A right off Old Airport Road, where he parks twenty feet from the plane on a pedestal—a 170 Freighter twin-engine aircraft. The first-ever plane to land at the North Pole in 1967. A testament to the region's aviation history, the old blue and red freighter now tagged with spray paint by bored teenagers. A place for them to drink during the summer but largely left alone in winter.

Brother Wolf

Kal turns off the radio, adjusts the heat, and removes the camera from its case. The LCD screen blinks on when he presses the power switch. Holy terror. Demon on display. Last picture taken. Kal scrolls back through the photos. Sees the creature make its approach in reverse. Switching scenes. Now a slideshow of three friends on a camping trip. Kal recognizing their faces from the news. It's the group from Denmark. Flashing through photos of their northern expedition: fishing, swimming, smiling, laughing. Moments of reflection. Repose. The group gathered around the campfire at night. These scenes intercut with stunning photos of the Mackenzie delta. Badger was right. It wasn't a bear. They were nullified by the nightmare. Reaper. Wraith. Kal goes back to the final photo. There it is. Wretched thing. Snarling. Smiling. Blood-stained fangs jutting out in every direction. Chunks of flesh caught between saw-toothed teeth. White gums leaking black ooze. Infection dripping from its mouth. A ghastly sight. Pupils pinned. Deep-set yellow eyes buried in their sockets. A man's face pried and pulled. Shaped into a muzzle. Pallid skin stretched across the skull. Lowered neck attached to a body covered in coarse black hair and matted black fur. This distorted form with elongated legs, torso, arms, and hands. Gnarled finger with serrated bone claws. The creature caked in blood. Kal can't believe what he's looking at. Can't comprehend. What the hell is it? Wendigo? Werewolf? One and the same. Poisoned. Possessed. This demented being. Beyond disturbed. How? How could that exist? To think this is what they saw in their final moments. Lives erased. Snuffed out. Awful. Evil. No. Not how this works. Like Lenny said—the spirit continues. Can't be claimed. Carries forward. Then there's Jake. Stuck. Imprisoned in a body no longer his own. Haunted. Tortured. Consumed by the curse. An incomprehensible scale of suffering. When did the parasite take hold? How? Why? What? Are there more? Questions at a clip. Pouring in. Kal rattled. Turns the camera off. Places it in its case. Locks the lid. Hands shaking, he cracks the window. Breathes in the cold air. If he's looking for answers, he knows where to look. Jake put it on paper. Kal grabs the spiral-ring notebook from the glove box. How does a man become a monster? About to find out. Kal opens the cover. Turns the page.

FUGUE

She blows out the candles on her birthday cake. Jude feels sick to his stomach. Maggie, little sister, the newest addition to the family, still smiling, still glowing from her special day. The gifts, the games, the celebration. No idea. No idea what's waiting. A forced performance. That's all it is. Eight and six. Two years apart. Two years praying for an escape, somehow, someway, avoid this day. It's terrible. Terrible what they do. What they did. Now he's expected to help. They can't do this. Not to her. Not to sweet little Maggie. Curly blonde hair, bright blue eyes, dimples. That giggle. Her laugh. Can see her spirit. Curiosity. A kindness to the child. Innocent. How could they? It won't make her stronger but it might destroy. Who knows how she reacts. Look what it did to Simon, the night terrors, the stuttering. Jude can't do it. They can't make him. But they can. They will. Sergeant Major will see to it. Honour thy father or suffer the consequence. Death, Jude can deal with. Disappear. Dissolve. It's the torture, the terrorizing for his transgressions that concerns him. There's no end to it and he can't fight back. He's tried. Too weak. Sergeant Major too strong. There's nowhere to run or hide. He's always there. Watching. Conspiring.

The birthday girl yawns, fighting to keep her eyes open while waiting her turn to wash up at the bathroom sink. Maggie dressed in a hand-me-down nightgown, two sizes too large, pooled at her feet. Sergeant Major, as always, stands by the door for inspection. Each time Jude glances over, Sergeant Major stares back stone-faced. Mother standing obediently beside him with those raccoon eyes and glazed expression; frail, frightened, defeated. How could God, the one they worship, all-knowing, all-loving, benevolent God, make this man his father? Wards of the state. Adopted by evil. How could the creator abandon them to this monster? Put them in this prison? They've done nothing wrong. Why are they being punished? Jude fights back tears. There's no going back now.

John, Luke, Margaret, Matthew, Mary, Simon, Ruth, Thomas, Jude, now Maggie. Always on their sixth birthday. Why six? Why? No explanation. None. Any mention of it within the group is strictly forbidden. John was chained in the bunker for months when he tried to run. Luke had his jaw broken, wired shut, after he begged Margaret to forgive him. Matthew was buried in the box for eight days for trying to warn Mary. They muzzled Mary because she couldn't stop crying, and starved Simon for asking why. Ruth was lashed across her legs and back for attacking Mother. When Thomas tried to run, they made him walk over burning coals. Jude knows this because Sergeant Major told him. A warning after the fact. Divide and conquer. Alone with their guilt. Their fear. Each child in isolation. Exhausted.

Eyes open in the dark. On his back looking up at the ceiling. Jude hears the turn of the deadbolt as the door opens. Mother aims the flashlight directly at Jude's face. He squints, trying to block the light with his hand. Mother holds it there. Jude gets out of bed, puts on his slippers, and follows her to the bunker.

Brought to a bucket of ice water in a rust-stained bathtub, Jude follows orders, scooping out the ice with a colander. When the ice has been removed, he stands in the corner while Sergeant Major, sitting naked in front of the mirror, applies his make-up, covering his face in a chalk-white foundation, then painting his neck black from under the chin to top of his collarbone. Jude imagines smashing a hammer into the back of his skull or sinking a knife into his back. Sergeant Major stands up, pulls on the black robe, walks to the back of the bunker, and opens the chest freezer.

Revulsion. Jude feels sick. He wants to throw up. The mask. That horrendous mask. Just looking at it makes him nauseous. How could anyone put that abomination on their face? A patchwork of skin stitched together from God knows what: pig skin, roadkill, roustabouts? Layer after layer. Lumpy, wrinkled, cracked. Wisps of hair still attached in sections. The melting sheen of frost makes the mask looks like it's sweating. Sergeant Major, back in front of the mirror, smearing fresh layers of lipstick around and around its awful

Fugue

drooping mouth. Iris open. Eyes black. Pupils so dilated it's as though there's nothing behind the mask.

Mother stands behind the camera. Brother and sisters in bed with their backs turned, feigning sleep, while Maggie softly snores from her back. Jude, placed behind her bed, stands with the bucket of ice water. Sergeant Major, in full costume, crouches down beside it. From all fours, he nods to Mother, who lights the string of firecrackers. On cue, Jude dumps the bucket onto Maggie's head. The water crashes, splashing off her face. Maggie wakes with gasp, coughing, choking. Sergeant Major calls out with a scraping whine.

"Maggieeeeee."

Sergeant Major rises above the bed. Mother shines the flashlight on the mask, illuminating the monster. Maggie screams. The monster leans in with a violent hiss. She screams again. Screams with such force it tears her vocal cord. The monster shrieks in response, raising its arms for the kill. Maggie's eyes roll back. Switched off. Shuts down. Sergeant Major drags her limp body out of bed and stands her up in front of the camera. Maggie's head flops to the side, the whites of her eyes showing, her mouth hanging open. Mother ignites the flash powder, triggering a burst of pyrotechnics in the T-shaped flash lamp. She holds it aloft for exposure and take the photo. Sergeant Major lets go. Maggie crumples to the ground.

Gone. Broken. A slack-jawed mute. Helpless. Incontinent. Fed by gavage. No bringing her back. Lifeless. Lost in a catatonic stupor. The blue of her eyes pulled back. Jude grief-stricken. Crestfallen. Crushed by the guilt. At night he kneels by her bed, begging, pleading, for her to get better, to forgive him. Promising to find a way out, to free them from their wretched confines, but there's no response.

The doctor suspects encephalitis lethargica is the cause for Maggie's condition. The origin of the disease is unknown. There is no effective treatment. All according to Sergeant Major, who seizes the moment to proselytize.

"This does not mean defeat. We will pray for our precious Maggie, fallen ill, as this tragedy unites us. Our family stronger for it as we shoulder the burden in providing her the best care possible. For there's no use looking to the outside for help. Strength from within—God willing, we can lead Sister Maggie back into the light."

Truculent, quarrelsome, combative, hostile. Accused of each, Jude takes the beatings and starves for his sins. Not that it matters. Not after Sergeant Major revoked his reading privileges. All he had. Prefer they kill him and be done with it. There's nothing left. Nowhere to go. Jude cherished the thirty minutes he was allotted to read to Maggie each night above all else. He tried to sell each story, enunciate every word, timing the pauses, punctuation, feeling, flow. A chance to communicate. Connect. And there were days he'd swear she was listening, retaining the words, absorbing the stories. The feeling so strong, at times, he'd look up to gauge a reaction that wasn't there, but it didn't matter. He knew there was a reason. Something to it. Rebuilding a broken bond. Piece by piece. Word by word. That was the intent. His purpose. His promise. Each day, without fail, by her side with a book. Sergeant Major saw it, sensed it, then severed the connection. Applying his favourite apparatus of control: "The Lord giveth, and the Lord taketh way."

On his eighteenth birthday, brother John is bequeathed a neighbouring parcel of land. The celebration takes place on site. Record temperatures. Sweltering heat. They wheel Maggie out from across the field for the celebration. Sergeant Major, holding a spade shovel, gathers the family around for his grand gesture.

"The land is John's to harvest, construct a home, raise a family on. A significant first step towards the community we must aspire towards. Strength in numbers. Each capable member of the family will lend their labour towards building John's home. If Luke continues to abide, to contribute, he will receive a plot of lands beside John's when he turns eighteen. No one breaks rank. Each gets their turn. Patience, virtue, industry—that's how we build our kingdom."

Sergeant Major hands John the shovel. John breaks the dirt, posing for the camera. Mother takes another picture of John holding his framed land claim. Jude bears witness, arms crossed, seething. How could John accept this gift? Surrendering his impending freedom for a parcel of land in the same prison. Trading independence for internment. Jude prayed John would leave and never come back unless it was to liberate them. Now big brother's smiling,

Fugue

bowing to the Sergeant Major. Ignoring the abuse for his own advancement. Coward. Jude walks away. Mother asks where he's going. Jude keeps walking. Sergeant Major commands him to stop. Jude kicks up dust and spits in the dirt. A direct act of defiance. Jude checks his shoulder, sees Sergeant Major tearing towards him. Runs. Blindsided by the sergeant. Knocked down in the dirt, dragged by his collar, back across the field to the bunker.

He wriggles, writhes, scrapes and claws, grabbing whatever's in reach, hanging on, refusing to go down those stairs. Kicked, punched, pummelled. His fingers pried apart, stomped on, broken. Jude screams. Keeps fighting. Resisting every step of the way until the tank is empty. Completely gassed. Exhausted. Nothing left. Brought down below, he collapses in the corner. Drenched in sweat, his cheek against the cool concrete, Jude listens to the running water as Sergeant Major fills the tub.

Held under. Thrashing. Lungs about to explode. Pulled out. Gasping for air. Pinned back down. Repeat. Again and again until Jude can't find the strength to raise his arms. Turning toxic, he blows out the carbon dioxide, inhales the water. Lungs burning. Like they're being torn apart. Sergeant Major rips him from the water, drags and drops from the tub. Two brutal chest compressions crack ribs, expel the water and everything else. Rolled onto his side. Coughing, retching, heaving, until his airway opens. Intake. Oxygen. Breath. That is all. Spent. Done. Unable to lift an eyelid, Jude hears footsteps. Sergeant Major walking away. Heading up the stairs. When the door closes behind him, Jude surrenders to the darkness.

He heard about the seizure after the fact. Ruth told him once he was released from the bunker. It happened when Sergeant Major dragged him down there. Maggie's eyes started fluttering, her body shaking, suddenly the pitcher of lemonade exploded. John and Mother were hit with the shrapnel. John had glass shards buried in his arm, Mother got one under the eye. Sergeant Major deduced that the pitcher shattered from thermal stress. Sweltering heat from the sun coupled with the surplus of ice cubes compromised its molecular structure. Ruth isn't convinced. She believes it was Maggie. Her seizure caused it. Happened at the same time. No coincidence. Can't be. Jude shrugs. Makes no difference. Sergeant Major's probably right. Blame it on the sun. Maggie's mind is as broken as that pitcher of lemonade.

New recruits. Brother Paul and Sister Emma are welcomed to the ward. Introductions are made. Paul, age four, sickly, malnourished, head shaved from lice. His sister Emma, still a baby at six months old, big brown eyes, cowlicked black hair. Jude stays silent, detached, while the others feign excitement. Sergeant Major cradles Emma on the couch, Mother and Paul beside him. Thomas wheels Maggie over as requested. Sergeant Major leans in with Emma.

"Look, Maggie, beautiful new blessings for our family. This is Emma and that's Paul—your new brother and sister. Their family could not provide for them so we welcome them into ours."

Maggie shudders. Eyes flickering, she falls into convulsion. Sergeant Major orders John and Luke to lift her up, lie her down on her side. They step forward, stopped in their tracks by the deafening shatter of glass. Mother screams, covering Paul's face. The baby starts crying. The seizure stops.

"Nobody move! Stay away from the broken glass." Sergeant Major hands Emma to Sister Margaret and moves from room to room. Heading upstairs, then returning minutes later.

"Shattered. Every window in the house. Interesting . . . very interesting, Mother. It appears our little Maggie has a magic trick."

Sergeant Major kneels beside Maggie's chair with his hands on her arm rest. "Isn't that right, Maggie? We're all very impressed. That was quite a statement you made. My question is why? Why would you do that? To your home? To your family? Someone's got to clean up this broken glass. Someone has to pay for new windows, new mirrors, and it won't be you, will it, helpless little Maggie? You scared Mother. Made your little sister cry. That's not allowed. Now what do we do? What's next?"

Sergeant Major stands up. Snaps his fingers in front of Maggie's face.

"Hello? Anybody home?"

He kneels back down and hangs his head.

"Mary . . . fetch me a glass of water. I'm feeling parched."

Fugue

Sister Mary returns from the kitchen with water. Sergeant Major takes a slow sip and stands up.

"Ah . . . that's good. Nothing beats a glass of cool, clean water when you're thirsty. We're lucky you didn't break all the dishes during your little tantrum, aren't we, Maggie? We'd have nothing to eat off. To drink from. Having said that, I'm perfectly willing to sacrifice this glass if it means communicating with my little Maggie. After all, what's one glass amidst all this destruction? So here it is."

Sergeant Major places the half glass of water on the coffee table coaster.

"Do what you did, Maggie. Show us another magic trick. I know you're listening. Speak up."

They wait for a response.

"Are you angry?"

The glass doesn't move.

"Are you sad?"

Not a ripple in the water.

"What is it? How have we offended you?"

Silence.

"Maybe you were just excited to see your new brother and sister. Is that it?"

Nothing but the whites of her eyes. Head tilted back and to the side.

"Speak, damn it! Speak!"

Sergeant Major picks up the glass. Flings the water in Maggie's face. Jaw clenched, he smashes the glass on the hardwood floor and grabs her arm rest.

"Deaf, dumb, mute. You can't hear me? You can't control it?"

Water dripping down Maggie's face. Sergeant Major shakes her wheelchair.

"Prove it! Prove your power!"

Jude can't take it.

"Don't touch her!"

He rushes in and Sergeant Major clobbers him with a backhand that drops Jude to the floor. Bell rung. Partially concussed as Sergeant Major continues shaking Maggie's wheelchair.

"Answer me!"

No response. Maggie's eyes rolled back. Body limp. Sergeant Major stops shaking the chair. Leans in close. Hissing at Maggie through gritted teeth.

"I know you're in there. You can hear this. You understand every word as you mock our family. Making us change your diapers. Laughing in your mind as we bathe, wash, and dress you. Forcing us to participate in this gross spectacle, this silly little performance of yours, but fair warning, dear, precious, little Maggie—another outburst like that and I'll break your neck. Better yet, perhaps I'll bury you alive. Dig a hole. Put you in it. Start piling on the dirt and see if that snaps you out of your little funk."

Still nothing. Sergeant Major pushes the chair away from him in disgust.

"Freak!"

Sergeant Major spits on the floor.

"Mother, I'm leaving. I'll be gone several hours. Children, help your mother, see to it this glass is cleaned up before I get back."

Maggie is moved to the bunker. Locked in. No one speaks her name. It's verboten. Sergeant Major keeps his key chain clipped to his belt loop at all times. Only Mother is allowed access to the bunker. Jude's stress, his concern for Maggie, grows with each passing day. Worried sick, stomach in knots, needs to escape, alert someone on the outside, but the distance between the property and town is too great. Sergeant Major would stop him before he got to the road. Jude is trapped under his rule. His watch. Shackled to the bed frame when Sergeant Major's not there or sleeping. Impossible to escape. Hopeless. Can't... Can't quit.

Weeks pass, then months. Jude fears the worst, that Maggie's dead, but continues his silent communion. Speaks to Maggie in his mind. Talks to her throughout the day and in bed at night. Telling her to stay strong, to survive, they'll get through this. He describes new lands, new locations they'll visit when they escape. Any time he reads, it's to her. Morning, noon, and night, he tells her he loves her, that she's not alone. There's no reply, imagined or otherwise, none needed. He will not stop. It's death or deliverance.

A year goes by. Halfway through the next one. Not a word mentioned of Maggie but Jude continues speaking to her. Keeping the connection, imagined or otherwise, as he bides his time seeking a means of escape. Awaiting the reveal, signal, sign. Understanding it may arrive in stages; he must be patient, perceptive, and ready to act when the moment arrives.

Jude sees it when Sergeant Major teaches Matthew how to drive the old Model T for his fifteenth birthday. Brother Thomas and himself are brought along for the ride. Jude listening intently from the back seat. Taking mental notes. The second he has a moment to spare, he jots down every detail on a piece of paper, later structuring a list of starting instructions on the flip side of the paper. Jude keeps the instructions folded in his pocket; any time he has a moment alone he reviews them:

Step 1: Make sure the key is off and the hand brake is engaged with the lever all the way back.

Step 2: Open the choke with left hand. Prime the engine by cranking the lever with right hand. Turn it over three times.

Step 3: Turn the key to battery.

Step 4: Make sure the spark advance lever to the left of the steering wheel is up.

Step 5: Barely open the throttle with the accelerator lever on the right of the steer wheel.

Step 6: Engage the crank, give the lever one half turn using left hand, grab the fender for strength.

Step 7: Advance the spark, pulling lever down until engine runs smoother.

Step 8: Engine running, switch the key from battery to magneto.

Step 9: Release hand brake. Press lever forward to ninety degrees to put car in neutral, then press clutch pedal down to go forward in low gear. Push the lever all the way forward for high gear.

Step 10: Pull the accelerator down—drive away.

Of course, none of this matters without the car key. He needs to get that key chain.

On the eve of Brother Paul's sixth birthday, Sergeant Major instructs Jude that he will be required to hold the bucket. Maggie's absence means the task is bestowed to him once again. Jude nods, outwardly accepting the assignment to appease Sergeant Major, knowing it won't happen. Not this time. Not another one. It ends tomorrow. Jude prays for a sign, the ability to recognize the moment and seize it. Lord, steady his hand. Grant him strength. He's got to get those keys. Has to.

Intense heat. Jude feels the sun burning his neck while shovelling and hauling dirt for the construction of Brother Luke's new home. Approaching lunch, Sergeant Major stops work early. Let the celebration begin. He instructs Mother to pack a picnic basket and for everyone else to grab their swimsuits and towels.

It's a ten-minute trek through the backwoods to the water. Sergeant Major piggybacks Paul, the birthday boy, on his shoulders. Everyone gets in the water, including Mother, who pins up her dress and wades in with Sister Emma, now two years old. The older boys wrestle and splash about. Sergeant Major teaches Paul how to float on his back, then spends several minutes launching him through the air into the water, sending Paul into fits of laughter every time.

When Mother starts unpacking the picnic basket for lunch, Sergeant Major challenges the older boys, John, Luke, and Matthew, to a race, swimming to the buoy and back. At least two hundred metres' distance. The contestants line up along the shore. Margaret announcing the race: Ready . . . set . . . go!

The challengers plunge into the water. The spectators applaud. Shouting encouragements. Sergeant Major's pants, key chain attached, hanging on a tree stump behind them. Jude waits until they pass a hundred metres, steps into his shoes, and excuses himself to use the washroom. Mother nods back, keeping her eyes on the race. Jude unclips the key chain from the belt loop, walks up the hill, out of sight, and sprints full speed through the woods.

Back at the house, Jude soaks the living room couch in engine fuel and takes a match to it. The burning couch catches the curtains. Flames spreading across the ceiling as he pours more fuel along the front and back porch. Sealing both entrances with a wall of flames, Jude rushes to the bunker.

Fugue

Heart racing, he unlocks the hatch. Finds Maggie near death, starved, withered, barely breathing, on a soiled mattress in the back room. Her arms are covered in burn marks; piles of spent wood matches cover the floor. His heart breaks, he wants to weep for the suffering she's endured, but there's no time. Jude grabs her arms, drags Maggie across the floor to the stairs, scoops her up, slings her over his shoulder, climbs the stairs, staggers to the garage, and flops Maggie down in the back seat of the Model T. Hands on knees. Heaving for air. Jude catches his breath, primes the engine, and turns the ignition.

Smoke rising. House ablaze. Sergeant Major roars his name. Jude jumps behind the wheel. Advances the spark. Releases the hand brake, puts the lever to ninety degrees, and presses the clutch pedal. The car moves forward in low gear when Sergeant Major bursts into the garage and punches Jude full force in the ear. World spinning, seeing stars, Jude is ripped out of the car, onto the dirt. Sergeant Major turns the engine off. Jude scrambles backward, too dizzy to stand. Sergeant Major pounces, repeated strikes. A brutal beating. Jude can't cover up. His brothers, pleading, begging Sergeant Major to stop. Nose broken. Eyes swelling. Jude pissing himself as his body goes numb.

"You want to start a fire? To burn our house down? You shall burn with it!"

Sergeant Major grabs Jude's hair and drags him towards the house. Jude hears his sisters screaming in the distance. Knocked senseless, motor function gone, he can't connect body and mind. Sheets of heat, crashing through, closing in, closer to the searing wall of fire. No. Please. Not like this.

Seized. Stalled. Dropped. Jude rolls over, looks up, eyes stung by the smoke. Sergeant Major stands before the flames, arms out, head back. Crack! Bones snapping in quick succession. Sergeant Major moving, twitching, contorting like a spastic marionette. Suddenly stops. Suspended by invisible strings. Starts vibrating. Shaking. Surge. Rupture. Burst. Sergeant Major's eyes explode from their sockets. Dangling from their optic nerves as bones bursts through skin. Compound fractures. Collapse. Strings snipped. Sergeant Major's mangled body in a crumpled heap before him. Pooling blood. Framed by the inferno. Jude in shock as Mother appears from the path. Stands up as she races towards him. Sees the slaughter. Shrieks. Dropped to her knees. Raised back up. Rattled. Skin starting to sizzle. Crack.

Splat! Another explosion. Turned inside out. Organs exposed. Brothers and sisters scream, cry, wail as Jude limps away from the carnage back towards the car. Maggie still shaking. Eyes flickering back. Jude takes her hand. Holds it.

"It's over, Maggie. We did it. We're free now."

A breeze rustles the leaves. Little sister lets go.

DIRGE

Two-lane highway. Cross into the Northern Territory at the 60th parallel. Driving a flat, tree-lined corridor, punctuated by small ponds and not much else. Brings me to the Deh Cho Bridge, which takes me across the Mackenzie River. Listening to an audio book on the American buffalo when I see a small herd of wood bison grazing at the side of the road. Press pause. Pull over to take a picture. The hulking bovines briefly look in my direction then go back to munching grass. Keep driving. Continue listening. Quite the history lesson. Coincides with the current assignment and my overall understanding of things.

Commonly referred to as buffalo, bison are the largest land animals in the Western Hemisphere. Their population in North America fluctuates between three hundred and fifty thousand and four hundred thousand. Of that total, thirty-one thousand wild bison remain. The rest are found on farms or ranges. At one time, bison roamed the North American plains with herds so vast it took days to pass them. Two technological advancements in the late 1800s dropped their numbers from ten million in 1871 to several hundred by 1889. One advancement was a new tanning method that allowed their soft hide to be made into tougher, more desirable leather. This made buffalo hide ideal machinery belting, a crucial component in a burgeoning industrial age. The other technology was the development of the repeating rifle, allowing hunters to kill buffalo in huge numbers. This efficiency turned the buffalo hunt into an outright attack. Train travellers going through the Midwest would shoot the beasts out their window for sport. The US army sanctioned the wholesale slaughter as a strategy to conquer the Plains Indians. Commanders ordering troops to kill buffalo in order to starve the Natives into submission. Plans for territorial conquest now matching market demand. Industry devouring buffalo hides, meat—then bone.

Photos from the late 1800s show men in suits and bowler hats standing proudly atop massive piles of buffalo skulls. These men were buyers. Selling buffalo bone by the ton. The bones shipped by train or steamship to facilities that would render them as fertilizer, glue, and ash. The bone ash consumed by the sugar, wine, and vinegar industries to shine their sugar and clear their wine. Makers of fine-bone china also entered the market. Requiring high-quality bones that weren't too dried or weathered.

This insatiable demand for the ungulate's skeleton was welcomed by farmers. The liquidation of buffalo herds had transformed the prairie/plains from a living highway to a literal bone yard. In many areas farmland had to be cleared of buffalo bones for plowing. Now there was money to be made for their inconvenience.

Buffalo bones were the first cash crop for many settlers, but they were rarely paid in cash. More often, bones were exchanged for receipts that could be used at any merchant if properly endorsed. If pickers were paid in cash, a ton of bones could fetch them a few dollars. That same ton shipped to rendering plants and furnaces was worth between eighteen and twenty-seven dollars. Boiled, charred, crushed, or powdered it was worth as much as sixty dollars.

During this massive bone harvest, wagon loads were brought to town where a local buyer would inspect them. Only bleached bones, free of flesh and oil, were accepted. Skeletons were purchased by weight, so inspectors would carefully examine them. Some pickers soaked bones in water to make them heavier, others would add sod under the bones for weight. At its peak, twenty teams per day were bringing in bones for weighing and unloading.

Inevitably, supply outstripped demand. Prices spiked when the supply grew short in 1890 but there were no more bones to pick. In short order, the fertilizer industry began crushing rock to obtain fertilizer phosphate and the bone trade turned from boom to bust. The buffalo population decimated with under a thousand left.

Brought to the brink, the bison were saved from extinction through captive breeding, farming, and land protection. Close call, though. Cautionary tale.

Dirge

Greed its own disease. Certainly has a way of distorting things. Manifests in many forms. I should know. My job would not exist without it.

Getting close. Last leg of the drive. The endless boreal forest giving way to a network of small lakes and pink rock outcrops. Dwarf pines, some shrubs, wild grass, and lichen cling to exposed rock. A surreal quality to this desolate landscape. Approaching midnight and it's still light out. True dark doesn't take place in the territories. Not this time of year. The night existing in suspended twilight from late May to early July.

Feels like I'm driving through a waking dream, when after sixteen hours on the road, I finally reach the "Diamond Capital of North America." Cruising past the airport with Long Lake to my left. To my right, I see the "Welcome to Yellowknife" sign posted in front of a Bristol freighter peeking above the pines. The blue cargo plane, with red-tipped wings and a blunt, rounded nose, now resting on blocks. Past that, I exit the highway onto the Ingraham Trail. This takes me to the Milner Lake access road. Off that, a dirt road that brings me to the cabin. Touchdown. Stretch my legs and back out. Spend another hour prepping the cabin and call it a day.

Next morning, I drive into town. Grab breakfast at the Gold Range Diner. Sipping my coffee while I scan the **The Yellowknifer**. Still front-page news: Search continues for Mati Cottrell and Claire Demming. "Three weeks ago, the sixteen-year-old Native girls snuck out of Mati's mother's house during a sleepover—they haven't been seen since." Police following various leads. No new information brought to light. Two more names for the database.

Pat down before I board the boat. No problem. Not yet. A beautiful afternoon to be out on the Great Slave. With braided black hair and polarized frames, Chief Sabourin sits proudly in the captain's seat of a brand-new twenty-five-foot Bayliner Cruiser.

I'm stationed at the back of the boat, surrounded by four overweight Native men Chief calls his cousins. Glum-looking group. Severe. One cousin in particular. Greasy mullet, wispy goatee, and a face blighted with pockmarks. Staring at me with stone-faced hate and a shotgun in hand. Pump action. All for show. Not worried about the gun. Not from this distance. With a heavy boot I'd push that rifle into his chest but it's not my intention to complicate things, and I'm fairly sure the other cousins are holstered under their hoodies. Best keep quiet. Ready to speak when spoken to. Thirty minutes from shore, Chief eases up on the throttle.

"Switch seats with him."

The older cousin with the harelip stands up and I move to the front of the boat.

"I gotta double the asking price."
"You've already been paid."
"That was the deposit."

Chief flashes a smile that puts his gold canine on full display.

"This is serious business here. A lot of risk involved."

He can barely keep a straight face while saying it and I let him know.

"Chief, you're getting greedy."

Watch his expression go cold.

"How the fuck can someone working for David fuckin' Drachmann accuse me of being greedy? Don't insult my intelligence. There's two hundred thirty-seven tons of arsenic buried under the ground at Giant Mine. The owners got their gold, made their money, closed the mine, and left a fucking mess behind for taxpayers to clean up. I know how this game works. Privatize profit. Subsidize cost."
"The council and community are well compensated."
"Are they now? Well, here's a history lesson for ya. When Giant Mine started operating, it would burn its tailings up the stack. That toxic smoke would spread over the area. Particulate falling to the ground. That practice continued until a Dene child died of poisoning from eating contaminated snow. That was 1951, the child's family was handed seven hundred and fifty dollars in compensation. It was gold then, now it's diamonds—Drachmann Diamonds. It's pay now or pay later. Either way, we're getting paid."

Dirge

Brought back to shore. Make the call. More money wired to the same account. Notify the chief. He invites me to a traditional feast at the bingo hall later that evening. When I arrive, he and his cousins are sitting at a banquet table near the front of the hall. Several buckets of KFC with all the fixings are lined up between them. Chief spots me at the entrance, tears into a drumstick, and waves me over. He nods to a cousin, who offers me his seat. Decline. Remain standing. Chief tilts the bucket of chicken towards me.

"Help yourself to some deep-fried raven."
"No, thank you. Prefer my fried chicken cold with hot sauce."

Chief shrugs his shoulders. Tossing the bone onto his plate.

"Fuck it. Let's go then."

Follow Chief's souped-up, chromed-out, white F-150 to Rae-Edzo. A small community located off the Yellowknife highway on the northern arm of Great Slave. Rae-Edzo, renamed Behchokò, previously known as Fort Rae, is traditional Dogrib territory. The population, just shy of two thousand, is still majority Dene. The area has two churches: St. Michael Catholic Church and Tilcho Baptist. There's also a gas bar, convenience store, family diner, and community centre.

Chief parks by the boat launch and I park beside him. See a Native man in his sixties, maybe seventies, smoking a cigarette in a scraped up, fourteen-foot aluminum boat tied to the dock. A Misty River with the classic blue and red decals. Get the impression he's waiting for us. Chief and a couple cousins step out of the F-150. Walk towards the boat. Follow them over. Nod to the man. Nods back. No introductions necessary. Stone-face motions for me to lift my arms for another pat down. Show him the 9 mm in a shoulder holster under my windbreaker.

"What the fuck is that?" Chief sneers.
"Insurance."
"Hand it over."
"Not happening."
"Then it's not happening."
"The money's been transferred. You got guns. I got gun."

"Fuckin' cheeky, huh?"

"No disrespect, Chief. Strictly business."

"Whatever."

Chief waves me onto the boat and we take a thirty-minute ride to an island near the opposite shore. Met by another cousin strapped with a Glock 10 at the floating wood dock. This one lean. Sinewy arms. Leads us towards a canvas tent where another cousin is posted outside on a fold-out chair. Chubby. Squat. Spitting sunflower shells onto the ground. Looking bored with a shotgun in his lap. Sees Chief. Stands up while the lean one pulls back the canvas doors flaps. Big reveal. There he is—Ethan Drachmann. Lying naked in the dirt with his hands tied behind his back. The current "warehouse supervisor" and heir to the Drachmann Diamonds family fortune. The son of David forced to piss and shit in the corner of the tent. Chief wincing from the smell wafting out.

"Fucking stinks."

Ethan's doughy body covered in welts, bruises, and bug bites. Razor bumps and patches of stubble across his chest, back, and belly. His curly mop of hair, slicked back in corporate headshots, now a poofy, knotted mess. Can see he's taken a beating: spilt lip, black eyes, broken nose. Buzzing in my ears. Mosquitoes starting to swarm outside the tent. Chief sparks a smoke.

"Glad I don't have to drive back with him."

Ethan isn't moving. Eyes open. Catatonic. Chief blows smoke in his face.

"Get up. On your feet."

No response.

"You fuckin' deaf?"

Still nothing. Chief nods to the lean one, who drives his boot into Ethan's back. Breaks the trance and maybe some ribs. Ethan gasps. Screams. Starts wailing. Rolling around in the dirt. Chief not having it.

"Shut the fuck up or you're getting another one."

Ethan whimpering with a suppressed whine. Chief rolls his eyes.

Dirge

"Pick him up."

The cousins hoist Ethan up under his arms.

"You have clothes for him?" I ask.
"Nope."

Lean one pushes Ethan out of the tent. Marches him down to the dock where the Misty River and its captain are waiting. Before we get in the boat, I untie the rope holding Ethan's arms.

"Jump in the lake. Wash yourself off."

No towels. Back in the boat. Ethan sopping wet. Shivering as we bounce over chop, driving into a direct headwind. Approaching the other shore, I see a few kids playing by the boat launch. The engine putters as we drift towards the dock. The kids staring at the naked white man in the boat. Ethan shaking now. Teeth chattering. Stone-face steps out first and shoos them away. I warn Ethan to watch for the glass as we pass a smashed vodka bottle on the way to the car. Unlocking the door for Ethan, I kneel down to retie my shoes and check the undercarriage for any devices. Inside the car, I turn the ignition.

"Crank the heat," Ethan orders.

I oblige. Checking my rear-view as Chief peels out in the F-150.

"What happens now?"

When the cloud of dust clears, I start driving.

"Did you hear me? What's the plan? Where are we going?"
"Tomorrow morning, you fly to Calgary and receive directions from there."
"Why not tonight? Just get the fuck out of here."
"No more flights."
"No more flights? Why aren't we using the private jet?"
"Not available."
"What the fuck do you mean, not available? It's a private jet."
"Your father's decision. He doesn't want you on the company plane."
"Why?"

"You'd have to ask him."

"Bullshit. I'm going to. This is fucking bullshit."

Ethan sulks in silence until we reach the intersection of the Ingraham Trail and 48th Street. If you take a right onto 48th Street, it takes you into town. I turn left.

"Where are you going?"

"We're staying at a cabin on Milner Lake."

"Why? Take me to my place."

"Precautionary measure."

"I'm supposed to show up at the airport naked? I need clothes."

"There's clothes for you."

"And how the fuck am I supposed to get on a commercial airline without my wallet, without ID?"

"I have your ticket and identification."

"What about my phone?"

"You don't need your phone."

"How do I receive directions?"

"Someone will meet you at arrivals."

"Fuck that. Give me your phone."

"Not happening."

"Give me your fuckin' phone."

Ignored.

"Give me your phone or you're fucking fired."

Ignored again.

"My father sent you. You work for me."

Ethan oblivious to the reality of his situation.

"Give me your fucking phone now!"

"Do not yell in my ear again."

"Fuck you!"

I turn down a gravel road just past Giant Mine. Pull over. Put it in park. Slide my seat back. Grab a fistful of Ethan's curly locks and start smashing his head against the passenger window. Crack the glass. Smash his face against the dashboard for good measure. Stop. Ethan in shock. Blood pouring from his nose. Covers his face. Folds over in pain, or pretends to, popping the door open and making a run for it. I remove the keys from the ignition and chase after him. Because he's running barefoot and in piss-poor shape, I'm on him in seconds. Drive my palms into his back. Ethan flies through the air, landing on his stomach. Sliding over the gravel, he springs back up and starts running. Kick his legs out this time. Drive my knee into his lower lumbar, grab another fist full of hair, twisting his neck back. Let him know.

> "Matters of my employment fall outside your jurisdiction. Recognize there's a difference between rescue and recovery. Realize you have no inherent value. In fact, you're a giant liability, which means you don't dictate the terms of our discussion. And that's all this is . . . We sit down, sort out some details, get your story straight, and go from there. Is that understood?"

Answers with a snivelling, "Yes," and I help him to his feet. Ethan's pale blob of a body tore up from the road. Gravel embedded in his skin. At a glance, you almost feel sorry for him.

U-turn. Back on the main road. Ethan staring straight ahead. Watery eyes. Runny nose. Lip quivering with a petulant scowl on his face. I see anger. Indignation. Underneath it all, fear. Can't hide that.

> "You are in . . . so much trouble. You . . . are . . . in . . . so much trouble."

His voice is shaky. Taking little gasps between sentences.

> "You . . . have no . . . idea . . . what you've . . . done."

Still doesn't get it. Zero situational awareness. Embarrassing for his age.

At the cabin, I find Ethan a change of clothes and heat up some chicken soup. Not hungry myself, I pour him a bowl and wait patiently at the other end of the table for him to finish eating. Halfway through, he looks up at me with soup dribbling down his chin.

> "Can you not stare at me while I eat? It's disconcerting."

I take the bowl and toss it in the sink.

"My father did not pay you to assault me!"

Ignoring another outburst, I sit back down. Get straight to it.

"Chief Sabourin saw you in your truck with Mati Cottrell and Claire Demming the night they went missing. Where are they?"

"I'm not saying another fucking word until I speak with my father."

"You're cut off. Daddy's done with you."

"You're a fucking liar!"

"I was sent here to clean up your mess. After that, you're on your own."

"Bullshit! Call him! Call him right fuckin' now!"

"He's not answering."

"Then we've got nothing to discuss."

"Then I grab the toolbox from the back of my truck. It comes with a hammer, pliers, and a butane torch."

Ethan whimpers in response.

"Perfect . . . that's just fucking great."

"Stop pouting. How did those girls end up in your truck?"

"Saw them stumbling down the street. Asked if they wanted a ride."

"You knew them?"

"We'd met."

"Where? They're half your age"

"At a party."

"Whose party?"

"I don't know. Some housing unit in Sissons Court."

"What were you doing there?"

"A friend invited me."

"What friend?"

"Doesn't matter." "I'll decide what does and doesn't matter."

Dirge

Ethan pushes the table into me. Tries to escape but I snag him by his collar before he reaches the door. Rip him to the ground. Starts shrieking so I take the boots to him again. That's when he breaks. Crumples up. Curled in the fetal position, sobbing hysterically. Seeing snot bubbles. Total mess. Once he's exhausted himself, I prop him up on his chair.

"Wipe the snot off your face."

He uses the sleeve of his shirt.

"Who's your friend?"
"Cayden."
"Last name."
"Margis."
"Cayden Margis."
"Yeah."
"How do you know him?"
"He works at the mine."
"Doing what?"
"Heavy equipment operator."
"You've got the girls in your truck. Where do you take them?"
"Corey's."
"Who's Corey?"
"Cayden's buddy."
"What's his deal?"
"I don't know."
"Sure you do."
"Local coke dealer. Sells steroids. Owns a tanning salon and a supplement store."
"What's his last name?"
"Stapp."
"Corey Stapp."
"Yeah."
"Why did you bring the girls back to his place?"
"They wanted to party. One of them was hot for Cayden."
"Cayden's at Corey's?"

"No. He's with me in the truck."
"What were you two doing?"
"Cruising around."
"Cruising around . . ."
"Nothing planned. Picked him up at his place. Went for a drive. Saw the girls and brought them back to Corey's."
"Because they're too young to get into the bar."
"No, that was just a place to go."
"Where does Corey live?"
"Kam Lake trailer park."
"What address?"
"Magrum Crescent. Can't recall the number right now."
"Who's there?"
"Just us."
"That's Mattie, Claire, Cayden, Corey, and yourself."
"Yeah."
"There's no one else there?"
"No."
"What happened?"

Ethan clams up. Cornered. Considering his options.

"Don't stop now. Let's hear it."
"Everyone's drinking. Corey's chopping lines. The girls are wasted. Dancing. Laughing. Having a good time until Cayden starts getting aggressive."
"Why? What's he doing?"
"The way he's talking to them. Asking the girls which one sucks dick better. If they take it in the ass. Making things awkward. Corey doesn't help. Thinks it's hilarious."
"How do the girls react?"
"They're laughing too but it's nervous. Can see their confusion."
"Then what?"
"Cayden backs off a bit, but the girls are a mess. Mati can't stand up. Keeps dropping. Starts mumbling she wants to

go home. Claire can't stand up either. See her slide down her seat with this blank expression. Totally out of it. Same moment Cayden slings Mati over his shoulders. Carries her off into the bedroom then comes back for Claire. Thirty minutes later, he leaves the room with his shirt off. Cracks a beer. Sends Corey in. Corey comes back. Tells me it's my turn."

Ethan stops. Stalling. Trying to recalibrate his story. I prompt him to continue.

"And the truth shall set you free."
"Find both girls unconscious. Naked. Claire's sprawled out on her back. Mati's face down on her stomach. I try to turn to leave but Corey pushes me back into the room. Cayden's behind him recording the whole scene with his phone. These guys are twice my size. There's nothing I could do."
"Nothing you could do . . ."
"They were going to hurt me. I was forced, they forced me, I had no—"
"No what? No choice? I know your profile, Ethan. Daddy's had to bail you out before."
"That was different—"
"Shut the fuck up. You did what you did. Then what?"
"I don't know . . ."
"Do I need to grab the toolbox? Start pulling teeth?"
"I leave. We leave the room. Keep drinking, doing lines, playing videogames. Eventually Corey goes back in to check on the girls or whatever. Sees Mati's stopped breathing. Scared she's dead. Cayden checks her pulse, confirms it, and without hesitation, smothers Claire with a pillow."
"Now you need to get rid of the bodies."
"Yeah . . ."
"Walk me through it step by step. Start to finish."

"We wrap the bodies in the bedsheets with duct tape. Load them into the back of my truck with two twenty-pound kettlebells and drive down to my boat. "

"Where's your boat parked?"

"The docks off Wiley Road."

"No one saw you?"

"No one there. Was like 2 a.m."

"Now what?"

"Transfer the bodies onto the boat. Corey wants to dump them in deep water. Knows where to go. Drive across Great Slave into Christie Bay. Reach the spot. Kill the motor. Drifting offshore. Depth finder's reading over two thousand feet. No wind. No waves. Lake's completely still."

"How long does it take to get there?"

"Around four hours."

"Continue."

"I'm on lookout while they tie the kettlebells to the girls' ankles. There're no other boats. No one on shore. All clear when I hear the noise. Something cutting through the water behind me. Spin around and see this mass of scales arching out of the lake and back down. It's at least six feet wide. Try to get the guys' attention but it's too late. Disappeared under the water. Rush to the sonar but there's nothing there. Cayden smacks me, tells me to quit fucking around, but I know I saw it."

"Let's get back the two dead girls you're about to toss overboard."

"That's it. We dumped them over the side of the boat. Drove back."

"You guys didn't go for breakfast? Grab pancakes?"

"No. Dropped them off and went home."

"Where did you drop them off?"

"Brought Cayden back to his place and Corey to his trailer."

"Where does Cayden live?"

"Ptarmigan Apartments.

Dirge

"What unit?"

"Twelve A."

"Let's go down the list. There's Cayden, Corey, Chief Sabourin, and his crew. Who else can connect you to those girls?"

"No one I can think of."

"You sure about that?"

"Yes."

Stay quiet. Cold stare. See if he coughs up another name. Ethan squirms in his seat.

"What now? What's next?"

I draw the 9 mm from my shoulder holster and fire four rounds into his chest. Easy cleanup. The cabin is rigged with dynamite. I light the fuse, drive out of the blast zone, and wait for the explosion. There's a deafening boom followed by a low rumble. The cabin obliterated in a cloud of smoke. Debris flying through the air.

Ethan stood a chance as an only child but with two brothers, both suitable heirs, he wasn't worth the risk to the Drachmann Dynasty. That being said, the job's not over yet. Check into a room at the Explorer Hotel. Consider my directive. Compose a list of questions and answers. Isolate the variables to the best of my abilities. Bullet point pertinent information to complete what's required. Know what's needed. Clear in my approach, I call my contact and brief him on my conversation with Ethan. Send a copy of the audio recording for conformation while keeping the original file as collateral. Communicate forward action for approval. Receive a reply within the hour. All clear. Informed Cayden Margis is working in camp and won't be back for another week. My preference is to deal with Cayden, Corey, and Chief in quick succession, which means I'm in a holding pattern until Cayden returns from the mine. In the meantime, I may as well enjoy some Northern hospitality.

Shower. Nap. Step out for the evening. Starting at the Gold Range. Drinking beer and shooting pool with some interesting characters. The house band playing classic rock standards. Bar getting busier. Louder. Picking up some hostile vibrations. Two groups mean-mugging each other. One set is seven surly-looking tradesmen still in work gear. Steel-toe boots covered in drywall dust. Place them in their thirties, maybe forties. Mostly white. Big fellas. Rough around the edges. The other set being nine young Native men, tatted up, wearing flat-brim ballcaps, baggy shorts, and wife beaters. Tensions escalating. The two groups talking shit over the music. Pinpoint a few bad drunks on either side looking to make a name for themselves. Can see it's about to kick off. Pay my tab when I hear a bottle break. Chaos erupts. Someone throws a chair. Fists flying. Blur of bodies. Bouncers rush in as the violence spills out onto the streets.

Melee. Ruckus. Stand back and watch things play out. Cops separate the warring factions. Two combatants in handcuffs. One of them is a haggard, middle-aged white man with shaggy hair, long goatee, and a giant beer gut. Blood pouring from his mouth. T-shirt hanging in tatters off his back. Got pieced up by a young Native with a shaved head and neck tattoo. Kid can scrap. His wifebeater's ripped in half but there's not a scratch on him. Still fuming, though. Hurling obscenities while the cops drag him across the street and jam him into the back of a squad car as four more cars pull up.

Exit the madness on Range Street. Walking back to the Explorer. Further down Franklin Avenue, I see a group of teenagers beating up an old man. Ugly scene. The man is drunk, concussed, or both. Stumbling around with his hands out. Scared. Confused. Can't understand what's happening. Getting peppered with punches and kicks when a wild swing drops him. From all fours, he tries to stand up. The man hunched over, wobbling on his feet, when this white boy with floppy hair kicks him flush to the face. Planks him. The man's arms shooting out to his side. Body stiff as he falls backwards in slow motion. Shithead teenagers hooting and hollering. Racing away on their skateboards. As they speed by me, I step into the streets and clothesline the kid who kicked him. Send some sharp kicks to his midsection. Lift the kid up by his shirt. Grab his throat. Dig my fingers into his larynx. Pinching off his airway, I see the fear in his eyes. Trying to pull my hand off his neck while his friends are screaming for me to let go. One of them has his skateboard raised, threatening to attack. Give him the nod but he doesn't have the stones. When the kid's eyes roll back, I lower him to the concrete. Takes a second to regain consciousness. Hear him coughing as I walk over to the old Indigenous man. Looks Inuit. Help him to his feet and hail a passing

Dirge

cab. I place him in the back seat and hand the driver a hundred dollars. More than enough for a taxi anywhere in the city. Suggesting the hospital, I tell the driver to take the old man wherever he needs to go. Tuck another hundred in the old man's vest pocket. Nods back. Not a word spoken between us. I continue the ten-minute walk back to my hotel room.

Lying in bed, I feel the beer sloshing around my empty stomach. Need something to eat. Some grease. End up ordering a medium Hawaiian from Bruno's Pizza. Does not disappoint. Damn good pizza.

Slightly hungover when I wake up. Dissolve an electrolyte tablet into my water bottle. Go back to bed for an hour. Feel better when I wake up. Ready for coffee. Put the kettle on. Pour myself a cup and check the news: 128 bison dead in a reported anthrax outbreak. The dead bison found northwest of Fort Providence, near Mills Lake, during a routine anthrax surveillance flight. Apparently, anthrax occurs naturally in the region. When high water levels are followed by hot, dry conditions, the anthrax spores in the ground become concentrated in low-lying areas. The bison inhale the spores and become infected. People with cabins in the area have been warned to stay away from the bodies. Anyone who comes across other dead bison told to call the Department of Environment and Natural Resources right away. In other news, Mati Cottrell and Claire Demming are still missing.

Blessed with beautiful weather throughout the week. Make the most of it. Hit the driving range at the YK Golf Club, hike the Frame Lake Trail, go for several swims at Long Lake, and take a trip to Cameron Falls. Also cross the street to check out the Prince of Wales Heritage Museum. Work-wise, I scout a few locations, make some mental notes, but that's about it. On my last day off, I pack some beers in the cooler and go fishing off the shores of the Yellowknife River. Bring a few condiments in case I catch something: butter, lemon, salt, pepper. End up hooking a northern pike. Once I fillet the fish, I place it on the pan and cook it up on my camping stove. Pike aren't so good if they've been frozen, they get a grainy texture, but when you fry them up fresh, they're not too bad. Similar to walleye or cod. Certainly can't complain. Enjoy the offering. Considering the last job, this one feels like a paid vacation. Killing the whistleblower didn't sit right. Admired her courage. Her conviction. There was poison in the water and she spoke up. Went public.

Embarrassed my employers. Cost them money. Damage was done but I still got the call. Told to make it look like an accident, so she was crushed by a rockslide mountain climbing.

That night, I looked in the mirror. Felt completely detached from my reflection. Cracked skin. Hair gone grey. Staring at this worn-out creature I've got to keep feeding. An accumulation of scar tissue facilitating a basic evil. No room for remorse. Everything excused by necessity. That contract plagued me for months. Couldn't eat. Couldn't sleep. Kept seeing her face. Two versions. Before and after. Damage done in graphic detail. Made aware early on that each kill leaves a mark. An imprint. Might not register but it's there. Understanding that, I was able to compartmentalize my emotions by acting as an impartial observer. Cordoning off what I can best describe as metaphysical feedback. That limiter allowed me to function in whatever capacity required and still enjoy the fruits of my labour. This one had me worried, though. Thought I was losing my mind. Nightmares are normal, every night normal, but her death disturbed me on a cellular level. A derangement stemming from an absence I can't properly speak to. Felt vacated. Empty. Hollowed out and haunted. Everything poisoned. My nervous system shot. Crippling panic attacks. First one sent me to hospital. Prescribed benzos. Made things worse when I wasn't on them. Walls closing in. Hell was a place and I was in it. Learning there are levels. Rapidly descending. One kill opened the floodgates to all the others that proceeded her. Tortured by demonic voices. Visions. Truly terrifying. Refused to pray. Couldn't. Wouldn't. Reached my breaking point. Ready to end it when I got the call for this one. Forced myself to answer. Won't say divine intervention but it's certainly been a welcome distraction.

Back to work. Waiting in the airport parking lot for Cayden's return flight from camp. When he steps out of the terminal, there's no mistaking him: six-foot-four, jacked up on steroids, and covered in tattoos. Inked-up arms, knuckles, and neck. Sporting cool-guy sunglasses with slicked-back blond hair that's shaved on the sides. Wearing black jeans, black boots, and a crisp white t-shirt. Watch him strap a wax canvas duffel bag to the back of his Harley, straddle the seat, and rev the engine. Bad-boy biker raised in an upper-middle-class family. Cayden's dad's a lawyer. His mom sells real estate. They cottage at Prelude Lake during the summer and stay at their home in Bermuda during the winter. An only child born with a silver spoon. Cayden

Dirge

seems to think he's the king of the jungle. Built like a superhero. Living like an outlaw. An alpha male able to bend the world to his will. A notion that can be erased in short order.

Post watch outside his building. After two weeks in camp, I'm sure Cayden's ready for a night out. Just past ten he steps out in a fresh set of clothes. All black now. Dressed like a doorman with some accessories: gold chain, platinum-plated watch, and what appears to be a skull-shaped silver ring. Crossing the lot, Cayden fires up his Harley and I follow him to Kam Lake, where he parks on the street in front of Corey's trailer home. Has to. Driveway's full. At the top there's a lifted metallic black F-150 Super Crew with a sporty-looking ATV sitting in the truck bed. Parked behind that, a cherry-red Mustang GT convertible. Cayden heads inside. Stand by until they step out thirty minutes later. Cayden now with a Nike gym bag slung over his shoulders. Can see Corey's a big boy too. Large frame but he's loaded with water weight and a thick layer of fat. Looks like he took the steroids and forgot to work out. Clearly spent some time in a tanning bed, though. Freshly cooked. His skin a deep red under the bronzing. The pig comparison an easy one to make with his slightly upturned nose, weak chin, and puffy face paired with these lumpy, bee-stung lips. Not sure if he was born with them or had injections. Either way, they're off-putting. Look wet. Like they're coated in lip gloss. This slob, all dolled up with his hair spiked and gelled. Wearing a pink polo shirt with the collar popped, white deck shorts, and shiny red high-top sneakers. Blinged out with several diamond-studded rings on his stubby sausage fingers. Watch him waddle to the driver's side of the Mustang and follow them for the next two hours as they make house calls: pick-ups, deliveries, collections.

Cayden uses his shoulder to bust the chain latch off one guy's door. Leaves carrying two soapstone carvings. Eventually they double back towards Kam Lake. Stopping at a trailer surrounded by twenty dog kennels and a chain-linked barbwire fence. The dogs, all husky mixes, bark, yip, howl, whine as Cayden and Corey cross the yard carrying the Nike gym bag. Leaving the trailer with another gym bag ten minutes later, this one Adidas. They bring the bag and carvings to Corey's. There a minute or two. Tail them downtown. Arrive at the local strip club.

TYRANT

Done waiting in my truck. Decide to check it out. Size things up. Everyone distracted by this scrawny fella in perverts' row, wolf-whistling at the dancer on stage. Won't stop. Keeps jamming his dirty fingers in his mouth, whistling at a piercing pitch. Cayden's not having it. Glaring at this silly character who's completely oblivious. Too busy enjoying himself. A lazy-eyed drunk with frizzy hair shooting out from under the sides of his ballcap. His entire outfit splattered in dry paint. Wearing jogging pants and a t-shirt several sizes too large that hangs from his sloped shoulders. Teetering in his seat, the fool finally stops whistling. Starts clapping and yelling instead.

"Yeah, baby! Shake that moneymaker! Daddy works hard for his money!"

Corey's getting a chuckle out of it, but Cayden's clearly not amused. Lazy-eye carries on until the girl leaves the stage. Puts an unlit cigarette in his mouth and stumbles over to Corey and Cayden. Pats Corey on the back. Seems to know them. Yammering away about something. Can't hear what's being said over the music. Lazy-eye starts gesticulating his arms wildly. His body language a mix of fear and fake indignation. Being accused of something he vehemently denies. Can see him backpedaling. Trying to explain himself. Pleading to Corey when Cayden drops him with a brutal sucker punch. Corey bursts out laughing. Lazy-eye tries to stand. Fails. Sitting there in shock, hand under his chin, blood pouring out his nose. Scooped up by the bouncers and tossed into the street. Corey still laughing, rubs Cayden's shoulders and orders a round of shots. Seen enough. Not the place. Slam back my beer, take a piss, and go wait in the truck.

Bar close. Still light out when they leave the club with the feature act. Bringing her to a bush party at these sand flats past the airport. Keeping my distance, I hang back by the tree line. Pull a pair of binoculars from the glove. Survey the area. Scan the crowd. It's mostly teenagers and young adults with some older dirtbags, like Cayden and Corey, scoping things out. All the action taking place in the centre of the sand flat. Everyone gathered around a massive stack of burning pallets. The outer circle bordered by a collection of cars and pick-up trucks with competing sound systems. Each trying to drown out the other while dirt bikes and ATVs buzz in and out of view.

Dirge

No surprise, there's plenty of underage drinking going on. See one kid puking in the sand, while another kid pisses on his back for an audience of cackling spectators. Twenty feet from that a girl, maybe sixteen, is puking from the back seat of a Toyota Camry. Vomit dripping from her long red hair. Moving on, I spot some troublemakers sneaking along the perimeter of the party, sniping people with a Red Ryder BB gun. The young shooters cracking up over their targets' pained reactions. Watch them shoot a tubby teenager with bad acne who charges them, fists flailing. This sparks a mini brawl that edges precariously close to the red Mustang. Corey screaming at everyone to "Back the fuck up!" and bitch-slapping a gawky teenager who bumped into him before spitting in his face. The kid's friends pull him away before it escalates.

The party still in full effect when a squadron of cop cars races past me to break things up. Cayden and Corey buddying up to one of the police officers. Obviously another juicehead. Swole from fluid retention, with inflated delts and traps. Sporting a spray tan, bald head, and chin-strap beard. Likely sell him gear or maybe it's the other way around. The cop chatting up the stripper before he's pulled away to collect teenage waste cases. Officers arresting teens covered in puke for a night in the drunk tank. Time to clear out. Cayden and the stripper sit inside the Mustang. Corey finishes his beer, tosses the bottle, and gets back behind the wheel.

Follow them to his place. Twilight hours. Take my time. Make sure no one else is showing up. Silencer attached, I commit to the moment. Make my approach. Easy access. No dogs and they forgot to lock the front door. Glide through, gun raised. Loud sex from the bedroom at the back of the trailer. Place is a mess. Piles of dirty dishes and takeout containers. Beer empties scattered throughout. On the kitchen table, a dusty skull-shaped ashtray, its open mouth overflowing with cigarette butts. Infomercials playing from a giant flatscreen TV in the living room. Framed posters of **Goodfellas**, **Scarface**, and **The Sopranos** hang from the walls. On the coffee table, a coke mirror smeared with residue, a razor blade, and a rolled-up fifty-dollar bill. Finger on the trigger, I make my way down the hallway to the far room. Checking the first bedroom and bathroom. Both empty. Continue to the back. Closed door. Twist the handle. Kick it open. Cayden's in bed with the stripper while Corey jerks off in the corner. Piggy looks up with his pants around his ankles.

"Who the fu—"

Three in the chest. One between the eyes. Cayden tosses the stripper off him onto the floor. She yelps in pain, landing awkwardly on her arm. I step forward. Sight set on Cayden as he curls up against the headboard. Hands raised trying to shield his face.

"I didn't tell them anything. I swear to God. I fed them a bunch of bullshit. The raid had nothing to do with me. Please, I—"

The bullet rips through his hand. Plant two more in his chest. The stripper knows not to scream. Neck strained. Staring at the wall. That's how I leave her.

One more stop. Drive down to Old Town. Streets are quiet. Chief's three-storey house sits atop a forty-foot rock face. Park on a side road. Walk up the winding driveway. All the doors at the base of the house are locked. Climb the stairs to the back balcony. Pop the lock on the sliding glass door. Step into the dining area with a clear view of the living room. TV showing a video feed from multiple angles inside and outside the house. See the shotgun on the coffee table. Stone-face snoring on the couch. Take aim and fire. The bullet pierces his skull, sinking into the arm rest. Above the fireplace mantel hangs a large picture of Chief Roy Sabourin at a pow-wow wearing a feathered headdress, beating on a caribou skin drum. Native art, artifacts, encased and framed throughout the house: arrowheads, antlers, furs, beaded flowers, Dene rattles, and dreamcatchers. Staged photos lining the wall as I move up the staircase: Chief with his chest puffed out, posing with politicians at every level of government. Pictures placed in ascending order, all the way to the prime minister at the top of the stairs. Roy with a shit-eating grin. Eyes beaming with pride. Made man. Top boss. Turning right when I hear coughing from a room at the other end of the landing. Listen through the door. More coughing. Push it open, gun raised, ready to fire. Looking into a master bedroom but the bed is empty. Realize Chief's in the ensuite bathroom. Hear him straining, farting, trying to take a shit. Kick the door wide open. Chief flinches. Covering up. Sees me. Sighs. Resigned to his fate.

"Fuck sakes. Least let my wipe my—"

Dirge

Brain matter on the backsplash. Message sent.

Ethan, Corey, Cayden, Chief: direct links to the murder of Claire Demming and Mati Cottrell have been eliminated. Drachmann Diamonds remains untarnished, shining brightly into the future. Who knows how they'll spin Ethan's disappearance. Don't care. My work is done. With a long drive ahead of me, I shower up at the hotel, catching a few hours' sleep. All it takes. Bags packed. Grab breakfast at the Trader's Grill before I hit the road. Reading a copy of **The Yellowknifer** while I sip my coffee. Still nothing on the missing girls. Says some bush fires are causing concern and the anthrax outbreak has reached record numbers. Four hundred sixty-three bison killed and counting. The article describing a unique procedure for disposing of the bodies. Each carcass injected and doused with formaldehyde to prevent scavenging and the release of spores. The carcasses then burned in a pyre using wood, charcoal, and diesel fuel. A standardized protocol with a semblance of ceremony. Better than being dumped off the back of a boat.

TEMPLE

Pressure. Digging into his back. Eyes open to a water-stained drop ceiling. Wind howling. Windows rattling. Hard rain. Rolls over. Knees in the dirt. Was lying on a pile of rubble. An aggregate of smashed concrete, chunks of drywall, splinters of wood and bent nails. Brushes off the debris sticking to his back. No shirt. No shoes. Tattered track pants. Where's his wallet? Phone? Scans his surroundings. Abandoned building. Factory? Half of the windows smashed out of their square steel frames. Glass scattered across the ground. Black mold climbing up brick walls. Turns to see his father seated behind a large rectangular desk in the far corner. Cold stare. Severe. Has to look away. Hangs his head. No explanation or excuse. Can't conceive of how he got there. Which is where? Another reclamation project? More property? Must be. Blacked out and somehow stumbled onto one of their worksites. Embarrassed. Ashamed. Exposed. Hears the door close as his father leaves the room.

Water streaming in through holes in the ceiling. Past the pipe and grating. Collecting in pools several storeys below. Recoils from a dead rat in the rainwater. Flutter of wings. Pigeons in the rafters. Raccoons crawling across the high beams. Rust reigns over the old generating station. Slowly corroding massive steel columns and girders. Giant blocks, slabs of cracked concrete with mangled rebar jutting out the top, are lined in rows along the dirt floor. Demolished formations awaiting disposal. Dust particles floating through the air. Soft glow through a giant grid. Rows of industrial windows lead to another door. Father waits. Exits.

Belted by the wind and rain. Huddled over. Arms clenched around his torso. Bare feet trudging through cold mud. Turns the corner. Facing a vast field of tall grass stretching towards snow-capped mountains framed by a pitch-black sky. In the middle of the expanse, an old red barn. Father halfway there. Trying to keep up. Temperature dropping. The wet ground now frozen. Cutting his feet. Burrs clinging to his tear-away track pants. Wind screaming across the prairie. Pushing him back. Whipped with pellets of rain turned to hail. Tries to shield his face. Chin tucked into the nook of his shoulder.

Exhausted. Shivering. Shaking. Frozen feet bleeding and blistered. Steps inside the barn. Shelter. Shielded from the wind. Father holds the lamp. Hangs it. Nods to the back of the barn. Spirits soar—Magnus! An old friend. All grown up. At least four metres in height. Several tons now. Sloping back with the high shoulder hump and long, curved tusks. Thank you, Father. Thank you. A humble bow. Limps towards the mammoth. Reading his body language. His hairy companion at ease. Approachable after all these years. Tail swishing, trunk low, with those lazy-looking eyes. Magnus lowers his giant domed head. Nudging in how he used to. A gentle gesture of affection. How he missed him. Overwhelmed with emotion. Sorry. So sorry. Should have never left. Back by his side. Won't leave him now. Never again. Running his hand through coarse fur, he pricks his finger. Burrs. Magnus is covered in them. Realizes his coat is in terrible condition. Matted fur. Patches missing. Scabs and lesions. Open wounds. Infected. One of them festering. Closer look. Maggots. Writhing with maggots. How? Who let this happen? He did. The guilt twisting his stomach. This beautiful beast left to rot. Suffering in his absence. Save him. Heal him. Have to. Hears a clicking sound as the mammoth's eyes go wide. Panic. Tusks strapped, wrapped with chains running to winch motors in the ceiling. What is this? Why? Father answers.

"Taking the tusks. I paid for him."

Booming clap of thunder. Sheets of hail hammering the tin roof. Motors on. Gears engaged. Spin. Coil. Snap. Tusks ripped from their roots. Magnus buckles. Blood spurting out of the sockets. Staring down in disbelief. Horrific betrayal. His soul screams. Shakes the foundations. Shot back into black. Gasping for air. Drenched in sweat. Heart racing. Disoriented. Swirling darkness. Spinning. Buzzing. Pulsing light from the intercom. First time he's heard it. Who? Why? What time? Don't answer. Leave it. Not going away. Might be an emergency. Has to be. Presses the panel.

"Hello . . ."

"Sammmmuel . . . wakey wakey."

His name from another life. That voice. Who else? Has to be.

"Uncle Vince is here to take you on an adventure."

Guests aren't allowed. Against policy. Sam exits the building. Sees Uncle Vince, window down, smoking, smiling at him from the back seat of an armoured SUV. He nods in acknowledgment. Approaching the vehicle when a rat scurries across the sidewalk, disappearing down a sewer grate. Vincent raises a tumbler of whiskey, jingling the ice cubes in the glass. Trademark twinkle in his eyes. Same wiry build. Sporting a sharp suit with a buzz cut. Sees the specks of silver in his hair but far less than before. Skin somehow tighter but not stretched. Natural. A few lines across the brow. Crow's feet in the corner of his eyes. Still looks five years younger than the last time he saw him and that was ten years ago. Vincent takes a drag of his cigarette and flicks it onto the street.

"Holt? Holt Womack? Where'd you come up with that?"

Vincent questioning his name change.

"Does it matter?"

"That depends. You the new sheriff in town?"

"What is this?"

Vincent sips his whiskey. Hissing from the after bite.

"Missed you at the funeral."

"Didn't get the invite."

"Take a drive with me."

"Need to be at work in three hours."

"Another low-end factory assignment?"

"Indeed."

"Ask me again why I'm here."

"Why don't you quit fucking around and tell me."

"Reparation."

"For what?"

"The will. You were robbed."

"Disowned."

"Regardless. There's a significant part of his legacy the estate doesn't know exists."

"Say it so I can go back to bed."

"Let's loop around the block and I'll break it down for ya."

Uncle Vince chopping lines of coke on the middle console. Beside him, a stunning woman in a high-cut white skirt. Staring out the window. Introduced as Ms. Clarke. Distant. Detached. Bored. Arctic-blue eyes and frosted cupid's bow lips. Straight platinum blonde hair with silky shine. Scooped neckline highlights her bust. A perfect handful. Exquisitely crafted. Smooth, sculpted legs. Crossed. Her skirt brought right to the edge.

"One for me . . . one for you . . ."

Vincent carving two large rails. Leans in. Snorts one. Reels back.

"Yee-hah . . . okay . . . yeah . . ."

Wipes his nose. Eyes watering. Nods to the next line.

"Help yourself."

"No, thanks."

"Something to drink?"

"No."

Vincent vacuums the second rail up his nose.

"Wooooof. There it is. Anyway, yeah . . . Your dad. At least he died doing what he loved."

"Flying his helicopter or looking down on everyone?"

"Ha! You're something else, Sam."

"And to think the program was actually working."

"Program?"

"Same one you're on."

"Whatever do you mean?"

"Dad looked ten years younger every time he popped up in the press."

"He did look great in those wedding photos."

Temple

"Yeah . . . really put the work in. Full head of hair. From grey to brown. Those saddlebags under his eyes are gone. The liver spots on his hands have disappeared. And miraculously, the old turkey wattle on his neck has tightened up."

"Makeup and photo filters."

"Bullshit."

"Said with such certainty, such disdain."

"Drinking from the fountain of youth, but dead is dead."

"Don't dance on his grave just yet."

"Why? He's planning a comeback?"

"Convinced."

"Of what?"

"The Atman."

"Which is what?"

"Reverie developed some kind of connectome. A neuro-mapping software that backs up your brain. Stores your memories. All that info ready for download when the time's right."

"Sounds like a scam."

"Maybe but that's the idea. Problem being his body was destroyed. Nothing to salvage. If he died from a heart attack, they'd fix the plumbing, attempt a reboot, but that ain't the case."

"So he's done."

"Left with a couple of options but they're not great. The androids are impressive but they're not there yet. Not really. Right now, the plan is to clone him with requested modifications. Once the clone has completed puberty, it'll be euthanized, and your father's file will be downloaded into it."

"Well, that's evil."

"Bit of a grey area."

"Sounds like murder to me."

"Could be construed that way but ultimately it comes down to patent and property laws."

"The lawyers found a workaround."

"They always do."

"Five-year hold on the estate. Then it's split in half. One half to be divided amongst your siblings. The other half held in safe keeping. A fifty-year trust while his team tries to bring him back. If not, it's redistributed amongst his heirs."

"All praying he stays dead."

"The estate is structured to protect against tampering. Any collusion or attempt to block his resurrection by the heirs will result in a forfeiture of future inheritance and make them liable for damages. That aside, let's get to the business at hand."

Vincent sparks another cigarette.

"Your father made a substantial investment in a project we kept off the books. Our first and only joint venture. Something you need to see in person."

"Do I?"

"If you want his half of the action."

Possessions packed: clothes, phone, toiletries. Sam notifies the building manager he's ready for inspection. Takes ten minutes to check the list. No damage to the unit. All clear. Good to go. Where, is the question. For what? Vincent refusing to spoil the surprise. "Buy the ticket. Take the ride."

Private jet fuelled and waiting. Drive onto the tarmac. Park by the plane. Four young women, porn star pin-ups in flight attendants' outfits, waving from the top of the air-stair. Vincent ushers Ms. Clarke past him.

"After you, my dear."

Letting her lead the way, Vincent nudges Sam with his elbow, nodding up at the view as Ms. Clarke climbs the stairs. Her glutes flexing in a skintight white skirt. Left cheek. Right cheek. Mesmerizing. The perfect posterior with a diamond-shaped gap between the legs. Ms. Clarke striding past the smiling attendants without pause while Vincent takes a moment for introductions.

"Good morning, ladies."

"Hello, Mr. Slade," said in unison.

"Please. Vincent or Vince. Whichever you prefer."

Giddy laughter from the girls.

"This is my nephew, Sam."

"Hi, Saaaam."

Sam gives a curt nod and steps onto the plane while his uncle carries on.

"And what, may I ask, are your names?"

"Rochelle."

"Yuri."

"Becca."

"Britney."

"Lovely. Now, it's a long flight, girls, so let's have fun with it."

Forty-one thousand feet in the air. Orange juice. Freshly squeezed. Rochelle bends over to fill Sam's glass. Plunging cleavage directly in his eye line.

"Thank you."

"My pleasure."

Vincent sniffs a bump of cocaine off his thumb.

"Raaaa! Wooo . . . okay . . . yeah."

Leering at Rochelle's ass as she returns the cart to the galley where the other hostesses are gathered.

"There for the taking, Sam. At least for the next forty-eight hours."

"I'm good."

"Don't be such a prude. Start with a massage. Bedrooms in the back."

Sam swigs back his orange juice, pulls on his headphones, and closes his eyes.

Slammed upwards. Dropped. Ribcage across the arm rest. Rude awakening. Screams from the back. Sam buckles in. Hears his uncle.

"Hitting some chop!"

Vincent shuffling down the aisle in boxer briefs. Shirt unbuttoned. Pants around his ankles. Holding a foaming bottle of champagne. Becca and Yuri crawling behind him, topless, smeared lipstick, trying to reach their jumpseats in the main cabin. Screaming with each jolt of the plane.

"Nothing to fear, folks. This plane is built and tested for—"

Bucked sideways. Vincent flung into an open seat. Somehow still holding the champagne. Takes a swig. Sight to see. Coke-ringed nostrils. Champagne running down his chin, neck, arms. Raises the bottle.

"Bring it on, baby!"

Trap door freefall. Shot back up.

"Woooooooo! Stomach-meet-throat. Helloooo!"

Ms. Clarke across the aisle, jaw clenched, gripping the arm rest.

"How we doing, Emi? I know how much you like—"

Another lateral jolt banks her head off the window. Vincent tosses the bottle behind his seat.

"We're alright . . . bumps and bruises. Scrapes and scuffs."

Rummaging through his pockets, he pulls out a crumpled pack of smokes.

"Some people pay good money for that kind of action."

Sparks a bent cigarette. Takes a quick drag, blowing smoke through the cabin.

Outside the vortex. Smooth air aside from the occasional shudder. Sam's heart still racing. Stinks like a skunk. Shirt soaked in sweat. Ms. Clarke, already over it, at work on her laptop. Pants pulled up, Vincent walks the aisle. Smoke dangling from his mouth. Shirt still unbuttoned. Beer in hand, he flops down in the seat across from Sam.

"Checked in with the girls. A little rattled but everyone's fine. Drink service will resume shortly."

Temple

Descent. The island comes into view. Sheer cliffs. Granite walls. Ice-capped mountains named after Norse gods. Flying into the fjord. Over the inlet. Crossing tundra with braided rivers feeding connecting creeks.

Landing gears engage. An airstrip lashed across the land. Pummelled and paved. Dashed white lines. The wheels touch down between its borders.

"Terra firma."

Vince drops a pill into the palm of his hand. Washes it back with beer.

"Summer solstice. That's as dark as it's going to get out here."

Caps the vial. Shakes it.

"One of these and it's lights out. Rest up tonight.
Rage tomorrow."

The plane slows to a stop. No terminal, just a control tower. To the side of the taxiway, a mass section of paved tundra lined with private jets, SUVs, ATVs, UTVs, helicopters, and heavy machinery. Toys and tools. Billons on display.

Tire treads across the land bridge. Adding new ones. Security drops them off at their campsite inside the corridor. Luxury yurts with rocket stoves and running water. Ms. Clarke cuts a direct path to her yurt while Vincent brings the flight attendants back to his. Further back, canvas tents for the staff. Smoke rising from their fire pit. Sam surveys the landscape. Sees an inukshuk placed on a pile of flat stones by the bank of a languid river. Water slowly churning. Their site is situated under the shadow of giant stone towers. Cleaved mountaintops dusted in snow. The uninterrupted west face stretched out before him. Its angular peak swooping upwards, above all, to the temple. A brutalist structure staking claim to the land. This marvel of engineering in direct defiance to the natural order. Those who brought it here bending the landscape to their will. Echoes from a rockslide. From one side of the valley to the other. Shifting topography. Alive. Awake. Eternal.

The patter of rain against his yurt. Calming acoustics. Doesn't want to leave his bed but has to pee. Gets up to use the washroom. Checks the stove while he's at it. Adds more wood. Sheets still warm when he returns to bed. Breathing in the cool fresh air as the rain lulls him back to sleep.

Grey skies. Mountains shrouded in mist. Intermittent rain. Sam steps inside the cook tent. Sees the ice queen sitting alone at the large wood banquet table. Sipping a cup of coffee. Staring at her phone. Ms. Clarke with her hair pulled back in a ponytail. Puffy pink down vest over a white alpaca sweater with grey hiking pants and boots.

Sam pours himself a cup of coffee, reads the options, and places his order with Umik, a local hire cooking breakfast on a stainless-steel charcoal grill at the back of the tent.

"Morning."

Umik nods back.

"I'll have bacon and eggs with bannock biscuits."

Another nod. Umik drops two more slices of thick-cut bacon onto the cast iron pan.

"Thank you."

Sam moves to the table, sitting across and several spaces down from Ms. Clarke.

"Good morning."

She looks up from her phone. Yet another nod, this one barely perceptible. Goes back to staring at the screen. Sam notices she's not wearing any makeup. Flawless skin. Not a single blemish. Roll out of bed radiant. Wonders what it would take. What does she need? Want? Expect? No chance he meets her criteria. No problem. Keep things casual.

"Sleep well?"

Silence. The awkwardness interrupted when Umik rings the bell. Breakfast served.

"I got it."

Sam brings their plates to the table.

"Thank you."
"No problem."

Pours himself a glass of freshly squeezed orange juice from the jug.

Temple

"Wonder if we'll see the sun today?"

Ignored. Sam butters his bannock. Spreads on some raspberry jam.

"Storm warning for late afternoon into the evening."

Delayed response. Now an official exchange.

"Could be the same front we flew through."
"Maybe."
"Intense."
"Exhausting."
"Vince seemed to be enjoying himself."
"Sure was."

Ms. Clarke, done talking, dips her toast in the rich orange yolk.

Eating their breakfast in silence when Uncle Vince saunters in.

"Umik, I just saw an Arctic fox sniffing around my yurt. Is that a good sign? We going to win some money tonight?"

Umik shrugs. Ms. Clarke leaves the table. Exiting the tent without a word. Vincent rolls his eyes. Pours himself a cup of coffee and takes a seat across from Sam.

"Hell hath no fury like a woman scorned."

Won't ask. Not taking the bait.

"Problem being she's very good at her job."
"Which is?"
"Arrangements."
"Arranging what?"
"Everything. Nothing. I don't know . . ."

Vincent sips his coffee.

"Big reveal today. You excited?"
"Bated breath."
"Ha! You'll see soon enough."

Waiting by the river when four utility terrain vehicles pull into camp. A tall man with slicked back, honey-blond hair and grey stubble steps out of the first UTV. Dressed head to toe in alpine tech apparel. Amber lenses resting on a Roman nose. Uncle Vince flicks his cigarette in the fire pit. Greets the man with open arms.

"Let's see those baby blues!"

Pearly whites with sharp canines. The man removes his sunglasses. Winks back with bright blue eyes.

"This man's a goddamn movie star!"

Shades back on. They greet each other with a firm hug and handshake.

"Gunner, this is Alden's son, Sam."

Gunner reaches out. Shakes hands with Sam.

"Honoured to meet you, Sam. Your father was a man of great vision. A mentor of mine in business and beyond."
"Sorry for your loss." Replies Sam

Vincent interjects.

"Bit of baggage between Sam and the old man."
"Understood. Family can be complicated."
"Shall we?"
"We shall."

Awaiting the arrival. Heavy cloud cover. Terrible visibility. Gunner in communication with air traffic control. A low murmur from his walkie crackling softly in the background. Vincent blasts a bump of cocaine off the back of his thumb.

"Christ almighty . . . what if it crashed?"
"No chance, boss. Military transport crafts carry heavy payloads in all kinds of conditions. The Hercules is a workhorse."

Action over the walkie. Gunner turns up the volume as air traffic control welcomes the aircraft into their airspace. Vincent bouncing his knee in anticipation.

"Here we go, Sam. Here we go."

Temple

On cue, the massive carrier bursts through the mountain fog.

"How much did we pay for that thing?"
"Guess."
"A yard."
"Well under."
"Eighty?"
"Sixty."
"What's the sticker price?"
"One point eight."
"Steeeeep."
"War is a racket but I've found some great deals."
"Haaa! Gunner, yaaa fuckin' swindler."

They meet the hulking aircraft at the end of the tarmac. Looking on as the cargo door is lowered. Twenty mercenaries in black combat uniform and body armour exit the hull in two files, forming a line on either side of the loading ramp.

"Time to inspect our precious cargo." announces Vincent.

Gunner driving between the lines and up the ramp. Inside the hull ten more mercenaries stand guard over of a twelve-foot by twelve-foot titanium cube equipped with biometric scanners, encryption pads, and vital sign monitors. Gunner, Vincent, and Sam exit UTV. The armed escorts step away from the cube as Gunner steps forward, reviewing the vitals with the chief physician and his team.

"Good numbers. Everything in accordance. Let's take a look, shall we?"

They switch the digital displays to a video feed from inside the cube. It takes a second for Sam to register what he's seeing. To separate the subject from its surrounding. An entanglement of wires, cables, cords, and tubes. All plugged into slabs of striated muscle sealed under powder-white skin. This being/biomass/behemoth covered in electrodes. Intubated and affixed to a mechanized throne.

"Resting soundly."

TYRANT

The abomination strapped and sedated. Chin on its chest. Gunner slides open the viewing slot. Peeks inside. Waves them over. Vincent ushers Sam forward. He looks through the frame. Facing the throne. Harsh lighting. Washed out. Green tint on bleached hide. Veins like garden hose. Knotted rope. Torrents of blood pushed through twisted vascularity. Pathways. Conduit. How do they fuel this beast?

"Starting to stir. A little early . . ."

A warning from the anesthesiologist as the beast opens heavy-set, blood-shot yellow eyes.

"No big deal but we need to make a move."

The monster struggling to lift its head.

"Take it to the temple."

Gunner ends the viewing. Shuts the slot. Vincent taps more cocaine onto the backside of his thumb. Blasts another bump.

"Yaaa . . . ladies and gentlemen, ODIN HAS ARRIVED."

Tearing across the tundra in separate vehicles. Gunner following the cargo. Sam and Vincent returning to camp. Sam staring out the window. Still processing what he saw.

"Awfully quiet there, Samsanov."

Vincent removes a gold flask bound in a leather casing from the jetted pocket of his jacket.

"Fifty-year-old malt scotch whiskey."

Takes a nip. Offers the flask to Sam, who waves it away. Still processing what he saw. Vincent tucks the flask back in his pocket.

"Are you brooding?"
"What the fuck was that?"
"The future of combat sports. Eight teams in an elimination bracket. An exclusive group. Think F-1. Consider the fighters cars. As they advance through the bracket, you can swap out

parts or replace the entire car. All dependent on performance and the degree of damage sustained."

"That's your joint venture? Some human-hybrid… fucking mutant freak show blood sport."

"I mean . . . it's one a hell of a show."

"Nightmare. That thing's a nightmare."

"Odin's a beast. We've got the best team on the circuit."

"Odin . . . let me guess, Dad picked the name?"

"Sure did."

"That thing's alive."

"Well, yeah."

"It's sentient."

"So are the cows slaughtered for steak."

"To live is to die, that's what you're saying?"

"Enough. Spare me the righteous indignation."

"Fuck you. Fuck that. I didn't sign up for this."

"Yeah, ya did."

"How?"

"You're here. What'd you think you were going to see?"

"I don't know . . ."

"You accepted the invite because you're bored and broke. Uncle Vince arrived just in time. Temple takes place once a year. This is the championship round eight years in the making. I brought you in to share this moment. Going for gold. For glory. So stop saying no and start saying yes. This ain't some morality play. We're in it to win it and blow our fucking minds along the way."

The walls of the lodge are adorned with stuffed head mounts, antlers, and animal hides. The team, their backers, and potential investors are gathered for a ceremonial dinner banquet. Freshly caught fish and game meat prepared by a highly decorated chef flown in at a premium. Gunner holding court at their table. Speaking to a bald, bloviated, and bespectacled executive. Sam recognizes this man as Barry Finkelman, the CEO of an asset-management firm with direct ties to the central debt merchants. A tall man with splotchy skin, beady eyes, and a bullfrog neck. Another operator in the consolidation scheme. Agents of inversion plundering nations. Feeding off the workforce. Deranged hoarders and their empty amusements. Offering nothing of value so they lie. Cast spells. Baseless projections. Fabricated earnings. False flags. Now this grifter wants to enter the arena. Have his own gladiator. Stake claim to an indentured avatar spawned from a lab. Finkelman fumbling the fork on the way to his mouth. A chunk of Arctic char bouncing off his chin and back onto the plate as Gunner continues his presentation.

"Consider the mechanics. It's more than stacking muscle. The number-one component for strength is where the tendons are attached to the bone. Leverage generates power. We're always making adjustments. Alterations. Trying to find the sweet spot. Expanding upon that—mind the modifiers. What's the trade-off? The tipping point? Muscle and tendon strength must be matched with the requisite bone density or you'll see fractures. If this balance is out of alignment, the muscles pulling on the tendons can snap bones. We've seen it. So now you increase bone density but you're presented with a new problem. Traditional instruments for surgery, for repair when required, no longer work. Need a new set of tools. Find what works. Precision lasers and diamond tips drills. Problem solved. Moving on. But wait . . . what are we missing? What else is affected?"

Barry baffled. Wipes the grease of his chin with a red linen napkin and shrugs his shoulders.

"Security. Implements of control. Standard bullets no longer work if a fighter escapes its confines and goes ballistic. Tranq darts won't put them down in time. So, what's the correction?"

Gunner waits. Barry answers.

"Better bullets?"
"Exactly. Armour-piercing bullets. No big deal. Add them to the armament. All set, right?"
"Yes?"

Temple

"Not so fast. You've increased bone density to account for strength, to carry extra muscle mass, but you've compromised your fighter's potential for speed and agility. Both essential in battle. Timing. Precession. Point being—optimal performance in the field of combat is an ongoing experiment. Disabling and destroying your opponent with ultimate efficiency the goal."

Gunner directs the wait staff to clear the empty plates. Finkelman motions a server to refill his glass.

"I'm curious, what's their level of intelligence? Is it something you can program?"

"Intellect is a fascinating subject. There's a widely distributed pattern of correlations with brain structures. Capacity corresponding with volume. They encompass almost all areas. For instance, a thicker temporal cortex is linked to larger, more complex dendrites of human pyramidal neurons. Larger model neurons are able to process synaptic inputs with higher temporal precision due to faster action potentials in larger cells. This enables more efficient synaptic information transfer."

"I just nod my head and pretend to know what he's saying," quips Vincent, garnering a chuckle from the group.

Ms. Clarke leaving the table as Gunner continues.

"Forgive me, I have a tendency to ramble regarding topics I'm passionate about. Yes is my answer to the question of programming. Anansi allows us to encode for volume and gene function to boosting cognitive ability. However, brain structure is not fixed at one particular developmental time point. Grey-matter volume changes throughout childhood as well as adulthood. It's influenced by learning, hormonal differences, experience, and age. When people acquire a new skill, juggling, for example, transient and selective structural changes are observed in brain areas associated with the processing and storage of complex visual motion. White matter also undergoes dynamic change in response to learning, stress, and social experiences. Taking all these factors into consideration, your fighter's cognition is a combination of coding and coaching. Nature and nurture."

Sam ready to leave the table. Had enough. Sick of these psychos dazzling each other with "science" and business acumen to disguise their depravity. Finkelman flushed in the face. Nodding along to Gunner's presentation before interjecting with another question.

"Do you breed for temperament?"
"Great question. How do you design disposition? What are the ideal traits applied to combat? Is a fearless fighter a good one? Do they need that fuel to motivate? Can an angry fighter harness their rage or does it blind them? Once again, there's a balance to be struck."
"Trial and error."
"Precisely. Learning as we go. We're at an interesting juncture with Odin. His processing speed and pattern recognition, two criteria crucial to combat, are far beyond any human mind. He absorbed his coaches' teachings within a matter of months. Professionals who spent a lifetime acquiring knowledge in the field. Odin's technique, his combinations, now light years ahead."
"Did you fire the coaching staff?"
"No, that would be folly. We're a team. This is a collaboration and they're highly involved in the process. Soundboards for us to understand what we're looking at. What's working and what's required. When to push. When to pull back. Resistance plus rest equals resilience. Strength and conditioning. Stress inducers. Cold. Heat. Exhaustion. Steel sharpens steel and diamonds are formed under pressure. Understanding that, we created an apparatus called the rack that hits every target."

"The rack?"

"Sounds fun," adds Vincent.

Barry chortles. Slugs more wine.

"It may not move the metrics for 'fun' but it has produced a marked increase in performance thresholds. An essential device for sustained improvement. Understanding the fighters can't spar past a certain point. Too strong. Too fast. Too vicious. The potential gains aren't worth the risk of injury."

"Is this the same Odin that started the tournament?"

"Yes, in fact. A rarity. Win or lose, the scale of damage usually dictates we cut our losses and move on. The fighter may be salvageable but it's better to start with a clean slate."

"Because of cost?"

"It's more a matter of time. If monetary concerns were an issue, we wouldn't be here."

Guffaws. Deranged. Demented. Done—Sam steps away from the table. Heads outside. Drizzling rain. Ms. Clarke smoking a glowing green vape under the overhang. Decides to approach her. Engage conversation.

"Not your scene?"

"Games. Always with their stupid fucking games."

"Need something to fill the void."

Ms. Clarke pulls the hood up on her rain jacket. Walks away while motioning for transport.

"What'd you say to her?"

Sam turns as Vincent puffs a cloud of cigar smoke into the air.

"You want a shot with Emi, you need to be direct."

Looks back and she's gone.

"Don't beat around the bush. Her time's precious and her patience thin. In case you haven't noticed."

"Fuck it . . . I need a drink."

"Yeah, you do."

Toasty warm inside the yurt. Yuri and Becca making out on the bed while Vincent snorts another line off Rochelle's tits. Sam sipping his beer as Britney grinds against his lap. Surrender so easy. Pour a drink. Pop a pill. Rip a line. It's that simple. Now he's in it. Complicit. Compromised. Weak. Should be ashamed but he's feeling too damn good.

Wide open. Fresh air fills his lungs. Amazing. The act itself. Breath in. Breath out. Helicopter standing by as his uncle smokes a cigarette in the wind and rain. Scoundrel. Rascal. Cad. At least he can laugh at himself. Admit the grift. Recognize the criminality. Not the old man. Fair gains. Hard fought. Always at war. Mergers and acquisitions. An ongoing assault against perceived enemies after his inexhaustible wealth. Anything excused. Exploiting resource. Crushing dissent. Ruthless. Denying impoverished populations access to clean drinking water because he bribed local officials for regional water rights. Dislocating villagers by burning their crops so he could purchase their land. A total psychopath. Cruelty a commendation. Caring is kindness and kindness is weak.

The chopper flies over the sheer-face granite walls of the land bridge. Going into cloud cover as Vincent snorts a four-inch line off the back of his cellphone.

> "Whoooopsie . . . ah . . . yeah . . . woah . . . big ol' gagger . . ."

Eyes watering. Cocaine flakes falling from his nose.

> "Yeah, so, wooo, yeah . . . fun fact. Our opponent is owned and operated by Berzin."
> "Shocker."
> "Right? Who knew the world's largest private military company would be into engineering genetic freaks for blood sport. Turns out they're quite good at it. Won the tournament the last two years but we're getting the belt back tonight."

Sam shifting from exhilaration to nervous anticipation.

Temple

"See, the old man actually poached Gunner from Berzin. Was actively pursuing Logos before the crash and wanted to plug Gunner in as a director."

"What a shame. Defence contractor would have been a real feather in his cap."

"Samuel with the sarcasm. Gunner's still pushing for it but there's a lot of ground to cover now that we've lost access to the larger accounts."

Through the clouds the temple comes into view. Hard lines. Raw concrete, steel, glass, and stone. The massive utilitarian amphitheatre built atop a disk-shaped platform anchored into the northern peak of a twin-peaked mountain. On the southern peak, a helipad connected to the temple with a span bridge built across the rocky saddle.

"Ain't it something."

"Sure is."

The temple in the path of a massive thunderhead pushing in from the north.

"That looks menacing."

Shaped like an anvil. Forked lightning shooting through its towering column.

"Sure does."

Vincent takes another nip from his flask as the pilot announces their descent.

Gunner waiting outside the landing zone.

"Gentlemen . . . Welcome to the show."

"How's our beast?"

"Snarling. In the chute."

"Ready to reclaim the kingdom."

"Chomping at the bit."

They cross the forty-foot-wide bridge towards the temple. Built their battleground on a mountaintop because why not? Trying to claim a place amongst the gods. Obscene excess in the face of wide-scale suffering. Sam feels a chill as they walk under its shadow. Met at the arched entrance by four strikingly beautiful women in sleek black dresses. Long legs and high cheekbones. None under six feet. Supermodels in contrast to Vincent's harem of porn star stewardesses. Each of the four women unique in appearance. One a Nordic goddess. Ethereal. Almost alien. Pale blues eye. Blonde-white hair. Another with porcelain skin. Raven-black hair and Cleopatra bangs. Luminous green eyes flecked with gold. The next appears Latin in lineage. Butterscotch skin. A thick mane of sun-kissed hair and welcoming, come-hither hazel eyes. Finally, the one with flawless sable skin. Hair in braids. Eyes like nothing he's ever seen. Gun-metal grey with traces of silver. Vincent takes the lead during introductions.

"Wow, wow, wow. What an arrangement . . .
Absolutely stunning."

Their servers smile and bow.

"I'm sure you've met Gunner. This is my nephew Sam and I'm Vincent."
"Freyja."
"Cleo."
"Octavia."
"Genevieve."
"An honour to meet you all. Please lead the way."

A black tunnel, lined with glowing kerosene wall lamps, lights the way to the emperor's box at the east end of the coliseum. Berzin takes the west. Finkelman and the other investors have their own room. Coaching staff watching from the lockup. This is theirs. Theatre seating. Black leather recliners with full view of the battleground. The girls take their place behind the bar. Sam standing before the battlefield. Ground level. The killing floor a massive circle. Bone white with a barely perceptible concave and propagating rings from the centre out. The combat zone surrounded by tinted black glass walls at least forty feet tall. Sam puts his hand on the glass to confirm it's there.

"Almost invisible . . ."

Pristine. Not a smudge, streak, or spot on it. Gunner raps the glass with his knuckles.

Temple

> "Self-cleaning blast-resistant glass. Damn near indestructible."

Deep rumble of thunder. The sky getting darker.

> "Darling, you have the most dazzling eyes. I'm sure you hear it all the time but it simply must be mentioned."

Vincent settling in at the bar.

> "Why, thank you, kind sir."

Cleo playing along while mixing a Manhattan. Gunner checks his watch.

> "Gentlemen, I need to check on our champion in waiting. Make sure everything's in order."

The watch grabs Sam's attention. Same black leather strap and watch dial with art deco font.

> "Your Rolex. That's a Cosmograph Daytona."
> "You recognize it?"
> "Serial number 6239."
> "Yes, I was meaning to tell you. Your father gave it to me as a gift after Odin's first victory. He knew we'd created something special."

Sam looks to the bar, making eye contact with Genevieve.

> "Could I get a beer?"
> "Of course. What kind would you like?"
> "Halderson, if you have it."
> "Indeed we do."

Genevieve brings over a perfectly chilled bottle.

> "Thank you."
> "My pleasure."
> "Alright, I must go." announces Gunner.
> "How long are we looking at?" asks Vincent.
> "That's what I'm going to check in on. Within the hour, I'd imagine."

Vincent nods, raising his glass to Gunner, who disappears down the darkened passageway.

The edge of the anvil creeping in over the open roof. Communal lines of coke carved up at the bar. Everyone with a drink in hand at Vincent's insistence.

"Girls, check this one out."

He holds out his phone, showing a photo of a stern-looking boy with a bowl cut standing beside a young woolly mammoth, its trunk wrapped around the boy's waist.

"Awwww . . ." The girls fawning over the picture.

"You know who that is?"

Before they can guess, Vincent points to Sam.

"Right there. That's Sammy boy with his best bud Magnus."

The girls double down.

"Awww. So cute . . ."

Sam wants nothing to do with the conversation.

"You see them in parks now but that picture was front-page news at the time: 'Alden Slade Brings Woolly Mammoth Back From Extinction.'"

"How big is Magnus now?" asks Octavia, the beauty from Brazil.

"He's dead," Sam answers. Chugging back the rest of his beer.

"Cancer, apparently."

"I'm sorry."

"Don't be."

Sam grabs another beer from the fridge. Snorts a line. Vincent breaks the awkward silence.

"He found out after the fact. Bit of sore spot."

Gunner enters the room, looking at his watch.

"What's the word? They give him the gunpowder yet?" asks Vincent.

Temple

Gunner holds up his finger, waiting for the cue. Seconds later, the hammer hits the gong. Dark timbre. Full resonance.

"About to begin."

He approaches the glass. Looks to the sky. The anvil above the arena. Everything eerily still.

"Just hanging there . . ."

Vincent snorts a line. Cleo hands him a fresh Manhattan.

> "You know, Sam, here's the hilarious part of that **Times** piece—it's complete bullshit. Your dad said Magnus was brought back using DNA from a mammoth's shin bone or some such nonsense. Total hoax. Magnus was an early Anansi experiment. They took elephant chromosomes, fucked around with the gene sequences, added hair, made a few more tweaks, and there's your woolly mammoth. Pushed it in the press and the public bought it hook, line, and sinker."

Of course. The old man still taking shots from beyond the grave. Believed the lie. Sam feels his temper flare. Stomps it down. Doesn't matter. Magnus was good. Magnus was true. That doesn't change.

> "We contemplated building a dinosaur theme park.
> Coded a very close facsimile of a velociraptor integrating sequences from a sandhill crane, a southern cassowary, and frilled agama."
>
> "A real Jurassic Farce," quips Gunner as the gong goes off for a second time. Vincent pointing his finger to the sky.
>
> "Sound the alarm!"

The arena flashing red. A booming bass drop shakes the foundation. Blaring horn blasts overlaid with wailing alarms. Sam covers his ears.

> "What the fuck is going on?"
>
> "All part of the show, Sammy boy!"

Lights out. Silence. White flash. Thunderclap. Cloud-to-cloud branch lightning flashing across the sky. The combat circle glowing white. Gaining intensity. At its peak projecting a towering column of light into the massive thunderhead. Two drones fly into the arena. hovering outside each fighter's chute.

Picture-in-picture. From his phone, Gunner displays the drone streams on the glass. Odin snarling. Barrel chest. Built like a silverback. Expanded ribcage connecting to enlarged vertebrae with built-up ligaments. A boulder of muscle strapped onto a fortified frame with inured tendons. On the other feed, Indra—the defending champion with its own augmentations. Extended torso with expanded wingspan. Stretched limbs. Reinforced joints. Rocking side to side. Light reflecting off lacquered exoskeleton. Midnight black. Cognac coloured eyes buried in a carapace. A face plate protrusion wrapping around the orbital bones connecting to its mandible. An amalgamation of a bull's frontal bone and insect clypeus.

The third and final gong sounds. Gunner shrinks the video displays. Sliding them to the far corners of the viewing window. A voice with deep bass counts down over the loudspeakers.

"Three—two—one."

Chutes open. Split-second charge. Full force. Midair collision launched with lethal intent. Flying knees and elbow strikes. Blinding speed. Jaw-dropping power. The initial exchange a blur. Blood spilled on both sides. The drones circling the fighters at a distance. Zooming in for closeups. Capturing the action from varying angles. The fighters measuring distance. Indra has the distinct height and reach advantage. Moving upright like a praying mantis with its arms raised. Odin on all fours, knuckles down, dragging, moving laterally. Circling each other, searching for an opening. See it. Charge, strike, break. Odin sliced open. Getting shredded by ridged shins and elbows. Unfazed but losing blood. Odin rushes in. Dodging the scythe. Ducking under raptorial appendages and rocking Indra with an uppercut. His opponent staggered, Odin shoots a double leg takedown. Lifting Indra off its feet onto its back. No hesitation. Odin immediately passes guard, raining down hammer fists. The carapace cracking. Indra getting smashed. Starting to split. In desperation, it wings a lashing elbow that flays open Odin's brow. Blood seeping into his eyes. Indra rolls its hips for the escape. Odin backing up. Blinking. Vincent springs out of his seat, spilling his drink.

Temple

"Can't see! Fighting blind!"

Odin wiping the blood from his eyes as Indra stalks him down. Whipping kicks into his kidney and liver. Odin trying to check them but can't see the kicks coming. Starting to fade. Arms dropping to his sides. Opening up his head to attack. Indra targeting the brow laceration with jabs. Peeling back the skin. Blood gushing from the wound. Pouring down Odin's face.

"This is bad . . . this is bad . . ." repeats Gunner.

A devastating combo ending with a left cross drops Odin. On his hands and heels, scrambling back to standing position. Indra timing it with a flying knee into his sternum. Odin crumples.

"He's done. He's fucking done."

Gunner can't watch. Hand over his eyes. Odin turtling as Indra picks him apart. Looking for openings. A driving straight punch bounces Odin's head off the canvas but the follow-up misses the mark. Odin turning his neck in time. Catching the arm. Indra recoils but Odin hangs on. Hooks his legs over the arm and neck.

"Caught him! Caught an arm-bar!"

Locked in. Loud crack as Odin snaps the arm. Letting go for a leg lock. Secures the heel hook. Indra rolls into it. Trying to escape the submission but can't post his arm to pull out. The broken limb folding ninety degrees in the wrong direction. Odin torques his hip. Falls back. Turning towards the heel. Tearing apart Indra's meniscus. Severing collateral and cruciate ligaments. Indra writhing in pain as Odin snags the other leg. Wraps it. Cracks it. Rolls away. Indra ruined. Attempting to stand. All its weight on one good arm. Odin circles his opponent. Takes aim and punts Indra in the face. A soccer kick snapping its head back.

"Damnnnnnn!"

Kill shot. Indra lays motionless. Odin, painted red, staggers backwards. Mouth hanging open. His hulking frame heaving for air.

"Dead . . . it's dead. He did it! We fucking did it!"

Hugs and high-fives in the emperor's box. Sam in shock. Stunned silence.

"Smile, Sammy boy! You're about to get paiiiiiid."

Flash of lightning. Crash of thunder. The anvil cracked open. Another gong strike officially ends the fight. Arena lights switched on as Odin's eyes roll back. Their champion collapsing in the downpour. A group of glass panels slides open, allowing access to the arena. Four APCs and two customized ambulances drive out to meet the combatants. Security exits their vehicles first. Guns drawn, they inspect the combatants before waving over the medics, who rush to the fallen fighters' sides. Odin going into convulsions. Vincent turns his back to the carnage.

"Alright, Gunner, turn it off . . ."

Gunner taps his phone and the viewing widow goes black.

". . . and let's TURN. IT. UP."

Vincent blasts his victory playlist through the sound system. Spraying the room with champagne.

"The king is back! We the champs! Fuck Berzin!"

Hoot. Holler. Drink. Dance. Sniff. Snort. Smoke. Repeat. Vincent carving up more cocaine. Sam on the down. Can feel the drop. Diminishing returns. Less time between lines. Needs to stop. Step back. Drink some water. Deal with the discomfort as they wait out the weather. Heart racing. Mind scattered. Anxious. Agitated. Trapped on a mountaintop. Stuck in this room. Vincent acting the fool. Shirt off. Swirling it above his head while the girls dance around him. Gunner his clapping monkey. Godawful music. Needs to get out. Go for a wander. Grab some fresh air.

Distant buzzsaw. Down darkened corridors towards the light. Sam makes his way through the maze onto the battlefield. Roof closed. Indra gone. Body removed. Medics surrounding Odin. Security surrounding them. Sam approaches the wreckage. A passing glance from security as he peers over their shoulders. Odin intubated. Rib cage cracked open. Retractor in place. Diamond-tipped surgical saws. Flecks of white. Bone fragments. Open heart still beating. Then it stops. The beast dying. A moment's pause interrupted by yelling in the background.

"Samsonite! What the hell are you doing out there?"

Temple

Uncle Vince standing inside the entrance to the arena with his arms draped around Octavia and Genevieve. Sam turns back to the murmur of medics. Odin dead. Done. An official pronouncement as the medics shift gears from rescue to cleanup.

Daylight. Depleted. Felt sick. Medics called. Sam administered an IV. The drip bag supplying vitamins, minerals, and electrolytes. Along with a low dose combination of sedatives, an anti-inflammatory, and anti-nauseant. Recovering in the recliner. Feeling better. Much better. The black wall once again a window. Overcast sky but the storm has passed. Vincent standing in silhouette. Staring out at the battlefield. Still going. Teetering in place with a drink in one hand and a smoke in the other. Just him and his uncle. Gunner disappeared. The girls gone. Vincent stumbles back. Finds his footing. Turns to Sam with glassy eyes. Nostrils crusted in cocaine.

> "Fuckin' boner pills . . . Keep fucking but my bag is empty. She's waiting for me to cum but there's nothing left in the tank. Down to last drop . . . Keep on pumping. Can't stop. Can't quit. Stick and lick and suck and fuck . . . I don't know, man . . . I don't fucking know . . . Killing time, I guess. What else . . . What else I got? Start a family? Maybe . . . might . . . Family the foundation. Everything else just . . . fluff. Build a home. Real one. Something right. Something true."

Vincent slurps back more booze. Drops the glass.

> "I'm fucked . . ."

Wrecked. His uncle can't walk so they wheel him out to the chopper with an IV in his arm. Accompanied by Nathalie, his hand-picked medic, an attractive brunette with a warm smile, who will be joining them for the return flight. Arrangements made. Money wired.

When they land at the airstrip, Ms. Clarke is there waiting. Vincent still too mangled to walk. Sam helps Nathalie transfer him from the chopper into his wheelchair. Ms. Clarke pointing her towards the private plane where their flight hostesses, back in uniform, are waiting at the top of the stairs. Nathalie slings her medic bag over her shoulders and pushes towards them.

"What a mess," observes Ms. Clarke with contempt.

Nathalie helping Uncle Vince up the stairs into the plane.

"Enjoy the fight?" Ms. Clarke asks Sam without making eye contact.
"Enjoy is not the word."
"Entertained?"
"Yeah . . . I suppose so."
"So you're aware, a return on the wager has been received and your winnings transferred."

Ending the exchange, Ms. Clarke makes her way towards the plane. Sam trailing behind her.

Cruising altitude. Nathalie reading a book at the front of the plane. Vincent passed out with his harem in the back. Ms. Clarke seated across the aisle from Sam. Earbuds in. Busily typing on her laptop. Sam resisting the urge to check his bank account. Not sure why. No reason. Decides to look. Logs in on his phone. Sees the number. Enough decimal points to ensure he'll never have to work again. Set for life, as they say. Now what? Sam looks out his window. Golden light cast through a bed of clouds. Rich man. Blood money. Can it be cleansed? Does it matter? Currency. Current. Token of exchange. Energy. Time. Time is money, yadda yadda. Must invest that energy into something good. Atonement. Make amends. How? Land. Land to grow on. Truth is in the soil. Food and shelter. That's the foundation. Build a community based on trust. Anchored in an honour system. Learn. Grow. Acquire new skillsets. Build new systems. Bullshit . . . The money is cursed. Can feel it.

Arrival. The plane slows to a stop. Big yawn from the back.

"What a night!"

Uncle Vince on his feet. Stretching out his arms in the middle of the aisle.

"Amazing what a little shuteye will do for ya."

Sam sees one their helicopters fuelling up outside the air hangar.

"What's the plan, Sam? Checking back in with the pod people?"
"Somewhere else I should go?"
"Take a trip to the old estate with me."
"No, thanks."
"We're selling it."
"Why?"
"The family couldn't reach an agreement to keep it. Doing a walkthrough for a joint appraisal."
"Have fun with that."
"You don't want to take a walk down memory lane?"
"I'm good."
"Are you?"
"Yeah."
"Surprise the siblings. Meet your little brother."
"That's on them."
"Do you enjoy the victim role?"
"Fuck off."
"Yes or no?"

Following the coastline. Passing over palatial estates. One stands out from all the others. Unmatched in size and scale. Sam sees the place he called home. Thirty thousand acres of beachfront property behind guarded walls with gun turrets. Within said walls:

- The main house, a colossal mansion with a helipad in the courtyard.

- Two warehouse garages housing hundreds of luxury vehicles and classic cars.

- Marina with a fleet of boats, including one the world's largest mega yachts.

- Aircraft hangar with a collection of classic twin-prop planes, helicopters, and a private jet.

- Eight-thousand-foot runway.

- Twenty-three-hundred-square-foot reception hall seating up to a hundred and fifty people with a massive limestone fireplace and projectorium.

-Twenty-one-hundred-square-foot library with domed roof and secret bookcases containing historical documents and rare manuscripts.

- Multiple swimming pools. One with a beach. The sand imported from St. Lucia.

- Waterpark with a grotto, waterfall, tube run, and slides.

- Rec centre with gym, racetrack, tennis, squash, and basketball courts.

- Ice rink.

- Archery range.

-Game park with go-cart track, four-lane bowling alley, pool hall, trampoline room, freefall simulator, and arcade with the world's most prized collection of pinball machines.

- Eighteen-hole golf course.

- Vineyard.

- Botanical garden with multiple greenhouses and koi pond.

-Wetland estuary running into a man-made lake stocked with salmon and sea-run cutthroat trout.

- High-yield pasture with grazing cows, sheep, and horses.

- Racing stable.

- Game reserve stocked with elk, deer, and bison.

- Zoo filled with exotic animals.

-Staff housing, a small section of the property positioned furthest from shore.

Descending into the courtyard, Sam can see armed guards strategically posted around the main house.

"See they've beefed up security."
"After the raid, your father went all in. Fortified the compound."
"Hex still the H.O.F.?"
"Dead."

"How?"
"Heart attack."
"Didn't think he could die."
"Escaped a POW camp in the territories and—"
"Claimed forty scalps along the way."
"Fucking maniac would toss his parachute from the plane and jump out after it for something to do."

Vincent points down to a young blonde woman in full stride from the house to the helipad.

"Hey, look, your widowed stepmother's coming out to greet us. Seems as though someone tipped her off to my surprise."

She stands outside the landing zone in a tight summer dress. Arms crossed under her breasts. Bronzed skin, blonde hair, blue eyes: the apex version of a California beach babe. Hyper sensualized. Absurdly desirable.

"How old's this one?"
"Twenty-four, I believe."
"A forty-one-year age gap."
"Correct, but he could easily pass for sixty."
"Lucky girl."

They disembark the helicopter. Make their approach.

"In fairness, she wouldn't exist without him."
"Ansari?"
"Custom design."

Within earshot, Vincent opens his arms.

"Raylee, my dear, you are a vision of beauty."

She blocks his advance with an open palm.

"Who's he?"

Ms. Clarke marches past them to address the rest of the family gathered with their teams of appraisers, agents, and lawyers.

"Raylee, this is Alden's first-born, Sam."

"He's not welcome here."

"He is now. This was Sam's home before you were born and you'll show him the requisite amount of respect."

"Why did you bring him here?"

"To see the property, the place he grew up, one last time before it's sold."

"I did not agree to this."

"I don't care. Now where's the little man?"

"He's gone with Hector to feed Temmu."

"Which one's that?"

"The Smilodon."

"Don't know—"

"The sabretooth."

"Ahhh, yes. Too big for the house now?"

"He was too big five years ago."

"Time flies. Start there, Sam. See Hector. Meet Gage."

"No, he's not."

"He is. That's his big brother. His blood."

"Excommunicated. Alden wanted nothing to do with him."

"Alden's not here right now."

"He will be."

"We can have that discussion if and when. For now, we're putting petty grievances in the past where they belong. Understood?"

"You have a duty to uphold your brother's—"

"Stop. Step back and recognize your place in the pecking order. Sam will see his brother."

Shift in tone. Non-negotiable.

"I need to be there."

"No, you don't, but feel free. We'll do the appraisal without you."

"I'm leading the walkthrough."

"Well, you can't be two places at once, Raylee, so take your pick."

Temple

The fleet of SxS ATVs has expanded. Sam selects the first in line and drives towards the zoo. Tailed by security in an SUV. Through the cast-iron gates, he follows the winding path, passing various enclosures—rhino, elephant, gorilla, giraffe—into the big cat exhibits: lion, jaguar, tiger. Rounding the bend, he's blocked by a pick-up truck backing a livestock trailer into the feed hatch of an enclosure. Sam parks the ATV. Security stopping ten feet behind him. A grizzled Mexican man with a heavily lined face steps out the pick-up truck.

"Hola, Hector."

The man turns to Sam. Takes him a second. Eyes brighten. His face softens.

"Samuel!"

Hug and handshake. Hector steps back, smiling.

> "¿Cómo estás?"
> "Sigue en pie."
> "¿Tú?"
> "Sigue en pie. Apenas."

A boy with brown hair and blue eyes appears from the other side of the truck.

> "Gage este es tu hermano mayor."

Sam waves to the boy, who glares back.

> "Hello, Gage. It's nice to meet you."

The boy assessing the situation. Looks to the guards, then Sam.

> "You're not supposed to be here."
> "I'm not?"
> "You're banned from the property."
> "Why's that?"
> "You betrayed our father."
> "How?"
> "By rejecting our claim."
> "Claim to what?"
> "How did you get here? Who allowed you onto the estate?"
> "I arrived with our always incorrigible Uncle Vince."

TYRANT

"The degenerate."

Gage turns to Hector.

"Offload the pig. Open the hatch."

Hector drops the automated ramp on the trailer and pokes the hog through the window bars with an electric cattle prod. The swine squealing, jumping out of the trailer into the feed hatch. Hector raises the ramp and opens the gate on the hatch. The hog now refusing to enter the enclosure. Hector hits it with another jolt, forcing it out. Hatch closed. Pig trapped. Pacing a strip of flat ground at the front of the exhibit, a fabricated section of canyon: dry brush, climbing trees, sculpted rocks, and a cave. The sabretooth stepping out of the cavern. Standing five feet in height from all fours at six hundred plus pounds. Thick neck attached to a wide skull with a broad muzzle baring eleven-inch upper canines. The apex predator looks down at its prey. In no particular rush, it climbs down to ground level. The frantic hog pinning itself in a corner as the cat stalks it down. From a crouch, the sabretooth springs at the swine, straddling its sides with striated forearms. Claws tearing into flesh. Driving large upper canines into the back of the pig's neck. Locked in. The pig crumbles under the cat's weight. The struggle soon over. Gage claps his hands. "Alright Hector, no need to ogle while he eats. Bring me back to the main house." He directs his attention to the guards tracking Sam.

"Do not let him out of your sight."

"Don't worry, they already heard it from your mother," Sam snipes back.

"My mother should have never allowed you on the premises."

"How old are you, Gage?"

"Irrelevant."

"The old man really did a number on you, huh?"

"He taught me well with the time we had."

"Think he's coming back?"

"I know he is."

"Then you'll never be king."

"I'm here to serve, you insolent fraud."

"Aren't we all."

Temple

Gage gives him the middle finger.

> "There ya go, kid. Have fun with it."
> "Fuck you."

Gage gets back in the truck. Hector offering an embarrassed shrug.

> "Good to see you, Hector."
> "**Igualmente.**"

Hector and Gage drive off. Sam turns to his security detail.

> "Where to now, boys?"

The question met with stone-faced silence.

> "Guess I'll lead the way."

Sam drives to the one place on the property that still holds meaning. The giant sycamore stands a hundred feet tall with a six-foot diameter across the trunk. Countless hours of his childhood spent with Magnus under the old tree. Sam would climb onto the mammoth's saddle, stand, then leap onto the first branch. Nestled in the crook between the massive branch and the trunk, he'd lean back and let his mind wander. Away from Father's foul moods and Mother's drunken states. Somewhere to escape. Alone and uninterrupted. He'd often read or eat a packed lunch up there. Worlds imagined in that tree: characters, concepts, and timelines. When he wanted to come down, he'd call Magnus. His loyal friend grazing nearby or flopped down under the sycamore's shade. The mammoth, heeding his call, would lower Sam to the ground with its trunk or lean in close enough that Sam could jump onto the saddle. Those were the days before darkness descended.

Mom drinking herself into any early grave while Dad berated her vice. Then the accusation. Stolen jewelry. The suspect's employees. New additions. A family living in staff housing: father, mother, son, and two daughters. The father a maintenance man, the son a groundskeeper, the mother and daughters part of the cleaning staff. Sam was friends with the son, Jair. A fellow teenager. Racing go-carts at the game park when Jair was rounded up by security and driven back to staff housing. Sam followed. Watching the ugly scene unfold. Security tossing the family's living quarters looking for the missing items. Marched them outside and made them turn out their empty pockets. Nothing was found. Humiliating.

Sam horrified by their treatment yet he stood by and let it happen. Embarrassed. Ashamed. The items found several days later. His wasted mother having transferred them to one of her secret safes in another paranoid blackout.

The family was still fired to save face. Couldn't be trusted. That's when he began to question everything. Learning how they made their money. Where it came from. Blackmail and blood were the foundations of their fortune. He would not abide. Was told to take it or leave it. So he left. Now he's back. No better for it. Thought he could make his own money. Couldn't. Not really. Sick of being poor. Tired of living paycheque to paycheque. Time stolen. No space. No privacy. Took the handout. Trust-fund tourist. Fraud. No excuse but now's not the time. Save the self-flagellation for another day. Sam kneels down. Pockets a small piece of rigid bark shed by the tree. Ready to leave, he places his hand on the sycamore, saying a prayer for Magnus when distant gunshots shatter the peace. Sam opens his eyes. Security with their guns drawn. Sights set. Three red dots floating on his forehead.

Vincent coughing up blood on the cobblestone driveway. Shot through the chest. Red running through the cracks. Appraisers, lawyers, and real estate agents all gunned down. The family lined up in the courtyard. Sam sees his siblings for the first time since his exile. Each with an armed guard standing behind them. Brothers Aaron and Eric. Sisters Alice and Evelyn. There they are. Shaken. Shook. A guard pushes him forward by jamming a gun muzzle into his back. Placed between Raylee and Gage at the end of the line. The child with a split lip. Trembling. Terrified. Holding court over the proceedings is Ms. Clarke and their new head of security. Somehow familiar. Shaved head, black beard, broad nose with a flat bridge bisecting his forehead. Same age but built for war. Shrapnel scarring across the left side of his face. Artificial eye with a red tracking iris. The right eye is brown with a Y-split above the brow. Suddenly registers. Remembers the mark. Jair. It's him. Imposter. Insurgent. Vincent wheezing. Choking. Pink froth running down the side of his face. Ms. Clarke nods for Jair to finish the job and he puts a bullet between Vincent's eyes. Ms. Clarke waits a beat. Begins.

> "Before we go down the line, I want you to know your children, the children you left at home with their nannies because you couldn't be bothered, will not inherit your empire. They will not avenge your death."

Temple

Brother Aaron snaps. "You fucking cunt, if you hurt my kids, I'll—"

Jair strikes him in the face with the butt of his automatic rifle. Aaron drops to the ground. Nose pulverized. Gushing blood. The colour drains from Eric's face. Alice aghast. Evelyn weeping.

"Thank you, Victor."

Emma addressing Jair.

"Look at me, Aaron . . ."

Aaron looks up at Ms. Clarke, the bridge of his nose busted wide open.

"You don't need to worry about your kids. They're already dead."
"You're lying."
"You'll never know." "Treacherous cunt . . . My family made you a fortune!"

Jair pulls the trigger. Aaron falls sideways. Sisters screaming.

"Hey Emi, how long have you known Jair for?" Sam stalling for time.

The question met with a cold stare. Keeps going.

"I know his story. What's yours?"
"Sorry, Sam. You took the money."
"And I can send it to you."
"You can't. The transfer went to a mirrored account."
"How's that work?"
"Stop delaying the inevitable."
"Put a bullet in my head if you have to. End it there. Don't kill the kid."
"How else do we erase your bloodline?"

Sam looks up to the big blue sky. Draws a deep breath into a sigh.

"What if I take you out for dinner?"

Ms. Clarke nods to Jair and it ends with the flash of a muzzle.

TWO TAILS

Retail parks, strip malls, and gas stations line both sides of the highway.
Black sky
No stars
The night illuminated by fast food placards and streetlights.
Stranded
Standing in a parking lot behind the golden arches.
Waiting without a ride or destination.
There's a smattering of vehicles but the lot is near empty.
A tiger appears from behind a parked car.
Watch it stride between light and shadow.
See the way its right shoulder drops.
Hobbled.
Missing a leg
with a bend in its spine,
stomach sagging,
mange,
dehydrated,
malnourished,
cloudy eye,
cataract.
Pausing with forty feet between us.
Its mouth hanging open.
Nose in the air.
Tracking a scent.
Don't turn my way.
Does.

TYRANT

Locked in.
Step back towards the drive-through.
Searching for something to swing.
Scan the hedges.
See it half buried under wood mulch.
A rusted piece of signpost snapped off at six feet.
That'll do. Has to. Pick it up.
The tiger stalks forward.
Weaving side to side.
Searching for the right angle to strike.
I'm talking, shouting, puffing my chest.
Jabbing the air with my signpost spear.
Letting it know I will swing. I will stab.
There's no free lunch here.
Acting brave but I know it's a done deal if the cat commits.
One step closer.
Drawing it towards the harsh light of fast-food America.
The patrons on the inside are oblivious,
but the customers lining up at the drive-through take notice.
Gawking.
Safe and secure in their cars and trucks.
Off the street and into my field of view,
a large corn-fed white boy in a sweat-stained ballcap, marked with the
fluorescent green insignia of a monstrous energy drink.
His friend with dark skin, a skinny teenager with a high-top fade and dirty
white sneakers.
Stoned. Seeking food.
Laughing, joking, oblivious.
Whistle through my teeth.
Catch their attention.
See the situation.
Stop.
Eyes wide. Pointing.
The tiger still zeroed in on me.
I nod to them.

Two Tails

No sudden motions.
Slowly stepping back.
Signpost aimed at the tiger.
Call for help.
People with guns.
I move around the bend.
Approaching the front entrance.
Front lot.
Busy.
Patrons parking outside.
See the threat.
Panic.
Commotion.
Clamour.
Movement.
Noise.
The tiger hissing.
Confused.
Overwhelmed.
Agitated.
Too many targets.
Triggers.
The tiger rushes a family raised on Happy Meals.
Stops on a dime.
Changes trajectory.
Darts towards a set of elderly coupon collectors.
Time to go.
Leave the lot.
Still holding my signpost spear.
Straight past corn-fed and his friend.
Leave the scene.
Amped up, they chase me down, jog over.
Trying to show me the footage on their phones.
Ignoring the chaos behind us.
The screams muted background noise,

TYRANT

as we walk and talk along the four-lane highway.
My adrenaline still pumping.
Prioritizing distance and space
Can't stop.
Stop.
Look up.
Standing in the middle of the sidewalk—another tiger
This one has all its legs.
Gazing across the highway, it turns to us.
No hesitation.
Full sprint towards us.
Closing the distance in seconds.
Primed to pounce, I swing the post, striking the tiger between neck and shoulder blade.
Enough force that it careens onto the highway.
Headlights.
Struck by a truck.
Tires over torso.
Twisted.
Crushed.
Tossed aside.
In a broken heap against the concrete median.
The tiger closes its eyes.
Dead.
Roadkill.
Corn-fed rushes onto the highway to inspect the damage.
Phone out.
Grabbing footage.
Headlights.
Clipped by a car.
Dead.
Roadkill.
His friend flinches,
winces,
looks away.

Two Tails

Hands on his head.
Fingers through hair.
Face twisting in anguish.
I don't know what to tell him.
Keep walking.
Continue.

THANK YOU TO JESSICA CRADDOCK